James Stenhouse is a retired Marine Engineer who, along with writing enjoys hiking and the restoration and maintenance of antique automobiles.

James lives in Nova Scotia with his wife, Joan.

This is a work of fiction. Names, characters, businesses, places, events and incidents are either the products of the author's imagination or used in a fictitious manner. Any resemblance to actual persons, living or dead, or actual events is purely coincidental.

CONCORDAT

James Stenhouse

CONCORDAT

Vanguard Press

VANGUARD PAPERBACK

© Copyright 2023
James Stenhouse

The right of James Stenhouse to be identified as author of this work has been asserted by him in accordance with the Copyright, Designs and Patents Act 1988.

All Rights Reserved

No reproduction, copy or transmission of this publication may be made without written permission.
No paragraph of this publication may be reproduced, copied or transmitted save with the written permission of the publisher, or in accordance with the provisions of the Copyright Act 1956 (as amended).

Any person who commits any unauthorised act in relation to this publication may be liable to criminal prosecution and civil claims for damages.

A CIP catalogue record for this title is available from the British Library.

ISBN 978-1-80016-571-7

Vanguard Press is an imprint of
Pegasus Elliot Mackenzie Publishers Ltd.
www.pegasuspublishers.com

First Published in 2023

Vanguard Press
Sheraton House Castle Park
Cambridge England

Printed & Bound in Great Britain

For Joan, and her unconditional love.

Chapter 1

She woke with the dregs of a dream draining away into daylight consciousness. Placing a forearm over her eyes she tried to recapture the essence of what had brought about the thrumming desire she felt throughout her body. Sweeping the sheet aside and shrugging off her nightdress she went to the bathroom and into a torrent of shower water so cold it made her gasp. It was too soon since the last and she needed time to plan and prepare. She needed to chill the urgency and heat her body was generating. Shivering, she was forced from the shower but inside her the heat and craving continued to grow. Never before had the need, the urge, been so strong. She knew she would surrender to them. It was hard for her to wait until nightfall. She needed the release it would bring, and the need grew stronger with each passing hour. Several times during the day she was tempted to rush out and find what she needed and douse the craving. She fought the impulse until darkness came.

She went to a place she had used once before. It was used mostly by business people visiting or passing through the city. She scanned the room and found what she needed sitting at the bar.

He had watched her come in and knew she would sit at the bar leaving an empty stool between them. She would order a gin and tonic with a twist, no ice. He knew she would comment to the bartender about how busy it was and receive, 'yeah, for a Wednesday' in response. He knew they would smile at each other in the bar mirror and lift their glasses in a reflected silent toast. He knew that when a couple came in, she would offer them her seat so they could sit together and casually move to the one beside him. He knew everything about her. He'd read her Life File.

She was dressed in an emerald-green satin dress that emphasised her figure and presented a dark cleft of cleavage. Her hair was Irish Colleen red that dropped to her shoulders in shiny waves and her eyes were vivid green.

A light freckling dotted her nose and cheeks. She was attractive without being beautiful but her whole appearance made her memorable.

When she moved to the stool next to him, he waited for her to speak. She always made the first approach.

After taking a sip from her drink she half-turned and said, "Hi, my name's Susanne." It wasn't. It was Cheryl.

He told her his was Tony and when she asked, he said he was an engineer in town on business for a few days. She said she worked for a pharmaceutical company doing most of her work from home. Another lie. She had inherited wealth and had no need to work. She led their conversation into personal areas. She told him she was divorced. Lie. She had never married.

He said, "Me too." He asked about children and was told none. He professed the same. When he asked if she enjoyed being single, she said yes, she liked being on her own and free to do her own thing. He echoed her thoughts on the freedom. They shared snippets of their lives. The likes and dislikes. Nothing too deep. They were playing the game and dancing the dance to intimacy, a dance she had done many times before.

Leaning close so that thighs and shoulders touched she asked quietly, "Have you become celibate since your divorce?"

Leaning in tighter he smiled and answered, "Not at all. It's one of the perks of being single again."

"How true," she said and in the shadow cast by the bar she ran a hand up his thigh towards his crotch. He was prepared for this, and she found a bulge that was hard and sizeable. After raising her eyebrows and forming a silent 'oh' with her mouth she said, "My place is only five minutes away, do you want to come for a cup of coffee?"

He squeezed her thigh and said, "Absolutely. Shall I ask the bartender to call a cab?"

"No need. My car's in the lot across the street."

Normally she would take more time with chatter and innuendo before making the invitation but tonight the craving was stronger than she had ever experienced. Just thinking about what was to happen as they hurried to her car was enough to bring an orgasm that caused her to gasp and stumble. He caught her arm at the elbow and asked if she was okay. Smiling she assured him she had never felt better and pressed the fob that unlocked her car.

Pamela who was interning at Retribution watched it all.

Chapter 2

Instantly he knew it wasn't a dream. The woman was too real — too solid — and the bed dipped under her weight. She was seated on the side where his wife, who was away visiting family in Scotland, would normally be sleeping. Reaching out a hand she touched the centre of his forehead with the tip of the index finger, and he flinched as every cell and nerve in his body flooded with a vitality he had never experienced before but when he tried to speak, he had no voice.

The woman smiled and spoke. "Hello, Richard, don't worry, you will be able to talk soon. I'm Ambrosine Light and I, for want of a better word, 'work' for an organisation called Concordat. Let's go to the living room and I'll explain why I'm here." He felt no fear or anxiety, he had an absolute certainty this woman meant him no harm.

When he came out of the bedroom pulling on a dressing gown, she was seated in one of the easy chairs, he took the other. Out of the shadows of the bedroom and in the light from a lamp she had turned on he could see what a truly attractive woman she was.

His mind registered this fact and she said with a smile, "Thank you Richard, I appreciate the compliment. Richard I'm going to sync with you. You don't have to understand what that means at the moment. When it happens, it will shut down the parts of your brain that would ask questions and seek answers and explanations. It is only necessary that you receive something that will study and record your brain functions during your daily activities. You will not be aware it is happening. I'm going to sync now."

He felt a faint shock in the spinal area below his skull and noticed the flash of a grimace across Ambrosine Light's face at the same moment.

"That went well Richard, you are receptive to syncing and it becomes less intrusive with use. When you wake up tomorrow morning you will have no memory of my visit and will go about your life as usual. I will return tomorrow night and we will sync again and depending on the results of your brain study we will either continue your preparation or I will say goodbye and leave you to the rest of your life."

He sat relaxed and unperturbed while she explained these things. Since the touch to his forehead, he had become aware of how things in the apartment he saw on a daily basis had become more sharply focused. Everything had taken on a crisp clarity. In particular he was drawn to the sounds made by the carriage clock on the mantle above the fireplace. The noise of its ticking had hardly been noticeable so precise were its mechanical components and which, as an engineer, he admired, but now when he paid particular attention to the clock, he not only heard an amplified ticking but also the background sounds of shafts turning in jewelled bearings and of gear teeth meshing and moving with micrometre precision to sweep the hour and minute and second hands around the numbered dial.

"That is your brain working at half capacity heightening your senses and why you can hear all the mechanical functions of the clock," Ambrosine Light explained. "And also why your brain will be able to accept and store all that I am about to transfer. It will take only a nanosecond, but you will experience a sensory and neurological flooding when the download inrush takes place. Transfer starts now."

He had a slight headache when he woke and took some Tylenol to relieve it. It didn't help which surprised him and the ache stayed with him all day.

Chapter 3

Knowing what was about to happen he stood in mock surprise when in the bedroom she first removed the wig that hid her real hair which was blonde cut short to just below her ears. Next, she removed green contact lenses and placed them in a container on a bedside table. Her true eye colour was a light, misty grey.

As she slipped out of the emerald-green dress she said, "I wear a disguise when I go out to find someone to have sex with. I'm well known in certain circles and if some of the gossipy bitches got wind of my activities it would be all over the place in no time. Also, if their limp dick husbands found out it would be like giving them open season to hit on me."

She had worn nothing beneath the dress, and he saw a body that was, for forty, trim. He knew she worked hard to stay in shape, and it showed. Everything about her was firm and toned.

She let him admire her and watched as his eyes roamed over her body then she said, "Okay, let's get those clothes off you." He helped by taking his jacket, tie and shirt off while she undid his trouser belt and undid the fly to push his trousers and underwear down over his hips. "Oh my!" came from her when his penis was revealed. She pushed him staggering backward to fall on the bed where she frantically tore the shoes and socks from his feet and yanked his trousers and underwear free.

"Move up the bed, stay on your back" she commanded. "I want this time to be my way." It was as she straddled him and took his penis to guide it into her that he started the cull. The body beneath her vanished and she was left on her knees unable to move. A man she did not recognise came to sit on the bed and rest against the headboard. This was not Tony. This was an older man. Handsome but showing lines that only age can engrave. His eyes were the outstanding feature.

The colour of blued glacier ice and which appeared every bit as cold as he very quietly said, "I am going to take you to the edge of death and make you suffer just as your victims suffered. After that you are going live an existence that will be far worse than dying. I can hear you asking, 'Is this a nightmare?' It isn't, and before you start begging, as I know you will, there will be no forgiveness, no stay of execution. Now I'm going to take you to your torture room and make you ready." He stood and taking her hand she meekly followed as he led her from the bedroom.

In the room below the garage, he watched as she strained against the manacles she had used to secure her victims. He watched as twelve times she suffered all the physical and emotional agony of her victims. He watched as her mind was torn apart and her body contorted in a rictus of ever-increasing pain. He brought the faces of the twelve into her eyes and the sounds of their pleading screams into her ears while her body suffered the same excruciating indignities that she had inflicted on them.

As the final agonised howl from her final victim faded, he tore the last remnant of sanity from her saying, "This is your sentence. You will die in an institution for the criminally insane at age eighty-six and at this time each day you will relive all the torture you have just experienced. You will not be able to take your own life to end the torture, your mind will never consider it."

The man who came to mow the lawns found her the next day wandering naked among the flowers and shrubs while tearing at her hair and repeating over and over that people were being killed in her head. The gardener called for paramedics and police and when the police as a matter of routine checked the house, they found the room beneath the garage along with the restraints and implements of torture. The dissected remains of twelve bodies, six male, six female, were removed from a well partially filled with lye and fitted with an airtight cover to contain the smell of decomposition. Video recordings of her depravity were found that caused even hardened investigators to become physically sick.

Life File Observers would visit her regularly to confirm the sentence was still in effect.

Chapter 4

The touch of her finger woke him the next night and he vividly remembered her previous visit. "Hello Richard. Let's sit in the living room again. I took the liberty of making tea and it should be nicely brewed by now if you want some."

He took time to dress in sweatpants and a tee shirt before joining her. She lifted the teapot and raised questioning eyebrows at him.

"Yes please."

He had his voice this time and he felt the same flow of energy and heightened awareness throughout his body as during her previous visit. The hint of a headache he had had all day and when fell asleep, was gone.

The tray with the tea things sat on a coffee table which was bracketed by the easy chairs on which they sat.

Ambrosine Light poured and added the exact amounts of sugar and milk he preferred before handing the china mug to him with a smile saying, "Yes, I know exactly how you like your tea and a great deal more." Pouring a little milk into her tea she inhaled the steaming aroma with a satisfied 'Mmm' and then sat back and crossed her legs.

Scrutinising him over the rim of her mug after taking a sip she asked, "Do you want to know what we found from our study of your brain?"

As before he felt no fear or anxiety. He knew he could trust this woman. "Yes, I do. I'm intrigued."

Ambrosine Light smiled broadly, "Good! Many people we approach are so freaked out by what's happening they make themselves believe it's all some sort of dream and refuse to go any further. Let me explain what it was that I downloaded when we synced last night. It was a program with algorithms that searched your brain for any weaknesses that would compromise or endanger you or Concordat going forward. I mean your whole brain was searched and not just the small amount that humans use when living." She sipped tea and waited for the question she knew would come.

"If a weakness is found what happens then?"

"I erase all memory of my visit and they continue on the path to their predetermined death."

This caused him to wrinkle his brow and say, "Predetermined death. You mean you know how and when a person is going to die?"

"Oh yes, we know that about everybody and I'm going to tell you about yours and the option you have. I'm going to sync now."

This time he barely felt the connection.

Chapter 5

"It went without a hitch, she thought all along it was real, but it was tough setting it up. As my report shows her mind was like a cess pit of degeneracy and insanity. I know we followed protocol but maybe we should have got to her sooner. I mean we knew what she was doing, and it was obvious the cops weren't getting anywhere linking the missing person's cases to her even with the pointers we provided. Perhaps the Protocols need some flexibility built in for cases like this. What she did to her victims was truly sickening. You know, women like her are more ingenious at covering up their crimes than men. Men act, often too quickly, whereas women, by and large, have more patience and plan more thoroughly. That and the fact society just can't seem to get its head around the truth that a woman can be as vicious as any man in such matters as torture and killing. And…"

Before he could expound further Amber placed a finger on his lips. "Richard, we are all well aware of your thoughts on these matters and you are not the first from Retribution to voice them but for now we have to Wipe you and let you get some private time. The Solons have been approached about protocol flexibility many times, but they feel it best to leave them as is and we can only accept they have a good reason for that. After all, we are not the only planetary system Concordat keeps watch over. Now, you know the drill. I'll sync with you and transfer the cull to records and that will leave your mind cleared and ready for your next assignment. Where do you want to be after it's done?"

. "In the hammock with Eleanor at my place on the beach."

Amber smiled. "I can do the hammock and beach, but I'll need to find out what Eleanor is doing and ask if she can join you. She will if she can, I'm sure."

He asked, "How did Pamela's appraisal go? She seemed to handle it okay."

"Gerald reports that she did well. Her neurological and physical readings were within required parameters. She showed natural responses to the sexual component in the bedroom, a voyeuristic horniness, and showed increasing compassion for the victims as the punishment played out. She considered the sentence suited the crimes and showed no sympathy towards Cheryl. I'll get the appraisal transferred to you and you can comment if you need to."

"Not necessary. If Gerald and the appraisal unit are good with her joining Retribution so am I. I was impressed with how calm and controlled she was during the whole thing. Let me know how she does with the rest of her induction into the unit."

"Will do. Enjoy your private time. The wipe starts now."

Eleanor joined him. He felt the hammock sway as he lay with eyes closed and said, "Hello lovely lady, I'm so glad you could make it."

She kissed his ear and whispered, "I can't stay long, there's a huge flap on and I only have a couple of free hours."

"I'm sure we'll make the best use of what time we have," he murmured.

Chapter 6

With the strict requirement that he not ask questions until she was finished Ambrosine Light began, "This is your predetermined death. One week from tomorrow on your seventy-second birthday you will start the journey into dementia and then the day after your eighty-eighth birthday you will die in a nursing home from respiratory failure brought on by pneumonia. In your case the loss of mental and physical capabilities will occur rapidly and after age seventy-seven you will be reliant on others to take care of your most routine and intimate of acts and functions. You are well aware of the anguish and stress this type of illness places on family members from your time as a volunteer at the hospice and similar will occur to your family. You will become aware of the perforations appearing in memory functions early on and will fight to retrieve what slips through. There will be minor victories that you and your family can celebrate but they will be brief as the event horizon of the black hole that is swallowing your mind expands. For eleven more years after all cognitive and physical functions have gone, you will, from a medical standpoint, be alive, but by any other standard you will not be living. This is the truth Richard, and this is how the last sixteen years of your life will play out unless you accept what Concordat offers you. This is their offer.

Concordat are prepared to spare you, and your family, all the years of dementia imposed by your predetermined death by providing an alternative one. In return, Concordat require your agreement to carry out any and all duties that they consider you best suited for." Uncrossing her legs Ambrosine Light sat forward in her chair and leaned towards him. "This is the alternative death. You will die from what will be determined at autopsy to be a blood clot in your brain. You will die in your bed next to your wife." Without taking her eyes off him she reached for her mug and drank some tea before settling back once more and asking, "Do you accept Concordats offer?"

Memories of his time volunteering at the hospice came to him. It would be particularly distressing for his wife and family during his final years when he knew he would lose all recollection of who they were. Richard was certain that he did not want his wife and family to go through that. He loved Jane and the rest of their family too much and did not want his final years dictating what they did with their lives. Also, he had always made it clear that he preferred to end his life on his own terms. Old age and infirmity held no attraction. He found it hard to understand why the accumulation of years beyond those where they could be counted as productive and of some accomplishments were so important to some.

And beyond all that he was convinced that by accepting the offer new avenues of experience and learning would be open to him, so he said, "I accept and I have one question."

"What is it, Richard?"

"Why me?"

Chapter 7

A short time after Eleanor, with reluctance, had returned to her work Amber contacted him.

"Sorry to cut into your private time but analytics and programming has found an inconsistency in a Life File. One that has been overlooked for years. It could be a one-off involving only this file but there might be others and the Solons want this investigated. A team has been put together to find out how this, let's call it anomaly, occurred and if more exist. Charlotte is team leader. I know you and she have history, but she wants you read in on what's been found then join the team and, if required, set up for a cull, or culls."

Still feeling the physical effects of Eleanor's visit on his body he stretched and swung his legs out of the hammock, "Where are the team?"

"At Charlotte's cabin."

"I have the location. I'll be right there."

When he arrived, the team members were on the porch admiring the view across a turquoise-blue lake with snow-capped mountains.

Victoria from Watchers remarked to Charlotte, "Gorgeous place, did you do it yourself or is it copied?"

Charlotte shrugged. "The cabin is a copy of one my uncle had, I liked it and it saved me having to design one and the view is nice. Maybe it's one I knew back in life." She gave a brief nod to acknowledge Richard's arrival and said, "Let's go inside and get started."

Charlotte was known to be all business and her organisational skills were second to none. With a brilliant mind but little in the way of social skills she had hated the schmoozing and politicking that had been part of her career tracks life side. Calling people out for talking bullshit had often stalled a promising move up the corporate ladder.

"I arranged for drinks and snacks so help yourselves then Jenny can give Richard the background."

Coffees and soft drinks along with sandwiches were collected from a buffet table. The group took up all the seats, so Charlotte wheeled a chair from her study. Sandwiches and drinks were still being consumed when Charlotte told them all to go verbal.

"Jenny, give Richard a brief outline of how you found the anomaly," Charlotte directed.

Hurriedly swallowing a mouthful of egg salad on rye Jenny began, "I was finishing up a new computer program which I call Wide Spectrum Single Constants. The purpose of the program is to find single common denominators which connect crimes that appear, from Life Files, to have no shared similarities. I know that observers already use a similar program, but this is more refined and searches wider parameters."

Jenny paused to take a mouthful of coffee so Charlotte took the opportunity to say, "Just get to the point Jenny; we don't need every little detail."

Jenny's mouth tightened at this curt admonishment and to show displeasure she put her mug on the coffee table with more force than was necessary. This show of truculence seemed lost on Charlotte.

"It was when I ran a full program test looking for any faults or false positives that flags began to appear beside numerous Life Files. The program was telling me that thirty-six people had been killed over a twenty-four-year period with no past or current Life File giving any indication of who the killer was. The program had found a single constant across all the deaths and that constant is a Doctor Brian Meldrew. Dr Meldrew has been in the vicinity at or near the time of death of each victim as determined by autopsy. All the killings, the murders, remain unsolved and most have gone cold life side." Having got to the point Jenny picked up the remains of her coffee and sat back.

Chapter 8

"Why you? It's because of the breadth of your life experiences." What he came to know as an Ether Screen appeared above the coffee table and felt no surprise at this happening.

"Here is a brief overview of the responsibilities Concordat have and how your life experiences can help in their mission. Take a look."

The scope of Concordat custodianships became immediately apparent as did the elements of his life that had prepared him for their offer. When the Ether Screen went blank and disappeared, he said, "I understand."

Amber smiled across at him, "Fantastic isn't it, what the human brain can absorb when some areas usually dormant are woken up. You saw and understood all that at almost time light speed."

He asked, "Which of those sections will I be working for?"

"Watching your Life File, we have you pegged for Retribution if you are accepted. It will all be made clear when you die."

He sat forward in surprise, "What do you mean? *Could* be joining and *if* I'm accepted. I thought everything was arranged and taken care of. I accepted the Concordat offer and did not expect, nor will I accept, these last minute 'coulds' and 'ifs'. I entered into our agreement with the understanding it will relieve my wife and family of the burden that my slide into and ultimate death from dementia would bring them. It's as first agreed, or you can erase all memory and go now."

Amber remained unperturbed by his outburst, "That is exactly the response we expected from you. Let me explain. Many who accept the offer are so enthralled by all the hoopla of me, or someone else, turning up and doing the forehead touching and heightened senses thing along with the offer and other stuff like the Life File and Ether Screen that they lose sight of what is being asked of them. Even after the Ether Screen presentation many do not ask the salient question, 'what will I be doing?' Some think it is a way of bypassing death and don't care what Concordat asks of them, they just want out of a future filled with pain or degeneration or both. Most want out for themselves and not for any benefit it would bring their family and others. Concordat are custodians of planets not just individuals but it is individuals like you that think and act beyond themselves that are needed to monitor the progress of a planet's lifeforms and sometimes to bring direction to, or in extreme cases, eliminate an individual lifeform."

Amber paused while he took this in then continued, "After you have died and been met by one of my colleagues you will be taken to an arrivals facility and there you will meet someone from transitions who will tell you all about Concordat and what we do and then review your Life File with you. It would serve no purpose to tell you more right now because we have to prepare your brain to assimilate all that's going to be flooding into it but in the nanosecond before your death you will remember all that we have done here and what I have explained to you. Nothing that happens will cause you pain or discomfort." Cradling her teacup in her hands she leant forward and looking directly into his eyes asked, "Are you satisfied with what I have told you?"

He answered, "I am. I believe you when you say no harm will come to me and now that I understand the reason for the 'could' and 'if' statement I'm willing to go ahead."

"Very well, Richard. I will visit you again in two days and we will review all we've spoken about and the decision you made. During that visit I will make the offer from Concordat again and you will once more have the option to accept or refuse and whichever your choice it will be final."

Chapter 9

Charlotte nodded towards Yuri from Life Files who took up the story, "I was called in to find out how the killings have remained hidden for so long. They had to have got past my observers and compilers who not only have direct observation but as Jenny pointed out they have their own search programs. I have no idea how this has been missed for twenty-four years."

"And that is why this team has been put together," came from Charlotte. "First, we need to know how this Dr Meldrew, assuming the results from Jenny's program are correct, how this doctor has kept his movements hidden from us and once we know that we can tell if he is a one-off or if there are more like him in the Life Files. Meldrew *should* have been flagged because his Life File exists, and it *should* have a record of him in the vicinity around the time of the deaths. I've got a meeting with a section head about another matter, so you carry on and bring Richard up to speed, Eleanor. You can stay here if you wish or find somewhere else and let me know. Any queries? No. Then I'll be on my way, and I'll hear from you later, Eleanor." After returning her chair to the study she stopped beside Richard and bent to whisper in his ear. He gave a slight nod and then she left without any words of goodbye.

"I've heard about her," came from Victoria into the brief silence following Charlotte's departure. "And it seems to be true. She is totally without social skills or a sense of humour. Richard, what was the whispering about?"

All eyes came to rest on Richard. "You're right about her lack of social skills, she's always been that way. But she does have a sense of humour."

Ted from Watchers asked, "How do you know that, about her sense of humour? Does anyone else know anything about her?"

Before the enquiry could be taken further Eleanor broke in, "That's enough. Let it drop. We have more important matters to attend to."

Victoria pouted and mumbled, "Bummer, I was looking forward to a wander down that memory lane," which brought a 'don't push your luck' glare from Eleanor. Victoria took a totally focused interest in picking imaginary lint from her skirt.

Eleanor turned to Richard, "For starters Victoria and Ted have already put full-time Watchers on Meldrew and any family members that live with him and told them to report every hour. Yuri has got Observers going back over all the periodic downloads taken from Meldrew and those from members of his family. They're looking for any collusion or even accidental connection that helped him. Jenny and Alan checked her program to make absolutely sure there was no strange glitch. All kinds of diagnostics were run but we needed to be fully convinced before we asked you to do a neuron search on Meldrew. If he *is* hiding thirty-six killings from us, then who knows what you will find when you go in. That's a broad stroke outline for Richard but has anyone got anything to add?" Silence. "No, then the rest of you can go back to your sections to keep digging into how this got past us, and I'll give you a call about getting together later."

The others left leaving Richard and Eleanor alone in the cabin.

"Thanks for stepping in, I should have kept my mouth shut about her sense of humour."

"You are welcome. It's sufficient that only the three of us know about the relationship, nobody else needs to." After a pause Eleanor murmured, "However, you *can* tell *me* what she whispered to you."

Moving to sit beside her he smiled and said, "Don't be so nosey but maybe, just maybe, I'll tell you if you are really good to me next private time." He got a hard punch to the bicep in response.

Chapter 10

On the day he was to confirm his decision to join Concordat he had returned from a trip to the supermarket to find her waiting in his apartment and he felt her syncing with him the moment he opened the door. This was the first time she had visited during the day. He nodded to her as he placed the shopping on the kitchen worktop. Removing his jacket, he hung it in the hall closet then went back into the kitchen to place the few foodstuffs he had bought into the fridge and cupboards before asking, "Can I get you something? Tea, coffee, soda?"

"Tea please. Some Earl Grey would be nice," she answered with a smile.

Nothing more was said while water was brought to the boil and the tea was allowed to infuse to a deep golden hue inside the glass teapot. He poured the aromatic brew into china mugs and added a half tablespoonful of sugar and some milk to one then just a dash of milk to the other. He carried both mugs to the living area and handed the one with a dash of milk to her then sat on the other easy chair. They both sipped and savoured the tea and he waited for her to speak.

She had first come to him ten days before while he slept and twice more since then. She had told him her name was Ambrosine Light (please call me Amber) and that she came from Concordat with an offer for him. He knew she was coming on this day for confirmation of his acceptance, she had told him she would.

"You have learned of the Concordat offer and what is required of you. You accepted the offer at my last visit. Do you confirm that acceptance now?"

Without hesitation, "Yes."

"Good. Six months from today you will die and someone from Concordat will come to assist in your transfer. It will not be me but someone from your Life File that has predeceased you. It will be someone you knew and were comfortable with. The choice as to who depends on their availability at the time."

From a slim document case resting against the side of her chair Ambrosine Light took a pale blue folder with the word 'Life File' and his name embossed on it. She had shown him the file before and although it was micromillimetres thin, his life history was contained within and any event could be extracted from it with every detail clearly evident. Below his name was the outline of a thumb.

"To seal your contract with Concordat and to confirm your acceptance of their offer please place a thumb in the space indicated and a record of your DNA will go to the Concordat archives. It takes only a nanosecond and you will not feel anything." He did as requested and Amber slid his Life File back into her document case.

"Thank you, Richard. The next time we meet it will be at Concordat, goodbye for now."

Picking up the document case and her mug she went to the kitchen and placed the mug on the counter then she let herself out of the apartment, unsyncing as she closed the door.

He sat silent and still until long after his remaining tea had gone cold. He sat as the first fractures of his mind started to open and particles of memory began to fall through.

He was not aware, but it was as Ambrosine Light said it would be.

Chapter 11

Later, Jenny contacted Eleanor by closed loop saying she and Alan wanted to meet with her and Richard away from the other team members. Eleanor told her at the diner.

They sat in booth five and ate lemon meringue pie.

Alan licked his fork and sighed, "Isn't this one of the great things about being with Concordat? Everything tastes just the same as when we were in life."

There were noises of agreement from the others. Jenny was a little slower, so they waited until with a last 'Mm-Mm' she put her fork down then Eleanor leaned forward with forearms on the table to say, "Okay you two, you've had your treat now tell us why we're here." Jenny looked at Alan and made a hand gesture that signalled 'go ahead'.

"I want us to go verbal and lifebrain, best to keep this between us for now." He waited until they each confirmed. "Jenny called me when her program first coughed up the flags about the killings and Meldrew and asked me to run an independent diagnostic. I knew Jenny was working on something, but she hadn't told me a lot about it so when we synced and she downloaded, I was amazed. A masterpiece, that's the only word for it. Anyway, Jenny told me to attack every line in the program, she wanted me to find any weakness or flaw. I ran every test and variable in the book, and some I created myself, and the outcome was always the same, a killing with Meldrew in the vicinity at the M E's estimated time of death. Eleanor, you told us to go back and run all the diagnostics again which we did, plus new ones Jenny and I thought up, and the results always come back to Meldrew. Somehow, he is hiding his killings from us, *or*, and I hate to say this, they are being removed from his Life File."

Before anyone could speak, Richard signalled the waitress over and asked for coffees all round and they sat in silence until they arrived then he said, "I can't believe that anyone in Life Files is involved. What would they have to gain? There is nothing that happens life side that directly affects observers and compilers, and we all know how closely Yuri monitors her Life File people."

Alan agreed, "I'm with Richard. The only Concordat people that have direct contact with life siders are destination consultants and Retribution personnel, and the Ret's only to plan and carry out a cull, *and*, Yuri moves her people around from file to file, they are never with one full-time."

Eleanor rotated her coffee mug between her hands, "All true and I'm inclined to agree that Yuri and her team would have found out if an observer or compiler is involved." Here she paused and looked into the dark reflecting pool of her coffee, "But what if an observer or compiler has found a way around the emotion block of Meldrew's particular file and is experiencing the same feelings and emotions that Meldrew does at the killing? What if one of them has become addicted to and complicit in the killings and is removing them from the file? Jenny, is that possible?"

Jenny took time to think this over, then said, "Perhaps. The emotion blocks are very strong, and we have no evidence that anybody in analytics and programming has found a way to circumvent them. However—if a way has been found then any of the observers and compilers could access a file at any time and alter it. If that's happening, we are about to stir up a real shitstorm."

Richard said, "Hold on. In order to get in and out of the file without attracting attention then knowledge of when a killing was about to take place, or had taken place, would be needed. Thirty-six in twenty-four is one every eight months. What I suggest is for Jenny and Alan to get together with Yuri and check the records to see if the name of an observer or compiler keeps coming up around the times of the killings."

Alan and Jenny looked at each other then began to talk together.

Eleanor jumped in, "Don't talk at the same time, we can't understand you. We're on lifebrain, remember."

Alan fell silent and Jenny said, "We can input a search addition that will tell us who the O and C's have been throughout the Life File." Rising from her seat she motioned to Alan, "Come on, let's go and get started."

Eleanor caught Jenny's arm saying, "Before you start, I want you to go to Yuri and explain what you are doing and why. Two reasons for this, first you won't be stepping on Yuri's toes and second, I want you to gauge her reaction when you tell her. If she is at all reluctant to help, let me know."

Alan was startled, "You don't think Yuri is…"

Eleanor interrupted, "I don't think anything at the moment Alan but until we know for certain that Life Files are not involved, we can't rule anything out. Get this done as quickly as you can and if we don't find in-house involvement then Richard will do a neuron search. We'll talk again later."

After they had gone, Eleanor and Richard ordered second cups of coffee. He mused, "If there is an in-house connection it will cause one hell of a shake up."

Eleanor agreed, "Yes and it will throw into doubt every protocol and procedure we use to recruit life siders."

Richard nodded, his face grim, "The requirement books would have to be rewritten. Are you going to tell Charlotte about this, about the possibility?"

"No, not right now. I'll wait until Jenny and Alan get back to me. I'd rather go to her with a firm result that Life Files *are* or *are not* involved."

They were silent as they finished their coffees then they left the diner.

It was when their waitress was passing booth five that she noticed the plates, forks and mugs and found the exact amount for the coffees and pie piled in the middle of the table and a twenty-dollar bill under a mug. Smiling she stuffed the twenty into her apron pocket. Walking back to the counter she tried to recall who had sat in booth five. She couldn't remember—which surprised her.

Chapter 12

It happened as Ambrosine Light had said. Before dawn November thirtieth, the day of his seventy-second birthday he died in bed beside his wife. Everything about Ambrosine Light's visits, the Concordat offer, and his acceptance came flooding back to him in the microsecond before the blood clot did its work.

A pure blackness surrounded the billion centillion particles that had flowed from his dead body, and which were now coalescing around the neural part of him that was witnessing the event. The final assembly was a body that was unmistakably his.

He was looking at an infinity of darkness when he was grasped by the shoulders from behind and a voice said, "It is remarkable isn't it? We know you've been lots of places on planet Earth so we figured we would give you a cosmic experience." The voice and the painted fingernails he could see by squinting downwards to his shoulder suggested it was a woman holding him. "Right now, you are looking out from the very edge of all universes to where there are no stars. There are star nurseries out there, but none have given birth yet, hence the darkness. When I turn you around you will recognise me because I'm in your Life File."

He was spun round and looked in amazement at a face he knew very well. "Welcome to Concordat, Richard," a woman he instantly recognised said. Before he could respond she kissed him full on the lips then held him at arm's length saying, "I'm the friendly face sent to greet you as Amber promised and I'm so glad you decided to join Concordat." Tilting her head from side to side she scrutinised his face before saying, "Goodness you have aged since we last saw each other, but never mind, that can be taken care of. How do you think I've stood up to the ravages of time?"

Eventually he overcame his surprise and found his voice, "Eleanor, it's wonderful to see you again and you look terrific and hardly any different than when we were last together, time has treated you very well."

"Thank you and we will have lots of time to catch up later but now we have to go to life sider arrivals where you will be introduced to Abigail from transitions who will process you but first, we need to get you dressed, you can't turn up naked the first time you meet Abigail. Think of the clothes you want to be wearing." He thought dark blue polo with jeans and sneakers and immediately he was dressed in them.

Eleanor said, "Okay, now you are decent, let's go find Abigail."

Chapter 13

Yuri had called in observers from off time to go through the years of periodic downloads of Meldrew and family once the common thread became known. She told them that analytics and programming had cause to believe that Meldrew was a serial killer, but that the killings were not making it into his Life File. Each had been given a five-year download period and told to scrutinise them for anything that looked out of place. Yuri was surprised when Jenny said she and Alan were on their way to see her, so far nothing had been found that would interest analytics and programming.

The analysts could see that Yuri was anxious in case anything pointed to wrongdoing by her people. Alan asked that the three of them go lifebrain and verbal then he explained Eleanor's directive.

Yuri stiffened when the possibility was raised that an observer or compiler could be involved. "I am sure no such thing has happened—I have absolute confidence in all my people."

Jenny said softly, "We don't think anyone in Life Files is involved Yuri, but we have to confirm it. I'm sure you see the logic, and it will save you and your people the necessity of reviewing all those records. Please have your observers shut down while we install our program into their download system."

Yuri squared her shoulders, "I'll have them disconnect and I'm sure you'll find none of my people are involved." Going out of lifebrain she synced with the observers and told them to take a break until she contacted them.

Alan and Jenny immediately synced together and entered the Life File system where they removed the existing observer and compiler program and installed theirs. At hyper speed it took little time for the central server neural hub to indicate the program was installed and ready to run. Jenny asked Yuri to pick a periodic download record belonging to someone already deceased. Jenny explained that it would be used as a test and control run to confirm that the program was listing all observers and compilers and the dates they were involved.

Yuri brought up the periodic download directory and scrolled through to stop at Malcolm Dennis. "Use that one. I followed it when I was a compiler and observer."

The names of those involved with the Malcolm Dennis record along with their date logs raced across Yuri's view screen. The final analysis from the program was that only the observers and compilers directly involved had accessed the Life File record.

Alan smiled at Jenny, "It works. It will give us what we need to know when we check out the Meldrew record."

Yuri asked, "Can I put my people back to work except for the Meldrew file while you check it out." Jenny answered, "Yes, of course. We will transfer Meldrew's Life File to analytics and programming and get to work on it." Yuri took Jenny by the arm, "I want to know the results from Meldrew's downloads immediately."

Jenny responded by squeezing Yuri's hand, "We know you do, and we'll let you know as soon as we can."

Yuri moved her people on the Meldrew file to others already in progress and directed the rest to go back to work.

Chapter 14

They were in a large room that, to him, seemed to have appeared around them rather than they moving to it. Through large open French doors, he saw a wide terrace and beyond its balustrade the deep blue of a calm sea.

Eleanor introduced him, "Abigail, this is Richard. He's a dear friend of mine. Richard, this is Abigail, and she will be taking you most of the way through transition. I've delivered him as promised, Abigail, so I'll head back to work." The two women hugged and Eleanor, after giving Richard a hug and kiss on the cheek, left through the French doors.

Abigail smiled and in a soft Irish brogue said, "Hello Richard. Let's go outside and I'll fill you in on what's going to happen."

The terrace was rectangular and formed of pink veined white marble five meters wide from the wall of the building and ten meters across the building façade. A balustrade one metre high lined the edges and had columns of the same pink veined marble supporting thick flat capstones of black marble. The terrace stood on a hillside that dropped steeply down one hundred and thirty-three metres to a cove with a white sand beach. How he knew these measurements to be exact he had no idea; he just knew that's what they were. He turned at the balustrade and looked back at the building which was built in the classic Mediterranean villa style. Two stories, large windows with slatted wood shutters, balconies beneath each upstairs window and painted brilliant white with trims highlighted in deep blue. More cliff sloped upward behind the villa which stood on a small plateau. He could see two tracks to the side of the villa, one switch backing upward to the cliff top seventy-six metres above the terrace and the other taking a meandering zigzag route down to the cove.

Abigail hitched herself onto a capstone and patted the space beside her in an indication that he should join her and for a few minutes they sat in silence facing the villa absorbing the warmth of the sun and feeling the gentle heat captured in the capstones.

Abigail said, "During the transition process certain episodes of your life will be seen that contain events that did not reflect well on you. How do you feel about that?"

Needing time to think he moved to stand and leaned with his hands on the balustrade looking out over the cove to the water's horizon. Abigail sat and waited for him to answer and seemed in no hurry for his reply which was to answer her question with one of his own, "Why is it necessary to do that at all, what purpose does it serve?"

"It serves the purpose of eventually getting rid of the clutter in your brain. Memories you want to retain will be retained and those you want cleared will be cleared. A very small number of persons you knew that predeceased you, like Eleanor, are already here and another purpose of the review is to reunite you with them if you have the desire to do so."

Stepping back from the balustrade he looked at Abigail and smiled, "I see. Well then, let's get on with it."

Chapter 15

Eleanor received reports from Victoria and Ted at Watchers that nothing unusual was happening with Meldrew or his family members. They were going about their daily lives and routines and all their actions seemed perfectly normal. The close watch would continue. Jenny reported the test run had been successful and suggested the team, with the exception of Yuri, be in attendance when Meldrew's records were run. Eleanor agreed and told them to gather at analytics and programming.

Alan said, "Yuri will be devastated if we find one of hers is mixed up in this, and she's upset she can't be here when we run Meldrew's records."

"She might be upset but she understands she needs to be at arm's length until we find out one way or the other so let's get started," came from Richard.

Eleanor nodded to Jenny who said, "Okay—everyone direct sync to viewer two, here's the Meldrew file."

There was a collective sigh of relief when the program found nothing to indicate anyone from Life File had attempted to alter or obscure anything in the records. The program did flag and confirmed what Jenny had first found—the downloads put Meldrew in the vicinity at the medical examiner's time of death and this was the only single constant across all thirty-six killings and across all twenty-four years.

They un-synced and went lifebrain and verbal. "How the fuck has he kept them hidden?" Ted asked.

Alan stretched and yawned before asking, "Eleanor, can I be the one to tell Yuri that Life File are in the clear?"

"Sure, go ahead and then both of you meet the rest of us at the diner. I think pie is in order while we discuss our next move which is most likely a neuron search by Richard."

When they were all at the diner selections were made and pie wedges consumed before the topic of the neuron search came up over teas and coffees. Eleanor pushed her plate away to make room for a mug of coffee and opened with, "When we do a search, we know what to look for and it's usually to confirm a decision to cull after all other options have been explored. This time we have no idea what we are looking for or what might be found so I want your proposals on how best to locate his hiding places and more importantly how we protect Richard while he's carrying out his search."

Yuri, looking much happier knowing her section had been cleared, spoke up, "I think Richard should do a recon. Go in and get the lay of the land and see if there is anything out of the ordinary like a hemisphere anomaly or synaptic crossovers. Anyway, I don't think Richard should go too deep the first time, we need to know more before he does that."

Ted chimed in, "I'm with Yuri on this. Look, everything about Meldrew scans normal so however and wherever he's hiding this stuff it must be very deep and certainly nothing that we've seen before. We need to probe first because it's possible that Richard could get trapped in Meldrew's hiding place."

Next was Alan, "We can ignore all the usual places killers use because they would have been found during periodic downloads. Do we agree on that?" Murmurs of assent from the rest of them, "Okay, that will narrow down the number of search areas. Now, we know that serial killers always want to relive the events so we can eliminate all areas incapable of retention and recall with emotions and therefore narrow the search areas even more which means less risk to Richard. What do you think?"

Again, murmurs of approval then Victoria — who had been finger doodling in slopped coffee — focused all attention on her when she said, "I think we should first figure out when he is likely to kill again. We need to get an idea of his schedule from the time of deaths in the autopsy reports and that will give us a guide to when he will do it again. We can't plan Richard's search until we know how much time is available before his next killing and we need to do it on Earth Time." She began finger doodling again, "I assume that Concordat wants him stopped *before* he kills again."

Silence hung over the table following Victoria's statement until Richard spoke up, "You're right Victoria, we have to know his next kill date. We already know he kills about every eight months, but we need a more exact time frame." Turning to Eleanor, "I think Jenny and Alan should work their analytic magic and come up with the exact number of earth days between each event. Once we have that we can add them to the date of his last kill and know, within a reasonable approximation, when the next will take place."

Alan and Jenny looked expectantly at Eleanor who nodded and said, "Go ahead you two, do it."

As Alan and Jenny were rising from their seats Yuri said, "I'm not trying to tell you how to do your jobs but if you don't find an exact number, I suggest you look for outside influences such as phases of the moon or numeric and alphabetic sequences or does a particular day or time keep coming up. I've seen a woman's menstrual cycle be the catalyst for killing."

Alan came to Yuri's seat and placed a kiss on her cheek saying, "Thank you, that's a great help." Yuri blushed.

As the analysts left the booth Jenny said, "We'll get back to you as soon as we get a result, Eleanor."

"Do that. I've got to report to Charlotte soon."

A large tip was waiting for their waitress who had no memory of who had occupied the booth.

Chapter 16

Abigail's skirt rode high up her thighs as she slid from the capping stones and he thought *mmm, nice legs.* Giving her hips a swish to settle the skirt she smiled and said, "Thank you kind Sir, I've always felt them to be one of my better features."

"Damn," he said. "Got to be careful what I think."

Abigail smiled, "Yes you do, for the time being at least."

Richard had had his back turned to the villa during this exchange and when he turned to follow Abigail, he found that two cinema style seats and a glass topped coffee table had appeared on the terrace.

"Before we start, I want you to meet David who will be operating the Ether Screen feed and monitoring your neurological responses and absorption rate as we go through your transition. David will not see any content from your file, his job is to make sure we don't neurologically overload you."

As Abigail finished speaking, a tall, tanned, blond haired man Richard put at about thirty dressed in pale blue board shorts and a Hawaiian shirt covered in multicoloured palm trees came from the villa. He smiled and held out a hand for Richard to shake and they did the 'pleased to meet you' exchange. David explained, "Absorption rate varies with the person, some are fast brains, some slow and neither of which is bad, but both have an impact on how quickly the individual's brain can be brought to fully functioning status. There are several steps in the process to fully functioning which will become clear as Abigail leads you through them. Abigail and I will be in contact throughout, and you will be synced to her and able to communicate. Rest periods will be taken with the number needed being determined by how your brain is reacting to the amount of inflow and the speed at which it is receiving and processing it. From Amber's visit reports and how Eleanor spoke when she knew she was to greet you we are sure you'll handle everything just fine. I'll leave Abigail to tell you about the rest of the process and I'll see you later." With a nod and a smile to them both David went into the villa.

"Let's sit down," Abigail said gesturing towards the seats. "Would you like a drink?"

He asked for coffee and no sooner were the words out of his mouth than a woman who he guessed to be in early forties appeared carrying a tray with a carafe filled with coffee and two mugs which she placed on the table saying, "I'll be back with milk, cream and sweeteners in a moment." Then she went back into the villa.

Richard turned to watch as she crossed the terrace and went into the villa then turning to Abigail said, "I know that woman from somewhere but can't remember her name. Is she someone from my Life File?'

"No, not directly but you knew of her during your life. She's Amelia Earhart the aviator."

"The woman that went missing attempting to fly around the world in the nineteen thirties. That's her? I knew her face meant something to me. How did she end up with Concordat?'

"I'm the best one to answer that," Amelia Earhart said as she came back onto the terrace carrying the milk and sweeteners. After placing the tray on the table, she offered Richard her hand which he shook in slack jawed amazement. "Pleased to meet you, Richard. All the theories about what happened are way off the mark. You'll know some of them I'm sure, so I won't rehash. Simply put, I had a heart attack and died, and my navigator, Fred Noonan tried to get us to Howland Island but because of navigation errors due to not taking into account prevailing winds he missed it and the plane ran out of fuel and crashed into the sea. Somebody from Concordat came to me during the heart attack and made me an offer. Unfortunately, Fred died in the crash and Concordat made sure he did not suffer. That's the story. I work in the preselection section at the moment looking over Life Files for suitable candidates to approach about Concordat. Yours was one of them. Interesting life you led. Anyway Richard, it's been good meeting you in the flesh so to speak. Enjoy your coffee. See you later, Abigail. Oh, and by the way, Richard I'm thirty-nine not early forties." With a final smile to both Amelia Earhart turned and went back into the villa.

"We should sit now," Abigail said gesturing to the chairs. "Amelia took you by surprise, she wanted to meet you and see the person she's been tracking through your Life File but the moment she entered the villa she was wiped. She now has no knowledge of you or your Life File. Help yourself to coffee then we'll get started."

Chapter 17

Eleanor had been contacted by Charlotte and told to come to her cabin to report on progress. This surprised Eleanor because she had expected to do it the usual way by distance syncing.

Knocking on the front door and hearing a shouted 'come in', she entered to find that in the dining area the table had been covered with a white linen cloth and cutlery for two laid out. Smells that made Eleanor's mouth water were coming from the kitchen. She was in the throes of taking her coat off when Charlotte popped her head out of the kitchen and said, "Make yourself at home and there's some bottles of stuff in the cabinet and ice in the bucket if you want a drink before dinner. Hope you like roast beef."

After answering in the affirmative Eleanor added some ice to a glass and poured herself a mineral water. "Anything I can do to help in there?" she called across the room.

"No. I'm good. Just dishing up, be out in a minute."

Charlotte spent the next while bustling backwards and forwards with salad and vegetables and finally a roast already carved into slices. She gestured that Eleanor should take a seat and then sat down herself before offering red wine. "Let's wait until after dessert before we talk shop."

Everything about the meal had been delicious and for dessert crème brûlée which Charlotte caramelised with a propane torch was made. A lot of trouble had been taken, even down to the wine which complimented the meal perfectly. Small talk was exchanged about their years in life and Concordat but with both steering clear of the common thread that ran through both their Life Files. After the meal and before coffee — both decided against brandy — they cleared away the remnants of their meal and loaded the dishwasher before settling down at each end of the sofa cradling coffees.

They were very different in looks and temperament. Eleanor a voluptuous beauty with a down-to-earth approach to things that belied her intellect. She was a people person and always keen to try new things. She could be forceful when needed but always tried to treat people with kindness and respect. Charlotte was attractive with a good figure although she thought her calves too big and her cheeks too chubby. Her IQ was off the scale. She often spoke without considering how her words might hurt and her ego was easily bruised. She looked at life very seriously and was known to hold a grudge. Both women featured in Richard's Life File.

Looking over the rim of her coffee cup Charlotte said, "Bring me up to speed on the case."

Eleanor told her about the program run that had cleared observer's and compilers of any involvement and the details of the meeting held to determine the best way to carry out a neuron search without putting Richard at undue risk. She explained what Alan and Jenny were doing in an effort to uncover the exact time between killings so that they knew when the next might take place and then plan accordingly. She said she expected to hear from analytics and programming soon. She went into detail about the input of each team member and the decisions made so that by the time she was finished her coffee was almost cold.

Charlotte said nothing during the report, she just sipped coffee and her eyes never left Eleanor. "I'm going to pour myself more coffee, yours must be cold so let me bring you a fresh one." Eleanor was perplexed, this was a new Charlotte, she had never known her to be so solicitous and friendly.

Returning with fresh coffees Charlotte handed Eleanor hers then sat and curled her legs onto the sofa. "It seems you and your team have everything well in hand and I'm glad that Yuri's people have been cleared. Jenny's program that found Meldrew is genius, but it has brought queries from the Solons as to why analytics and programming had not thought to create it sooner. We suspect Meldrew is a serial killer from evidence that he was close at the time but until the results of the neuron search are in, we have no direct proof. If proof is there then every Life File we have, living and deceased, will have to be rescanned looking for the method Meldrew has used to evade the observers and compilers." Charlotte placed her cup on a side table, then said, "The Solons want every precaution taken during the neuron search. They want a second operative in there who will have a neural connection, a hard link, with Richard during the search. It will be a lifeline that can be used to retrieve Richard if he gets into trouble. I told the Solons I believe you are the best one for the job, so I've come to you first. How do you feel about it?"

Eleanor let this sink in then answered, "I'm not sure. I mean I'm pleased that you and the Solons think I'm up to the task, but I've never heard of it being done before—so is this a first?" Charlotte gave a single nod. "I see, then how do we know it will work?"

"We don't. If anything does go wrong then you, or whoever it is with Richard will have to work something out on the spot. The neural connection is the best plan we have and for it to have any chance then someone needs to be in there with him."

"Has Richard been told about the plan?"

"Yes. I discussed it with him before inviting you here and he's on board. Of course, he wanted to know who would be with him and I told him I would be talking to likely candidates. He's waiting to hear from me."

"Did he give any suggestion, or even hint, as to who he wanted with him?"

Charlotte shook her head, "He didn't. He wouldn't bring pressure to bear that way."

Eleanor swung her legs off the sofa and went to French doors through which she could see the moon silvered mountains and lake and stood for some time. Charlotte sat quietly and waited.

Returning to the sofa she sat and looked at Charlotte. "Yes, I'll do it."

"Thank you. I felt you would and I'm sure Richard knew you would be one of those I'd chosen to speak to." Charlotte lowered her head and in a soft voice said, "If you had said no then I was going to do it. Richard should have someone with him who knows him well and has been close to him just in case anything goes wrong." Lifting her head, she smiled, "You are a far better choice, I would never have made it in Retribution, I'm too squeamish. Do you want to tell him or shall I?"

"Let me do it, we'll have things to plan and talk about."

"Very well. Not much more we can do until analytics and programming are heard from so why don't we have a brandy now and relax."

Eleanor accepted and as Charlotte made her way to the liquor cabinet, she thought in wonderment at what a different person Charlotte was when it concerned someone close to her heart. It seemed the Charlotte of the Concordat wore her abruptness and seeming lack of empathy like armour to cover her vulnerability.

Chapter 18

Richard poured coffee and Abigail who already had hers waited until he sat back in his chair and took a drink. It tasted exactly like Tim Hortons coffee, his favourite brew from his local fast-food place.

Cradling her coffee mug between her hands Abigail began, "The dog and pony show isn't necessary. We could simply take a person from their body and sit them right down here, but we put on the show to gauge the person's reaction. You are showing remarkable equanimity for someone that has just gone through all that hoopla. You show very little in the way of surprise at what's been happening or what you've been told or who you have met, with the exception of Amelia perhaps, or the explanations given. You seem to take it all in your stride and exhibit no apprehension or anxiety. Why is that?"

He took some time to consider his answer and Abigail waited, "As I died, I remembered clearly the offer I had accepted and knew in that moment that there was nothing I had any control over. Once before I was in a life-and-death situation over which I had no control, and the final outcome was in the hands of others. There was nothing in my life that had prepared me for that situation. There was nothing in my experience or what I knew that would change the outcome of the circumstance, so I made peace with that and put my life in the hands of a pilot and co-pilot who had the training and experience to save me and my fellow passengers, if that was at all possible. That episode must be in my Life File and Concordat must know the impact it had on my life and the stoicism with which I approached my life after the event. Is that not clear from my Life File?'

"I haven't seen your Life File," Abigail responded. "Transition reviewers, that's my position at the moment, don't have any prior knowledge of the type of life a newcomer has led. We need to approach each transition without any preconceived ideas or notions. After your transition is complete David and I will have filled our quota — we only get to do five — and we will be transferred to other departments. Transfers within Concordat are common until the most suitable department where an individual can excel is found. It might seem to be a very trial and error system but it's amazing the talents that come to light that were hidden or not given the opportunity to grow during a life. Thank you for the explanation and I'll look for the incident you mentioned as we go through your review."

"If you haven't seen my Life File, how do you know there are events or episodes that reflect badly on me?" Richard enquired.

"Everybody has things and events in their lives that they prefer not to be reminded of Richard. Nobody has a perfect life." Placing her mug on the table she called to David, "Please set up the Ether Screen and prepare to sync and run Richard's Life File. I'll give you the go ahead once I've explained to Richard what to expect."

"Roger that," David's voice came from inside the villa. "Here comes the screen and let me know when to start."

A large clear screen looking very much like an ultra large heads-up display appeared above the coffee table. There were a series of lights and symbols pulsing around the edges and in a lower corner the trace lines of what seemed to Richard to be his heart rhythm. He thought it bore some resemblance to vital signs monitors he'd been hooked up to in hospitals. When asked, Abigail confirmed it was indeed similar but to a far more sophisticated degree.

"I'm going to sync with you and David now and once we have checked our connections we'll get started. You'll get the hang of it as we go along and feel free to ask questions and seek clarification. We have all the time in the universe so no rush. Okay David, here's the sync and let's check to see what the starting absorption rate is for Richard."

Chapter 19

Messages had gone out from analytics and programming to all team members that Jenny and Alan had results from the timeline search and wanted to meet immediately. Eleanor, who was still with Charlotte at the time, told them all to meet at her apartment on Chowringee Road.

It was a spacious apartment and modelled after one her parents had owned. All the windows were open and large fans lazily mixed the warm and pungent air into the sounds of Kolkata at night. Richard knew the apartment well; he and Eleanor had first met in Kolkata. Eleanor clapped her hands to silence the chatter and when she had everyone's attention, she told them to go verbal and called on Jenny and Alan to tell what they had found about Meldrew's killing cycles.

Jenny started, "All references to time are Earth Greenwich Mean Time. The killings all happened in Britain starting in nineteen-ninety-five. We found the date of the first killing from the autopsy report, so we plugged in some lines of program that looked for similarities, or exacts, in time between killings over the twenty-four-year period. The first killing occurred on the first of January 1995 and from the body temperature at the scene the autopsy report says at or shortly after midnight. The second death occurred on the second of August, ninety-five, with a time of death put between one and two a.m. The third was April third, ninety-six, with time between two and three a.m. The fourth on December fourth at approximately four a.m. I'm sure you can all see a pattern emerging here. Eight Earth calendar moths plus one day plus one hour. We found that to be consistent —give or take an autopsy hour or two — across all killings and across all twenty-four years. The six extra days for leap years during that time became part of the cycle. Alan can tell you the rest."

"It works out that he is on a cycle of three kills every twenty-four months plus the additional twenty-five hours added from the previous kill." Alan paused to look around. "Okay, I see by your faces you want the bottom line. Earth date now is September twentieth and if he does not deviate, he will kill again between September twenty-sixth and thirtieth. Can't give an exact date because autopsy dates and times of death are probably *not* one hundred percent accurate." Murmurings broke out as they all took this in, and Alan gave them some time before continuing, "To check that we had not overlooked any factor that drives his compulsion to kill at these times we searched police records and autopsy reports for any consistent similarities across dump sites and their locations, we also looked at age and a hundred other markers including hair and eye colour, height, weight, body type, tattoos and even down to schooling and similarities in family upbringing and found none that were consistent across any of the victims who present the only other commonality in that they are all female. Nothing was found that points to *why* he uses these time periods we only know that he does."

Eleanor nodded toward Jenny and Alan saying, "Thank you, that's really good work, you two." Both smiled in appreciation. "All right team," Eleanor continued. "In earth time we have six days — give or take Alan and Jenny's autopsy fudge factor — to find out why he's killing and how he's keeping it from us. I want us all on earth time when working the case, the countdown has started. Yuri, get continuous real time downloads from him and get together with Richard tomorrow to take him through Meldrew's Life File and those of his family including his mother and father and any siblings, we need to be sure he's acting alone. Victoria, Ted, put Watchers on Meldrew's friends and colleagues. If he's in any clubs or fraternities, I want the members watched. Take an overview of his habits and routines and if you suspect anything put your people on the scene. Jenny and Alan, throw your net wider, go beyond the twenty-four years, maybe he practiced before deciding on the eight-month schedule so go way back even into early puberty and look for any cases that bear any similarities to the methods of killing we know he has used. Team, we need to know everything about this man. If he's having sex with his secretary or anyone else, I want to know the colour of her panties. One more thing, I met with Charlotte, and she told me that because we do not know what we will find during the neuron search the Solons want a neural lifeline attached to Richard whenever he does a search and it's been decided I will be going in with him to provide the line." Startled looks greeted her announcement and Richard smiled a smile that said he knew she would. "If the worst occurs and Richard or I or both do not make it out then Amber will perform a cull immediately. Okay that's about it for now so I'll let you get to it, and we'll meet again tomorrow. Richard, please stay, there's a few things we need to go over."

As they filed from the apartment Ted whispered to Victoria, "Yeah, I'll bet they have some things to go over, I'd like to take the minutes of that meeting." Victoria poked him in the ribs with an elbow and shushed him.

Chapter 20

Again, the slight jolt as the sync took place. David reported the connections were good and he was about to run a trial episode from Richard's Life File to confirm voice and visual continuity and get some neurological response base readings. Abigail said to go ahead.

He was in the boxing ring in the school gym sparring with someone whose face and name he could not remember. He had boxed from ages thirteen to fifteen and done pretty well at his school's level and winning his weight class one year. He heard the voice of the phys ed teacher telling him to keep his guard up and to move in fast with quick jabs to the body while telling his opponent how to block the punches. He saw, heard and even smelled everything with crystal clarity and even the voices and noises coming from others in the gym could be heard and understood clearly. He felt the sweat running down his cheeks and the pressure on the soles of his feet as he danced around the ring in pursuit of his opponent. Sharp bursts of pain were felt when a blow landed on him. He could feel the effort of his muscles working and was aware of the messages his brain was sending to all the areas of his body that made the act of boxing possible. A bell sounded and he and his opponent went to a corner to drink water and have their faces wiped while listening to the teacher give advice as the roles of attacker and defender changed for the next round. The teacher slapped each on the shoulder and told them to start boxing in the centre of the ring when the bell sounded. As he took up his stance and stared into the face of his sparring partner the screen went blank and faded away.

"How was it, David?" Abigail asked.

"Fine. Everything was there. I got all the emotional and physical responses expected and Richard managed to reach seventy percent of Light Time absorption rate."

"That's good. Thanks David. I'm going to explain the rest of the review set up to Richard now but if I miss anything that you think is specific to Richard jump right in."

"Okay, will do."

Abigail explained that although every moment of his life was recorded in his Life File much of what was considered to be without particular merit and was mostly common throughout any life had been left out of the review. All the 'boring parts' as Abigail put it with a smile.

She told him, "Observers have marked some events as being of importance to you and with outcomes that moulded your character in ways that would be of benefit to Concordat."

She paused to drink some coffee, then, "As your brain, all parts of it, becomes increasingly active you will experience the contents of the review with a clarity of emotion and physicality you have never known before. Every sense will become fully awake, every emotion fully felt and realised. Everything will be there, the good and the bad. You will see people and things you were not aware of at the time. Things that you are proud of and those you are not. Things accomplished and those that failed. Every moment of love you showed and every moment of hurt you brought, every second of hate you felt, it will all be there. All the joy and the pain will be felt again but this time with more intensity. You will see again the faces and hear the voices of those who impacted on parts of your life."

Here she stopped and gave Richard an enquiring look that invited him to speak.

"There is much about my life I am not proud. I've done things that hurt myself and others, often badly, so why it is necessary to relive them in all the detail you've outlined when there is nothing I can do to change the events. Also, the fact that you and David will be sharing those times with me makes me feel uncomfortable."

"Valid concern. David, come out and explain the reasons behind why we look at the good, the bad and the ugly."

Chapter 21

As directed by Eleanor, he met with Yuri to go over Meldrew's Life File. They decided to meet at her penthouse. It was a corner suite and the view across the city through the floor to ceiling windows was spectacular. A large balcony with potted shrubs and loungers wrapped around the two outer walls. He thought the interior decoration and furnishing to be very Yuri, mostly white with subdued blues and greys. There was a touch of the oriental about the place, and it was apparent that a lot of thought had gone into the lamps and ornaments that sat on various surfaces as well as the art on the walls. The living, kitchen and dining areas were open-plan which gave a feeling of airiness and space. Four doors, which he presumed led to bedrooms and bathrooms, were flush mounted to the two interior walls. Yuri invited him to sit wherever he liked and offered tea and coffee. He sank into a white leather easy chair that he found more comfortable than its design suggested and accepted coffee. "A little milk and a level teaspoon of sugar, am I right?"

He smiled and said, "You got that from Eleanor, that's cheating."

Yuri, who had seemed a little nervous when she opened the door visibly relaxed and smiling back said, "Busted." While Yuri busied herself getting the coffees he remarked about the view and complimented her on her choice of colours and furnishings.

"I'm glad you like it," she responded from the kitchen, pleasure evident in her voice. "In life I lived in a walk-up brownstone that froze in the winter and baked in the summer and I swear every meal by every tenant was boiled cabbage and that got mixed with the odour of urine from all the cats in the building." Continuing to talk she brought the coffees, "I used to look at ads for penthouses in the papers and dream of owning one someday. Anyway, Patricia from destinations came to me soon after the tumour in my brain was found and offered me Concordat so here I am."

Tasting his coffee, he raised the cup towards her saying, "Perfect."

They made small talk about their time in Concordat while they drank coffee and when Yuri had taken away the cups, she invited him to join her on a sofa while she brought up an Ether Screen and prepared to show highlights from Meldrew's Life File.

"Brian Meldrew. Neurosurgeon. Forty-six. Married twenty-two years. Wife's name, Constance. One child, a daughter Amy, age eighteen." As Yuri recited this information pictures of each person assembled on the screen. "On the surface a normal family with a successful father, a mother who quit working to be home during her daughter's childhood and now does volunteer and charity work and a daughter with good grades who will soon go to university. Of course, there have been the usual family frictions and arguments but nothing more than most go through. Although one in particular involves Constance's sex life. Each parent is on good terms with the other parents' and family. I can show you selections from our periodic downloads but from my experience, and that of my observers and compilers, there is nothing that points to Meldrew being a serial killer." A pause, "Even so, I've called in all my people from private time, and I've got them going over the records looking for anything the least bit off kilter but so far, nothing. If you can give me a direction we need to go or something you think we've missed, I'll bring it up."

Richard enlarged each face on the screen and studied them as if in larger-than-life format he could drag from them some previously unseen clue. Slouching deeper into butter soft leather cushions he expelled a long whistling breath and sat silently looking at Meldrew, his wife, and daughter.

Yuri sat still and silent until he spoke, "Yuri, you say there's nothing to find from their Life Files and I believe you. Unfortunately, it means that Eleanor and I will be going in blind with no idea what to look for or where to look." He took his eyes from the screen and turning his head to look at Yuri asked, "Do you have someone you can put in charge of the day-to-day running of the Life File section?"

Questioning wrinkles appeared on Yuri's brow before she answered, "Yes, I can hand it over to Charles."

Sitting up straight and turning to face her, he said, "That's good, because I want you to pick two of your top people and I want the three of you to scrutinise every move Meldrew, his wife and daughter make. No one else, just them. We have a few days before the neuron search and if there is something off kilter, I trust you to be able to find it." As he finished speaking, he placed a hand over hers to give a gentle squeeze and saw the palest pink of a blush infuse her cheeks. Still with his hand on hers he mused, "Of course we don't know for sure he is a serial killer. All we are going on is analytics and programming common denominator, but I trust Jenny and Alans take on the situation as much as I trust you to find something if it's there." Giving another squeeze he asked, "Can I have another cup of your delicious coffee and then how about a tour through the rest of your apartment?"

Chapter 22

David came from the villa and leaned against the balustrade, "There are two reasons Richard. One is to use past experiences as the datum marker from which we can measure the rate at which your brain ramps up to its full operating capability. As the review goes on you will see and experience many things that were happening around you, but which did not register at the time and of which you mostly took no notice. These things, people and events will be become more and more evident as your brain works its way towards full capability. I will monitor how quickly you start to identify them. You see, not all brains have the same capacity to utilise all that's available to them. With some the neurological make-up, the internal pathways, are not numerous enough, or in some cases not strong enough, to bring the brain to one hundred percent efficiency. The review will tell us if yours is capable of reaching that highest level. The second reason. When the review is complete your brain will be cleared of all clutter in order to free up neurological capacity that will be used to carry out whatever it is Concordat requires you to do. However, you will be able to retain some memories of past events and peoples. How many will depend on the review results. Abigail will tell you all about that once it is complete. Those are the reasons, and we hope they put you more at ease but there is one more thing you should know which I'll let Abigail explain and I'll get back to my control station."

David glanced towards Abigail who gave him a smile and a slight nod then he stood from the balustrade and went back inside.

Abigail sat forward to rest her forearms on her thighs and looking directly at his face said, "Observers and compilers who assembled your Life File and transition people like David and me cannot judge or have any opinions about the persons or the events in the file. What occurred and to whom are simply facts in a Life File. Our brains have been neutralised in those areas capable of judgement or opinion on any part of a Life File. I see concern on your face but don't worry—that will be reversed when we are reassigned. Also, after each review, transition personnel are cleared, what we call 'wiped' of all that file's contents. David and I will have no memory of you or your file when you leave us. If we meet again, we will need to introduce ourselves as if we had never met." Sitting back, she relaxed into the cushions and said, "David, please bring up the ether screen."

The review started with a picture of a ship. It was named City of Newcastle and was berthed in Royal Albert Docks, London.

Chapter 23

Later, when he had left Yuri's apartment, he decided to hike one of his favourite trails, so he closed all connectors with the exception of the one with Eleanor and messaged her of his intention. He knew she would not disturb him unless absolutely necessary. To him hiking was walking zen. He lost himself in mindfulness and each step was being in the moment. He hiked the Cape Chignecto coastal trail for eighteen kilometres from Red Rocks to Big Bald where there was a cabin in which he would spend the night. He knew the trail well and never tired of its rugged beauty. Arriving at the cabin he poured spring water that was barrel stored over his body to wash away the sweat and trail dust then prepared and ate his evening meal. Afterward, he sat on the cabin porch sipping on a mug of tea and watched the sunset across the Bay of Fundy. The silence was absolute with even the squirrels detecting his mood for tranquillity had ceased their chatter.

Sitting relaxed in an Adirondack chair and feeling the tiredness of hard hiking fatigue he watched the sun drag the last of daylight below the horizon and the sky turn from fiery reds to cobalt blue and then an ebony blackness that had uncountable pin prick holes of starlight. Words from Omar Khayyam came to him—'Be happy for this moment. This moment is your life'.

In sleep he dreamed of Yuri. He had stood beside the kitchen breakfast island while she perked fresh coffee and they talked about her work in Life Files and his in Retribution and when the coffee was poured, she said, "Bring it with you and I'll show you the rest of the apartment."

One of the doors leading from the living area led to a guest bedroom with ensuite, another to a half bathroom, the third was an office cum den and the fourth opened to the master bedroom with a connecting bathroom. Both bedrooms had outside walls with large windows offering wonderful views over the city. The colours, furniture and accessories spoke of the same care and attention to detail evident in the living area. During the tour he became more aware of how attractive Yuri was. What she wore was far removed from her dowdy work clothes. White silk blouse and lacy camisole with a pleated skirt of the palest blue that reached to just above her knees and swirled out when she turned. Her legs were long and shapely, and her toes sparkled with gold nail varnish. He complimented her again on her choice of decoration and furnishings.

They were in the master bedroom and he asked, "Is this all your work or did you use an interior designer?"

"All my own work. I'm not very socially active," she replied as if that explained everything.

He raised eyebrows in a show of surprise, "You're a very attractive woman. You must get invitations."

In an effort to hide her discomfort she reached for his coffee cup saying, "That must be empty, I'll take both to the kitchen."

Handing over his cup and in an effort to give her time to compose herself he asked, "Do you mind if I use your bathroom?"

Looking down at the cups she mumbled, "Go right ahead." Then turned and left the room.

He relieved himself then took his time washing and drying his hands. Looking in the mirror above the sink he wondered why Yuri was so uncomfortable accepting compliments from men. Leaving the bathroom and preparing to say his farewells he was surprised to find Yuri sitting on the edge of her bed. Closing the bathroom door, he inclined his head to the side and smiled an invitation for Yuri to speak.

Dropping her chin to her chest the deep breath she took was loud in the quiet room and when she exhaled it ruffled her blouse. Still with head down she began to speak. It was almost a whisper, so he went and sat beside her, and she stiffened when his weight moved the mattress.

"When I was in the brownstone dreaming of apartments like this, I was very different to what you see now. My father abandoned us when I was a baby and my mother died of an overdose when I was nine. I bounced from one foster home to another and at sixteen fell in with a pimp who promised to look after me but instead turned me into a whore. I was not attractive, not even very pretty, but at sixteen I had developed a good body and that was all that mattered to the men who paid to screw me. Sometimes I'd ask them to tell me that I was pretty. They could be saying, 'Come on bitch, you can screw better than this.' But what I heard was 'you are beautiful and the best lover I've ever had'." Tears were pouring down her cheeks unheeded and soaking into her blouse. "By twenty-four I was burnt out with drugs and alcohol and my pimp kicked me out. I walked the streets taking whatever money was offered me for sex acts and my landlord would cover the months when I couldn't make all my rent if I let him fuck me or give him a blow job. When I was twenty-eight, I started to have blinding headaches that sometimes lasted days and that no amount of alcohol or drugs could stop. I had no medical insurance, and all the ERs did was send me away with painkillers and tell me to quit drinking. In the periods between headaches, I carried on doing my thing, drugs, drinking and turning tricks. It was when I collapsed in an ER from what was thought to be an epileptic seizure that an MRI found the tumour in my brain. It was inoperable and they gave me four to six months. I had no family to go to, no one to help me so I left hospital with a pocket full of pain killers and decided that I would find a man and take him to my place then take all the pills and die while he screwed me. It was while he was pounding away at me and calling me his 'bitch, whore' that Patricia came. I thought it was the drugs taking effect, but she spoke to me in my head saying, 'give me just five minutes of your life and perhaps something can be made of your death.' I could see her plainly inside my head and the sound of her voice and the expression of pure sadness on her face as she looked at me gave me strength to push the man off and tell him to get the hell away from me. He must have seen Patricia's eyes looking out through mine and that warned him not to mess with me. He pulled his trousers on and grabbing up his shoes he gathered his coat and left while calling me nothing but a prick teasing whore. I gave Patricia her five minutes." Turning her tear-streaked face towards him her voice quavered when she said, "Patricia and the others in transition were cleared of my Life File so you are the only one that knows my story. I kept those memories to confirm just how far I've come since those days."

Lifting her hands from where they lay on her lap he spoke gently, "I am honoured that you chose to tell me, and you are certainly not that woman any more. What I see is a beautiful and gentle lady who, I think, wants to experience the pleasure that sex can bring but is afraid that it will be like it was in life. I think you feel that way because you chose to keep the memories of that time in your life. Believe me when I say no one in

Concordat would hurt you that way. Give yourself the freedom to explore wherever your feelings and desires take you. Become part of it. Let this Yuri chase away the memories of that Yuri."

With tears still spilling from her eyes she pulled his hands towards her and murmured, "Will you help me explore my feelings and desires?"

Chapter 24

David paused the review at the beginning of Richard's forty fourth year saying that Richard's brain was beginning to have minor cross connections and it was time to take a break.

Abigail acknowledged with, "Thank you, David. I'll take Richard for some R and R and let you know when we are on our way back."

"Okay. I'm off to visit Aditi. See you later."

Abigail asked, "How are you feeling Richard?"

"Amazed, astounded, thrilled and more alive than I ever was in life. I didn't want to stop but with this new brain I'm getting I could see what David meant about cross connections. I was trying to go too fast too soon. Tell me, how long did that take? We must have been here ages to get from my early twenties to forty-four."

"Not as long as you might expect but let's go somewhere more relaxing. I've set up a marquee on the beach in the cove so how about a swim and something to eat and then I'll tell you about Concordat time."

They made their way down the path to the cove and as Abigail had said there was a large marquee style tent set up on the white sand beach. The sand inside the tent was covered with brightly patterned rugs and there were large cushions scattered about. A table with various foodstuffs and drinks stood in the shade provided by the marquee and two lounging chairs sat on the sand outside.

"How do you prefer to go swimming Richard? Board shorts or skinny dipping? If you want shorts check the hamper under the towels. Me, I prefer skinny dipping." Without any sign of embarrassment Abigail removed her skirt, blouse and underwear then ran into the water. Shedding his own clothes, he followed her into the sea.

The temperature of the water was perfect for energetic swimming, so he dived when the water reached his knees and then swam away from the shore with long and strong freestyle strokes. Swimming until he began to lose breathing rhythm and his strokes became uncoordinated and sloppy, he turned to float on his back and breathe deeply until his pulse rate dropped and his breath became regular. He was staring into a cloudless blue sky and luxuriating in the feel of the water caressing his body when Abigail swam up and began to tread water beside him.

"Still pretty good Richard. Not quite as fast as when you swam competitively but the technique and power are still evident."

"Thank you. Water has always been my element. I always loved being in and on it."

"That was apparent from your review. Now, how about a race back to shore? It's only a couple of hundred metres. Are you up for it?"

He answered, "Sure." And no sooner was the word out of his mouth than Abigail took off.

She easily beat him and was sitting in water to her waist when he gasped his last few strokes to finish and sit beside her. As he sucked air into his lungs and tried to calm his breathing Abigail beamed at him then said, "What kept you?"

Around the gasping for air he asked, "Where did you learn to swim like that? That was Olympic speed."

"I just thought that I wanted to swim that fast, so I did. Don't ask right now, there are many wonderful things available from Concordat and you will learn about them from me and others as you work through your transition. Be patient, more preparation is needed. Let's dry off and get some food then I'll tell you about Concordat time."

After drying off using towels piled on the hamper, they dressed then taking a tray each they gathered food and drink and made their way to the loungers.

"Nice try earlier Richard but you're not quite there yet," Abigail said before popping a piece of honeydew melon into her mouth.

"Ah, you mean my thoughts about your figure. Yes, sorry about that. I did try to keep them quiet."

"No need to apologise. I'm glad you find it attractive. It was chosen with that response in mind. That will also be explained as we go along but for the moment let's eat and then I'll explain about time here."

Chapter 25

When he woke there was a ground mist flowing in undulating silence towards the Bay of Fundy cliffs one hundred metres distant and there it dropped like a silent waterfall to the beach and water below. Stepping down from the porch the mist swirled and parted about his legs as he went to the water barrel to wash and get water for morning coffee. Morning mist usually held the promise of a warm, sunny day.

Before the climb out from Mill Brooke on the last leg of his hike he contacted Eleanor and told her he was on his way back and she replied asking if she could join him at the top and walk out with him. He said he would be pleased to have her company. The Mill Brooke climb and the one from Refugee Cove were two of the steepest and longest on the trail and always took a lot out of him, but he knew at the top of Mill Brooke the trail levelled off into an old growth of maple wood which was one of the prettiest parts of the whole trail. He spotted Eleanor sitting on a windfall waiting for him as he made the turn at the top of the climb. Eleanor had a day pack and was dressed in shorts and tee shirt with sturdy hiking shoes and socks. As always, her smile of welcome made his heart lift.

Patting the trunk beside her she said, "Hi there, sit down and take a load off." Unbuckling his pack, he dropped it to the ground and sat beside her.

Wrinkling her nose, she asked, "Have you been wearing the same clothes the whole time?"

Lifting an arm, he sniffed the pit, "I can't smell anything and why would I change clothes on a two-day hike?"

Waving a hand in front of her face she said, "Stay where you are I'm going to move up wind of you. Sometimes the enhanced senses can be a drawback. I've iced tea in a vacuum flask, fancy some?"

"Mmm, please. The first time I came here it was with the kids and I remember sitting on a deadfall much like this and telling them about a

Garden of Tranquillity I visited in Kamakura, Japan. This has much the same effect on me; such beauty and peace with everything exactly where it should be, a place of perfection."

They sat for some time in silence and listened to the maples murmuring in the breeze. It was Eleanor that eventually sighed and said, "Time to go, we have work to do."

Slinging packs onto backs they buckled up and started the walk back to Red Rocks. The final decent to the beach before Red Rocks took them down to McGahey Brook and he told Eleanor he intended to shower in the waterfall just upstream from the brook bridge.

Eleanor was enthusiastic, "I think you should, and I'll rinse your clothes while you wash."

The cold water made him catch his breath when he first stood naked under the torrent but then became refreshing as he felt the sweat and, he had to admit, smell sluice away. He had his head back and eyes closed and was basking in the sensuous pleasure of water running over his body when Eleanor pressed herself against his back and hugged close. "I laid your clothes on some rocks in the sun and then wondered what we could do until they dry. So here I am as naked and as wet as you and open to suggestions."

Turning in her arms he made a forlorn face and, in a voice, full of dejection said, "I seem to have suffered a severe case of shrinkage from the cold water so I am going to have to rely on you to do something to correct the matter."

Pushing a little away from him she looked down, "Mmm, well I'll see what I can do, quickly on your back in the grass over there and hopefully it's not too late."

It wasn't and the recovery was much enjoyed by both of them. After, when they were dressed and shrugging into packs Eleanor remarked with feigned off handedness, "Met Yuri earlier today and she mentioned you had visited her apartment, she said she really appreciated you going over and that you had helped her a lot. I was surprised how different she looked. Touch of make-up and really fashionable clothes. She looked very attractive. Seemed more alive and had a look of dreamy satisfaction about her. Women notice these things. Wouldn't happen to know why that might be, would you?"

Turning away and starting to walk toward the beach he said, "No, don't have a clue."

He could feel Eleanor sticking her tongue out at his back and then saying sotto voce, "Yeah, I bet you don't."

Chapter 26

"How long do you think it has been since Eleanor brought you here and we started the review?" Abigail asked after they had finished their meals and were sitting relaxed on the loungers.

"From where we are in my life, I think that even with improving brain absorption I'd guess three to four days. It's hard to estimate because nothing changes in this place. I'm not overly physically tired. The sun seems fixed in the sky, there seems to be no tide movement and what clouds there are don't appear to move or change shape."

"Yes, that's how it seems. There appears to be nothing to focus on that gives any indication of time passing. Even shadows don't lengthen or diminish. You are still viewing time from an Earth time perspective which is a construct built around the orbit of a planet around a star. Here time is flexible. It can be compressed and stretched, it can be slowed and accelerated, and it can appear to be stopped. You will be able to control all forms of time after your brain reaches ninety-eight percent capability which it appears from David's observations so far it is well on the way to doing. Getting back to my question and your response of three or four days. The answer is the equivalent of twelve Earth hours. We've covered over twenty years of your life in that time and your brain capacity and capability has increased to the point where you can see and comprehend everything that is passing across the Ether Screen at many, many times the speed it was able to absorb even when at its most active during your life. What I am telling you will become much clearer as we move through your review and, if your brain allows, the controlling and changing of time and many other things will become second nature to you. Here's a small demonstration. Watch one of the clouds."

He glanced up to a cloud shaped like a large banana that had stayed stationary above the horizon during their time on the beach. It startled him when it suddenly moved rapidly many kilometres to another point on the horizon and became more like a moth or butterfly in outline.

Abigail was about to speak but Richard raised a hand in a gesture that indicated he had something to say. "I felt a shift in my mind at the same time as the cloud moved. A shift or movement is the best I can describe it. It was as if my mind caught up with time that had passed. There seemed a moment of extreme activity in my brain when that cloud moved or am I mistaken?"

Abigail swirled the ice remaining in her glass of Pepsi before answering. "No, you're right. Before we left the villa, I suspended that part of your brain function that is aware of the movement of time through the tracking of natural phenomena such as the shifting of clouds and shadows. You can see now that the sun and shadows have moved. Everything else we have done since leaving the villa we have done in Earth time—the type of time you are most in tune with at the moment. The suspension I mentioned is called a synaptic pause. I closed that memory synapse at the point you registered the cloud, shadows and position of the sun but allowed everything else to register in real time. The 'shift' as you call it was me opening that synaptic path and allowing that part of your brain to catch up with the time we are presently in, the here and now. What you experienced was, in effect, the pausing of time governing your visual references of sun, clouds and shadow that indicate the passage of time."

Richard made no response but went to the table and selected pieces of fruit to bring back to the lounger. He used his fingers to eat the sweet and juicy slices, pausing occasionally to wipe juice from his mouth and fingers with a linen napkin he'd found on the table. Abigail busied herself with collecting more food and ate it without any sense that she expected him to respond to her explanation about Concordat time. They were still synced, and she knew that Richard was taking time to mull over what she had said and whether or not to ask for further explanations and clarifications.

When he finished eating, he placed the plate and napkin on one of the rugs that formed a floor for the tent and said, "I'm going to see what else I learn before asking questions or wanting explanations and answers that might become self-evident as we proceed."

"Okay," was all Abigail said.

Settling back into his lounger Richard closed his eyes and thoughts of Eleanor came unbidden into his mind.

Chapter 27

The team met with Charlotte at her cabin to go over plans for the neural search. Charlotte began in her usual no preamble way. "Ted, Victoria, what have Watchers found?"

Ted reported that life in the Meldrew family went on as normal. Nothing of outstanding interest had happened and certainly nothing that indicated planning for a killing. Victoria told them the same applied to relatives, colleagues and friends. All interactions appeared perfectly normal and innocent.

"Yuri. Anything come from the continuous downloads?"

Yuri reported nothing had come from the downloads that showed any leanings towards killing or collusion to kill among any family member. They all appeared to be perfectly normal and no more flawed than the majority of humans. Yuri spoke with more authority than they had heard from her previously. Yuri had changed and some had remarked before the meeting how attractive she looked and had she altered her hairstyle and where did she get such lovely clothes. She was not beyond blushing but was pleased about the attention. She had made sure to be close to Alan.

"Jenny, Alan, anything new from analytics and programming."

Both shook their heads and Jenny told them that regardless of what improvements, alterations or additions they made to Life File programs nothing came back indicating how Meldrew, or anyone else for that matter, was hiding the killings. Always the results came back to only Meldrew being in the vicinity every time a killing occurred.

"Then we are no further forward and can't give Richard and Eleanor any ideas of what to expect when they insert and do the search. Right, can anyone think of anything we could have tried regardless of how off the wall it is?" Silence greeted the question. "Okay, this is what I want leading up to the insert. Richard, Eleanor, Yuri, Alan and Ted, I want you to work together learning everything about Meldrew and his immediate family from the day they were born. Put your combined minds together and pick every record and download apart. Look for any clue that will help at insert. The rest of you continue to monitor and get more people if needed. Richard, Eleanor please stay behind. Thank you all, but does anyone want to add anything?"

Yuri raised a hand and Charlotte nodded for her to go ahead. "At a previous meeting Eleanor said she wanted to know everything about Meldrew from current downloads even the colour of his secretary's panties if he is sleeping with her. He's not but she likes bright red hip huggers. I just wanted to let you know how thorough we are in Life File."

This was a very different Yuri and some mouths dropped open and a stunned silence followed her announcement then the tension that had been in the room vanished and there was laughter and applause with Charlotte joining in and saying, "Thank you Yuri, your thoroughness is noted."

Richard told Alan, Ted and Yuri to meet with him and Eleanor later at the diner and he'd be in touch with a time.

When the others had left, Charlotte offered them drinks with Eleanor accepting a glass of chilled white wine and Richard asking for sparkling water. Charlotte joined Eleanor with a glass of wine and after taking a sip said, "There's been a change to the plan. The Solons now require that if anything happens during the neural search that makes it impossible for one or both of you to withdraw then an immediate partial cull is to be carried out. We are not to wait for a member of the Retribution team to insert and do it. They want to install a spinal cord destruct mechanism which will destroy Meldrew's mind and leave him in a vegetative state at the first sign that one or both of you are in distress and cannot return. The Solons think it better to destroy whatever is hidden than to allow him to continue. Also, they do not want the rest of the team to know about the device."

It was long seconds before Richard said, "I cannot speak for Eleanor, but I knew from the start that there could possibly be only two outcomes *if* he *is* a serial killer. We find his hiding place and get out, or he traps us, and we destroy him and us. I'll accept that. I've a lot to thank Concordat for." Turning to face Eleanor Richard asked, "What about you? Still want to be in there with me, now you know that if the lifeline is blown, we both won't make it out?"

Without hesitation Eleanor replied, "Of course I'll be with you. I owe Concordat a lot too and if I have to go then there is no one else I would rather fragment with. Anyway, other than Charlotte, who else would put up with you under such circumstances? They'd probably cut the line just to get away from you."

Charlotte who had just taken a mouthful of wine snorted it down her nose at Eleanor's remark then all three laughed.

Chapter 28

The gentle shaking of his arm brought him from his reverie, and he opened his eyes to find Eleanor standing over him. "Hi there. Abigail caught you thinking about me so she gave me a call and as I have some free time, we decided I should visit. Abigail is off to meet a friend so she un-synced and we are verbal. I can't sync with you while you're in transition.'

Finding his voice after the surprise of seeing Eleanor by his lounger he said, "What a wonderful surprise. I was just lying here with my eyes closed and thinking about you, but you already knew that from Abigail."

"Move over and let me sit. Yes, and of course she saw us together during your life review, so she knows it was a special time during both our lives. We were so good for each other at the time, but it could never have lasted long term and we both knew that. We were very naughty at times though, weren't we?"

"Very! Remember under the floating pontoons at Kolkata Swimming Club. Thank goodness it was dark, and the pool lights didn't reach that far."

"I know," Eleanor laughed. "Getting out of my one-piece bathing suit wasn't too bad but putting it back on in the water afterwards was hilarious. After we did it the first time, I put it on back to front, so I had to take it off again and then we did it again because we were both horny with the fumbling around and feeling each other. Why nobody heard the snickering or saw the disturbance in the water I can't understand."

"Great times."

"Great times indeed. Now, how about a walk on the beach while we reminisce? I've a couple of hours before I need to get back."

Swinging his legs from the lounger he stood and reached out a hand to her saying, "Sounds good and maybe we'll find a pontoon or even a raft moored out there somewhere."

Linking an arm with his, Eleanor pulled tight against him and said, "You never know, maybe we will."

They walked in water up to their ankles and talked about the times they had spent together in Kolkata and in England when she was at university doing her doctorate and he was on leave. Their relationship was never one of clinging need on either of their parts. They each found in the other an easy companionship that was without restrictions when apart and full of wonder and exploration when together. They both agreed it had been a sexual revelation for both of them. They both had experience before they met but what they found in each other was a free-flowing exchange of ideas and experimentation.

Eleanor tugged him to a stop and moving so that she could look at his face she stretched her arms over his shoulders and out behind his head and linking her hands she let out a long sigh and said, "Oh Richard, wasn't it a shame that our relationship could not last. We had such fun together and the loving was spectacular, but we were both far too headstrong about career and life aspirations to make the compromises a long-term relationship requires." Letting her arms fall to his waist she pulled him close and kissed him gently on the lips then turned to his side and took his hand and started walking again.

Kicking water that made sunlight sparkled droplets ahead of them he asked quietly, "How did you die?"

"Cancer. Attacked my brain and it spread quickly, it was inoperable. I was only in my forties. Barry came with the offer. Die sooner and before the pain became unendurable or suffer and waste away. I never gave it a second thought and chose the offer."

"Did you marry?"

"Don't know. Perhaps. I preferred to have that part of my Life File deleted during transition review. It's a personal choice they give, and I must not have wanted to carry that particular baggage around with me in Concordat. If it helps you to decide then most people delete that part of their life from memory. It makes it easier to have relationships involving intimate acts."

He stopped in surprise at her words, and she turned her face to his and smiling said, "Oh yes, we can fuck here and it's just like back in life—maybe a little better."

Richard gave a hearty laugh, "You haven't changed a bit. No bullshit just straight to the point. It really is wonderful seeing you again."

Eleanor raised an index finger, and a slight frown creased her forehead then she said, "Abigail wants us back. Time for you to continue the review."

Turning they walked hand in hand with the easy closeness they had always had back to the tent and to Abigail who was waiting.

Chapter 29

It was pies all round again, this time blackberry apple as recommended by their waitress whose name tag announced was Sherri. Coffees and teas followed with Sherri telling them she'd be back later to top up.

When personal preferences for milk or cream and sugar had been taken care of Eleanor looked toward Yuri and asked, "Yuri, is it possible for you to sync us all together and take us through the Life Files of Meldrew and his immediate family and close relatives, either by birth or marriage, and do it at Time Light speed?"

"I don't see why not," Yuri replied. "But as you know when Life Files are reviewed when entering Concordat, the Time Light speed is adjusted to suit the incomer's cerebral absorption rate so it will be necessary to run them at the slowest absorption rate amongst us."

Glances passed between them with each wondering who absorbed the slowest and then Richard spoke, "Look, all our rates will have changed since coming to Concordat so let's have a third party, who will be wiped afterward, take absorption readings from us individually then without telling us the result pass the slowest reading to Yuri without naming anyone." There was unanimous agreement and Yuri said she would get Charlotte to designate who would take the readings and ask that Charlotte herself take care of the wipe afterward.

"How long to set this up?" Eleanor queried.

"Not long. No longer than four or five earth hours, or faster if we all go back to Concordat time," Yuri answered.

"No, stick with Earth time. That's what we're working to now and until this is over. We know that jumbles can occur transiting backwards and forwards across time sectors," came from Richard.

"Want me to get started now?" Yuri asked.

Which received a, "Yes please," from Eleanor.

Yuri gulped some coffee then with an, "I'll be in touch soon." She left the diner.

Alan, who was watching Yuri through his reflection in the diner's night darkened window as she crossed the parking lot and disappeared in shadow said, "I wonder what brought about the change in Yuri."

Richard winced as Eleanor kicked his shin under the table and remarked innocently, "Yes, I wonder that myself. I hope something really special happened but that's her business not ours."

Sherri pocketed the large tip left in booth five when she collected the plates smeared with blackberry and apple pie and the five empty coffee mugs. Money to the amount of the bill she had no memory of writing was in the middle of the table and she had no recollection of who had been in the booth, but the tip money was real enough.

True to her word Yuri contacted them after four hours to say the absorption tests were arranged and gave each one a time they should appear at Life Files to meet with Rose who had been selected to run the tests. She admonished then not to arrive early; she did not want any paths to cross. Yuri would be tested first.

Ted had offered to arrange the venue for the Time Light sync and had chosen a room in the villa that they all knew from their own Life File reviews. The open French doors let a soft breeze into the room which held five adjustable loungers with plump cushions. On the balcony outside the room a buffet table had been prepared for after. Hunger and thirst were often an after effect of Time Light procedures.

"Great choice Ted, it's just as we remember it," Eleanor said as she looked around the room then went onto the balcony to investigate. "Just what we need." Ted smiled and thanked her.

The other three arrived together and echoed Eleanor's words of praise. Alan was particularly pleased about the path leading down to the bay and voiced, "I'm going for a swim when we're done."

Yuri and Eleanor separated from the others and talked between themselves until Eleanor turned and said, "Yuri will have the button on this. She is the most experienced in running Time Light reviews and has arranged for a Life Filer to monitor all of us while we are in sync. The Life Filer will not see the review but if they detect any undue stress or unusual cerebral activity in any of us, they will inform Yuri directly who will make the decision to un-sync that person if she considers its necessary. Everyone okay with that?" All agreed. "Okay, let's get settled and see what Meldrew and his family have to offer."

Once settled comfortably with loungers adjusted to their liking, Eleanor nodded to Yuri and each felt the slight jolt as the cortex syncs took place and a large Ether Screen appeared on which the Life Files of Brian Meldrew and his family passed at Time Light speed.

Chapter 30

Abigail and Eleanor hugged saying their goodbyes then Eleanor gave Richard a light kiss before starting up the track back to the villa.

Going to the table Abigail took a can of Diet Pepsi from the chest containing ice and soft drinks. It passed through Richard's mind that even after all the time it had sat there the ice showed no signs of melting.

Popping the can open Abigail drank then gave a soft burp before saying, "I'm glad Eleanor was able to visit but now it's time to get back to David. He's all set to continue." Drinking more of her Diet Pepsi she put the can on the table, and they went out of the tent and onto the track to the villa.

David was leaning with his backside against the balustrade and greeted them with smile and, "Ready to go again? The way things have gone so far, another six Earth hours should cover it. Richard, your absorption rate has been increasing exponentially and I'm able to continually increase the speed at which your Life File passes, and your neurological read outs show minimum stress levels." Stepping away from the balustrade he walked towards the French windows and said, "Let me know when you're ready to start Abigail." Before going inside.

When they were both seated, Richard felt Abigail syncing with him and then she called to David, "All set." Immediately the Ether Screen came alive.

As more and more areas of his brain that had lain dormant began to activate the visuals of his life took on a clarity beyond clear and all emotions, whether pleasurable or disturbing, gained such intensity that at times he felt they would overwhelm him. And bordering all that he had experienced directly were persons, places, things and actions that he had been completely unaware of or had dismissed at the time but which in some way, to a greater or lesser extent, had impacted on his life choices and decisions. He was aware that Abigail was also experiencing the sharper emotional and sensory aspects. The highs seemed higher and the lows lower.

The final ether image was the closing of his eyes as he fell asleep on the night he died. As his eyelids closed out the last of the dim light that seeped around the bedroom drapes the Ether screen went dark then vanished.

He felt Abigail un-syncing but neither one moved nor made any comment. He just wanted to sit and come to terms with the way he felt. He felt utterly calm but at the same time had the underlying impression that if action was needed, be it physical or mental, his body and mind would react with outlandish speed. He had never felt so utterly and completely alive in every sense of the word.

David came from the villa carrying two glasses filled with a tawny liquid and with moisture clinging to the outside which he handed to them, "Brought you some iced tea. I thought you might like it while the two of you go over things. As for me, I'm done except to tell you everything went extremely well. Richard, you are now at ninety-eight percent of max brain utilisation. Abigail will explain how and when those other two percent will be activated."

Wiping his hands down the sides of his board shorts to get rid of the moisture from the glasses he reached out a hand to Richard and as they shook, he said, "It's been a pleasure meeting you Richard and I found your review very interesting. There were some outstanding neurological readouts. Now I'm off to get wiped, or as it's referred to by those who go through it regularly, I'm off to see the scrubbers. If we bump into one another, we will have the pleasure of meeting all over again." David bent to kiss Abigail on the cheek and say it had been lovely working with her, she smiled and responded in kind.

Abigail sipped at her iced tea and then leaned her head against the back of her chair before saying, "We have come to the point where you have the option to retain or discard some or all of your memories. There is an enforced period for reflection. A time for you to ponder on which memories are important to you and which are not. Once the decision is made it cannot be reversed. The memory goes or stays, no second chances. I will be with you, and you can pick a place or places that had particular significance in your life, and we can go there if you think it will help you decide."

Richard asked, "Can you provide background to what happened to cause certain events and memories? Things that I was unaware of at the time?"

"Yes, that can be done but only if the person or persons involved predeceased you and came to Concordat. It's known as third-party information and permission has to be given by the party or parties for you to see that part of their Life File. Permission is not often granted. Do you have something specific in mind?"

"I do, but first there is a place I would like you to take me. I'm sure you'll recognise it from the review."

Chapter 31

Afterwards on the balcony they each selected a drink and food from the buffet then found a place to stand or sit that gave separation from the others. Nothing had been said since the end of the reviews. Time was needed to process what they had experienced and for all the emotional turbulence to settle. Richard was leaning on the balcony balustrade lost in thought and gazing out across the sea when Eleanor came and sat on the balustrade beside him. "Ted and Alan are wondering what hit them."

Richard turned to sit beside her. "Yeah. They watch and analyse but never get to know the innermost thoughts and emotions of the person, just the external movements and actions."

Yuri wandered over while popping a strawberry into her mouth, Richard and Eleanor sat silent while she sucked the juice from her fingers. She inclined her head toward where Ted and Alan stood several feet apart and said in a low voice, "The boys are having a hard time sorting it all out so perhaps we should take a time out for a swim or a walk on the beach until their minds settle down."

"Good idea," came in unison from Eleanor and Richard. Eleanor went to Ted and Alan and told them about taking a break which was greeted with enthusiasm. Alan came to Richard and Yuri, but Ted was talking earnestly with Eleanor who made some response that brought a smile to Ted's face and he hurried back into the villa. Richard gave Eleanor a 'what was that all about' look when she joined them.

"Ted asked if his friend Christopher could join him for the break and I said 'sure' but talk about the reviews was taboo, he promised he wouldn't, and I trust him. He's arranging a place for them to meet and I said to be back in one Earth hour."

Yuri piped up, "I'm going for a walk on the beach and then a swim—does anyone care to join me?"

Alan immediately stepped forward, "That sounds wonderful, and I'll join you." Yuri smiled and reached for Alan's hand to lead him to the track down to the beach.

Richard chuckled, "That worked out well. Not sure how much walking and swimming they'll get done though."

Eleanor grabbed his hands and pulled him up from the balustrade, "Never mind those two. I can see a cave in the right-hand arm of the bay I want to explore and it's an easy swim. You up for it?"

"Sure, let's go exploring." Then in a parody of Groucho Marx he raised his eyebrows and held an imaginary cigar to his mouth and said in a voice mimicking Groucho, "Who knows, maybe there will be something else up for it when we get inside."

With laughter in her voice, she pulled him towards the track saying, "You really are incorrigible."

The others were climbing the final few metres to the balcony when Ted came from the room. The break had refreshed them all and they decided the balcony was a good place to continue working. Chairs were brought together around a table holding a pitcher of iced tea and glasses.

Eleanor began, "Richard and I talked it over and what we want is for you, Alan, to give us your take on Amy then Ted, you give us yours on Constance and then Yuri you do Meldrew. Tell it in your own style but leave out the small stuff. When each of us has finished giving individual reports we'll do a combined critique. I've been in touch with Jenny and Victoria telling them to keep digging into the daily activities of Meldrew and family and to follow any lead no matter how tenuous. Yuri, Charles is doing a good job and he's aware you could be away for some time. Also, Charlotte has been given an update and approves of our approach and is continuing to check our Life File recruiting and admission protocols. Okay Alan, what's your take on Amy?"

"All I saw was the growing to young womanhood of a normal healthy female. Healthy inasmuch as there were all the usual frictions, mood swings, sullenness, rebellion, sexual exploration, hormonal upheavals and angsts that most youngsters experience but underneath that is a very warm love for her mother and father and a gratitude for what they have done for her. As with most of her generation she is attached to her cell phone and tablet and follows some social media sites. As a child she was always 'daddy's little girl' but now at eighteen has a closer bond with her mother and appears to be leaving the 'all about me' phase behind and is becoming more empathetic. Her academic grades have been consistently good, and she has offers from two universities and is considering a degree in psychology. Amy has never wanted for any of the staples of life, she has been well sheltered, clothed and fed and her parents have loved but never spoiled her and made sure her grandparents did not. At eighteen and although still a virgin she knows her body intimately and gets pleasure from it. There are friends both male and female with whom she has an active social life. She swims with a local competitive team but more for the health aspect than competition." A pause to pour and drink iced tea then Alan continued, "She is developing a strong sense of self-worth and she is more stable and well-adjusted than some of the young women my own daughters called friends at her age. Bottom line, from what I experienced of her during the review, both physically and emotionally, I am convinced there is nothing in Amy's Life File that indicates she is in any way involved with what we suspect her father does. I saw no dark side to her nature and any animosity she holds never goes beyond fanciful thoughts of revenge which are soon discarded, and she moves on. Did you see her differently?"

Head shakes from the others. Eleanor turned to Ted saying, "Your turn now."

Chapter 32

It was exactly as it was on that day.

He grasped the veranda railing as his legs became unsteady and his senses reeled just as they had when he had come here in life. He lowered himself gingerly to the step just as he had all those years ago and felt the same overwhelming sense of perfection and peace that his eyes and mind tried to grasp.

They sat on the top step of four that dropped down to the edge of perfection from a porch that surrounded the building. A weathered wooden fence bordered this perfection on three sides with the fourth border being the building containing a single square room that had such plainness and simplicity that it emptied the mind of all distraction and prepared it for what came when a shoji panel was slid aside, and the garden was revealed.

Abigail sat beside him and she too saw and felt the beauty and serenity of the place.

Sand had been raked into loops and swirls of perfect symmetry that flowed around lichen mottled standing stones of weathered granite. The stream that flowed flat across the space provided a mirror that reflected the trees and bushes that stood tight against the fence. White and pink cherry blossoms were petalled daubs against the pale-blue sky and a soft breeze rittle-rattled reeds at water's edge. Small islands of perfectly manicured grass dotted the sand and gravel sea and on one that divided the stream a Buddha sat in quiet smiling serenity. Everything in this place was exactly where it had to be. The singular was reliant on the collective to bring about the harmony of the whole.

Abigail laid a hand on his arm and squeezed gently, "I can understand why you wanted to come here. It was apparent from the review that it was a special place and time for you. Now, what is it that you need third-party records for?"

"You saw Rose, the girl I had my first real romantic and sexual liaison with and how she abruptly walked out of my life, well I was never convinced the explanation she gave me for breaking up was the true one. Can you find out if Rose is with Concordat and if she is then ask her if what she told me was really the truth."

"I can do that. If she is with Concordat, I'll need to connect and talk to her about your request. Most third-party access requests are turned down. Give me a moment and I'll see what I can find out."

Richard sensed that Abigail was no longer completely with him. It was as if a part of her had left even if externally she looked the same. He sat and let his senses be drawn into the perfectness of the space before him. Time served no purpose in this place, so he had no reference to judge how long that part of Abigail had been away, but he knew the moment it returned.

"Rose is with Concordat although that is not the name she uses, and, she has agreed that you can see the true reason she left you. She feels that you deserve that truth. She says that lying to you had never sat well with her."

Richard nodded, "Okay. How are third-party records handled?"

"You will see through her eyes and feel through her senses. You will be Rose. I'll see what you see, and you can leave the record at any time, just say 'out' and I'll shut it down. Ready?"

"Yes."

She told him she was breaking off their relationship, that it wouldn't work, that she had realised she didn't love him and didn't want to see him again and that he was not to try to get in touch. He saw his expressions and body language as she told him this, standing outside a pub they had arranged to meet for a drink after she had finished work and before they went for a meal. He was tanned from the summer sun and his hair was bleached to almost blond. In the seconds as he stood speechless with mouth open, she turned and hurried, almost ran, towards a car parked nearby and with a last glance at him she pulled the passenger door open and ducked inside to sit staring out the windshield as the car was driven away by a woman already seated behind the wheel. Her vision blurred as tears fell from her eyes. A hand appeared at her thigh to give it a gentle squeeze and he heard, 'You did the right thing. What you had wasn't fair on either of you. You'll feel better after we get to my place.' There was only silence and the view through the windshield until the tears abated and the car pulled up outside a terraced house. They both exit the car, and he feels the woman, whose face has been obscured, take Rose's hand and leads her into the house and straight upstairs to a bedroom. Rose's face is cupped in gentle hands and thumbs wipe away tears that still linger under her eyes and all the time the woman is saying it will be okay, that the right thing had been done and he feels kisses to cheeks and lips and neck. He senses the arousal in Rose as fingers undo the buttons of her blouse and reach around to undo the clasp of her bra. The auburn hair of the woman is seen as her head moves down and he feels the kisses and soft teeth tugs to each nipple. Rose stands perfectly still staring at her face in a mirror above a dresser. More shudders are felt as the woman's fingers begin to explore and Rose's reflected image fades as she closes her eyes.

"Abigail, out, please!"

Abigail was aware that Richard was reflecting on what he had experienced and sat quietly beside him until in almost a whisper he said, "She should have told me. I would have understood. I would have preferred that than to be left wondering if it was my fault. It was months before I came to terms with it. It hurt me deeply as things like that do when you're that age."

Chapter 33

Ted took a drink and settled back, "There was nothing in Constance's life up to the time she married Meldrew that pointed to a killer mentality. Middle child bracketed by two brothers in a well-respected and reasonably wealthy family. Father a surgeon and it was at a hospital function that Constance, who was going into nursing met Meldrew. Two years of courtship followed during which time Meldrew started to make his name in medical circles and Constance completed her training. Constance was twenty-six when she had Amy. The marriage has had the rocky patches that most marriages seem to encounter and overcome but one lingers. Constance adores sex at seemingly any time and in all its variations while her husband's libido, never as active as hers, seemed to vanish after she became pregnant. Following the birth of Amy — an event that did nothing to dampen Constance's sex drive — she supplemented the supply by seeking pleasures outside the home. When her husband became aware — he walked in on her and an electrician at the house to fix the dishwasher — an arrangement was made. She could continue her exploits as long as they were discreet and did not interfere with the raising of Amy. The arrangement continues to this day with rumours and innuendo sometimes circulating but not proved. I see a woman that is unfulfilled by marriage but who found motherhood and the raising of her child satisfying. Thoughts of divorce are there for when Amy goes to university and begins life on her own. There is nothing in her relationship with Meldrew that suggests the closeness necessary to be a participant in or even accessory to the killings and certainly not to ones that occur at such regular intervals. What do you all think?"

"I agree with you Ted, she has no connection to the killings," Eleanor replied. "Did the rest of you see anything?"

All responded in the negative, so Eleanor said, "You have the floor Yuri, what did you get from Meldrew?"

"Keeping in mind what Meldrew is *suspected* of and the fact that if true he has successfully kept it hidden, I looked for any neurological catalyst that drives him to kill at such precise intervals and what was different about him compared to other serial killers we have reviewed. The cerebral, neural and synaptic activity we receive and record from healthy brains are crystal clear and sharp edged and for the majority of the time that's exactly what Meldrew's are like—*but not always*." Yuri knew she had their full attention and took time to drink before continuing, "In the five days before the times we have for the killings some of the sharp-edged clarity is lost and a very faint distortion occurs which remains until Meldrew has left the area of the killings then it clears. Now when I say faint I mean *very, very faint*. Reviewed at Time Light speed, and during periodic downloads under our present programming, it would easily be missed but I stayed with his brain records during our review and nanotime sliced them looking for anything hinky and that's when I noticed it. We don't nanotime slice every brain at periodic download unless something gets flagged and obviously Meldrew's didn't raise a flag. I have no idea about the cause, but it seems to originate at the brainstem and cerebellum juncture. From the timing of the distortion, it must have something to do with why he kills. It always appears five days before the event and begins to fade immediately after."

Eleanor let out a whistling breath from between pursed lips, then, "Yuri, you know what this means don't you?"

"Of course. Hundreds, if not thousands of killers could have slipped through. New programs and protocols will have to be put in place for the observers and periodic downloads along with every ongoing Life File needing to be rescanned under the new P and Ps. What a mess and on my watch. Someone needs to tell the Solons and we need Alan and Jenny to come up wi…"

Eleanor broke in saying, "Hold everything. Let's not get distracted from our main task by going off at tangents about new P and Ps and letting the Solons know. That's not our job, our job is to confirm whether Meldrew is, or is not, a serial killer and although the evidence Yuri has found is compelling it only points to his possible guilt; it does not confirm it. We've assumed all along he is a killer, but we have yet to determine the why of them or the areas inside his brain he's planning them. Only when we have that knowledge can new P and Ps be drawn up. Yuri, I will get your findings to Charlotte and tell her we are going ahead with a neural search, and it will be her job to tell the Solons about all the rest. We stay together and stick to our job. Understood?" Nods all round. "Good! And all that aside you did one hell of a job finding that, Yuri." Alan reached out to squeeze Yuri's hand and got a broad smile in return.

During the silence that followed, Richard got up from his seat and walked to the balustrade and resting his hands on the warm marble he looked out across the bay to the sea and said, "Constance and Amy have nothing to do with the killings, we all agree on that, and from all reports there is nothing unusual happening between Meldrew and any of his relatives, friends or colleagues and no connection between any of them and the times and places of the killings. They were nowhere near Meldrew during those times. It all comes back to him, and a search is the only way we can move forward, we need what he has locked away and Yuri has given us a place to start." Turning to face them, "Eleanor, you and I need to do some trial runs to test the safety hook up and we'll need Yuri on the outside monitoring and recording all our moves. It can be done on Meldrew before the distortion can't it, Yuri, while his brain is in normal mode?"

"Certainly. I'll set things in motion when we leave here."

Eleanor leant forward and slapped hands on her knees, "I think we're done here. Ted and Alan, you get back to Jenny and Victoria and brief them on what's been found and what we are doing about it. This doesn't mean we can back off on surveillance or looking for loopholes in our P and Ps so keep on top of it. Yuri, contact Richard and me when you've set up for the trial runs. I'm going to see Charlotte; she'll want a face-to-face report. That's about it except to say a big thank you to Ted for arranging our meeting place, a perfect choice." Ted beamed.

Chapter 34

"You have to take into account those times Richard. Homosexuality and lesbianism were considered crimes and if word got round it could, and did, ruin lives and careers. Society was not as accepting as thankfully many are today. And would you really have been that understanding? We've seen in your Life File references to 'homos' and 'dykes' and the sneers as the words came from your mouth. You are saying you would have understood then but you're doing it from the standpoint of the wisdom and acceptance you gained over the years. You did not have that in your youth." Abigail paused and reaching an arm around his shoulders she hugged him to her and said, "Rose has been brave enough to show you the truth and you can now decide if it is a memory you want to retain or discard when the time comes to decide."

Abigail sensed he was ready to leave this place and in one accord they stood and side by side walked back into the room and slid shut the shoji door.

"Anywhere else you would like to visit?" Abigail asked.

"Yes. There was that run-down shack on a beach in Trincomalee bay in Sri Lanka. You know I found it while exploring when we were loading there. The shack itself wasn't much but the beach was in that small, sheltered cove and there was that tattered old hammock someone had left strung between two palms. I'd like to revisit that place to lie in the hammock like before and give some thought to the memories I want to retain."

Abigail said, "Sure." And they were there.

The cove, the beach, the palm trees, the hammock and the shack. "I'm not climbing into this hammock," Abigail remarked as she peered at the frayed and stained canvas. "Time for a new one. Go check inside the shack Richard there should be one there suitable for couples. There should be pillows as well."

He also found a cooler filled with soft drinks.

Erecting the new hammock in the shade of the palms they settled into it and with heads propped on pillows sipped their cool drinks.

"Will I be able to do this, pick a place and go there?" Richard asked.

"Certainly, when you are fully up to speed. We don't rush the last two percent upgrade. It needs to be done with caution. It's remarkable what a difference in performance those two percent make. We take the time we are having now to let your synapses and neurons and all your other brain stuff settle down after the Life File review. You are not aware of it but there's a lot going on up there, lots of changes. We know from past experiences that dumping the two percent in too soon and too fast causes some very bad side-effects. I'll be told when the final upload will take place."

With surprise in his voice Richard asked, "Am I being monitored right now?"

'Oh yes. As long as we are synced all your brain activity is going back to transition control. They'll tell me when you are ready for the final upload."

"So, this control place knows everything that we say and do? You and I are never alone for a moment? Let's say, hypothetically, we decided to strip off and make love right here in this hammock transition control would know what we were up to? Is that right?"

"No. They would know by the increased neurological signal activity that something was happening, but they have no way of deciphering what that activity is. They would see rises in the excitement levels and the peaks during orgasm, assuming hypothetically they occurred, but would not know the reasons. There are literally trillions of reasons why neuro activity increases. Those in transition control are what is called neuro-blocked for the time they work there. They see what's happening neurologically but have no idea what is causing it."

"Okay, I understand. And now I am going to do what I did last time I was here and that's go for a swim."

Abigail gave an enormous stretch while saying, "Enjoy. I'm going to stay and relax and soak up some rays. I think I'll set up a blanket in the sun and take the pillows."

Standing they stripped and draped their clothes on the hammock then he headed for the water, and she took the pillows to a blanket on the beach.

Later, lying with her eyes closed she said, "Don't you dare! I know you're thinking of dripping water on me."

"Damn, can't get away with anything," he said feigning petulance.

"Dry off first and then I'll let you join me on the blanket. I'm too relaxed to move. There's fruit and sandwiches under the palms if you're hungry. Bring me some grapes please."

Trying for obsequious he said, "Yes, my lady, right away. Your wish is my command." Her laughter followed him as he dried himself while walking to the food.

Soon she felt his weight move the blanket as he stretched out beside her.

"Here are your grapes. Open wide, I'll pop one in."

Keeping her eyes closed she opened her mouth, and he dropped a grape into it. "Mmm, thank you. That tastes wonderful."

"Plenty more, I've brought a handful." He dropped them one by one into the valley created by her belly button.

There was a ripple of muscle as each grape fell but instead of dropping the last grape, he squeezed it so that juice burst out and then slid it slowly over her abdomen onto her ribs then between her breasts and over throat and chin to drop it in her mouth. With his forefinger he followed the trail of juice back down to take another grape and follow the same route back to her mouth. He did this five times before she said what was becoming increasingly apparent by how her breathing was becoming more rapid and the way she grasped the blanket and tensed the muscles of her buttocks each time he guided a grape over her, "Unless you want to take this to the hypothetical outcome we discussed earlier you had better stop because that is making me very horny."

Sliding another grape between her breasts he dropped it into her mouth and as she closed it to chew, he kissed her hard and tasted the sweetness of the grapes. She opened her mouth to him, and their tongues tangled amongst the grape pulp and juice before she pulled him on top of her and the remaining grapes were squashed in the press of their bodies as she opened her legs to accept him.

Chapter 35

Eleanor invited Charlotte to meet at the Kolkata apartment. When the door was opened to her knock, she was assailed with the spicy aromas of curry dishes and Eleanor greeted her wearing a cobalt-blue sari edged with gold thread. "Please come in," Eleanor invited with a smile, "Make yourself at home while I bring the rice to the boil. Would you like a drink? Help yourself to whatever's on the cabinet. As you can probably smell I made curry tonight as a thank you for the wonderful meal at your cabin. Oh my! You do like Indian food, don't you? I should have asked before making it."

Charlotte gave a slight smile, "I like curry as long as it's not too hot and I like egg and dahl and tikka masala."

Obviously relieved Eleanor said, "They are two of the dishes I prepared along with a vindaloo and butter chicken. I thought we'd eat Indian style using our fingers but if you're not happy with that, spoons and forks are available. I have a ton of naan bread too. How do you feel about the finger thing?"

Charlotte hesitated a moment then, "Why not, let's get messy."

Eleanor took a step back and looked Charlotte up and down before saying, "How about we dress you in a sari, might as well fit right in with the meal and the country."

"Oh, I don't know. I mean I've never worn one and have no idea how it goes on," Charlotte said as she looked down at her dark brown sweater and slacks outfit with matching sandals.

"Nothing to it," Eleanor exclaimed and taking Charlotte's hand she tugged her into a bedroom with a large closet full of sari wraps, petticoats and blouses. "You are an autumn person so we should go with this one in golds and browns and yellows. Now, out of your clothes except for your panties if you prefer to keep them on."

"Even my bra?"

"Yes, even your bra."

Charlotte shrugged and was very soon standing in only her panties while Eleanor cast an appraising look over her body.

"Mmm, no need for any support under the blouse, you're quite firm up top."

Charlotte glanced down and said, "That's more to do with the Concordat allowing age and figure adjustments than to any natural propensity on my part."

From the closet Eleanor selected a petticoat and blouse in gold for the undergarments and a blending of browns, golds and yellows with fine brocade stitching at the edges for the sari. "Here, this should fit you perfectly, it was my sister's, and your bust size is about the same, petticoat first then blouse, and I'll help with the winding and draping of the sari."

When satisfied Eleanor stood Charlotte before a full-length mirror fitted to the closet door. Charlotte twirled saying, "It's gorgeous and feels so light that it's like I'm wearing gossamer." Smiling from behind Charlotte's shoulder Eleanor whispered conspiratorially, "If you want to get the real feeling of softness and comfort, I suggest you take your panties off."

Charlotte's eyes widened in the mirror then reaching down she pulled the petticoat and sari material to her waist and slipped her panties off. "Oh yes," came from her when she dropped the materials back down, "That does feel sensuous."

Eleanor gasped and said, "Oh shit, I forgot the rice," as she sprinted for the kitchen. The rice was a little stodgy but not enough to spoil the meal.

They talked about the Meldrew case with Eleanor giving the latest updates and results during the meal and they ate from a large pewter platter loaded with all the curries, rice and chutneys and tucked in using fingers and envelopes of naan bread to get the food to their mouths. Chilled sparkling water was used to cleanse the palate between the different curries and Charlotte took a liking to buttered chicken but found vindaloo too hot. When they had eaten their fill and after rinsing their fingers in water bowls, they decided to delay the dessert of sweet honey dumplings until later. Eleanor whisked the platter away into the kitchen and returned with a tea set and a pot of tea.

"Care for some?"

Charlotte who had moved from the table to a large sofa accepted, "Yes please. The meal was delicious, thank you."

While Eleanor poured tea, Charlotte ran folds of her sari through her fingers, "The material and embroidery are so perfect, tell me about it."

Passing a cup of tea to Charlotte, Eleanor sat with hers and pulled her legs beside her on the sofa, "There are many different types of saris made in many places. Style and material vary greatly and are often dictated by religious belief or cultural norms. That particular one is a Banaras style, and they are famed for the brocade edging. It was made and bought in Varanasi. It was one of my sister's favourites and she would be pleased to see you wearing it. The one I am wearing is from Varanasi too."

"It's lovely and the colour really suits you," Charlotte said reaching for the brocade edging and asking, "What exactly is this pattern? I've been intrigued by it all evening."

Smiling hugely Eleanor straightened out a section of brocade and held it for Charlotte to examine. "Look closely and tell me what you see."

Charlotte moved to within inches of the brocade and looked closely then she raised her eyes to Eleanor and then back to the pattern asking, "Am I really seeing what I think I'm seeing?"

"Tell me what you're seeing."

"Well, not to put too fine a point on it I see figures having sex in all sorts of positions."

Eleanor laughed gleefully, "Absolutely right, they are all figures from the Karma-sutra," then with a wink, "I've worked my way through a few of them."

Charlotte slid more brocade Karma-sutra through her hands and without looking up said, "I think I'm ready for dessert now, looking at these is getting me hot. Oh dear! Did I just say that out loud?"

Eleanor gathered her sari to her, "Dessert it is." And rising from the sofa she bent to whisper in Charlotte's ear, "The Karma-sutra does not require that the parties be a man and a woman."

Later as they lay relaxed on the palette of colourful saris that painted Eleanor's bed Charlotte murmured, "The dessert after dessert was better, you tasted so good."

Eleanor moved to brush her lips across Charlotte's breasts then down across her stomach saying between kisses, "I — want — more — dessert — please."

Charlotte breathed, "Help yourself."

Chapter 36

Afterwards they walked into the sea to wash away sweat and grape residue. "Darn grape pips get everywhere," came from Abigail as she splashed water to wash one from her belly button.

Richard laughed and said, "We should be thankful it wasn't watermelon. Imagine getting those seeds in certain places."

Abigail grimaced, "That doesn't bare thinking about."

After drying off they returned to the hammock. Richard sensed that Abigail was waiting for him to speak. She was lying on her side with a leg across his thighs and an arm draped over his chest and a cheek against his shoulder. He had an arm beneath her neck and was gently stroking her back.

In a voice that resonated with sexual afterglow he said, "That was remarkable. Is that part of the transition protocol to check how heightened my senses are becoming? Because if it is mine must have gone off the charts. I have never felt so much sensual pleasure. You brought feelings and sensations that I have never experienced before. You were amazing."

"Mmm, it was good, wasn't it? And no, it's not part of the protocol. I've been sensing the sexual urges building in both of us and this seemed the perfect place to explore them. A sexual component often arises during transition, but it can be subdued if it is not a mutual interchange. You are the last of my five transitions and because we are wiped after each one, I can't tell you how many I've had sex with. I could well have subdued the urge in all of them or had sex with all of them, I don't know. I experienced your sexual exploits during the review, and you seemed to particularly enjoy those in Japan, so I wanted the woman's experience of them and that's why I guided you to do to me what they taught you to do to them and vice-versa. It was spectacular."

For some time, they lay quietly until Abigail moved to swing her legs over the edge of the hammock and sat up saying, "We need to go back to the villa now and there you will pick the memories you want to retain and those you want cleared. After that I will tell you about the changes that are going to occur in you and what Concordat expects from you. I have been informed that you are very nearly ready to accept the final two percent download and once that occurs a section leader will take over from me."

The sun was about to disappear below the sea horizon and some stars were already visible in the darker cobalt of the sky when Abigail asked on their return to the villa, "Do you prefer to stay out here on the terrace or go indoors?"

"I'm happy to stay out here for now. If I get chilly, I'm sure you can rustle me up a sweater from somewhere."

"I'm sure we can. I'm going to get into a sweater and slacks now, this skirt and blouse are a wee bit thin for evening wear outside. Cashmere sweater and cotton slacks. That's better. Now to your memory task. I'm aware you've given a lot of thought to what goes and what stays, and the final choice is yours. However, what you choose to keep can have an impact on which section you go to in Concordat. No Richard don't ask. I am not permitted to guide your choice in any way."

"Do I need to tell you verbally which are to go and which I want to keep, or will you know through being synced?"

"Through being synced, and you only have to indicate the ones to go. The rest will remain. You believe you have chosen what to keep and what not to keep but when your memory trace is run many more will surface that you have long forgotten but which remained stored in the recesses of your brain. You will need to choose from those also. There are millions of memories stored of which a good number are those you didn't even know you had kept. Even at the speed your brain now operates it will take some time. I'll help at the start, but you'll soon get the hang of it as you bring your more proficient brain into use."

Richard relaxed into his chair and Abigail reached for his hand to give it a squeeze and then hold it. "Right, here we go."

Chapter 37

Eleanor contacted all team members and said to meet at the diner at eleven that night. Sherri praised the apple and rhubarb pie, so it was that all round with the inevitable coffees and teas.

When forks had scraped the last remnants of pie from plates Eleanor began, "I met with Charlotte and brought her up to speed on what we have so far. She tells me the Solons are in agreement that we need to discover more about the distortion Yuri found before doing anything with the P and Ps but that they want it taken care of as soon possible. Jenny and Alan, you are to pick someone from analytics and programming and take them through the program that flagged the Meldrew constants. Charlotte wants back up in case anything happens to you two while analysing whatever Richard and I dig up on Meldrew. Don't both look at me that way. We have no idea what Richard will find; we could be opening a Pandora's box, so we need to cover for any eventuality. Whoever you pick, tell them it stays with them until they are told differently. Ted, Victoria, you can take your people off relatives, friends and colleagues of Meldrew, there's no need now for the depth of scrutiny you've had them under so go back to the normal Life File surveillance protocol for now. However, you two are to stay glued to Meldrew because we need to know if anything external changes in the run up to the killing date. Any tiny shift in his routines, what he wears, the route he drives to work, does his morning coffee change, how he closes the front door, anything at all no matter how small. We know that if they do happen, they must be very, very slight changes otherwise observers would surely have noticed them at periodic downloads. Yuri, Richard and I will work on the best and safest way we can think of to search Meldrew. Assuming our timing is correct there are still a few days before the distortion occurs, so we have time for trial and refinement of whatever we pick as our final strategy. We'll start on that tomorrow. That's about it except to tell you that the Solons are fully aware of our progress and have passed along through Charlotte their confidence in this team and they look forward to a successful, and above all, safe, outcome."

At the moment Eleanor finished speaking the diner door opened and Charlotte came to their booth. All heads turned in surprise and Alan, Yuri and Jenny moved closer together to make room for her.

Sherri arrived asking, "Do you want coffee honey?"

Charlotte took the mug from her saying, "Yes please." Sherri smiled and moved away.

"I don't want to disturb you, but I need a word with Richard."

Eleanor recovered from her surprise and said, "Not disturbing us at all, in fact we were just finishing up."

Abruptly from Charlotte, "Good, then I won't keep the rest of you any longer," then she stood and let everyone but Richard slide from the booth and leave the diner.

Richard smiled and said, "We have to stop meeting like this; people will talk."

Charlotte shrugged, "From the looks they gave when they left the talk has already started. Anyway, I'm here because I was with Eleanor recently and she told me about the distortion and etcetera, etcetera and well…" she tailed off.

"Well, what Charlotte?" Richard asked gently.

Tears welled in the corners of her eyes, "Please be very careful. I know we did not part on the best of terms or under the best of circumstances, but I do still care about you. I didn't come to you when you were suffering and you asked for my help but if you have any doubts about this whole business come to me, please."

Reaching for her hand he squeezed gently, "I still care about you too, but I don't have any doubts. I'm in safe hands because you picked the right people for the job. I also know you would not allow anything that put any of us at undue risk. There really is only one way to get to the bottom of this and that's a search and we will prepare for it as well as we can. Okay?"

She nodded so he said, "Shall we finish our coffees then take a walk in the moonlight and remember great times we had… like on the flight back from Spain?"

Thumbing the tears from below her eyes she smiled and said, "That was very mischievous of us wasn't it, doing it in the toilet."

Sherri found the bill payment and tip in booth five and wrinkled her brow trying to recall who had sat there.

They walked in the moonlight with arms linked and reminisced about the good times they had together and not about the bad ones. She guided him to a wooded parkland path and took his hand to lead him through moon dappled darkness to a dell surrounded by old growth trees and carpeted with soft moss where she threw her arms around his neck then kissed him hard and when she pulled away, she asked, "Do you remember what I said to you on the plane coming back from Spain?"

"Sure, I do. We'd been talking about joining the mile high club and you said 'I'm hot and horny and I need to do it right now' so we did in the rear toilet of a seven-forty-seven. No way would I get rid of that memory."

He could see the whiteness of her teeth as she smiled and said, "Well I'm saying it again." So, they did, on a bed of moss with a wide-eyed owl as an uncomprehending voyeur and with all the frantic energy and abandon that was them before.

Chapter 38

He heard Abigail tell him, "Richard, use your brain as if it's a filing cabinet of memories. You are going to get rid of all the memories that are simply clutter or unwanted. Memories that you don't want to carry with you in Concordat for whatever reason. Think of it as memory shredding. Once gone they can never be recalled. What you retain is up to you. Happy, sad or a combination it's up to you. Those you keep will stay with you and cannot be altered or discarded in the future. I know you already have a partial list of memories you want to retain. They became apparent during your Life File review. Ready to start?"

He gave a quick acknowledgement and pulled the file for his first memory.

During the process he felt his mind becoming increasingly liberated as discards flew from the files. It amazed him just how much memorialised junk he had carried around. The wasted brain space and activity required to store and occasionally retrieve much of what was dross shocked him.

As Abigail had predicted his speed of retrieve-scan-retain or discard increased exponentially during the task, but the sun was in the ascent when gentle pressure from Abigail's hand, which had remained in his throughout, and a soft, "All done Richard," brought him back to the terrace when the last memory had been scanned and his choice made.

Releasing his hand Abigail said, "That went well Richard. Would you like tea, coffee, something to eat before we go on?"

He became aware that he was now wearing a dark-blue woollen sweater and asked, "Did you rustle this up for me?"

Abigail nodded, "It can turn chilly here during the nights, so I thought it best."

"Thank you and I'd love a cup of coffee and a double chocolate doughnut."

"Help yourself from the table by the French doors. I'll get myself some tea."

He leant against the balustrade while he drank his coffee and ate the doughnut. Abigail gazed out over the bay below and to the cobalt-blue horizon line of sea and drank tea from a fine china cup.

Richard asked, "How long did it take to unclutter my memory?"

"Twenty-nine Earth hours."

"Wow! That long. So, what's next? Do I get that extra two percent? Am I ready for it?"

"I am told you are ready for it but the decision as to whether or not you get it is not mine to make. Very soon I will be handing you over to a section head and he or she will make that decision. I'm waiting to hear who the section head will be so how about we go back down to the cove and relax and maybe have a swim."

The tent and loungers were there as before, and Abigail said nothing before shedding her clothes and wading into the sea. He sensed that Abigail was carrying a feeling of melancholy about with her and that she preferred to have some distance between them. When he entered the water, he swam a distance that took him away from where Abigail was floating motionless on her back. As always the act of swimming invigorated but now he could feel every nerve and muscle and action in exquisite detail. He could feel the molecules of water separating as his body slid between their layers and he felt the balancing effect of gravity and buoyancy as the mediums of air and water interacted on his body. He swam parallel to the shore with modulated speeds as he tried each stroke in turn and wondered at the efficiency and speed he could attain with all of them.

After a particularly fast stretch of butterfly, he heard Abigail call to him as she left the water and went toward the tent, "Come to the tent Richard, the section head will be arriving soon, and we are to meet here." He waved in response and swam to shore.

When he reached the tent, he found Abigail was dressed in black slacks, white blouse and black jacket and on her feet black patent leather low-heeled shoes. He thought her outfit very business-like.

Taking a cue from her he asked, "How should I dress? You look like you're ready for a board meeting."

"Smart casual will do for you. I'm like this because I don't know where I'll end up. I'll be wiped and reassigned and I want to be dressed in something that fits in wherever I go."

He chose brown loafers, navy-blue slacks and an oxford button down shirt in light green and blue check.

Abigail tilted her head to the side and her brow furrowed then as she straightened, she said, "The section head is on the way. Coming down the track now. They haven't said who it is."

Chapter 39

"Looks good," from Richard. "You've put him deep so no residual flickers of disturbance remain when he wakes?"

Yuri confirmed, "He won't know anything other than he's had a good night's sleep."

Victoria confirmed that Watchers were with Amy.

Eleanor looked at Richard and smiled, "Let's go and take a look around." They inserted into Meldrew.

The recon went well, and several escape routes were considered and tested until a final choice was made. Connections at the cerebellum were normal, which they had expected, and gave no clue to what they might find when the distortion occurred, but they felt they were as well prepared as possible.

Eleanor asked, "Any readings he knew we were in there?"

Yuri shook her head, "None at all."

They went to the diner and joined the rest of the team. Sherri bustled over with mugs and a carafe full of coffee and when asked the pie of the day replied, "Pecan, and it's the best you will ever taste."

Alan laughed and said, "You say that about all your pies," and Sherri shot back sternly, "And have I ever lied to you, Sugar?"

Jenny poked Alan with her elbow saying, "She's got you there; she never has."

Sherri marched away with head held high to collect their slices of pie and they sat quietly until they were delivered. They talked between bites.

Eleanor, "There are six more days until the next killing if he keeps to schedule and we know the distortion starts five days before the event so we should see it soon. Is that right Yuri?"

"Yes, if he doesn't deviate it will show up tomorrow," Yuri responded.

Richard raised his fork to indicate he had something to add and swallowed before speaking, "We have Meldrew in the area of the killings because his name came up as the common denominator and it came up because *why* Jenny?" Jenny looked startled at the question and hesitated to answer but Richard pushed, "Come on, because *why*, Jenny?"

"Well because he *is* the constant, or at least his *name* is."

Richard looked around and saw frowns of puzzlement, "We kind of stopped there didn't we. We had Meldrew in the areas at the time of the killings and he was the only constant. But what if he *isn't* the only one?" Richard paused and sipped coffee to let this sink in, then, "What if the *places* where the killings took place also have a constant, and a common denominator? Yes, they are spread all over the country miles apart and are a mixture of cities and towns but that does not mean that there is nothing that connects them. If there is a constant, then we might find out *why* Meldrew was there and perhaps *why* he killed." Here he held up a hand saying, "Hold on Jenny, I can see you are bursting to tell me that we already know why Meldrew was in these places, you've already found that out, but that is the Life File record Meldrew slid past us before Yuri found the distortions and I believe those records are a cover for what really happened. Eleanor, I think Jenny and Alan need to put all the information about the places into their program along with every permutation they can come up with to find any commonality between them and I suggest they start with the very precise time frame he is using and see if the dates and times are particular to each place." Forking pie into his mouth he spoke round it, "Who knows, maybe we'll find out the next killing place."

Jenny and Alan looked expectantly at Eleanor, "Do as Richard suggests. Get Emma to help you. Emma is the one you picked to train like I asked, isn't she?"

Jenny and Alan both answered, "Yes."

"Good. We know you'll do the best you can." The analysts left with Jenny stuffing a last piece of pie into her mouth.

The remaining team members sat in silence lost in their own thoughts and drank coffee until Eleanor spoke, "We have one day and unless analytics and programming find something that changes things we go in as planned so all we can do is wait. Take a little time to yourselves but stay open for my call—in case Jenny and Alan do come up with something."

They all made moves to leave the booth, but Eleanor caught Richard's arm and said, "I need you for a little while longer."

Pulling a face and shrugging his shoulders in mock resignation he wished the other three a pleasant rest and sat down.

Chapter 40

They stood outside the marquee and looked up the track. A figure was about halfway down picking steps carefully with the aid of a walking stick. Richard saw Abigail visibly stiffen when she realised who it was. She whispered, "That's Per Lundquist. He's the senior section leader and in life as a business executive he was known as the smiling executioner. The company he worked for sent him round when costs needed cutting and efficiencies increased."

She got no further before Lundquist stepped onto the sand and pointing with his cane indicated they should follow him to the marquee.

A wicker chair was waiting for Lundquist, so he sat and asked, "Abigail, are there drinks in that cooler? If so, please bring me Mountain Dew and one for you and Mr Fleming if you desire one. I believe there will be a glass chilling in the cooler for me. I enjoy the drink more from a glass."

Abigail glanced at Richard who said, "Diet Pepsi please." Then she got the drinks and a Perrier for herself.

Lundquist thanked her and wiping the condensation from the bottle with a linen handkerchief he poured a small amount into his glass and took a sip that he rolled around in his mouth as if it was a fine wine before swallowing. "Please, both of you sit down."

Richard immediately thought, *he wants us on the loungers because they are lower and...*

Lundquist interrupted, "I've seen your Life File Mr Fleming and I know your dislike for those who manoeuvre seating, desk and office arrangements so as to force those they perceive as subordinates to look up at them. However, that was not my intention in directing you to sit. Had you remained standing I would have been uncomfortable looking up at you. But if you consider there was some ulterior motive, I will happily provide chairs the same height and style as mine. In fact, I will do that anyway." The loungers vanished and in their place two chairs identical to Lundquist's appeared under them. "There, do you find that more equitable Mr Fleming?"

All this was said in Scandinavian accented English with humour heard in its tone and seen on Lundquist's mouth and in his eyes. Before Richard could respond Lundquist smiled broadly at him saying, "Quite right Mr Fleming, I'm not someone to be fucked with. That was what you were thinking wasn't it?" Richard nodded and kept quiet.

Lundquist turned his attention to Abigail. "Thank you, Abigail. As always, your work has been excellent but now you must be wiped and move onto your new section. You will be working with the psychological analysis section. This move is viewed as being permanent. I hope you are pleased."

Abigail beamed. "Yes, very. Thank you."

"You earned it. Your section leader is waiting for you at the villa so say your goodbyes to Mr Fleming and go meet him."

Richard and Abigail stood and embraced then she left the tent and began the climb to the villa. She did not look back. Her wipe had already begun.

Lundquist drank more Mountain Dew and placed the glass beside the bottle on the carpeted sand of the tent then draped the linen handkerchief he had used to wipe the condensation away over the arm of his chair. They sat looking at one another, Richard sitting upright with hands on his thighs and Lundquist leaning slightly forward with his hands crossed on top of the handle of his cane.

"Mr Fleming," Lundquist began. "Concordat followed you throughout your life and from the time shortly after you started your career as a Marine Engineer it has been thought by the various observers and compilers involved with your Life File that you would be a suitable candidate for our Retribution section. Amber, Eleanor and Abigail are drawn to the same conclusion. Eleanor, one of several section heads within Retribution division and whose opinions on such matters I regard highly has put a strong case before me to place you in her section."

Removing a hand from his cane and not taking his eyes from Richard, Lundquist reached down and picked up his glass, sipped more drink and replaced the glass. His hand returned to his other on the cane and he continued.

"Abigail will have mentioned the transferring of persons to different positions throughout the Concordat organisation until the right fit is found. Retribution is not like that. Those that join Retribution remain in Retribution." Lundquist leaned forward to emphasise his next point. "If, after training and brain optimisation you fall short of the required standards by even the smallest margin you will undergo the ultimate wipe and return to being dead. The next phase of your — let's call it training — is in the hands of Brian and he will answer all the questions that are swirling around in your mind but which I elected to mute so that you wouldn't interrupt me every nanosecond."

Lundquist stood and Richard followed suit then Lundquist reached out a hand which Richard grasped and after a brief handshake, Lundquist smiled and said, "One more thing before I go; I was part of your Life File, a part you decided to discard from memory, but I retained that part from my Life File because I found our interaction at the time to be both uplifting and, at times, frustrating. You were very different from those I was used to dealing with. Don't let Concordat, Eleanor or me down Mr Fleming."

Lundquist left the tent and began to walk along the beach throwing back over his shoulder, "I'll take a little walk I think, such a beautiful spot. Brian is on his way down."

Richard turned to see someone the height and bulk of an NFL defensive guard coming down the track from the villa.

Chapter 41

He sensed that Eleanor had something to say that was important to her but was struggling with the words and her emotions, so he sat and waited.

Picking up a paper napkin she started to tear it into narrow strips and said, "I know why you intend to place the destruct mechanism in the vertebrae between where I will be and where you will enter. You hope that if Meldrew does trap you and you have to sever the nerves in his spinal column my position might give Yuri time to get me out." Pausing, she added another strip to the growing pile on the table, "I'm right, aren't I?"

Taking the pile of strips, he began to align them side by side and answered, "Yes." Without looking at her.

Anger flushed into Eleanor's face and voice as she turned to him, "That's it! That's all you have to say. How dare you! It's not your decision to make alone, I'll be in there with you so I should have some say in any escape plan hatched to save me and leave you. And, on top of that you told Yuri about the mechanism when we were told specifically not to tell anyone. Did you really think she wouldn't tell me?" Her voice softened a little as she said, "I'm sure you did this with the most noble of motives, but you should still have come to me first."

Taking the last piece of napkin from her fingers he aligned it with the others before saying, "I'm sorry."

Eleanor waited for more, but he was silent as he squared off the napkin strips. "There's nothing else you want to say?" she queried.

He said, "I have a statement and a question."

Eleanor with exasperation fast taking the place of anger, sighed, "Okay, let me hear them."

"Not much time left. Want to go and fool around?"

He got "Oh yes please!" in immediate response.

They went to the apartment in Kolkata because that was the city where it began for them.

It was Alan who called and told Eleanor that a constant had been found linking the places where the killings had taken place and she told him to contact the rest of the team and meet at Richard's beach house. She sent Alan directions.

Richard and Eleanor arrived unnoticed, and the others were standing in lagoon water to their knees talking amongst themselves and looking around. Richard shouted from the patio deck, "Hey, you lot, time to get down to work."

None, with the exception of Eleanor, had been to the beach house before and all commented on the beauty of the place. Richard, in response to a question from Victoria, said it was copied from a place he had found in Sri Lanka during his travels. Having told them there were drinks in the fridge and to help themselves he gathered together a selection of rattan armchairs with thick cushions. Once drinks had been selected and poured Eleanor pulled the seats around a large low, glass topped table and requested them all to sit. After she sat down Jenny became busy tugging on what looked to be one of the narrow ribbons used to attach the cushions to the chairs but as more of the ribbon was revealed it turned out to be a skimpy, floral patterned, bikini top. Jenny held it up for all to inspect and raised questioning eyebrows.

"I wondered where that had got to," came from Eleanor as she retrieved it from Jenny without any sign of discomfort or embarrassment, "I don't often wear it here, only when we have visitors, the bottom should be around here somewhere." Throwing it onto the shelf beneath the table's glass top she enquired, "Who's starting, you Alan, or Jenny?"

Alan started. "It was a combination of two things. One was Richard's suggestion about looking for any constant between the places where the killings took place and the second was Yuri's suggestion that a numeric trigger could be involved. We tried all sorts of permutations and got nothing until Emma, you'll remember she's the analyst we're training on Jenny's program, she said we should try adding the numbers of his time frame which is eight months, one day and one hour, which gave us ten, and see if that corresponded with anything to do with the murders and we found another constant. Every town and city where a killing took place has a total of ten letters in its name even if the name has more than one word."

Alan sat back to allow this to sink in for a few moments then Jenny continued, "There are one hundred and twenty-two places in his country with ten letter names so deducting thirty-six we have eighty-six remaining possibilities where the next kill will take place. We also ran the names of the places against the names of victims, when they were known, to see if they matched alphabetically but they did not, and the place names first letters use only eighteen of the twenty-six letters of the alphabet. Anyway, we now had two constants, Meldrew, and the killing places with ten letter names, so we searched for more commonality and as before with regards to sex, age, hair colour, ethnicity, gender and all the other markers we found no similarities that applied to all victims. Do any of you have any ideas or suggestions that will narrow things down?" Jenny asked in conclusion.

The only sound was the clinking of ice against glass as drinks were sampled and then Ted spoke up, "Can you get Emma to telesync a listing of the places and the times of the killings to a view screen here?"

Alan answered, "Yes, we can do that. What do you have in mind?"

Ted was noncommittal, "I'd like to get a look at what Emma sends before I say. I might be barking up the wrong tree."

"Okay, I'll get Emma to send what you want," Alan confirmed.

The tabletop turned opaque and became a view screen with place names and estimated killing dates and times shown in two columns. Ted looked at the information then telesynced with Emma and asked for a listing of the eighty-six places not on the killing list. Emma did this and the information became a blur as Ted mind moved it around the screen while the others watched in anticipation. When he was finally satisfied,
Ted brought the scrambled rush of place names and numbers to a halt and aligning them to his liking he began to speak, "He's killed thirty-six times and the place names' first letters have used only eighteen letters from the alphabet, two eighteens are thirty-six and as you can see from the columns he is using the same first letters but at the beginning of different names *in alphabetical order* and to me this means that his next killing place will start with an A. I believe he is about to start another run of eighteen killings." A slight pause, "There are only two place names of ten letters starting with A and he has already used both so in order to follow his alphabetical urge he will, I believe, return to the first place he killed. The second letter in the place names appear to be irrelevant because they have not followed in

alphabetical order. It is only the first letter, the number of letters and the time frame that appear to trigger his acts." Ted took a last look at the screen and nodded to himself, he was satisfied, and then he sat back.

Eleanor selected the first place name, and enlarged it to fill the screen, Accrington.

Richard looked towards Ted and said, "Great work Ted, that's a huge step forward." Ted acknowledged the compliment with a smile and Richard continued, "You seem certain that he will go back to Accrington and not simply choose the third B place on the list to begin killing again, why's that?"

Ted replied, "Because I think he is working to an eighteen-letter alphabet made up of first letters of the place names and to leave out the A would ruin his alphabet."

Richard nodded, "Makes sense. Emma, have there been two killings reported in Accrington eighteen months apart that fit Meldrew's schedule?"

"Hang on I'll check." The screen confirmed there had been.

Eleanor broke the silence that followed, "That's all good as far as it goes but we are discussing this as if the Meldrew we know is committing the crimes, but we have no evidence to substantiate that. We had the constant which placed him in the vicinity and now we have the place name constant but still no proof he did the killings. The Solons will not sanction a cull on what we have so far. For the time frame and alphabet theory to be true, Meldrew would have to show signs of an obsessive-compulsive disorder that drove him to follow those exact agendas. Has any one of us seen him display any OCD tendency in his normal everyday life? I haven't. The real proof must lie in the distortion that Yuri found and is due to start again tonight. We now have where he will kill if Ted's deductions are correct, but we still do not have the reason why the time frames are so critical or how he has kept the kills hidden from us. We still need to search. Richard and I will insert tonight at twenty-two hundred with Yuri monitoring us and downloading everything that goes on. Jenny and Alan, with Emma if she can help, you are to transcribe and analyse downloads and report back to Yuri if anything concerns you that could compromise our safety. Ted, Victoria, put watchers on Meldrew's immediate family and in-laws. We found nothing connecting them, but I want them watched when the distortion begins just in case they do become involved. If any of them show anything but normal brain function, tell Yuri. We have eight hours before we insert so take some self-time and sync with Yuri at twenty-one-thirty. Richard and I will sync at twenty-one forty-five. Any questions? None? Okay, I'll get in touch with Charlotte and give her an update then talk to you all before we insert. Enjoy your self-time."

Chapter 42

Reaching out a hand the size of an on the bone smoked ham he smothered the one Richard offered in return and gripped hard enough to make Richard wince.

"Hi ya! I'm Brian. Per Lundquist told you about me, right? I'll be taking you through what to expect when you're uploaded with the last two percent and run some drills that get you used to the Retribution play book."

Richard stepped back in order to take in this giant of a man from the top of his dreadlocked head to the size sixteen Nikes on his feet. "Sheesh," he breathed. "You are one big man, and I will most assuredly do whatever you tell me."

Brian grinned hugely showing magnificently white teeth then slapped Richard's right bicep hard enough to make him stagger a step sideways and said, "I'm sure we'll get along just fine. Eleanor tells me you are a smart guy and to expect lots of questions which is good, questions bring clarification. I heard from Per that he knew you at Life Side so you can expect that he'll be watching closely. Anyway, enough chatter, time to make it happen. I'm not cool with this place. I like my own spaces so let's go to one of them and get down to business."

They were squatting with backs against a graffiti covered wall that formed part of the supports for an elevated highway. Every inch of concrete space was filled with graffiti in never ending kaleidoscopic bursts of colour. They were the only two in the place and Richard noticed the lack of traffic noise from the roadway above and he was about to mention this when Brian placed a hand on his arm and said, "Close your eyes and keep them closed until I say to open them, okay." Richard nodded and closed his eyes.

He felt Brian punch him gently on the thigh and say, "Open your eyes."

The space was now filled with people who were all frozen in time and space. Before Richard had a chance to comment Brian began speaking and pointing, "See that skinny girl with the big tits over there? She's fifteen and turning tricks to feed her habit. That's her pimp standing beside her. The kid doing the jump on the skateboard, he'll be killed in a drive-by shooting. Those three with their heads together, the ones in the cut off tee's, they're gangbangers who will rape a young single mom for two days in front of her six-year-old son that they tie to a chair. That old homeless guy laying out his bedroll will freeze to death during a blizzard and the mangy mutt with him will die alongside. Buddies to the end. Those two standing by that column, he's a pusher and she's his junky whore this week who'll blow him behind that dumpster for a nickel bag, next week it'll be another. The cop over there, he's here for his pay off from the pusher. His partner doesn't give a shit because he collects from pushers three blocks down. When that guy over there gets caught by the four guys chasing him, they will kick him so hard they will break his jaw and three ribs. He looked at one of the guy's girl the wrong way so they will teach him respect. When his bones heal, he will ambush one of the four, break his skull with a baseball bat and then cut his balls off and leave him to bleed to death. That will start a gang war that will end up with seven dead. That girl spraying graffiti will paint a sick caricature of a rival gang's head honcho and when word gets around who did it, they will track her down and empty a can of spray paint into her mouth and pussy and then they will push the can into her. She won't be able to talk or have kids. See that fine woman about to walk out and onto the sidewalk, that's my sister and she fucked to make money to feed her two kids. She died of aids. One of her kids went to jail for life and the other slit her wrists. All these people lived in or hung around my neighbourhood. I knew some of them. Close your eyes again."

Richard did and then when told he could open them the tableau of frozen motion persons had gone, and the space was empty. Richard had the faintest sense that those he had seen in the space had stayed with him.

Brian draped an arm around Richard's shoulders and with sadness in his voice said, "C'mon brother, let's go somewhere and get us some coffee." They both stood and walked from the concrete and graffiti space.

Chapter 43

After transmitting her update Eleanor reported, "Charlotte wants to be there when we insert so she'll join us just before we sync."

Richard who was clearing the table of glasses and distributing the chairs around the patio said, "I figured she would. She's taken quite a liking to you since you had her for a meal in Kolkata. I suspect both of you ate well that night."

Eleanor threw a seat cushion that hit his head and retorted, "You've enjoyed many a meal from us yourself so you can't blame us girls if we eat out every now and then."

Later she lay with her head on his chest and murmured, "Well that should hold us for a while. I have that lovely, drained feeling, all warm and complete, how about you?"

"You remember the night I stayed over at your parent's apartment in Kolkata, and you woke me up by sneaking into my bed?"

"Of course, I do, it was delicious and all the more exciting because we tried to keep quiet so as not to wake my parents. Well, I feel just the same now as I felt then, wonderful." She kissed his chest and said, "I never told you but many years later my mother confided she did hear us, and it was fortunate my father was a heavy sleeper. My mum was very broad-minded."

He gently stroked her back, "She was also very beautiful, and you inherited her looks."

Moving to rest on her elbows she smiled and said, "Well thank you kind Sir, she was very lovely in many ways."

At twenty-one forty-five Yuri confirmed that the rest of the team was synced and ready and that Meldrew and his wife were having their usual nightcap before retiring. The Watcher's confirmed that nothing out of the ordinary had changed in the Meldrew's nightly routine or that of their relatives.

Richard and Eleanor were preparing to sync when Charlotte arrived. She began in her usual no small talk way saying, "Good luck you two, we want you back safe and sound." Then her voice began to shake as she said, "*I* want you both back." Then turning to Yuri, "Watch over them well, please."

"We all will," Yuri said quietly and with feeling, then she synced them into her monitoring and download circuits. Charlotte left after telling Yuri she would be at her cabin and to call her when it was over.

Eleanor went into Meldrew's lumbar vertebrae and Richard into the start of his cervical vertebrae and once situated Eleanor sent the safety neural connection up to him through a spinal nerve conduit they had picked and tested. Yuri reported that their entry had not caused any reaction in Meldrew's brainwaves or nervous system. Richard and Eleanor settled down to wait until Meldrew fell deeply asleep.

It was twenty-three-twenty when Yuri told them that Meldrew was in deep sleep and Richard could start his search. "You've got ninety minutes," came from Yuri.

"Okay," from Richard. "That should cover when the distortion starts. I'm going to get in position now. All set Eleanor?"

"Yes, take care," she replied.

Downloads would show it was at twenty-three forty-three on September twenty-fifth that the distortion at the junction of the spinal cord and cerebellum began and was complete at midnight which was when Richard began to search.

He was only nanoseconds into his hunt when he exclaimed, "What the hell! Yuri, I don't know what is happening here, but the distortion is not just around the cerebellum, it's everywhere. It's strongest and slightly opaque and more noticeable at the cerebellum and then becomes totally transparent as it spreads. Eleanor, I'm not in any danger and I need you up here to take a hemisphere because I won't have time in ninety minutes to transmit what is happening on both sides. Leave the neural line in place."

"On my way," came from Eleanor.

"Yuri, can you double stream record what Eleanor and I are getting?" Richard asked.

"Setting it up now, Alan will take Eleanor's and we'll pass both to Jenny and Emma."

"Good. So, Eleanor, which side do you want? Left, or right?"

"I'll take the right, I'm more into creativity and arts than science and math."

"Fine. Yuri, tell us when he is about to leave deep sleep and we'll meet back here to exit."

"Will do on that and I'll let you know if anything else disturbs him."

Eighty-eight minutes later they completed the search, exited and un-synced.

Eleanor immediately contacted Charlotte to report the search was complete, that she and Richard had suffered no harm and that the results were with analytics and programming. Relief was apparent in Charlotte's voice. "Good, I'm glad it went well. I'll let the Solons know. Get back to me with whatever analytics and programming find."

Chapter 44

"This coffee is great, but why a bar?"

"Hey, I'm like you man, a sober alcoholic, more than twenty-five Life Side years. One of the reasons I was chosen to guide you, although I prefer the title 'mentor', it has a nice ring to it. Kindred spirits man—pun intended.'

It was a deep narrow place containing a long bar with four booths facing it. The walls, ceiling and light fixtures were stained brown from the smoke of countless cigarettes and the sharp smell of spilt alcohol permeated the wood of the floor and the bar.

"Terry, the owner, that's him talking to Malcolm down at the end, makes the best coffee and always has some for Malky the Alkie, that's what the locals call Malcolm, when he comes in as soon as Terry opens. Tells Terry to put some 'sugar' in it. That don't fool anybody, the regulars all know it's a shot of rum he wants. Terry's a recovering alcoholic and runs meetings twice a week in the back room before he opens. Some find it strange an alcoholic owning a bar and having AA meetings. Kinda diametrically opposed isn't it. Selling the stuff that feeds the addiction and offering the steps that can sustain sobriety."

They sat drinking their coffee from thick china mugs and Richard was sure he felt the atmosphere and history of the place seeping into him. Many people, mostly men, it was that kind of place, came and went. They would have a quick drink or two before moving on to whatever awaited them in their lives. There were always two or three that seemed to be semi-permanent fixtures sitting at the bar usually nursing beers with whisky chasers. They ebbed and flowed during the day with Terry always greeting them as if old friends and asking, "How ya doin' today," before serving them. A few women came in. Mostly as the evening wore on into night and most were tired looking working girls who wanted the boost of alcohol before facing another night of hustling for tricks. Terry treated these women with respectful courtesy and most responded with a tired smile that for an instant flashed a beauty that was now long faded across their faces. Terry told them to be careful out there when they left. Terry never left. He drank coffee and ate bar snacks and attended to the chores. If a patron appeared to be getting too drunk or too rowdy, he firmly and gently led them to the door. They sat until Terry ushered the last customer through the door and watched him clear tables, wash glasses, wipe down the bar, sweep the floor and do the myriad of other things necessary to prepare the place for the next opening time. They sat even as the lights were turned off and Terry left after setting the alarm and giving the door an extra shake from the outside to make sure it was securely closed on its two deadbolt locks.

"Richard, why did you choose to keep your memories of your time as a performing alcoholic?" Brian asked.

"I keep them because I fucked up big time. I caused myself and others a lot of pain. It took many years for me to come close to making amends to those I hurt. Some accepted and some told me to go screw myself. I considered myself one of the fortunate few. I accepted help when it was offered, and the fellowship steps helped me to climb out of the bottle. I need to be reminded of what I am, an alcoholic, even after thirty plus years of sobriety. I'm not sure, but I think that will be as important to me in Concordat as it was in my life. You still refer to yourself as a sober alcoholic so perhaps I am right in keeping those memories alive and that even in Concordat it's still a day at a time."

"Smart thinking. Memories of my time performing have helped me. Let's get out of here."

They left the bar space.

Chapter 45

Watchers continued to monitor Meldrew and family with observers taking continuous downloads from him. The team joined Jenny and Emma eager to learn why the distortion occurred, what it meant and was it the place of concealment for the killings.

Jenny was in a state of high excitement. "You are never going to believe what we've found," she burst out as soon as they arrived.

But before she could continue Richard said, "Manners Jenny. Please introduce us to this lady who I assume is Emma."

Jenny was contrite and said, "Oh, I'm so sorry Emma. I'd forgotten they only know your voice so let me introduce you to the team."

Striking best described Emma. Tall and slim with the fine features of those found in some North African nations she had a brilliant smile and dark eyes that danced with humour.

Eleanor, who was a hugger, stepped forward and gave Emma one saying, "I believe it's you we have to thank for coming up with the numbers' thing. Nice one."

Emma responded to all their hellos and good to meet yous with, "I've heard a lot about you from Jenny and I'm thrilled to be working with you all."

With the formalities over Jenny told Alan to look at his view screen, "What do you see?"

Alan looked for some time and mind moved portions of Richard and Eleanor's search downloads into various configurations and overlaps then he turned and in hushed tones said, "Meldrew has two DNA strands and two spinal cords running in parallel."

Jenny and Emma high fived and grinned.

They had gathered in what could have been mistaken for a company board room with its large oval dark wood table and wooden chairs with padded leather seats. In fact, it was a meeting room housed in what at one time had been a hospital for the insane. Richard had given them directions and said to meet there.

Yuri looked around appraisingly at the carved wood panelling and leaded windows and remarked to Richard, "Why here? It's obviously old. What special meaning does it hold for you?"

"It's a place where I used to spend time back in life. The people that came to this room helped me turn my life around," Richard answered as he took a doughnut from a tray and coffee from an urn on a worn, battered and cigarette scarred sideboard. Yuri was about to ask for more detail but Eleanor who had overheard their conversation caught her eye and shook her head in a 'let it drop' signal.

Supplied with doughnuts and coffee they sat around the table and Jenny brought up a holographic projection of Meldrew's brain that hung and rotated at the centre of the table.

Jenny began, "We've enhanced what we initially thought to be a distortion but now realise is an additional cortex layer. As you can see it covers every surface of what we call his *original* brain and only to a depth that does not impinge on the skull or cause undue pressure on the cerebral fluid. Richard and Eleanor's search records allowed us to microslice and theorise that this *additional* cortex material increases in functional strength and becomes the dominant brain matter over the days and hours leading up to a kill. Because of its lack of depth and transparency observers didn't pick up on it and it caused no discernible change because the original brain *mass and output* drowns out and hides anything that the much smaller mass of the layer puts out. *That's* how the killings stayed hidden and once the additional material receded the record was taken with it."

The hologram image changed to what they all recognised as a DNA helix and Emma took up the account, "We next looked for the source of the additional cortex layer. Where did it originate and how did it travel to the original brain? Nothing within a human body can store and sustain cortex material other than the brain itself so we looked at what initiates all growth and function, namely DNA. On the surface his DNA helix looks perfectly normal, but nanoscale dissection found this." A second DNA helix became highlighted. "This second helix is imprinted into and encapsulated by Meldrew's *original helix*. Sequencing the strands, we find the original is responsible for Meldrew's normal daily functions, the ones we see in all downloads, nothing out of the ordinary, but the *imprinted* strand differs in that it contains a sequence that drives his need to kill. A sequence very common among serial killers, sociopaths and psychopaths. What we *don't know* is how it got there or why it only becomes active in the five days before a killing."

As the rest sat and digested this information an animated hologram appeared showing the progress of the additional cortex layer across all areas of Meldrew's brain from its start at the cerebellum to its completion at the frontal lobe.

"We have no verification but this is what we think is happening," came from Alan. "Five days before he kills, the, let's call it *rogue* DNA, introduces the covering layer and assuming, as in the past, that we are unable to observe or record any plans made for his next killing we will have to go live and physically monitor his every move in the hope we find out who the victim is in time to save them. However, and this is the part that hurts, we must be missing something. There has to be something that is the reason he kills to such an exact schedule. Something that will not let him deviate. If we don't find it, then in order to save the victim a cull will be needed and once that happens, we will lose any chance of finding his reason why. We need the 'why' so we can tell our new Life File programs and protocols what to search for. So, if you have any ideas no matter how squirrely they seem, let's have them."

Chapter 46

It was a messy space. There was untidiness everywhere.

An apartment. Old building because the rooms were high ceilinged and the windows tall and narrow. The view to other buildings, mainly roofs, suggested a top floor flat. Bed unmade; clothes thrown to land near but not in the open-topped laundry basket. Shoes kicked off and scattered in the entrance hall. Kitchen waste bin overflowing with folded pizza boxes and take away meal containers. Crusted mugs and plates piled to tap height in the sink. Empty wine and liquor bottles filling a large black garbage bag. Dust on every surface. Bathroom fixtures and fittings covered with soap and shampoo scum. Vanity mirror marked with water streaks and dried droplets. Toothpaste uncapped and dripping into the sink.

In the entrance hall a young woman sat on the floor with her back against the door and legs stretched out down the hallway. Her head covered with unkempt blonde hair drooped to her chest. She was dressed in blue hospital scrubs. A whiskey bottle lay horizontal in the vee formed by her legs. It was almost empty and some of its contents had run out and stained the blue material of the scrubs. On the floor was an empty pill bottle. A few small white tablets clung to the whiskey-soaked material below her chin. A scalpel lay in her left hand and a deep gash ran up the veins from the wrist of her right arm. Blood had congealed around her and the metallic aromas of blood and whiskey covered her like a shroud.

It took two hefty police officers to force the door open against its deadbolt and break the safety chain free from the frame then to push the body to the side sufficient for one to stick his head in and then immediately pull back and radio in to report a dead body.

It was the only flat on the top floor. A friend just dropping by for a visit saw the blood pooling outside the door. She knocked and called her friend's name. Getting no response and because of the blood she called the police.

Then there was only the dark stain barely visible on the dark wood of the hallways parquet floor. Cleaning, clearing and repairing had been done.

It was a lived-in space. Tidiness was everywhere.

She had killed herself to escape just as her younger sister had done.

Her sister turned to drugs early in her internship. Both had been groomed to enter the medical profession. Their parents were surgeons following in their parents' footsteps and the sisters were to do the same. Their father was disappointed that one of them wasn't male, he made that quite clear, and their mother often spoke of how she suffered during each pregnancy. They were to make up for the father's disappointment and the mothers suffering by becoming renowned surgeons and specialists. Something their parents could be proud of. It was more than expected of them—it was demanded.

The sisters hated medicine.

"This is in my Life File. I kept the memory. I knew Marie the elder sister. I was her sponsor at the time she killed herself. Her parents blamed her for her sister's suicide and said she was weak and if she hadn't been an addict herself, she could have saved her. The parents never showed any love or gave any support. It was all about them and the shame it had brought. I tried to help Marie. It wasn't enough."

"Can't say that," Brian said softly. "What you did for Marie was enough. It's up to the addict whether they accept. Who knows, maybe offing the parents would have saved her and her sister. I've taken a look at their Life Files and they were a couple of self-absorbed assholes without a shred of caring or empathy in them."

With a last look at the stain beside the entrance door they left the space.

Chapter 47

Charlotte broke the silence after Alan's plea, "I have to report to the Solons and get clearance for a Life Side operation so keep working on finding the missing piece that leads to 'why'. I'd hate to have to cull before we know. I'll get back to you with the live op authorisation." And with that she stood and taking another doughnut from the tray on the sideboard, left.

Meldrew's holographic brain continued to animate and revolve above the table as in ones and twos they drifted to the sideboard to get refills of coffee and select another doughnut. As if seeking inspiration from a Delphic oracle, Alan was peering closely at the junction of the spinal cord to cerebellum when Yuri came to stand beside him and said, "I have an idea but need your computing expertise to prove it right or wrong. Can we go to analytics and programming and I'll explain?"

Asking Yuri to wait a second Alan went to Eleanor and interrupted a discussion she was having with Victoria. Taking Eleanor to one side he explained Yuri's request and asked her approval which Eleanor readily gave. Many questioning looks followed them out the door and Eleanor shrugged off enquiries.

A brainstorming session was in progress with all sorts of ideas and speculations being thrown around when Yuri and Alan returned looking extremely pleased with themselves.

Making the others wait while they got coffee and debated which doughnut to have it was Richard who said, "There is only one thing that would make you two look so pleased and keep us hanging like this. You've found Meldrew's 'Why'."

Alan spoke around a mouthful of doughnut, "Yuri seems to have found the 'why'."

Two words appeared above the holographic image — Gestation Period — and underneath: eight months plus one day one hour.

"Explain," came from Eleanor.

Yuri explained, "At the beginning I mentioned numeric triggers and I've been thinking about and working on them since Emma came up with the ten factors about place names. I concentrated on Meldrew's downloads and those of his family looking for any dates of significance that could be a trigger. I looked at everything and anything where numbers were concerned but nothing stood out. That is until today when it dawned on me that maybe it was a pregnancy term. Alan and I just reviewed the Life File of Meldrew's mother, Frances Rudge nee Meldrew." A picture of a plain stocky woman with a scowl on her face superimposed itself on the view screen numbers. "This is his mother and from what we gathered from her Life File a thoroughly unpleasant woman and one not considered for entry into Concordat. Download records show she carried Meldrew for eight months, one day and one hour from the moment of conception, eight, one and one. We, Alan and I, believe this to be the trigger. It was a difficult pregnancy, and she was induced to give birth early because the doctors were concerned for her health if she carried to full-term. As it was the baby weighed ten pounds and seven ounces, big for such a small woman at only eight months." Meldrew's mother disappeared from the screen and Yuri said, "Alan, you do the next part please."

Alan swallowed the last of a honey glazed doughnut and started, "This is pure conjecture because we have no direct proof, but Yuri and I think that the embedded DNA, the second strand, is that of a twin that was absorbed by Meldrew during the gestation period. There are slight differences in the DNA strands so they would have not been identical twins but still quite close. That's not unknown. The main characteristics and features are almost identical, but differences are discernible, a cross between fraternal and identical twins. I must mention again that all this is supposition and guess work on our part, but Yuri and I believe that the five days prior to the birth when we know doctors started giving inducing drugs is now the preparation time when the other implanted and imprinted Meldrew gets ready to be — and we know this sounds crazy — gets ready to be born as the other Meldrew and kill in revenge for never developing and coming to term as a twin. Anyway, that's what we think."

Jenny was the first to speak. "Not crazy at all. Our records are full of the foetus of a twin being absorbed into various parts of the host anatomy, even some into the brain, so it's not a huge leap to what Yuri and Alan suggest. It's as good an explanation as we've been able to come up with."

Richard was next, "Okay, so we accept that premise of the 'why' and we think we know the 'where' which is Accrington and the 'when' four days away but to complete the puzzle and make it useful to analytics and programming and programs and protocols we have to find the reason behind the selection of place names with ten letters. Is there anything in his parents past that will shed light on that?"

Jenny and Emma locked eyes and Jenny said, "Our turn now Emma, let's see what we can find in the records." As they were rising to go Eleanor spoke, "I've just heard from Charlotte and we have the go ahead for a Life Side op so keep track of where the rest of us are and let me know what you find." Jenny and Emma gave acknowledgement and hurried from the room.

He'd told his wife and daughter he was going to Manchester to consult at the neuro centre of the Royal Infirmary. He was often called to consult so his wife was not surprised. Constance enquired how long and got four or five days in response and that he would call when on his way back. She had his cell phone number, but they never communicated while he was away. As Ted had predicted he went to Accrington and at a pub that rented rooms signed in as Liam Coward paying cash up front for five days.

Chapter 48

It was a white space. White on white on white. An infinity of white without shape or form. Where within this space they were located Richard could not gauge. Brian was standing next to him and that was his only point of reference and even 'standing' was a subjective choice. There was no sense of anything solid beneath his feet.

Then from a place within the space a column of men and women approached and passed in front of them. They made no sound and cast no look they just walked by to another place within the space and were gone.

"Those, Richard, are the Earth's paedophiles. Surprising number. All shapes, sizes, races, genders. All with one thing in common, they prey on young children. That sickens you doesn't it, Richard? Hold your thoughts and questions, there's more to see."

From another place in the space men, women and youths emerged to file past them and then were gone out of the space.

"Abusers, Richard. Physical, sexual and mental. You saw how young some are."

Then, from many places in the space came column after column with Brian identifying each one. All who did or caused harm to be done to others passed by. Brian pointed out two particular columns. "Those are the politicians that do harm under the guise of government and those are the lobbyists who represent the manufacturers and associations greasing the palms of the politicians that want only to protect their own interests and retain power."

The space emptied.

"Take me to one of your spaces Richard. A place you felt comfortable and at ease." Here Brian smiled. "Take me to your happy place. Things I need to tell you."

The space changed.

Richard, who was sitting on a bunk with legs dangling, stretched out his arms and said, "Welcome to my happy place."

Brian, who was on a daybed, looked around in surprise saying, "I did not expect this and I'm not a good sailor so be warned."

The space was small containing only a chest of drawers cum desk, a chair and a daybed with drawers under, a bunk also with drawers under, narrow wardrobe, wash basin with a mirrored medicine cabinet above. Bulkheads and deckhead were panelled in varnished light wood; the deck was covered with green linoleum tiles and a small brown rug lay by the bunk. All the furniture and trim were also varnished light wood. Two round portholes provided what natural light could enter. An overhanging deck above the portholes kept the space in shadow most hours. Four small squares of material matching the colour of the deck tiles served as curtains for the portholes. Electric lights above the wash basin and on the deckhead were required to be on must hours. There was a reading light at the head of the bunk. The whole space was perhaps four meters square.

"This is my cabin on my first foreign voyage ship. In life I always came back here in my mind. This was my escape from all the fucked-up stuff that went on in my life. The place I yearned to return to. The career I wish I had never left. In my mind I sailed all my voyages over and over again. Come with me out on deck, we're about to cast off."

He stood at the railing in his new uniform with the half-diamond gold braid backed by purple at the wrists designating him a junior engineer officer. It was oh-five-thirty hours and a warm June night by London standards when lines were let go and tugs pulled his ship away from the dock and guided it through locks from Royal Albert docks into the Thames to point it seaward. The trembling rumble of the main engine was felt through his feet and a breeze caused by movement as speed increased ruffled his hair and shredded the exhaled smoke from his cigarette. He knew in his heart that this was where he was meant to be. From the moment he first set foot on the deck he knew that ships and the sea were in his destiny. Taking a last lungful of smoke, he flicked the remains of the Benson and Hedges out over the waters of the estuary and watched as the glowing tip cartwheeled in an arc to a watery extinction. He stood at the rail to watch his first sunrise at sea and until at fifteen minutes to eight he went to change from uniform into boiler suit and make his way into the engine room for his first watch at sea. Life was good.

Back together in the cabin Brian said, "Man that was liberating! I liked your 'fuck it all' attitude at the rail. There must have been some serious shit that went down in your life that you wanted to leave behind. Good thing your feelings about ships and the sea turned out right. Your retained memories confirm that. I'm finding this place a little cramped, I'm not good in small spaces, so how about we find a quiet spot, on deck? Just keep the weather calm is all I ask."

Chapter 49

The autopsy revealed he died from myocardial infarction. The medical examiner had recorded his surprise to tape, "Bloody hell! His heart looks like it exploded." And indeed it took several hours to find and remove all the debris from the chest cavity.

An emergency call for an ambulance had directed the paramedics to a room at the Lancaster Arms pub. The caller, a female, hung up without giving a name. Later they found the call originated from a phone booth two hundred yards from the pub. Paramedics found a naked male spreadeagled on the bed like Da Vinci's Vitruvian Man and grasping a sharpening steel in his left hand. Checks for pulse and breathing indicated he was dead, but they tried defibrillating anyway without effect. Moisture around the pubic area and on the bed sheet seemed to indicate recent sexual activity. The presence of the sharpening steel was reported to the police who dispatched a detective and a crime scene photographer to the pub. Finding no external injury or any indication of foul play the detective had photographs of the scene taken and released the body to the medical examiner who had been summoned to determine time of death and then do an autopsy to find the cause. No identification of any sort was found but the owner of the Lancaster Arms told the police that the man had checked in as Liam Coward and paid cash up front for five days and he did not know if a woman had visited the room because to get to them you went down a hall past the toilets and then upstairs. People used the toilets all the time so anybody could walk up to the rooms without being noticed. Most likely the man had been with a prostitute and died while performing. Tracking down who was with him at the time would be next to impossible, the working girls and pimps wouldn't talk. Bad for business somebody dying on the job. The sharpening steel gave no clue as to why he was grasping it. Fingerprints taken from the corpse were not in any police data base. Further enquiries were put on hold until cause of death was confirmed. Massive heart attack.

Chapter 50

They sat on a bench on the boat deck aft of the accommodation block and looked out over the stern to where an arrow straight wake marked their progress across a sea as smooth and reflective as silvered glass.

Brian, sitting relaxed with arms outstretched along the back of the bench and legs crossed asked, "Where are all the questions Eleanor told me to expect? They are in your head, I know that, but you keep filing them under selected and rejected. You seem to prefer to wait and see if the answer becomes self-evident as we go along and that's not usually the case with new entries. Most want answers now and are impatient to get past what they think of as uninteresting stuff and get to all the magical things their new brain will allow them to do. How come you're not?"

"Eleanor was speaking of a different me, an earlier me, one that did ask many questions about many things. I changed. My being here is a result of the most unselfish thing I ever did, and you already know what that was. The fact that everything Amber said would happen at the time of my death did happen made it clear with utter certainty that there was no purpose in asking what lay ahead or what the outcomes might be. I knew that questions and their answers would not dictate, or even sway, what purpose I would serve in Concordat. So, even with my selected and rejected file I prefer to see how it all plays out, no questions asked. It is sufficient to have experienced all that has happened since Eleanor met me and that I am now beside you on this ship and I see no reason to question how it all came about."

They both sat in quiet companionship until Richard stretched and said, "I want a snack and something to drink, how about you?"

"Sure," came from Brian. "There's a great diner a lot of the guys go to when working a case. They serve bitchin pies, and the coffee is real good. You okay with that?"

"Absolutely."

When they entered Sherri said, "Hi, take a seat. I'll be right over."

Brian asked, "What's the pie of the day?"

"Pecan," came from Sherri as she followed them to a booth with two mugs and a pot full of coffee. They both agreed on the pie.

Brian poured sugar into black coffee, stirred, sipped and then said, "I liked the way you handled yourself when we went to the different spaces. There were all sorts of reactions going on in your mind. You ran the gamut of all the emotions from fury to sympathy but never let them get in the way of a rational deliberation and response. Your reaction centre is still in Earth mode, part of the two percent yet to be upgraded, so your responses were good for that type of brain function."

Sherri arrived with pieces of pie and said, "Enjoy, guys. You've tasted none better."

Nothing more was said until pie and first cups of coffee were finished and Sherri had been signalled to bring top-ups. Pouring she asked, "How was the pie?" and got 'great' and 'fantastic' in response. "Told ya. Nobody does pies better than Antonio."

Brian burped into a napkin, "Man that was good. There's still more stuff to cover but I have to give an interim report to the Transition people, so I'll go see them and catch up with you later. In the meantime, a lady called Isabel is on her way to see you and have a chat. Nothing heavy, just points to be cleared up. Here she comes now." Brian indicated a woman hurrying across the diner parking lot with an umbrella shielding her from the rain that had begun to fall. "Lovely lady, you'll like her."

Isabel stopped at the counter to speak to Sherri then made her way to Brian and Richard. Both men stood as Isabel propped her umbrella, a golf size one, against the table end and then removed a bright-yellow waterproof coat and hung it on a hook fastened to the booth dividers. All this done she opened her arms to Brian, and they hugged. Stepping back Isabel eyed Brian up and down, "Been a while Brian but you're still looking good. Roger must be taking good care of you. Give him my love."

"He is and I will," Brian said with a smile then, "Isabel this is Richard, Richard meet Isabel." As hands were offered and shook Brian said, "I'll take off now. Okay if I borrow your umbrella, Isabel?"

"Sure, go ahead and keep it. I'll get another from somewhere if needed. People leave them lying around everywhere," Isabel said with an impish grin.

Sherri approached with a pot of tea and a pastrami on rye sandwich for Isabel as she seated herself opposite Richard. He shook his head when asked if he wanted more coffee.

"We can talk while I get through this sandwich. They have the best pastrami here."

Richard responded, "Okay."

He put her age at early to mid-fifties. He thought petite described her best. Minimal makeup, short hair turning silver. Muted-yellow blouse with light-blue camisole visible underneath. Dark green ankle length slim cut jeans and black court shoes. As if making some sort of statement she wore glasses with hexagonal lenses in frames that were bright purple. He had noticed all this while she greeted Brian. Everything about her seemed perfectly proportioned but something about her face was not quite right. Then he got it, it was her nose, it was slightly too big. Without the distraction of the glasses, it would be more apparent.

Isabel dabbed at the corners of her mouth with a napkin to remove breadcrumbs, smiled and said, "Got me. I inherited the nose from my father. We all have it, my siblings and me. I wear outrageous glasses to distract from it. A silly vanity of mine. While I appreciate the 'petite' sizing I'm a bit above that, but not by much though, I want to make that clear. Again, vanity. As for age, spot on. I chose me at fifty-one. I like the age. Knowledgeable but still willing to learn." She pushed her plate away and bobbed the tea bag in the pot before pouring. "Brian warned me that you are a man of few words, so I'll return the favour and get to the point."

Chapter 51

It was almost his time. He was ready for his birth and for the task ahead of him. On the train to Manchester, he hid behind a newspaper while the subtle changes took place. His nose a little longer, ears flatter to the skull, eyes a less vibrant blue, lips and cheeks a little fuller, hairline higher and grey gone from the temples. None of the changes were extreme but combined they presented a face that was not Meldrew. Indeed, he thought it handsomer than Meldrew. His reflection in the carriage window smiled back at him. At Manchester he took a commuter train to Accrington just twenty miles away. He needed to start his hunt. Using the name Liam Coward, he took a room at the Lancaster Arms and paid cash for five nights. The room was small and as crooked as the building itself with a bed that squeaked but he didn't care, it was only to be his base for the hunt. Who he was to find was never clear at the outset but the moment he set eyes on them he knew beyond doubt. That's how it happened. He hunted and he found. This might be the time the other Meldrew did not come back.

He started his hunt by waiting until the evening crowds began to fill the pubs and clubs then he set out. Taking just one sip from the rum and coke he bought at each place he searched for his quarry. It was at the fifth he found her, working behind the bar.

He ordered his drink and as she pushed a glass under the rum optic, he remarked how quiet it was. After splashing coke into his glass and placing it in front of him she said, "Early yet, it'll pick up later on. You're not from round here, the accent, what brings you to Accrington?"

"I'm up here from Hull to see my daughter," he lied glibly. "She's a nurse at the infirmary in Manchester and she's on nights so we get together during the day."

"How long are you here for?"

"Another three days."

"Got to get back to the wife?"

"No, I'm a widower, she passed two years ago, cancer."

She placed a hand to her chest under her throat and said, "Oh, I'm so sorry. I didn't mean to pry."

He gave a wan smile, "That's okay, I'm out tonight because Evelyn, that's my daughter, said it was time I went out more and socialised so here I am. My name is Liam."

"Pleased to meet you Liam, I'm Sarah." A couple entered so she excused herself and went to serve them.

He guessed her age at mid-thirties. He got a better look at her figure when she moved away to serve the newcomers and was pleased with what he saw and looked forward to seeing more of it. There was no wedding band, so he surmised she was probably separated or divorced given her age. She made time to talk to him between customers and as she had predicted it got busier as the night wore on. He nursed his drinks and when it became so busy that they had little chance to talk he said cheerio and at her prompting promised to drop back for a chat the following night.

Having slept well he spent the next day looking for a killing site. Late in the afternoon he found it down an alley at the back of a block of newly renovated apartments. A 'For Rent Furnished—Immediate Occupancy' sign with a phone number was attached to railings at the top of steps leading down to a basement flat. The curtains at the windows made it appear lived in and at night it would be dark and secluded. He went down the steps and looking through a window could see it was not being lived in, it was too tidy. For confirmation he took the sign with him and found a phone booth to call the number. He told the person on the other end of the line he might be interested in renting the apartment and when asked gave his name as James Crown. Asking if it was presently occupied, he was told 'no'. He voiced satisfaction at this and said he would call again to make an appointment to view it with his wife.

He ate supper at a fast-food place. Some special deal made up of a cheeseburger, fries and a drink. He didn't care about the food which was slathered with some sauce supposed to bring flavour to the cardboard and sawdust taste of the meat. He was filling time before going back to The Viaduct pub to see Sarah.

There were only half a dozen drinkers when he walked in shortly after six with only one sitting at the bar. She recognised him immediately and without being asked poured a rum and coke and smiled when she put it on the bar as he hitched himself onto a stool.

"Hello Liam. Glad to see you're taking Evelyn's advice again and getting out."

He smiled back and paying for his drink said, "Hi Sarah. You remembered what I drink, that's nice, thank you, and how could I not take her advice when it means seeing my favourite lady bar tender?"

Doing a mock curtsy she laughed and said, "Thank you, always nice to be complimented."

Until the time the place became busy, they made small talk on all sorts of subjects and he learned she was indeed divorced, no children. In the course of their conversation, she mentioned she was not working the following day. In a break between customers, he asked in a voice full of nervousness and hesitation if she would like to have dinner with him the next night.

Her face lit up and she said, "I'd love to!"

He feigned relief, "Wonderful. You pick the place; I don't know any good restaurants here. Pick whatever food you like, I'll eat most."

"How about we meet here tomorrow, say around six-thirty, have a drink and then I'll take you to my favourite Chinese restaurant. It's nothing fancy but the food is really good. We can walk to it from here."

"Perfect, six-thirty it is. Thank you, I'm really looking forward to it."

As he made to leave, she caught his arm and leaned across the bar to kiss his cheek and murmur, "So am I."

He walked to the flat and stood in the shadows observing the activity in the neighbourhood. There was a light above the door to the flat which dispelled some of the threshold darkness and which he would remove before he brought her there. Only basement flat entrances were on the rear of the building; all others were accessed from the front through lobbies. No security cameras were in evidence. Satisfied that there was little foot traffic, and after ten-thirty none at all, he returned to the Lancaster Arms at eleven.

Chapter 52

Isabel asked, "How do you feel about coming into contact with persons you knew Life Side?"

Richard looked out of the window next to the booth. It was night now and rain was still falling. He and Isabel were reflected in the night darkened and rain-washed glass and he saw her raise her cup to her lips.

Turning away from the window and facing her he replied, "I'm fine with it."

"Mmm, few words indeed." Isabel then, "Don't you want to know who they are?"

"No. I'll deal with it when the time comes."

"There are three women in particular you might be required to work with. One is Eleanor who would seem not to pose a problem, but the two others might. From their Life Files they seemed to hold some animosity towards you. Does that alter your decision?"

"No. As I said, I'll deal with it when the time comes. Assuming that time ever comes the way things are going."

"Very well. I'll carry that back to those in transition handling your case."

Isabel made to move from the booth but Richard reached to place a hand gently on her arm and say, "You know we are not finished here yet, don't you?"

"Yes, I do. Okay, get it off your chest. Better to verbalise it than have it circling around in your brain. I much prefer to talk about these things than reading thoughts. Some people are so messy up there."

"I'm going to get more coffee; would you like more tea?' Sherri responded to his raised hand and he ordered more coffee and another pot of tea. They sat in silence until Sherri had brought the drinks and left.

After swallowing a mouthful of coffee, he started, "Since from almost the moment I arrived here I've been told about this last two percent. Abigail,

David, Per, Brian, all going on about the final two percent and how I have to be prepared for it and checking if my brain can handle it and what a difference it will make. Isn't it about time we cut to the chase? I'm done with the carrot and stick thing and all the jumping through hoops of which you are the latest. You didn't need to come here to tell me about women from my past. Brian could have done that unless it was thought a straight woman would connect with me more than a gay man on that subject. But I don't think that's the case. I think *you* are the final decision maker. *You* are the one to say, 'Give him the last two percent, or, forget about it and put him some place ninety-eight is sufficient.'" Pausing, he drank coffee and looked for reaction on Isabel's face, there was none, she simply sipped tea and looked placidly back at him. "You have the advantage over me because you can close your mind to me while all the time knowing what is happening in mine. Am I right? Are you the one who'll make the decision?"

"Yes, I am. And you're right I didn't have to come here tonight, Brian is perfectly capable of telling you about women with whom you had, let's say, past dalliances that did not end well. I only come to meet those who are being considered for Retribution section. We, by that I mean Concordat, have to be very sure about who we place there. All those you have spent time with and who have seen your Life File, including Per, they all highly recommend you but it's my decision that seals it and that's why I'm here. I wanted to check you out myself. Ether Screen's and neurological printouts are all well and good but nothing like getting up close and personal on the outside and looking around on the inside. You will receive Retribution centre two percent. Not all minds in Concordat were created equal and the final two percent upload is adjusted to suit the individual. All this and more will be explained before and after the upload and I can assure you that you will find the results far more spectacular than your ninety-eight percent brain can imagine. Now before Brian returns with a two percent uploader, I think we should have a piece of pie to celebrate your acceptance into Retribution section."

Richard rose to go to the counter to fetch the pies and Isabel smiled broadly when he remarked, "Vanity or not I love those glasses, really funky."

Chapter 53

He dressed casual in navy-blue slacks and black loafers with a white shirt open at the neck and a hound's tooth sport jacket. For colour a bright red handkerchief was stuffed into the breast pocket of the jacket. He arrived before Sarah and chose seats at a table away from the bar telling the man behind it that he would order when his friend arrived. He was looking at his watch at ten-past-six and wondering if he'd been stood up when Sarah hurried in all apologies for being late.

Taking her coat off she called to the barman, "A rum and coke and my usual please Keith." Keith nodded and said, "I'll bring them over." Her usual turned out to be chilled white wine and when Keith brought the drinks, he said he'd run a tab until they left.

They touched glasses and said, "Cheers." Sarah said, "I've been feeling nervous about this all day, it's a long time since I've been out with a man so if I become a chatterbox drop a hint and I'll stop." Looking into her wine glass she continued with sadness in her voice, "My husband used to call me that, and lots of other things besides."

"How long since the divorce?" he asked quietly.

"About the same since your wife died, two years."

"Well, here we both are after two years getting out again." And lifting his glass he said Bogart style, "Here's looking at you and to a beautiful friendship."

Sarah touched her glass to his and smiled saying, "I'll drink to that."

Sarah assured him they would easily get a table at the restaurant, so they had another drink and talked. He made up stories and she told him of her life, nothing too personal, until she excused herself to go to the lady's room before setting off to eat. He admired her as she walked away. The looks he had admired previously were even more attractive now. With the exception of her bust which was more than ample her figure was slim and shapely. A hint of lacy bra could be seen through a white blouse with the dark line of deep cleavage evident. A grey skirt that hugged tight and ended just above the knee emphasised her bottom and thighs while high heel shoes sculpted her carves. Her lips were full and painted bright red to match her nail varnish and the slight lines evident on her face, and which she had not tried to hide with excessive make-up, actually enhanced her mature good looks. Her hair was glossy auburn parted in the middle and flipped upwards at her shoulders. He thought she could definitely be the one. He helped her on with a jacket that matched her skirt and settled the bill with Keith and with them both saying goodnight they left for the restaurant.

She was right, getting a table was not a problem and from the way she was greeted it seemed she was a regular and valued customer.

When they were seated an elderly Chinese lady in a cheongsam came to their table and bowed and while handing out menus said, "Nice to see you again Sarah and with a friend, how wonderful."

"Thank you, Mama Hong. I told Liam that this is the best restaurant in Accrington."

Mama Hong clapped her hands and laughed saying, "Then I go tell cook make sure everything extra special for you. I come back soon to get order."

Sarah made suggestions on what to order and he went with her choices. The food was plentiful and delicious, and they stuck with water to drink agreeing to stop in somewhere for a nightcap after the meal. Sarah wanted to pay half the bill, but he wouldn't hear of it saying he had invited her out and therefore it was his treat. She agreed but only on the condition she bought the nightcaps, so he accepted her offer. He paid with cash. Mama Hong was at the door when they left and wished them goodnight adding, "Mr Liam, you take good care of Sarah, she my favourite." He smiled and assured her he would which brought a little colour to Sarah's cheeks.

Taking his arm, she told him of a nice quiet place to get a nightcap within walking distance, so he told her to lead the way.

It was busy but as she had said, quiet. The patrons were by appearance mostly business people. Banquets and chairs were covered and trimmed with red leather and background instrumental music played softly. The men tending bar wore black trousers, white shirts and red waistcoats and one greeted Sarah when they walked in.

"Hello Michael, good to see you again. This is Liam."

Michael said, "Please to meet you. What can I get you?"

Sarah spoke up, "A rum and coke and house white please," then pushed money across the bar saying, "I made a deal, Liam got the meal, I get the drinks."

"Have a seat, I'll bring them to you," Michael said as he rang up the money and gave change.

When they were seated, he looked round approvingly, "Nice place. Do all you bartenders know one another?"

"I spent some time working here but left because I got fed up with being hit on by tipsy businessmen, and a couple of times, tipsy businesswomen. I like the Viaduct and the hours suit me, but you can't beat this place for a quiet drink."

The clock hanging behind the bar showed ten. Another three hours and he would know. He continued to fabricate stories of his life and work while she opened up about her husband and their acrimonious divorce. He could see the wine was having an effect as she became more relaxed and did not withdraw when their legs touched. She was by no means drunk but certainly at ease. As an opener to his final gambit, he asked how far away the address of the basement flat was. He explained it was his daughter's flat. She said he would need a taxi and because her home was not far past, she could share it with him. He promptly agreed that was a good idea. It was all coming together beautifully. The way it was happening she could definitely be the one. They had one more drink and then Irish coffees, which he insisted on paying for, before Sarah asked Michael to order a cab. Michael advised ten minutes for the cab and after donning their coats and wishing him goodnight they waited outside with her arm entwined with his and hugging close.

Near to the basement flat he asked if she would like to come in for tea or coffee knowing full well a woman of her experience would understand what such an invitation meant. After a suitable pause indicating consideration of his offer, she squeezed his thigh and agreed that it would be a shame to end the night so early after she had had such a lovely time.

If she had refused, he would have been forced to seek a victim from the streets as he had done before. Not the best outcome but it was demanded by the timing and he dared not deviate.

It was eleven-fifteen when they stepped from the taxi. One hour and forty-five minutes.

Chapter 54

Isabel and Richard were halfway through their pie when Brian and a man he introduced as Sam Ng joined them.

Sherri hustled over with mugs and coffee but Sam asked for tea and he and Brian declined the pie. By the time coffee and tea were brought Richard and Isabel had finished their pie.

Isabel made ready to leave and Brian moved to let her slide from the booth and stand to don her waterproof and pick up the umbrella that Brian had thoughtfully returned with.

"I'll leave you to it. My approval for Richard to enter Retribution and receive the necessary upload is now in transition placement records so do your thing Sam. Brian, you stay with Richard during the upload and when it's finished, I want Takahara to take Richard on his introductory outing. Good to meet you Richard and we'll see each other again, I'm sure." Turning to leave she paused to wink at Richard and say, "Good luck handling it when the time comes." Then she left the diner.

Brian and Sam cast looks of enquiry Richard's way after Isabel's last remark. Richard did a shrug of 'I don't know what she's talking about' and Sam laughed and said, "You aren't fooling either of us."

Brian leaned across the table towards Richard, "It's a relationship thing, isn't it? Even here those things can get messy."

"Okay, okay, let it drop please," Richard exclaimed with exasperation tingeing his voice, then, "So, tell me Sam what's the next step?"

"The next step is to go to a place where you feel very comfortable, and the surroundings are familiar. Somewhere you and Takahara can keep returning to between introductory outings if you want to. Do you have such a place?"

"I do."

"Good. Take us there."

Exact amount for the pies, coffee and teas lay on the table in booth five along with a twenty as a tip. Sherri murmured to herself, "Starting out to be a good night tonight." Then she called to Antonio who was at the grill, "Hey Antonio, do you recall who sat here?"

Antonio looked over, shook his head and shrugged saying, "No idea."

Sherri said, "Me either."

Basement room. A dozen easy chairs and two sofas gathered in a rough 'u' around a low table. At the open end of the 'u' was a desk with two chairs. Fifteen people, men and women, were milling about, chatting and eating doughnuts and drinking teas or coffee brought from the coffee shop close by. Two small windows set high in a wall framed the darkness outside. At exactly eight o'clock a man stepped to the desk, raised a gavel and brought it down to quiet the room and announce that the meeting had begun.

Brian knew immediately where they were. He explained, "This is an AA meeting Sam. This room is full of caring and sharing. Isn't that right Richard?"

"Yes. It was in many rooms at meetings like this that I felt most at peace with myself. These are the people that helped me climb the steps to become a recovering sober alcoholic. There was always someone there for me at my darkest times. I love these people."

Brian patted Richard's shoulder with a ham like hand, "I'm with you there my brother. It was a group of drunks that saved me."

"This is a first for me," came from Sam. "I've never done an upload during an AA meeting. Do you guys feel what I feel, a certain serenity vibe in the room?"

"Uh-huh," came from Brian and Richard as they smiled at each other.

Brian became absolutely still and tilted his head to the side as if listening then straightened and informed Sam that Takahara was waiting for the call after upload.

"Great," came from Sam. "Let's get started. You've some idea Richard, of how improved your brain has become. You bringing us to this room is testament to that but this next improvement upload will fire up neurons that Life Siders aren't even aware of and it will be a massive jolt to your brain. Brian will keep an eye on everything and shut me down if anything starts to overload. I'm the conduit that feeds the upload to your brain. Here we go."

Chapter 55

Earlier that day he had come to the flat and removed the bulb from above the entrance door and after putting duct tape on one of the small panes of glass above the lock to deaden the sound. He had broken it and reached in to turn back the deadbolt. Picking up the glass and tape he put them in a rubbish bin standing against a wall that faced the steps. Stepping inside he made a quick tour. From the front door he went down a short hall with a galley kitchen on the right and doors to bedroom and bathroom straight ahead and one to the living room on the left. Furnishings were minimal but looked comfortable enough with a sofa and easy chair, coffee table in front of the sofa and a drop leaf dining table and two chairs in an alcove in the living room with office grade carpeting in beige. He particularly liked the thick lined curtains at the window and doubted any light would escape them when closed. A double bed, wardrobe and a chest of drawers almost filled the small bedroom and there was only a shower beside a toilet and vanity in the bathroom. The bed had a duvet and two pillows in covers on it, which would serve his purpose. The kitchen held a stove, sink, washing machine, kettle and assorted cups, plates and cutlery. All very like what a young woman renting and on her own would choose. In a kitchen drawer he found weapons he would use and one in particular that he chose for the killing. Satisfied with what he found he clear taped plastic wrap over the hole left by the broken pane so that to a glance from above it would appear as glass. Taking a cardboard strip from his pocket he folded it until by trial and error he found the right thickness to hold the door closed without the lock. He found a convenience store nearby and bought coffee, milk and sugar which he took back to the flat, they were props and indicated that someone lived there. He bought a toothbrush, toothpaste and toilet paper at a chemist to place in the bathroom should the woman want to use the toilet. Again, a sign that the apartment was lived in. There were towels already hanging from rails in the bathroom. He placed the folded cardboard on the threshold under the door and closed it tight against it when he left. He had not been aware of any foot traffic outside while in the flat. The only issue over which he had no control was if the realtor was showing the flat the next day. He would be able to tell by inspecting his preparations the next night before picking Sarah up. If the cardboard and plastic were disturbed, he would have to convince her to take him to her place.

"Darn kids! They've taken the bulb from the light again. My daughter says they do it as a lark. Take my hand and I'll lead you down." Doing as he asked, she then waited while he made a show of unlocking the door while blocking her view. Disappearing inside he said, "Wait a sec and I'll turn a light on." Light from the living room was enough to illuminate the hall and he ushered her in and locked the door. "Go into the living room and have a seat while I make some coffee. It's only instant I'm afraid, how do like yours?"

Removing her jacket, she hung it over a dining chair and answered, "White no sugar please." Then went to sit on the sofa.

From the kitchen he called, "If you feel cold the thermostat is on the wall by the door."

"No, I'm fine." Then, "How come no TV or stereo? I'd have thought those to be absolute musts for a young woman. I know I couldn't be without mine."

"That's one of the reasons I'm here. I told Sarah to pick them out and I'll pay. You know what it's like just starting out, not much money left over for things like that. Anyway, they should be delivered before I leave tomorrow," he finished as he came from the kitchen with their coffees. "Here you are, hope that's enough milk."

"Its good thank you, now sit down and relax," she said patting the cushion next to her. "I'm not really a coffee fan and we both know why we are here. Why don't you kiss me and see where that leads?"

He put both cups on the coffee table and took her in his arms. Her lips were soft, and her tongue probing and she offered no resistance when he unbuttoned her blouse and unclipped her bra to set free breasts that still held firm with nipples that were proud against his hand. She bade him stand and undoing his fly she set free his hard member and murmured, "Oh my, isn't that lovely." Taking her hand, he led her to the bedroom where they rushed to undress then fall naked onto the bed. The back lit dial of his watch showed eleven fifty when he took it off and pushed it under the pillow. Seventy minutes.

She was in control the first time, riding him with head thrown back and telling him, "Squeeze my boobs." As she plunged and withdrew and gyrated whispering, "It's been so long, this is so good." Until her body tensed and then shuddered into orgasm.

Kissing and fondling and coupling they explored each other with him staying her when he neared orgasm saying, "Not yet. I love the feel of you when you do but I want to really please you when I do." He felt his time nearing, and he manoeuvred her so that she was on her knees and he entered her from behind.

Head and forearms on the bed she gave muffled, "Yes, yes, harder," as he thrust against her. His rhythm increased and she rose to her hands to forge backwards to meet him and it was as he came that he grasped her neck and pressing on the arteries in her neck he held her with his weight on her back until she passed out and her struggles ceased.

Coming round it took seconds for her to realise that she was bound and gagged with duct tape. The duvet and pillows had been stripped from the mattress and she lay with tape running from ankles and wrists to anchoring points on the wrought iron head and footboard. A pillowcase was draped over a lamp on the chest of drawers allowing subdued glow to illuminate the bed and she saw on the fringe of light that he was sitting on a dining chair brought from the living room.

He was naked and checking the watch he had worn earlier. At her muffled exclamation and movement within the limits of her bonds he raised his head to smile and say, "Perfect timing, fifteen minutes to go and you need to be awake and alive for the stroke of one, barely alive will do but alive nonetheless." She squirmed and pulled against the duct tape lashings to no avail and without voice could only plead with her eyes. He stood and picking a knife from a selection by her feet he checked the edge with his thumb and in a conversational tone said, "You know, seeing your breasts move and hips rise as you struggle almost makes me want to mount you, and you can see that I'm ready to do that, but I can't." When he continued it was with a very different tone, "You see, even in your present predicament you might get pleasure from it and it is pain that I need to bring you. Yes, lots and lots of pain. The same pain my mother and I felt when she gave birth to the other one. The other one that hid me from her and took from her all that should have come to me, that would have made a whole me. It is through your pain that I might be born and take from the other one what should have been mine. I am a part of him, and I need to be free." Checking his watch his lips moved as if counting down and he placed the tip of the knife among the pubic hair at the opening of her vagina. "Now you will feel the pain my mother felt as I open you as she was opened." He lifted a sharpening steel from the bed and held it before her eyes. "You will feel the pain of her hours of induced labour compressed into minutes and at the exact moment the other was pulled from her I will destroy your insides with this just as hers were destroyed. I have tried for my birth many times and I want you to be the one that gives me the power to take over this body and be the one I was meant to be." Laying the steel aside and using his forearm and weight on her chest and belly to force her against the mattress he said, "Time to start your labour, Sarah. Time to set me free."

They took him when the knife touched her flesh.

Chapter 56

It was as if his brain caught fire. A lightning strike of energy flooded into it and everything his brain had been and now would be was revealed. The capabilities spreading throughout his brain that for his entire life had been woefully underutilised were amazing. His senses became exceptionally acute and others that he had been unaware of became noticeable. As it absorbed more and more of everything a brain is capable of processing, he worried his cranium would explode from the pressure of it all then he heard Brian say, "Easy, relax Richard, it will be over soon." And it was, and the feeling of pressure faded.

"That went well," Sam stated. "You're up to max and all your readings are normal. Feel any different?"

"Oh yes! I can feel individually each breath these people take; I feel the air moving. I can smell vodka mixed with the cola that woman keeps sipping from her water bottle. Each time a vehicle passes outside I can hear and see that crack in the wall open and lengthen by the very tiniest amount. I give it two years and they'll need to fix it. And…"

"Slow down Richard," a smiling Brian interrupted. "Sam asked how you feel, a simple 'fine' would do. We know about the rest of it. Been there, done that."

"Sorry, I'll try to curb my enthusiasm. Didn't both of you feel this way when you were done to the max? This excitement, this wanting to explore and use it all, to see what you could do?"

"Of course," Sam responded. "And that's why Takahara is on his way. He's going to give you the ten-cent tour, show you what you can do and most importantly how to control it."

"Takahara. That a first or last name?" Richard enquired.

"When asked he says 'Just name. Not first, not last. Just name,'" Brian answered.

Then Takahara was there.

He bowed to each of the three in turn and murmured, "Kon'nichiwa," and was responded to in kind.

"Brian, Sam, thank you for your service to Richard. You must go now to be emptied."

Richard raised questioning eyebrows at Brian and mouthed 'emptied' to which Brian mouthed 'wiped' and Richard understood.

The faces of Sam and Brian took on a look that signified their wipes were already in progress and they turned and going to the door opened it and stepped out into the night. Nobody at the meeting was aware of the door opening and closing. The sharing went on uninterrupted.

"Let us have tea," came from Takahara. "It will give time for us to relax and compose ourselves before we start our journey." A tatami mat and all the necessities for a Japanese tea ceremony appeared and Takahara began the intricate steps that make the ceremony an art form. Brian knelt facing Takahara with hands on thighs, backside on heels and back straight. When Takahara bowed his head and offered Richard a Chawan containing a small amount of green aromatic tea he bowed in acceptance and holding the bowl in both hands he swirled the tea around and inhaled the aroma before taking a small mouthful, swallowing, and uttering a quiet 'Aah' of satisfaction. Takahara nodded, satisfied, and lifted his own Chawan to drink.

Their tea consumed, Takahara did the ritual washing of the bowls then, "I am with you because I learn when Life Side you visited Japan number of times. Many places. You intrigued by the culture. Found it very much to your liking. Also found certain women very expert in pleasure practices. Buddhism appealed, the Zen practice particularly. One time you find serenity in Kamakura Garden and you search for same ever since. Think of me as your Sensei. You have many powerful weapons at your disposal now, I will teach you how and when to use them and, very important, how to control them."

Since Brian and Sam had left Richard had remained silent. His mind was becoming more settled and his senses less acute. He was finding he could filter out all extraneous background activities and narrow his focus to a single point of concentration. He focused on Takahara.

"Make yourself aware of the woman in the red jacket and tell me about her from the aura that surrounds her," Takahara directed.

Richard did so. Information poured into him from her aura that was made up of muddy colours that swirled about her. Thirty-three, divorced, one child, a son living with his father, home a basement bachelor apartment, two months behind with the rent, minimum wage job stocking grocery shelves. Longest time sober since attending meetings three months twenty-two days. No sponsor. Lots of debt. Takahara broke in, "Enough. Now focus on entering her mind and tell me her thoughts."

"How do I enter her mind? Do I sync with her and if so, how?" Richard asked. "It's always been others syncing with me, I've never done the syncing."

"Yes, sync with her. Connect with her at the spot you have been synced with since arrival. Think of that spot on her, you will connect."

It worked as Takahara said. He focused on the spot below her cerebellum and saw the most fleeting of confused expression cross her face then he was inside and eavesdropping on her thoughts.

Jesus Christ! How much longer is this old fool going to go on about his bad old days, I'm having a fucking bad day right now. If I didn't need Tracy to give me a lift, I'd get up and walk out. I don't know why I came back; meetings do nothing for me except bore me. If my shit of an ex would cough up more support, I'd be fine. Get out of my crap apartment, buy new clothes and find a better job. Oh, come on! Not another three-week sober drunkalogue! I'm not sharing, I don't want to extend this torture. I wonder if Jeff will be home. He's always good for a drink and a laugh. Maybe I can borrow from him to put toward the rent. I've paid him back in kind before. I wonder if he'll go for that again. He's not the worst fuck I've ever had. Come on! Come on! Close the damn meeting say the prayer and let's get out of here. Blah, blah, blah, blah, amen. Good, Trace is putting her coat on, not hanging about but I'll have to put up with all the bullshit about what a great meeting it was and how much she got from it. I'd love to tell her what a waste of fucking time it was. I need a drink.

"Enough. Leave her," Takahara ordered.

Chapter 57

They gathered round the bed. Sarah was still secured and Meldrew was draped across her with knife in hand between her legs. Both were breathing softly and regularly, as if sleeping.

The Life Side operation had gone as planned. By body hopping they had been able to observe him from the time he left home until they took him. He was theirs now.

On the train, at the Lancaster Arms, the pubs and clubs he visited in his search, the meeting with Sarah, his search for and finding this place all had been seen and recorded. They were the customers in the pubs, the taxi driver, the annoying little child on the train, the man behind the counter in the convenience store, pedestrians he passed in the street, diners at the Chinese restaurant—they had been in all of them.

Eleanor broke the silence, "Richard, move him off Sarah so we can release her and when we have her dressed, I want Alan to take her home. I'll make sure she thinks you are Liam, and her last memory will be of how good the sex was. He told her he was leaving today, and she will believe it was a one-night stand. I'll erase this address, so she won't come looking."

Yuri and Alan untied Sarah and moved her to the living room to dress her and awaken her on the sofa sitting next to Alan and buttoning her blouse. "That was so good Liam. I wish you could stay longer."

"Me too but I have to earn a living and I'll come by the pub next time I'm visiting Evelyn. I've called the taxi company we used earlier and it's waiting outside."

She made no comment when Alan got in the taxi with her or when he opened the door to her flat and led her to the bedroom where trancelike she undressed and climbed naked into bed. There were no signs of her bondage on wrists or ankles. Alan was satisfied and returned to the others.

The flat was without any sign of what had occurred there. Door window fixed, bed remade, milk disposed of and the coffee and sugar in a kitchen cabinet to be found by the next tenant. The bulb returned to the outside light and the rental sign took its place at the railing. The knives meant to cause Sarah pain were again in the drawer with the exception of the sharpening steel which they intended to take with them.

Meldrew was dressed and lying on the living room floor when Eleanor made arrangements for his transfer to Concordat. Richard remained with Eleanor when the rest returned to Concordat for Meldrew's arrival. Eleanor told fragmentation to go ahead and transfer. Meldrew became a centillion points of matter that flared briefly then vanished.

"He's gone from here, how does he look at your end?" Eleanor queried.

Ted came back with, "Looks good. He came together well."

"Fine. Richard and I are on our way. Everyone meet us at Richard's beach house."

Charlotte joined them and when all were seated Eleanor began, "Okay Jenny and Emma what have you got on the ten letter place names?"

An exasperated sigh came from Jenny, "We've got nothing. We found nothing before the operation, and we have nothing now. We followed everything he did and thought and scrutinised it down to minutest detail and ran it through every computational algorithm we had, or devised, and still nothing."

Charlotte spoke up, "Will having him here help? I assume the DNA and covering survived the fragmentation."

Emma confirmed, "They did and now we have to find a way to separate without harming either one of them."

"We are under a time constraint," came from Yuri. "Earth time he's two days away from being back home and if he doesn't get in touch with his wife, she will at least try to call him. He needs to be back, dead or alive, before she gets concerned and starts looking for him."

Victoria asked, "At separation will we have two Meldrews? I mean in the physical sense."

Alan answered, "Possibly. It could be that we give the other Meldrew the birth he's always wanted but at what stage of his development we can't say. He could be a baby or a grown man."

Charlotte voiced in all seriousness, "Or a teenager! How awful would that be?" Laughter greeted her remark and the last of the tension generated during the operation seeped away.

Richard had gone to the fridge to get a drink and he addressed them through the kitchen window, "Let me throw this at you. What if killer Meldrew has been tapping into decent Meldrew's intellect but hasn't been able, or hasn't bothered, to reach the intellectual stage of born Meldrew." Coming back and resting against the rail of the patio he continued, "The two Meldrews have been together since conception and must have, to some degree, matured in parallel but I think the unborn quit learning when he was able to manipulate decent Meldrew and begin killing. The numbers and letters and places are all that killer Meldrew has to work with intellectually. They are simply props to manipulate Meldrew to be at a certain place at a certain time. His prime purpose is to kill on the anniversary of his non-birth when his energy is strongest, and he can take decent Meldrew over. It's the psychopath DNA marker that drives his urge to kill. He says he's avenging for the pain his mother went through but that's the justification a psychopathic serial killer *would* use. In reality his birth would have been him taking over decent Meldrew full time and I believe he did hope that would happen. If we are to learn anything from this episode that will help programs and protocols, it has to come from the fact that decent Meldrew knew nothing of the acts or of the twin within. Brilliant as Jenny's program is it was through killer Meldrew's inability to move decent Meldrew outside a specific radius after the killings because of timing, and Meldrew becoming decent Meldrew again, that allowed the program to pick up on it." He could see all of them were absorbing his theory and had questions. "I've one more thing, then I'll shut up. There has to be a record of killer Meldrew hidden away inside decent Meldrew and we need to find it so that Life Files can look for it immediately when a file is opened and if they find it then watch and act accordingly. Finding it while killer Meldrew is with us is, I think, our best chance." Moving from the railing Richard returned to his chair.

To forestall any torrent of questions or criticism Eleanor rapped on the glass topped table, "One at a time people. Let's hear what Jenny has to say first, it was her program that put us on his trail." Handing Jenny a drinks coaster Eleanor explained, "This is the talking coaster. Whoever is holding it cannot be interrupted and once they have passed it on, they cannot speak again until all have spoken. The coaster always goes to the person on the left. If you have nothing to say simply pass it on. Right Jenny, tell us what you think."

Chapter 58

"We should leave this place now," Takahara told Richard. "It holds nothing for you once the meeting is over. It is the people that give it purpose."

They were walking down a busy street he recognised as the Reeperbahn in Hamburg. Crowded as the sidewalk was, they were never jostled or bumped or had to step aside to let others past. They flowed through the throng unacknowledged. Multi-hued auras were everywhere. Each had an individual resonance, a wavelength of sound all its own. They combined in a babbling cacophony that assaulted Richard's newly enhanced sense of hearing and he was finding it unbearable when Takahara said, "Think to silence it, Richard." He did and it was like hitting the mute button. The people and their auras remained but the noise was gone. Then he became aware that it was only the aura noise that had stopped, traffic noises and those of people walking past and talking remained.

Takahara plucked a pinch of aura from a man passing by and gave it to Richard saying, "Don't worry this will be a momentary lapse of memory to him if he even notices it is gone at all. I'll return it to him. Auras are the biographies of a person's health and welfare. Think of them as ledgers of their lives, a history of the past and present. You read the aura ledger of the woman at the meeting. The ledger entries showed her past marriage, where her son was and the debts she owed among other things. Auras are a biography of what has occurred or is still occurring. This small piece tells us that Manfred, the man's name, has been unhappy at his work for some time. He considers doing something about it but hasn't so far." Takahara took back the piece and tossed it over his shoulder then smiled at Richard and said, "It will find Manfred again."

"How come I didn't hear the woman's aura and why was hers the only one visible?"

"I muted hers and hid the others from you. That and the sync with her were demonstrations of your new abilities. You saw from her what had happened, what was still occurring and her thoughts at that very time. She will have acted on some and others were just flights of fancy. Those acted on will be in her aura. And, of course, everything will be in her Life File. Notice the different colours of the auras Richard, you will learn what many of them signify and what shades are of particular interest to observers and compilers, and which can be of use to Retribution in certain cases."

They walked on heading towards the dock area with Richard scanning aura colours that ranged far beyond any natural light rainbow spectrum he had seen Life Side. Gradients of lustre from shining brilliance to drab dullness were visible and Richard quickly came to understand it was the mood and thoughts of the person that dictated which colours dominated at any one time.

"That's right Richard, mood change, aura change, thoughts change, aura change. Thoughts affect mood. So many colours. Each meaning different thing to different people. A colour that show person happy because good deed done can also show torturer happy at thought of pain about to inflict. In time you learn subtle differences. Let us sit on bench over there."

A woman sat at one end of the bench drinking coffee from a Styrofoam cup and thinking about what she and her boyfriend would do after they ate supper at her flat. She shivered in sexual anticipation and a passion colour flooded her aura then faded as she stood to drop her cup in a garbage can and start walking away from the bench.

"She's going to a store to buy items for tonight's supper with her boyfriend. She's not quite sure yet what to cook but a bottle of wine is definitely on the menu. She is looking forward to having sex after the meal," he related to Takahara.

"Good Richard. Now isolate an aura and fade all the others. Use pinpoint mind. Does not matter who."

He picked a man waiting at a nearby tram stop. "What do you mean, 'pinpoint mind'?"

"Close mind to all else around. Focus on connecting with his mind. Bring your mind energy to narrow conduit, to 'pinpoint', so nothing else interfere in path to his mind then you enter easy."

Richard made a focused visualisation of all his mind energy entering the mind of the man at the tram stop and it happened. All other auras faded. The man made a slight hiccupping motion when Richard connected. He was inside and outside the man at the same time and in an instant knew everything about the man and was disgusted by what he found. He wanted to harm this man.

"Easy Richard," Takahara admonished sternly. "Do not move against him. Come away from him—now!"

What he had seen stayed with him when he withdrew. "Shit! That was awful. You must have seen what I saw Sensei. How can he do such things and more importantly—why has he not been punished for them?"

Takahara sat silent and impassive for some time while the human life of Hamburg flowed around them and then he cleared all auras and stilled all noise to say, "That man was in the line of paedophiles that passed you and Brian in the white space. I could punish him on the spot, hurt him badly, even cull him, I have that power but that is not the Concordat way. If I did hurt or kill him Concordat would immediately send someone to reverse the hurt or to return him to life. All other avenues to bring him to justice must have been explored and shown to have failed before Concordat will sanction a cull. He is under investigation as part of a bigger operation that is targeting paedophile rings and their distribution of child pornography. If the police and courts are unsuccessful in a prosecution, then that is when Concordat will consider stepping in. If he does go to jail, we might still deliver on him the hurt and damage he is doing to children. His fellow inmates will surely be those that hate paedophiles, don't you think? Control, that's what you must learn Richard, control."

A tram pulled silently to a stop and the man climbed on board and still without sound it took him away.

"Come Richard, let us take a little ride."

Chapter 59

Jenny took the coaster and started, "I agree with a lot of what I've heard and particularly about needing to find a marker that Life Files can identify at the outset. I also agree we got lucky picking up Meldrew which was in no small part due to my program but also due to killer Meldrew's time constraint as well. Whether or not his development is, or has been, stunted only extraction of his hidden record will confirm or disprove. Perhaps he is far more intelligent but again only separating and analysing the two Meldrews will find that out. Right now, I believe we should work on finding the best way to separate the DNA strands without damaging either one." Jenny handed the coaster to Yuri who was seated to her left.

"Life Files are working in the dark. We're casting about trying to find this marker but have no idea where to look. Is it in the DNA strand or is it in the brain or is it in the cortex covering? We had no reason to doubt our programs and protocols and thought we had everything covered — we've picked up serial killers many times — so what, or where, is so different about Meldrew, and how many more like him might we have missed? As I pointed out before we need to move on this because we need to get him back."

Yuri handed the coaster to Alan who passed it on to Ted saying, "Jenny covered it as far as analytics and programming is concerned."

"Nothing has surfaced from our Watchers that indicates any family member or relative is involved with Meldrew. They have been totally unaware of what he has been doing while away and obviously in the past he has acted in a perfectly normal manner when he returned. Yuri, am I right in thinking observers would have picked up on any strange or suspicious behaviour after he got back?"

Yuri nodded and confirmed with, "Yes."

Ted continued, "Okay, which to me begs this question; how does Meldrew slip back into a normal life routine without some residual awareness of what his body had done? If he has had the kind of energetic sex he had with Sarah then surely his genitals — which are not exercised that much with Mrs Meldrew — should give some indication yet he has never been recorded wondering about any soreness or abrasion in that area. I say 'body' because it appears his mind was controlled by the other Meldrew." Ted passed the coaster on to Charlotte.

"In one very important respect the operation was a great success, you saved Sarah's life and that was the primary objective. I take the point about returning him and if we have to destroy killer Meldrew in order to save the other because we run out of time then we must do that. The Solons are firm on that point and they realise that it could be some time before we have another combination of good fortune like Jenny's program found. Do what you can in what time is left but we need a live Meldrew back home on time." Charlotte handed the coaster to Emma.

"Assuming we separate successfully and assuming we send decent Meldrew back home with no ill effect do we have any idea what having killer Meldrew's DNA and records in our analytic systems might do to those systems? Maybe they could introduce some sort of virus. Perhaps it's best we find a way to keep both of them here until we set up a separate and controlled environment for the separation." The coaster passed to Eleanor.

"All valid points and suggestions but it seems that however we go about this we come up against a time factor. Meldrew has to go back before the Lancaster Arms or his family or his colleagues start wondering where he is. We are fortunate that Constance Meldrew doesn't normally contact him while he's away but some sort of emergency could change that so at best we have a little under two Earth days. Analytics and programming will have to put in place what safeguards and firewalls they can and Richard and I will go in to guide in the separation as best we can. We will be dealing with two Meldrews and can't afford to destroy any of the originals' DNA or cortex because we can't send him back with any physical or mental disability. Analytics and programming, how quickly can you get set a separate firewalled environment?"

Jenny answered, "Two maybe three Earth hours. We'll need to build an electronic barrier and do all our work inside it."

Eleanor acknowledged with, "Good, get to it."

All were making movements to leave and arranging to meet at analytics and programming when Richard announced he had something to say so they all sat down again. "I have an idea that will give us more time with Meldrew. I can take his place."

Silence and looks of perplexity greeted this announcement but before any voices were found Richard picked up the coaster and said, "Let me explain. I have already seen Meldrew's Life File along with those of his family when we met at Ted's villa so I know his routines and relationships. Part of my abilities as a Retributionist is to body alter so that anyone looking at me will see the original Meldrew and I can mimic his voice characteristics by copying his vocal cords. With access to his Life File, I'll be able to function at his work and I'll know all his memories. I'll blend in for as long as you need him then we can arrange a switch." He put down the coaster.

Charlotte was the first to speak, "So you would take over Meldrew's life doing everything he does and acting exactly as he does. You are confident his family won't know the difference?"

Before Richard could answer Eleanor broke in, "What if worst case we have to cull them?"

"I'm sure his family won't notice any difference and in the case of a cull we will have to come up with a scenario where Meldrew dies while away from home and we do a fragmentation body switch."

Yuri jumped in next, "If you go who helps Eleanor during the separation?"

"Amber. She's more than capable."

Alan spoke up, "It *will* give us the time we need to do the job slowly and methodically and to set up substantial firewalls and security."

Nods and murmurs of assent met this statement before Victoria said, "It's a great idea. Gives us all the time we need but what happens if Richard aka Meldrew gets knocked down and killed or has a life-threatening accident or illness, we can't just whisk him back. Ted and I can watch him and report but won't be able to interfere directly."

Richard answered her with a smile, "I appreciate your concern Victoria, thank you. I will be extra vigilant and take all the precautions I can."

"Will we continue to run Meldrew's Life File with observers and downloads while you are he?" Yuri asked.

"Absolutely. What I do as Meldrew needs to go on record," Richard responded.

Eleanor spoke directly to Jenny, Alan and Emma. "Okay, go and get started on your firewalls and other stuff and the rest of us will be along once Richard is back in Accrington as Meldrew and we've tested sync links and put Watchers in place." Turning to Charlotte, "Are you happy with us going ahead?"

"It seems the best approach even with the possibility of risks we have yet to consider or encounter. The Solons will understand our reasoning and Richard's volunteering. Much of what Concordat does and stands for on Earth rests on the outcome and we need the marker that Meldrew has kept hidden. I'll inform the Solons now."

Chapter 60

The Shinkansen Hayabusa bullet train was splitting the air apart with a streamlined proboscis and creating a pressure wave that pushed outward from its sleek flanks and then vacuumed inward when the last coach passed. Inside they rode in a smooth almost silent cocoon of speed where the outside close at hand is just a blur flung back past their windowed vision and the far distance slides clearly from frame edge to frame edge. They are riding from Aomori on Honshu to Hakodate in Hokkaido and will pass through the Seikan tunnel that connects the north and south islands of Japan.

"You were in Yokohama station at the time the first bullet train started service and stared in amazement — along with hundreds of others — when it passed through on its way to Tokyo. You have kept that memory, Richard."

"I have. This train is equally impressive and there was no bridge or tunnel between Honshu and Hokkaido when I first came to Japan early in the nineteen sixties. I visited several times during my life, but it was never enough Sensei."

"I bring you to this train because it is one of the fastest forms of land transport available to the people. A form of transport that along with air travel has become to be thought of as a necessity, but fast as they are this train and a jet aircraft cannot match the speed at which we can move. You and I Richard have country hopped. One second there, the next second here. We move faster than any train, jet or rocket and even light. Let us go to another of your places. So far you have been my passenger but now your turn to carry me. Once more I tell you control all important. Once more pinpoint mind needed. Select exactly where you want to go, I mean exactly, not close to or near so and so, but exactly! I say again, control, always control."

Warm water to their knees. Sound of surf breaking on a reef behind them. A crescent of beach rimmed with palms facing them. Clear blue sky above with a yellow white sun hanging above forested mountains rising from behind the beach palms. A ramshackle shack part hidden in the palms.

"Sorry Sensei. A hundred metres short. Meant to arrive outside the shack."

"First time not bad. You need to narrow pinpoint mind. You should have picked exact grains of sand to arrive at. But I not have to take over like with some. One almost put us in live volcano going to island in Indonesia. Let's go to beach, refreshments wait for us."

Wading from the water they made their way towards the shack and it took Richard by surprise when he saw the hammock Abigail and he had shared swinging gently in the warm breeze. Bottles of water stood beside the blanket shaded by palms that he and Abigail had used when satisfying the wants and needs of each other. Richard was not surprised to feel the chill of the water and he and Takahara opened a bottle each before sinking to the blanket.

"I know you came here with Abigail and it not surprise me when you choose this place again. It is very beautiful and peaceful," came from Takahara as they both knelt Seiza style and sipped water. "I know you wish to say something Richard. Please, say what is in your mind. It is most important that you do."

Chapter 61

Accrington train station had been chosen as the place for him to transfer. They'd used a toilet stall which he left carrying a travel bag containing clothes identical to the original that Meldrew had carried with him. He called Meldrew's wife to tell her he was about to travel back and expected to be home by seven. There was no surprise or questioning tone in her voice during their brief conversation, no indication that she found his voice different. She hung up after saying she'd see him later and have something ready to heat up for his evening meal. The Watcher saw her turn to the man in her bed and say, "He's coming back but not until this evening, so we have time until before Amy comes in from school."

To the world he was in every physical respect the original Meldrew. Before boarding the train, he and Emily tested their sync-link. Emily would be his contact while Eleanor was working on Meldrew. The link was good and Emily informed that Life Files were already recording and downloading. Thanking her he boarded and settled down for the journey to Meldrew's home.

Yuri had prepared an edited version of Meldrew's Life File for Richard to download. All the 'non-essential stuff'— as Yuri referred to it — had been removed with only thoughts, facts and events of importance implanted into Richard for retrieval if required. Richard knew that the acceptance of him by Meldrew's family was crucial if their plan was to work. Checking Meldrew's watch he estimated in one and a half hours he would know the answer. He had bought a newspaper with national circulation and read it to find out what was happening in the wider world. It appeared to be — as usual — all fucked up.

Amy heard his key in the door and greeted him with a hug when he stepped through, "Hello Dad, how was the trip?"

"Pretty busy but worked out well," he said dropping his bag and hugging her back.

"I've got some supper for you heating on the stove, chicken pot pie and veggies," Constance announced coming from the kitchen and pecking him on the cheek. "Hope that's all right."

Kissing her cheek he confirmed, "That will be fine. I didn't eat on the train; food hasn't improved any. Let me freshen up and change and I'll be right down." Picking up his bag he went upstairs.

Constance and Amy went back into the kitchen and had shown no hint of suspicion that he was anything other than their husband and father. When he came down and went into the kitchen his meal was on the table and Constance was pouring him a glass of wine. The façade of a happy marriage was being kept up for the sake of Amy.

Amy had a heavy after school workload and spent the evening in her room doing homework and projects. Constance watched television while he went into the den to catch up on mail and hospital emails. At ten-forty Amy came in to wish him goodnight followed soon after by Constance saying she was going to bed to read before sleep. He said he would be up as soon as he finished replying to emails and wished her goodnight.

Before he transferred it was arranged that anything related to Meldrew's work would be handled using a direct feed from records in his Life File which meant that Richard had access to all the knowledge and experience Meldrew had amassed in his career to the time he was taken. Nanosecond hesitation would occur when verbal responses were required while the information was located then transmitted by Emily but it would not be noticeable to Life Siders.

At eleven-thirty he closed his laptop and made his way to their bedroom. The lamp on his bedside table was burning and Constance was motionless and breathing steadily deep in sleep. He undressed and hung his clothes in the walk-in closet and deposited his underwear and socks into the laundry hamper. He slept in pyjama bottoms only and he pulled on a fresh pair. He knew that fresh linen would be on the bed and still crisp from ironing. Constance always changed the sheets when he had been away. She did not want the fragrance of her sexual exploits to be noticeable. She remained true to their agreement. Their king-size bed provided ample room between them and he settled without disturbing her and turning on his left side as Meldrew always did he turned off the lamp and the Meldrew part of him fell asleep.

Chapter 62

"Please say what is in your mind Richard. It is most important that you do."

Richard spread his arms wide in a gesture that took in the palms, the beach and the lagoon and said, "None of this is real in any fundamental sense, is it? I find it impossible to accept that what I have seen and experienced is bound by any of the accepted laws of nature or physics."

When Takahara spoke it was no longer with the idiomatic syntax that was the caricature version of a Japanese speaking English. He spoke in Japanese… and Richard understood him.

"Those laws are a Concordat construct. They are provided so that humankind can make sense of how the galaxies and universes formed. All the conditions for evolutionary life on this planet were put in place by Concordat and it was always intended that primates should become the dominant species. Several extinctions were carried out before a suitable mammal evolved during the era of the dinosaurs. In order for the mammals to flourish the dinosaurs were destroyed and changes to the weather patterns, atmosphere and tectonic plate movements were made. You could liken it to a 'tweaking' of the planet's ecosystems. From its position in its solar system to evolutionary outcomes nothing on or about the planet happened by chance; you are no longer constrained by that construct."

Takahara reached for his water and drank deeply then after placing the bottle in the sand he took a handkerchief from a sleeve of his robe and dabbed the corners of his mouth before saying, "What has been achieved by the dominant primate, Homo sapiens, has come about from an evolving brain that is — even amongst the most highly intelligent — only fifteen percent operational while yours is now one hundred percent. The abilities and capabilities of a brain increase exponentially as more and more becomes functional. It will be many millennia before Homo sapiens attain a fully functioning brain… unless they drive themselves to extinction before that. You, through Concordats intervention, have avoided the evolutionary time scale." Takahara fell silent.

Rising from beside Takahara Richard left the blanket and shedding his clothes as he went, he walked across sun warmed sand into the lagoon. Wading to hip depth he fell backwards to float relaxed in the waters supporting buoyancy. A slight raising of his head brought Takahara into sight still sitting Seiza style on the blanket but he sensed that his Sensei was not with that body but that he had taken — that was the only word he found suitable — his mind and travelled somewhere else. He wondered how many Takahara there were in this world. No! Not world—dimension! Of course! That's what it must be! Concordat was in another dimension and he and perhaps all the others could pass freely between it and Earth and, possibly, anywhere else. Hadn't Eleanor told him he could visit again the place where she had met him after his death? The AA meeting, Hamburg and the Shinkansen train were all real and with the capabilities of his fully functioning brain he could see, hear and sync with every aspect of the evolving primates called Homo sapiens.

When he returned to the beach Takahara informed him, "I am leaving you now Richard. My task of monitoring your brain functions and sensory outcomes after the final upload is complete." Here Takahara gave a rare smile and said, "It is quite the revelation when the understanding of another dimension comes. Eleanor from Retribution — whom you know well — will be taking over to introduce you to the other sections within Concordat and explain what they and Retribution do. I am the only person you have come into contact with during transition that will have any memory of you and when we meet again, we will do so as friends." Clasping his hands in front of his chest Takahara bowed from the waste and Richard returned the gesture with both saying, "Sayonara." Takahara turned and walked into the palms.

He heard his name being called from the lagoon in a voice he recognised and shading his eyes against the reflected glare of the water he picked out Eleanor standing on an outcropping of coral on the lagoon side of the reef. She waved and shouted, "Come and join me." So he did.

Chapter 63

Analytics and programming told Eleanor that they had finished isolating the Meldrews within a closed matrix and with the safeguards they had installed felt confident that whatever happened during or after the separation it would be contained and not infect any Concordat networks. Eleanor notified the rest of the team along with Charlotte and Amber to meet at analytics and programming.

Jenny gave the briefing. "Everyone to verbal and life brain please. Alan and I will insert at the sacral division of the spinal cord and make our way up the cord to where it joins the cerebellum checking the cord connections as we go. Our progress will be shown on a hologram for you to follow. We will not attempt any separation of the cords; we will just record any encasement and or absorption. We believe that when the rogue DNA kicks in so does the secondary spinal cord which then takes over Meldrew's bodily functions and alters his looks and creates killer Meldrew. Once we are at the cerebellum we will split up and function test synapses, neurons, neurotransmitters and all the rest across the brain hemispheres both through the covering and the brain under it and by doing this we hope to find the cache where he's been hiding the killings from us. We are hopeful to locate the cache in the areas responsible for memory in the medial temporal lobes which have the limbic system with hippocampus, amygdala etcetera. Real time recording flow will take place and those two gentlemen over there, Toby and John, will monitor Alan and me and be ready to retrieve us if anything poses a danger. The area of original Meldrew's hypothalamus that controls sleep and awakening function, the ventrolateral preoptic nucleus, has been neutralised to keep him inert and alive and we hope that it has the same effect on the other Meldrew. In the event that we are threatened John or Toby will tell Amber who will trigger a spinal cord severance and cull him. The Meldrews will stay on Earth time but once Alan and I prepare to enter we will go to Light Time and you will need do the same to keep up with us on the hi-litre but you will not be able to contact us directly, we want all communication within him kept to a minimum. That's the plan for this insert and when we have looked at the recordings we will — hopefully — be able to see how best to separate."

Charlotte asked, "Can we immediately change our programs and protocols once you find the cache?"

Alan answered, "Yes, once we find the location the P and Ps can be enhanced to target that area in all brains."

A hologram of a spinal cord and brain appeared when Jenny and Alan synced and Jenny said, "Everyone to Light Time operation." Then, "Put us in there, Toby, and start recording." Amber moved to stand beside Toby and John.

A red and a blue dot appeared on the hologram and began to move up the spinal cord. In front of Toby and John was an Ether Screen across which all the information transmitted from Jenny and Alan passed at Light Time speed. A secondary view screen showed Meldrew's vital signs in Earth time. Amber was charged with monitoring this screen for any signs that Meldrew was aware of the analysts and becoming agitated or attempting to wake up.

A continuous flow of verbal information came from the analysts which the recordists acknowledged and occasionally asked for a rescan to clarify or confirm. Wonder was noticeable in the voices of Jenny and Alan as they explored and reported on what they were finding as they ascended the spinal cord and column.

Separating at the cerebellum they each took a hemisphere and started circuit testing first at the junctions of the cortex overlay then intending to move on to the original brain. As the approaches to the portions of the brain involving memory were reached Amber noticed a rise in Meldrew's heart rate and blood pressure. Amber pointed this out to Toby who passed it on to the analysts. Alan and Jenny decided to leave the memory areas alone and asked if the heart rate and blood pressure dropped. Amber reported they did. The analysts decided to probe the connections between the cover and original brain at the memory centres and asked Amber to report which area caused the biggest increase in heart rate and blood pressure. It took them several nanoseconds to test probe the six areas of memory and it was probing that area involved with episodic memory, the medial temporal lobe, that heart rate and blood pressure increased the most. Toby advised no further intrusion into that area until all recordings had been studied and a nanoslice inspection of the memory centres carried out. Alan and Jenny agreed and moved to other areas.

The analysts withdrew from Meldrew at their point of entry and went along with the others to Jenny's boat to relax and recover while a preliminary study of the recordings took place.

The sea was calm as it always was and there was plenty of room on the after deck to accommodate them all with bikinis and board shorts being the preferred attire.

Charlotte who had taken a leaf out of Eleanor's book and wore a floral bikini opened the conversation, "Jenny, Alan, from what you saw and experienced give us your best ideas of where he's hiding the killings."

Chapter 64

Eleanor dove from the outcropping and swam to meet him. They met mid-distance between beach and reef and when they stood to embrace the water was mid-chest on him and shoulder level on Eleanor.

Eleanor smiling broadly pushed away to arm's length to say, "Let me take another look at you. Takahara reports all went well and he's handed you over to me to get you settled in. First on the agenda is you need to drop a few pounds and a few years. Let's go to the beach and I'll explain." Swimming side by side they made for the beach then to the blanket under the palms.

When they were both seated Eleanor began, "This is my age thirty-eight body and you last saw me at twenty-eight. I did stay in shape and inherited good genes from my mother. Anyway, one of the benefits that Concordat provide is the ability to have a full body makeover to look as we did between the ages of thirty and forty-five. If you got here earlier than thirty you are stuck with what you've got. You won't see many below thirty… not enough life experiences to be of interest to Concordat. Give some thought to which year you want and we'll see to it. Of course, I'm assuming you don't want to remain a seventy-something-year-old.'

"Why not? Takahara must be at least eighty and he gets around okay and Abigail seemed to find me satisfying from a sexual aspect."

"That was a disguise. Takahara is really forty here and was eighty-five when he came to Concordat. That's what you saw. He thought you'd feel more comfortable if you thought you were engaging with someone around your own age. It's something we do often when working a transition. With regards to Abigail don't pat yourself on the back too much. Certainly, you performed surprisingly well but during the act it was not you that Abigail was seeing. In her mind and visually she was with someone else entirely. Someone much younger."

"Spoiler alert! Way to demolish a guy's self-esteem. Okay. I'm beginning to feel like Alice, things are getting curiouser and curiouser. What other benefits accrue from the younger body makeover?"

Eleanor smiled widely and took his face in her hands then winked and said in her best femme fatale voice, "You get back all the vitality and urges that your body had at that time but with the added bonus of enhanced sensory responses. You know what I mean, sailor?"

"I believe I do and it certainly needs investigating. In life, I was four years older than you, so I choose to have my forty-two-year-old body back. I looked pretty good then. At least the ladies seemed to think so."

"Oh, you vain man," Eleanor said while pinching some of his belly fat. "Forty-two is after my time in your Life File so I'm interested to see how you looked. Stretch out and relax. You are going to feel all sorts of movement on your skin and in your body but it's not an unpleasant feeling. Close your eyes. Now, search your memory for one of you naked at age forty-two. Raise you right index finger when you have one. Good. Hold that image. I'm going to sync with you and tell transition to start the change."

Richard felt a shifting and tightening throughout his body and what seemed like a re-energizing of blood flow to organs and extremities. It ended with the tightening of his hands into fists then opening to rest on the blanket. Eleanor touched his shoulder and told him it was finished and that he could open his eyes.

Sitting up he looked at his more youthful body. It was slimmer with muscles toned from swimming and playing squash racquets. While not exactly a six-pack of muscle his stomach was flat and without flab and his chest muscles taught, no man boobs. Touching his scalp, he encountered the hair that he had shed in his elderly years. Fingertips found the goatee beard and moustache he sported in his memory and the lines on his face were far less pronounced even by touch. Standing he asked, "How do I look?"

Eleanor tilted her head to one side then the other and directed him to turn around slowly. He completed a slow revolution to end up facing her. "You look good. Older than the last time we were together of course but still handsome. Two things never changed over the years. One is your eyes. They always remained the same vivid blue. The other is your backside, it was always flat and flat it remained. I called you 'satchel arse' and it still applies," she ended with a smile.

"Yeah, it was never a backside worthy of the word. Can you conjure up a full-length mirror so I can take a look at myself?"

"No need. Use your mind to step outside yourself and look. Think that is what you want to do. Another bonus that comes with a fully functioning brain."

He thought it and it happened. Eleanor was right, he did look good for a forty-two-year-old man. He was sure the genes on his father's side had something to do with that.

Eleanor spoke to him, "Stop admiring yourself and get back here. We have a lot to cover but there is one thing I must check out before anything else."

Eleanor took his hands in hers and said, "I want to know if the forty-two-year-old you is as good as the thirty-two-year-old I knew. Would you like to find out if the thirty-eight-year-old me is as exciting as the twenty-eight-year one? I have memories that are making me horny as hell."

In response he went close to her and while nuzzling her neck below her ear undid the back strap of her bikini top and then slid thumbs into the bottom to slide it over her hips and let it drop down her legs. She shook the top from her shoulders and kicked the bottom aside. He was naked from his lagoon swim and was hardening when she reached down. She held him as they dropped to their knees on the blanket and then stretched out facing one another. He kissed the breasts he had known so well and she sighed while continuing to fondle him.

Chapter 65

He was in the shower when he heard Constance call about going down to fix breakfast and on the way knock on Amy's door saying, "Time to get up, I'm about to make breakfast."

Constance was in a robe when he came into the kitchen saying, "Good morning," and got a brief smile in acknowledgement. Minutes later just as the toast popped Amy came clattering down the stairs with wet hair and tucking in her blouse.

Giving her mother and father a kiss on the cheek and a murmured, "Morning." She grabbed a piece of toast and slathered butter and honey on before taking a bite and gulping orange juice. Meldrew had his usual coffee and soft-boiled egg and toast. Constance just had coffee, she preferred to wait until she was alone to have breakfast at a leisurely pace. Amy chattered on about school stuff and the latest thing to hit Facebook while she ate cereal and toast then finished a glass of milk in three swallows before jumping up and grabbing her coat and backpack and yelling, "Bye." she left letting the door slam behind her. Meldrew wrinkled his brow at the noise while Constance said, "Teenagers, what can you do?" and smiled into her coffee.

Constance had offered a brief, "Bye, have a good day," from upstairs when he picked up his briefcase and called to her that he was off to the hospital.

On the drive to the hospital Richard considered the reason why Brian Meldrew was to all intents and purposes a celibate. It came down to low testosterone which a course of patches and several other treatments had failed to increase. The level jumped and then plummeted again during the treatments and rather than go through the disappointment, and embarrassment, of, as Constance had so indelicately put it, not getting it up most times when she wanted sex he preferred their present arrangement. The other Meldrew had no problem in that area as they had witnessed with

Sarah which caused Richard to wonder if he had got the lion's share of testosterone. It was something he would enquire about when analytics and programming had finished their searches.

His work at the hospital went smoothly with never any indication that staff and colleagues found him different. Even his interns and patients accepted him as Meldrew and the direct link to Meldrew's Life File medical work data performed well. After rounds at the hospital he drove to his private practice office to be greeted by his secretary Elaine, she who went commando on Fridays, and Iris his nurse. His trip was enquired about and then he was brought up to date on appointments for that day. He was aware of one that Meldrew did not like but she was wealthy and came to him for every little headache convinced she had a tumour. She was youngish and called Bonnie Banks and had a body that spoke well of the cosmetic surgeons she frequented and being used to men wanting to get into her panties so she could not understand why Meldrew seemed uninterested. It seemed her life mission was to change his mind. Iris referred to her as Mrs Balloon Boobs. Behind her back of course.

After seeing the patients and once more fending off Bonnie's advances he settled into Meldrew's office to reply to emails and telephone consult with colleagues who had sent him medical histories of persons with strange symptoms and seeking advice. There were two that intrigued and he arranged for them to visit.

At five, Iris and Elaine opened his office door and wished him goodnight and see you tomorrow, he wished them a pleasant evening.

Living in Meldrew's home and sitting in Meldrew's chair at his practice and doing his work at the hospital was far different to reviews from Life File downloads. He was beginning to take on Meldrew's persona and not just the thin veneer necessary to fool people but a deeper one that gave him more understanding of the man and how having the other Meldrew inside had affected him without him even knowing it.

The soft chimes of the front doorbell roused him and he went to it wondering who would visit him after office hours. Neither Elaine nor Iris had mentioned a late appointment. He found Charlotte standing outside when he opened the door. She smiled and asked, "Can I come in doctor? I'm here to give you the results of analytics and programming first search and I've told Emily to take a break until I call her. I want to get your feedback about what they found."

Getting over his surprise he smiled, said hello and then ushered her into Meldrew's office and offered her a seat.

Chapter 66

Afterwards, Richard suggested a swim, Eleanor agreed.

Following their swim and from retained memories they made small talk about the years since they drifted apart while allowing the sun to dry them and then selecting what to wear. He was told casual was the main theme with Concordat unless someone wanted a change and went all back in life business clothes. That never lasted long he was told. It became skirt and blouse for her and slacks and short sleeve shirt for him with black slip-on shoes for both.

Eleanor explained what was to happen next, "We are going to my place, somewhere I'm sure you will recognise, and you'll meet the leaders of the other Retribution teams. We all work very closely together because sometimes our areas of operation overlap. No one you work with in Concordat has your complete Life File history but the possibility exists you will meet someone... like me... who shared part of it and retained the memory so be prepared for that to happen. Right, let's go and introduce you."

He did recognise Eleanor's place. It was the apartment in Kolkata, then known as Calcutta, that her parents had for the times they were not at the plantation house in Sahar Ganj.

Eleanor opened the door and ushered Richard inside. Eight people were in the room standing and sitting and many had cups of tea in their hands. The buzz of conversation died when Eleanor coughed to attract their collective attention. "Hi everyone and thanks for coming. Glad to see you found the tea things and from the crumbs on your saucers someone found my secret cookie stash and I bet it was Juan."

A smiling man who was unmistakeably Latino held up a hand and said, "Got me, but come on, in the drawer under the stove! That's the first place a good cookie thief looks."

There was laughter as Juan came forward to hug Eleanor and shake Richard's hand saying, "Good to meet you, Richard."

One by one Eleanor introduced them. Juan was head of the central and South American section. Cheng the Republic of China head, Valtieri of the Eastern European section, Nelson, covering Africa, Yvette, the Western European area, Mohammad from Middle East, Rashni covering the Indian subcontinent and surrounding area, Akiko the Far East section, Piri from Oceania, and finally telling him her section… Britain, Ireland and North America.

After greetings were exchanged Eleanor said the gathering was mainly to put names to faces and explained to Richard that geographical overlap often occurred and in areas where coverage was thin, particularly remote islands and sparsely populated regions, any available personnel could be called in to operate under the direction of the section requesting assistance. It was also explained that each section had five Retributionists excluding the section head. Richard spent some time talking to each section head and found that switching from one language to another was fast and seamless. He learned that the number of cases where a Retributionist was required was fairly constant across each section although population density and the quality of local law enforcement did have an impact.

His last conversation was with Akiko and throughout he felt something tugging at his memory. He retained many memories of his times in Japan and the Far East but none showed Akiko. "You are thinking we have met before Richard San, isn't that so? Think Moji the Grey Parrot Bar a long time ago. I was your first Japanese girl. I remember you were very gentle. I recognised you by your very blue eyes and the scar beside the right one. You have a few more lines on your face but still the young Richard underneath."

"I have your face in my mind now from that time but your name wasn't Akiko it was Eri and you told me in your Kanji it meant Blessing and Reason. I see nothing in your face now to remind me of Eri."

"I was attacked by a man who was obsessed with me but that I did not like. He cut my face and chest very badly and told me that he would make me ugly so no other men would look at me if he could not have me. He was right, his attack left me badly scarred. I was found and taken to hospital. I surely would have bled to death if not. I wished I had died when I saw what he had done to me. What you see now is what Concordat gave me copied from a mature woman in a fashion magazine, her name was Akiko. I like it."

"I am so sorry that happened to you. I went back to the bar a year later and Mamasan told me you had left and didn't know where you had gone. I was disappointed. You taught me such a lot the two nights we spent together. Did they ever catch the man that hurt you?"

"No. Police didn't put much effort into crimes against bar girls back then. I tried to hide my ugliness away from everybody by going into the mountains and begging sanctuary at a nunnery. Conditions were primitive and without the proper medications my wounds turned septic and I was close to death once more when Harold visited and told me about Concordat and how I could avenge victims of crimes like mine by bringing justice to the perpetrators. I accepted and the nuns buried my dead body the next day."

Akiko reached up to touch the scar beside Richard's eye and smiled, "I kept some memories of my time before the attack and the nights we spent together are among them. You were so gentle when so many men were rough — and — you were so eager to learn. You made it feel we were making love and not just a night of fucking. Richard, you will do well in Retribution. Please visit when you can." Joining the others by the door as they prepared to leave, she waved goodbye along with the rest and then they were gone.

Chapter 67

"So you think he's been hiding them in Meldrew's episodic memory bank?"

"Yes," Charlotte answered. "That's where heart rate and respiration rose whenever they got close to those connections between the overlay and original brain."

Richard mused, "Then why doesn't original Meldrew remember them? Episodic memories go way back and we know original Meldrew can remember back to early childhood."

"Analytics and programming think that other Meldrew has a separate episodic memory store in the hippocampus fed from the overlay where the memories of his killings go and are unknown to, and unreachable by original Meldrew."

Richard rested his arms on Meldrew's desk and considered what Charlotte had said, "I guess that makes sense. If the overlay controls and directs the memories into his own cache, then original Meldrew would not have any memory of the events. But wouldn't that leave gaps in Meldrew's Life File for when the killings took place?"

Charlotte concurred, "That's what analytics and programming are investigating right now. They think killer Meldrew has been planting false memories through the overlay of original Meldrew doing other things during the killing times. These are what are in his Life File."

"So what are your plans now?" Richard asked.

"We were hoping you could give some guidance. You spend a lot of time in other people's brains before a cull and know how to get around without being noticed so is there any advice I can pass on to Jenny and Alan?"

"I need to think about what they've uncovered so far so how about I call Constance and tell her I have to attend to a patient at the hospital and I'll be there most of the night. It happens quite often so she won't be too surprised then we can go have a meal and talk about options for Alan and Jenny."

He called Constance and when questioned if he wanted something left out eat when he came home told her he would grab something at the hospital cafeteria.

From Meldrew's Life File he chose a Thai restaurant, The Golden Elephant, a short drive away and took himself as himself and Charlotte there.

During the meal they talked over several options Richard put forward. Each had pros and cons but always looking to the safety of Alan and Jenny as the primary objective. Drinking coffee after their meals they decided on one particular course of action that he considered posed least risk to the analysts and original Meldrew.

Signalling for the bill Richard suggested they go back to Meldrew's office and contact the team.

On the Ether Screen projected to Meldrew's office everyone was gathered around Eleanor and they said their hello's before she spoke. "You have a suggestion how we can recover Meldrew's killing cache and find the marker that Life Files need to look for. We're all ears."

"First a question for Alan and Jenny. You feel sure the killing memories are in the medial temporal lobe? That they're tucked in beside original Meldrew's episodic memories?"

Alan and Jenny glanced at one another then Alan answered, "Yes, to both. The reactions we get when we approach that area, we don't get anywhere else. Results so far point to it being the place."

Richard continued, "You have Meldrew in suspension one day before he was due to return home, which is day four of five in his killing time. That's right, isn't it?" Eleanor confirmed it was. "Okay, then this is what I suggest. Put him in a duplicate of the Lancaster Arms and Accrington then bring him round to the point where he believes he is heading home and his killing time is running out in real time then at the moment the brain canopy starts to withdraw sever killer Meldrew's spinal cord. Cull him but without harming decent Meldrew then put him, decent Meldrew, immediately back into suspension. If you are right about where the killing cache is, you can retrieve it from Meldrew at your leisure because he doesn't know it's there. We don't care about the DNA and spinal cord absorption because Jenny's program can be altered to pick up on the event during gestation now we know what to look for. Finally, we can target scan all the medial temporal lobes in Life Files to see if any more like Meldrew have slipped through. That's it."

Eleanor said, "We need to be sure we can cut killer Meldrew out and not harm the other. If we go with it, we will need to plan how to get Meldrew back and you out. We don't have much time left. We'll talk about it and iron out some details and get back to you."

"I'll wait here with Richard," Charlotte said. "Get back to us as quickly as you can."

"Will do," came from Eleanor as the Ether Screen went blank.

Chapter 68

They busied themselves clearing away the cups and saucers and sweeping up cookie crumbs before Richard said, "I'm surprised at how few Section Heads and Retributionists there are to cover such a large population that's growing all the time."

Eleanor responded as she plumped up cushions on sofas and chairs, "Think of us as the final option. Concordat's success rate in leading terrestrial law enforcers to persons of interest is impressive. It's remarkable how often an overlooked clue comes to light, or a cop decides phone records need one more look or a face appears on CCTV footage that was missed at first viewing. The same happens with cold cases. Often it is how the case officer approaches the evidence or constructs the timeline that unearths a lead that ends in a conviction. Concordat plays a hand at such times." Pausing to look around she nodded with satisfaction and said, "That's better, they're a messy bunch."

Richard came from the kitchen where he had been washing and drying cups and saucers while Eleanor tidied the living room to say, "You changed some of the furnishings but I remember the apartment well."

Eleanor came and took his hand saying, "I'm sure you'll remember this," and led him to what had been her bedroom. She went to a fan that hung above a single size bed and pulled the cord to switch it on. The four paddles began to turn with what seemed a tired reluctance and a single chirping noise kept time at a certain point during each lazy slow rotation.

Richard laughed, "You kept the fan! How that chirping noise irritated me at first but you said if we moved to keep in time with it we could call it our rhythm method."

Eleanor reached for the cord, "Yes, but one of us would always pull the cord and turn it off when things got really active. But we must move on. Next stop Life Files."

Life Files was located in a crescent row of eleven regency style houses that looked out over a fenced park. Everything was immaculate and obviously well maintained. All the houses were painted cream with dark-green trim and doors that were reached by five steps rising from the sidewalk with the door and the steps of the middle house, number six, being slightly wider than the others. Not flamboyantly wider, just enough to signify that this was where the offices of the section head of Life Files worked. A gleaming brass plaque inscribed with 'Life Files Section—Please Knock' in black letters was positioned beneath a large iron doorknocker in the shape of a crouched lion. Standing before the door Eleanor murmured, "Yuri the head of Life Files is a committed Anglophobe and very much into all things regency," then she lifted the knocker and let it drop. The deep bass noise it made could be heard reverberating inside. As the sound faded the door silently opened and they stepped into a grand entranceway with marble on the floor and off to one side a staircase curving its way to the second floor. From inside it was obvious that the outside appearance of separate dwellings was a façade and in fact all behind the front walls and doors was common connected area rising three stories. A woman rose from a desk in a glass enclosed office immediately ahead across the hall. Richard guessed her to be mid-thirties as she walked briskly toward them saying "Eleanor, it's been far too long and this must be Richard your new recruit." There was a brief hug and air kisses for Eleanor and a brisk handshake for Richard.

Yuri started right in, "Charles will show you around Richard while Eleanor and I have a chat and I show her my latest acquisitions." A man approached them from the office next to Yuri's. Tall and slim he wore a paisley pattern waistcoat, white shirt with an ascot at his throat, trousers sharply creased that narrowed from hips to ankles and had notches where they met highly polished black lace-up shoes. Richard thought of him as being 'dapper' and everything about him was exact and polished from the cut of his silver dusted hair to the shine on his perfectly manicured nails. He did not offer a hand in greeting but instead bowed slightly from the waist. Eleanor linked an arm with Yuri and said, "Let's leave them to it. We'll have coffee and take a look at the new things in your collection."

Turning away the women made for Yuri's office and Charles led Richard to the staircase saying, "We'll start at the third floor and work our way down."

The curvature of the building was obvious as they walked past rows of Ether Screens running Light Time speed downloads into Life Files. Charles informed that each Ether Station handled five million Life Files. Observers, each responsible for a bank of five Ether Screens, would respond to a signal that the programs and protocols within the download algorithms had found something outside the norms of humankinds sociably acceptable behaviours. Most times, Charles explained, it was an aberration in behaviour that did not occur again but a watch flag was put on it anyway. He went on to explain as they went down a floor that if the aberration was picked up again the Life File was transferred to the flag watch department who monitored the Life File closely and who could — if the abnormal behaviour continued or escalated — call on Watchers section to look into it first-hand in real time. Flag watch and Watchers Section took the first floor and the ether screens were less in number and could be seen to be running far fewer Life Files and on many Watchers' screens only one Life File was showing. Arriving back on the ground floor Charles explained that suites of offices were kept there for use by Retribution sections if they required one in the planning of a cull. He told Richard that ten suites were presently in use.

Then as an aside he said, "No offence but I try to keep as far away from Retribution as I can. Some of their operatives frighten me even though I know they wouldn't harm anyone in Concordat. It's just you all seem so single minded when planning and carrying out a cull." Richard assured him no offence was taken and thanked him for his tour and explanations.

Charles acknowledged Richard's thanks and did his slight bow from the waist saying, "You're welcome," then turning on his heels he went towards his own office as Eleanor came from Yuri's.

Chapter 69

Eleanor and the team were together on the screen, "Jenny and Alan are happy to go with your plan Richard but want two extra days with Meldrew to check he's fully functioning before sending him back. Are you okay with that?"

"Sure. I can stay that long but what if Meldrew isn't up to scratch after he's sent, what's the plan then?"

Eleanor answered, "It depends on how incomplete he is. If it's some minor loss of motor or cognitive control, we will arrange for a mild stroke or similar nervous system breakdown while at work to explain it and if it's a major deficiency he will die under some set of unfortunate circumstances while you are away from his home and we do an exchange."

"All right, I guess we'll cross that hurdle if we come to it. When will you start?"

Alan spoke, "His final killing day starts tomorrow Earth time, your time, and we want to be installed early so we are fully prepared for when the canopy starts to retreat. We will have him follow his exact timetable and expect the withdrawal to occur sometime during the train journey which would be the reverse of the change travelling to Manchester. We will reconstruct the surroundings he knows from his stay so when we wake him, he will be in the flat and about to kill Sarah and from there it's his schedule we will follow."

"Can you make it real enough for him to actually believe he is killing Sarah?"

Jenny answered, "We will unlock his mind at the point he laid the knife on her and he will do what he intended to do but only as a mind projection of what he had planned. He will believe it's real."

Charlotte asked, "Are you prepared to cull him, Amber?"

Amber, who had been standing in the background confirmed, "All set. We've picked a spot where the two cords can be separated enough to sever killer Meldrew's without touching the other. As soon as Jenny and Alan are out, I'll cut the spinal cord."

Emma took a step forward and said, "We have made one change to your plan, Richard. You said to sever as soon as the canopy started to withdraw but we think it better to wait until it has totally withdrawn and we can be sure that good Meldrew's brain is fully back before Amber severs." Giving a grim smile, "Don't want a half and half Meldrew, do we?"

Richard nodded, "Good point. So Jenny and Alan will monitor the canopy and as soon as it retreats to the spinal cord and clears the cerebellum they'll tell Amber and she will sever. Have I got it right?"

"Yes," from Eleanor. "Emily will keep you informed of what's happening as you go about Meldrew's business. We can't connect you direct."

"Understood. And by the way, Emily is doing a first-class job. I'll thank her personally when this is over."

Yuri smiled, "I'll pass along your compliments. She'll go far, that's why I put her with you."

"And speaking of Emily it's time to call her back and I need to get back to being Meldrew. If anything changes, please let me know immediately. Talk again after the cull."

Charlotte told Eleanor she would be at her cabin until they activated Meldrew. Eleanor acknowledged and amid goodbyes from the team the Ether Screen disappeared.

"Well, I better get back to being Meldrew and go home to Mrs Meldrew and Amy," Richard said. "I can see why she has sex with other men, Meldrew seems to have no interest at all. It's not as if she's a bad looking woman, quite the opposite. Divorce is definitely in the air when Amy goes off to university. Shame."

"Just don't go out of character when you're with her, we don't want you surprising her in the middle of the night," Charlotte teased.

"I'm shocked you would even think that. Me, of all people."

"Yes, of all people particularly you! Keep your hands, and other parts of your body, to yourself."

Saying goodbye at the door Charlotte vanished into the shadows and

Richard got into Meldrew's car to drive home.

Constance and Amy were asleep, so he quietly undressed and slipped into bed.

Chapter 70

They were on the steps outside Life Files when Richard said, "Yuri sure doesn't come across as a bundle of laughs and what about those clothes. Even a regency dress would have been an improvement. Almost as if she goes out of her way to appear dowdy."

Eleanor bypassed his remark to ask, "How did you get along with Charles?"

"Fine. I like him despite some of his mannerisms. I have a feeling he has a fear of being touched. Why he would have that in Concordat I've no idea. He was excellent at giving me a good sense of what Life Files is and does and how it operates."

"Good, that's what we wanted. I find it hard to get excited about Yuri's regency stuff but she's a sweet person under the dowdy exterior. You'll find out that even in Concordat its different strokes for different folks and many keep the phobias and mannerisms they had in life, they're like old friends. I think Yuri likes the regency world of Jane Austen and the strong women that Austen wrote about. I do agree she doesn't go to any lengths to look attractive but that's her choice and she does one hell of a job at Life Files. Not a lot gets past her people."

"Okay, duly noted. Where to next?"

"Analytics and programming. I've told Jenny and Alan we're on our way and goodness knows where they're hanging out now."

They were hanging out in a gym. It could have been a school or college gym, it was hard to tell, and they were going one on one in basketball. Jenny was the epitome of the California girl. Tall, tanned, blonde, blue eyed, slim with large breasts, long legged, big mouth with lots of brilliant white teeth. Alan was shorter than Jenny by two or three inches, black curly hair, eyes dark like espresso shots, a Zapata style moustache hung from his upper lip and his body was all hard sinew and defined muscle. Jenny was the less mobile dribbler of the two and used her skill with the long shots to score while Alan moved hard and fast to the net then sprang upward to dunk the ball with force. Both played fast and were covered in sweat and the squeaking of their sneakers on the hardwood floor echoed from the walls.

Jenny gasped, "Be right with you. It's best of five and I've got him on the ropes, one more time in the hole and I win."

"No chance, you've got to get past me first and I'm fixing to steal," came from Alan as he bounced about on his toes. "Bring it on."

Jenny brought it on, spun past him and made the shot. Alan bent over with hands on his knees and wheezed, "Oh man, she gets me with that move every time."

They were still breathing ragged when they came to where Eleanor and Richard sat in the bleachers to say hi and that showers were in order before, as Alan put it, the ten-cent tour started.

"Come on through and we can talk in the changing room while we shower and dress," Jenny suggested.

Without any sign of embarrassment Alan and Jenny stood side by side in the showers and sluiced the sweat from their bodies and once the rinsing was over and the water turned off, they each grabbed a towel to dry off and Jenny asked, "Is there anything in particular you want us to show Richard or just a general overview Eleanor?"

"Just a general outline will be fine," Eleanor answered. "A lot of what you do is pretty esoteric but I'm sure Richard will ask questions if he needs something explained."

Alan clapped his hands and said with gusto, "All right! To the anal cave everyone!" And Jenny groaned and rolled her eyes in a signal that she'd heard that far too many times.

It wasn't a cave. It was a series of large pods of various colours arranged in a circle and connected by pedway's housed in clear acrylic shafts. Inside the circle was a terraced lawn with shade trees and flower beds while outside grassy meadows merged into woodland and that into slopes rising to snow-capped mountain peaks. The terraces were filled with men and women engrossed in reading and typing and scrolling on tablets or simply relaxing.

Alan turned to Jenny and asked, "Are you okay showing Richard around alone? I want to take Eleanor to the simulator and get her opinion on the program we're testing. We can meet up on the lawn after you've shown Richard around."

"Sure, that's cool."

Jenny took Richard into a mint-green pod and told him that each pod was staffed by personnel of a specific ethnic group and culture. She explained that analytics and programming function was to spot trends changing or occurring in random Life Files and to find any posing a threat to the overall wellness and safety of a particular person, group, race or culture.

Passing from pod-to-pod Jenny went on, "Populations are becoming increasingly mobile and intercultural and interracial partnerships more and more common and while that is a good thing overall — more inclusion — it does feed the rise of radical groups. Also, by majority the rich countries keep getting richer and the poor poorer. Trafficking in drugs and people also impact on the cultural mores of a race. We increasingly find a need to integrate analysts of different ethnicities, races and beliefs to work together as the offspring of intercultural couples become a larger part of the planet's population. We take all the data we can and where trends are spotted that indicate a shift towards increased harmful activities, we advise Concordat. With regard to your particular section, we do very little specific analysis unless a case crops up that is outside the norm of behaviours and it requires the reason or cause to be found before a cull so that programs and protocols can be altered to flag similar aberrations in the future and review Life Files for any that slipped through in the past."

Moving from pod-to-pod Richard was struck by the quiet industry going on. No noise, no rushing about, no raised voices—everything calm and orderly. It was a common thread that ran through everything he'd experienced since his arrival. He would talk to Eleanor about it.

After circuiting the pods, they exited onto the terraced lawn and sat relaxed on the perfectly manicured grass.

"What do Concordat do with all the analysis you produce?"

"They take it into consideration when placed against the larger picture of their evolutionary plan for the planet. Concordat have not tended to make wholesale changes since primates started their evolutionary journey. However, they will make singular adjustments by removing persons who cause harm and who are not brought to justice by the lawful, and sometimes unlawful, means available to the population. That's where Retribution come in but only after all other means have been explored and were unsuccessful. Life Files will have told you the same thing."

"Yes, they did."

Jenny, who was wearing a shirt tied below her breasts and khaki shorts, bare feet — all very west coast girl — stretched out with hands behind her head closed her eyes and said, "Eleanor is the one to ask about what triggers a cull. All I know is that a whole bunch of boxes have to be ticked before Solons will give the go-ahead."

At that moment Alan and Eleanor exited one of the pods and walked over.

Chapter 71

The corpse from the Lancaster Arms still lay in the morgue. The address written down at check-in did not exist. His clothes could be purchased at any one of thousands of stores. His body carried no distinguishing marks or tattoos. His wallet contained only a little money, nothing else. All efforts at identification had failed. No fingerprints or DNA were on record nationally or internationally. Pictures shown around the area of the Lancaster Arms produced no results and nor had the questioning of the prostitutes and their pimps who patrolled nearby. Pictures were put in newspapers and on television and again no result. It seemed John Doe would carry that title to his grave.

Sarah, who worked behind the bar at The Viaduct pub, saw his picture in a paper and after reading the police request that anyone knowing this man come forward murmured to herself, "Not bad looking, I'd have remembered if he'd been in here." Then she folded the paper and handed it to one of the regulars saying, "Here you go Fred, have a read while you drink your pint."

The medical examiner was unequivocal in his report, the man's heart seemed to have exploded even though examination of the tissue and muscles showed no indication of illness or disease. Blood and toxicology screens turned up nothing. No blood disorder or drugs. Stomach contents found the remains of a Chinese meal and alcohol. Policemen were dispatched to show pictures of the man at all Chinese restaurants without success. Thai restaurants were also canvased with the same lack of success. To the police it seemed that this man had wandered around Accrington as if invisible. His picture was put on television nationwide, nobody came forward to identify him. His body was placed in storage and if not claimed within thirty days he would be buried in an unmarked grave unless the coroner demanded it be kept longer while further investigations were carried out. The sharpening steel was put in an evidence locker. No mention of this piece of evidence was ever made public. Already the police were moving on to more pressing cases. After all—he'd died from a heart attack.

A young newly married couple rented the basement flat and noted on the furnishing inventory that a sharpening steel listed under kitchen contents was missing. The landlord said he was sure there had been one when he took inventory but that he would supply another. When vacuuming under the bed box spring a cardboard cylinder about two inches deep was pulled out by the suction nozzle. On the inside was the name of a manufacturer of duct tape. The husband, who was doing the vacuuming, tossed it into the bag reserved for paper to be recycled and carried on vacuuming. The bed linen and duvet that came with the flat were placed in a plastic bag and stored on the top shelf of the linen closet. The couple used linens they had received as wedding presents.

They liked the flat, it was a nice quiet neighbourhood. Nothing much ever seemed to happen there.

Chapter 72

Jenny still had her eyes closed so Richard tapped her shoulder and said, "They're coming," and they both stood.

They all hugged farewell after Eleanor and Richard had offered thanks for the tour and visit to the simulator which Eleanor reminded the analysts to let her know how the trials turned out. They promised they would. Alan and Jenny went from the lawn into a bright orange pod.

"Now it's time for Watchers with Victoria and Ted," Eleanor said. "I've been in touch and they want us to join them at an active site so you get a better introduction into what their section does. They're watching a human trafficking group. They'll explain when we get there."

It was seven-thirty on a wet and blustery morning when they met Victoria and Ted in a café on the fringes of an industrial estate and directly across the road from a transport company's warehouse and parking yard. Eleanor was greeted with hugs and Richard with warm hellos, handshakes and 'good to meet you'. The Watchers had already been seated in a booth by a window overlooking the street and when Eleanor and Richard sat down the waitress bustled over with coffee to fill the empty mugs already on the table asking, "Anything to eat folks?" Eleanor asked for rye bread toast with honey and Richard the pancake and bacon breakfast with maple syrup. Ted and Victoria already had the remains of eggs, bacon and hash browns in front of them.

Victoria started to explain the situation. "That transport company is bringing in girls from Europe and grooming them for the sex trade. They have legitimate contracts to haul freight for companies all over the continent and have dozens of trucks on the roads at any one time but they restrict the human transportation to only four trucks each week and never use the same trucks twice in a row."

When Victoria stopped to fork hash browns into her mouth Ted took over, "They change the trucks around but only four drivers are involved, the rest of them don't know about the human cargo and are only involved with the legitimate side of the business. The business is owned by a husband and wife and it's the husband that arranges to collect the girls through mob connections usually in former eastern bloc countries but it's his wife who grooms them and sells them on. The trucks carrying the girls only arrive after dark when the yard is quiet and back straight into the warehouse dock out of sight. We know there are soundproof rooms under the warehouse where the girls are used and abused and kept drugged until they are ready to sell on.

Victoria took up the briefing and Ted went back to eating, "The clientele want them the younger the better and pay big money. There are only three main purchasers and once the deal is made the girls are drugged and shackled into one of two unmarked vans and delivered to various addresses around the country. The vans only travel at night when traffic is light and always with another van as backup in case of breakdown or accident and always on minor highways away from motorways. The truck drivers act as delivery men."

Richard interjected, "You found out about this from Life Files, all this activity would have shown up, but how long have Concordat known about it? This sort of trafficking has been going on for decades, if not longer."

Ted wiped his mouth with a paper napkin before saying, "Centuries actually, it's an extension of the slave trade. The buying and selling of humans. To answer your question—we've known about this particular operation for two years and although there are dozens of similar operations running in this country, all of which we are watching, this one supplies to a particularly nasty sort of buyer. The girls are used in S and M porn and snuff films. We are also watching another operation that deals in boys and young men."

"And they weren't taken down years ago—why?"

Victoria answered, "Because they are being protected by someone high up in law enforcement. Someone who is into hurting girls and snuff filming. Whatever assistance Concordat has given in the way of clues and direction to law enforcement they have been blocked from further investigation or side tracked by this ranking officer. The head of the sex crimes unit no less. How's that for putting a fox in charge of the hen house?"

Pushing his empty plate away Richard leaned forward, elbows on the table, "Then why don't you just kill the fuckers? That's what Retribution section is all about isn't it, Eleanor? Getting rid of the bad people."

Chapter 73

She was still now. He stood back and surveyed his work. His penis and scrotum were covered in blood. Blood that had flowed from the cuts he made had soaked the mattress and he had entered her as she bled and when he had finished, he pulled away and slowly and deliberately pushed the sharpening steel into her all the time watching the pleading agony and fear in her eyes until only an inch of handle was visible. He saw death suck the light from her eyes. Now he was angry at her. He knew it had not worked, that she had not been the one to give him full control and that he would have to hide once again within the other. He silently raged at her and crashed a fist into her face with sufficient force to break her jaw. That made him feel somewhat better, so he went into the bathroom and showered.

He left her there and went and found a café that was open and ate a leisurely breakfast. He had paid for his room in advance so when the Lancaster Arms opened, he collected his things and left without seeing the owner. At the station he boarded a train to Manchester and there another to Meldrew's home. Not long after the train left Manchester, he felt the change starting so he put the newspaper he had bought for the purpose in front of his face and felt cheated as the other one took over once again.

When the canopy had fully withdrawn and Brian Meldrew was fully formed Amber waited for confirmation that Alan and Jenny were clear then she cut the spinal cord of the killer.

Emily told Richard the cord had been cut and the team were monitoring Meldrew. Later she informed him that Eleanor would visit him at Meldrew's office that evening to give an update.

Richard called Constance and told her he would not be home until nine or later and told her not to bother with a supper for him. He got a laconic, "Okay. See you later," before she hung up without saying goodbye.

The doorbell rang at six and he guided Eleanor into the office.

"Meldrew seems to have come through it without any ill effects." Eleanor began once she was seated across the desk from Richard. "We have him in a deep sleep mode and from the recordings all his brain functions are normal."

"When will you bring him out?" Richard asked.

"Earth time the day after tomorrow. What we intend to do is return him to this office after you have seen the last of his patients and see how he reacts. He will be retro implanted with all that you have experienced while taking his place."

"So no discernible difference since the other was culled?"

Eleanor shook her head, "None that are apparent at the moment, but we might see something when we begin waking him."

"What about the store of killing memories?"

"Alan and Jenny are recovering them now. They are doing it a year at a time, working backwards to the first, and checking for any disturbances after each one. They're at year twelve and so far, no change. It seems more and more likely that original Meldrew knew nothing about them."

"Any analysis being done on the retrieved memories?"

"No. We want to get them all and sequence them from first to last."

"Are targeted scans being done on historical and ongoing Life Files to see if there are more like him?"

"Not yet. We need to be sure, as much as possible, that his hiding place is the only one likely to be used by others."

Richard steepled his fingers under his chin in a very Meldrew like way before asking, "What happened to the severed spinal cord. Is it still there?"

Before answering Eleanor stood to reach across the desk and pull his fingers from beneath his chin saying with a smile, "Stop playing Dr Meldrew. The cord is being absorbed into surrounding tissue just as damage from a bruise does over time and we expect it to eventually disappear. Now enough talking shop, let's go eat."

They decided on steak.

Chapter 76

Eleanor popped the last piece of her toast into her mouth and swallowed before responding to Richard, "That's not the Concordat way. Every terrestrial means of bringing justice must have been tried and have failed before the Solons will consider a cull. We've made this point several times and this case is not at that stage yet. Tell him Ted."

"There are a lot of bad people involved and all are protected by one person. Now, because all the usual lines of enquiry we have dropped in front of the sex crime squad have been stymied by the top officer we are going to attack him directly. The faces of the persons involved in the making of the S and M porn are never on camera and bodies are covered by body suits to hide tattoos and distinguishing marks, they are cagey bastards." Ted paused to signal the waitress for more coffee.

Victoria took up the narrative. "We know from the officer's Life File that he has a small tattoo on his right forearm in the shape of an owl and beneath it the words 'ever watchful'. It's faded a little over the years but still quite visible and we know the tattooist — since retired — that did the work. A drawing of the tattoo will be sent to an officer on the sex crimes squad from an unknown source with a note saying that the man who has the tattoo is involved in the making and distribution of S and M videos with young girls. No fingerprints will be found on the paper and the envelope will be covered in prints from many hands, none on any criminal record. Copies of the tattoo will be sent out as a matter of procedure to all sex crime units asking for information and before the top officer becomes aware of its existence. He'll be away at a conference and its three days later that he becomes aware of it. After all, why would he be advised at a conference of one of many tips that come in?" Victoria looked to Ted and gestured for him to continue.

"A police sergeant soon to retire and putting in his last months behind a desk at a station many miles away will be the one to pick up the faxed copy of the tattoo. This police sergeant knows the tattoo from somewhere, but has trouble remembering, exactly where. The fax is copied and distributed to relevant personnel at his station and he goes about his business. But he can't get the picture of the tattoo out of his head. Snippets of memory keep coming back until he slaps the desk and out loud says, 'That's where I've seen it.' And goes to search out the head of the sex crimes unit at his station. You see where we are going with this don't you Richard?"

"I think so. Once he passes the information along about who has the tattoo he is sworn to secrecy. This is a very sensitive matter and must be handled with great delicacy. He shows them a tattoo he says was done at the same time at the same place during the same intake at police training college. The tattooist is retired but still alive and will recognise his work and will have kept a pictorial record of all his work. He will confirm the sergeant's story. How to prove it? Can't just walk in and say roll up your sleeve. Need just cause or a fortunate happenstance occurs that requires the arm to be uncovered when an officer who recognises the tattoo is there and is able to confirm its presence. An investigation would then start that uncovers the cover-ups and suspects are rounded up. I'm sure Concordat will provide a sufficient and clear evidentiary trail to get convictions. Am I close?"

Victoria and Ted exchanged 'well that was impressive' looks and Eleanor settled back in her seat with an 'I told you so' look on her face.

Both the Watchers drank the last of their coffee before Ted said, "That's one scenario we have in mind and you hit the high points Richard and added a couple we might use. As you can see a cull, though quick, is used only as a last resort. Concordat want the terrestrials to figure things out for themselves and with our help if necessary, so that their law enforcement and justice systems can be seen to be working."

Victoria signalled the waitress over and asked for the bill. Jenny paid in cash with a hefty tip and they all smilingly thanked her before getting up and leaving. Later, their waitress could not bring their faces to mind.

They parted outside the café walking in pairs in different directions after saying they must all get together when this case was closed. Each couple faded into the misty rain that had been falling all morning.

Chapter 77

Charlotte arrived as they were extracting the first killing memory and isolating it. They now had all twenty-four killings with each secured inside an individual data casing. Approaching Eleanor she asked, "Can I report to the Solons that the Life Side operation was successful and that Brian Meldrew will be returned to his family having suffered no harm?"

Eleanor responded, "You can tell them that the operation to save Sarah was successful and that the cutting of the killer Meldrew's spinal cord seems to have caused no ill effects to Brian Meldrew but we are keeping him for thirty-six more Earth hours to monitor him while we gradually wake him and then if all is well we will transport him."

With the exception of Emma, Emily and Richard the rest of the team were present and Charlotte addressed them, "You have all done exceptional work carrying out a very unique operation and when you have finished your analysis of the killing memories we can improve our procedures and protocols to find such events in past, present and future Life Files. I am sure we all look forward to a successful outcome. I'll leave you to get on with your work while I report to the Solons. Thank you."

Telling Eleanor she'd be in touch Charlotte left.

Silence followed Charlotte's departure which Alan broke saying, "High praise indeed. Not overly effusive but praise nonetheless and as she said, 'time to get back to work.' Eleanor, it's time to start bringing Meldrew out of deep sleep. I suggest we leave the analysis of the hiding place and the killings until we have him safe and sound back home and Richard back with us."

"Agreed. Let's run through the drill once more. Jenny, you first."

Jenny began, "Over several hours we will introduce brain activity that takes him from deep sleep into stage one light sleep then to stage two light sleep then stage three deep sleep then back to light sleep and once again back to deep sleep. Stages one through four are non-REM sleep and stage five REM sleep. During REM sleep we should observe him dreaming and that should give us a good idea if any change has taken place since the cord was cut."

Yuri was next to speak, "Observations and recordings will be made as if following a true Life File periodic download, with observers looking for any unusual activity particularly in the area of the medial temporal lobe. This Life File record will be kept in isolation from his previous downloads until we are sure there is no cross contamination from the killer Meldrew."

"We have little to do but look and learn at this point," came from Victoria. "Our work will start when Meldrew is returned home and a full-time Watcher program is put in place. Changes in previous body language plus any to actions and routines will be priority."

Looking at Meldrew's sleeping form Eleanor said, "Good, so let's get started and unless we have something to report that directly effects Richard, we will leave him and Emily to live the life of Meldrew."

Over the course of thirty-six Earth hours they brought him through five of his regular average sleep cycles of seven hours and fifteen minutes and held him at point of wakening fifteen minutes before the end of the fifth.

Jenny finished scanning the latest download and told them, "Nothing showed up that causes us concern. His brain activity is normal throughout all sleep cycles and Yuri is happy with what the observers are seeing. His dream sequences are well within healthy brain parameters although the sexual content of some took us by surprise given his lack of interest in the real thing."

Here Yuri interrupted to tell them, "We checked his file for previous sexually explicit dreams and found during puberty he was subject to them as well as wet ones but that they decreased and vanished at the time we estimate his alter ego began to make an appearance. Perhaps now he is alone his libido has reignited."

"Maybe," came from Alan. "Perhaps Constance is in for a surprise when she gets him back."

Eleanor stopped further speculation, "We'll find out soon enough and if we're all confident he is free and clear it's time to arrange his transfer and let Richard know he's coming. Jenny, contact transfer section and set it up for eighteen-hundred Earth GMT, destination Meldrew's clinic office. I will be with Richard during transfer and I'll let Charlotte know. I'll be in touch as soon as he arrives and Richard and I see how he reacts. Time now to feed all that Richard has experienced into Meldrew, we want the exchange to be as seamless as possible. I'm off to join Richard."

When Eleanor arrived, she found Richard in contact with Emily and streaming all his experiences as Meldrew through her to sleeping Meldrew. When streaming was complete, they positioned themselves across from the desk and chair where Meldrew was due to arrive. A message from Jenny that he was on the way came as a kaleidoscopic fragmentation of energy pinpoints assembled themselves into Brian Meldrew who, when fully formed, picked up the pen that Richard had been using and continued to write in the patient's file that Richard had been updating. They watched as he finished writing and placed the papers in his out tray to be filed by Elaine the next morning. Pushing back from his desk, Meldrew stretched and worked his shoulders to relieve muscle tightness, the exact tightness that Richard had been feeling, then he phoned his wife to tell her he was leaving and heading home. In response to a question from Constance he said, "Pork chops are fine. I'm on my way."

They watched him leave after setting the alarm at the front door. He was making his way to where he parked his car when they handed him over to Watchers and they returned to Concordat.

Chapter 78

They went back to the Kolkata apartment. Eleanor stopped at a curry house nearby and got a chicken tikka masala and a beef vindaloo with naan bread and sweet mango chutney while Richard went to lay out plates and drinking glasses for iced water from the fridge. They ate sitting cross legged on the floor using fingers and scoops of naan bread. They had tea after and then moved to the sofa with Eleanor leaning against him with his arm on her shoulders and her legs curled on the cushions. They were quiet and allowed the sounds of the Kolkata night coming in through the open window to surround them.

In a murmur Eleanor asked, "Why did you retain only one memory of Jane and why did you just share it with me?"

"Because I want you to know that there was another woman in my life that attracted me as much as you did."

"But why is that short memory of the two of you in that tiny room for smokers all you want to remember her by. She was very beautiful and it was such a calm beauty, even I can sense that."

"I felt it best to remember just the moment when I saw her and she smiled that wonderful smile and said hello. That is all I need. I don't need to know what came after, if indeed anything did."

"You did that with many other memories too, didn't you? You distilled them to a single moment or event."

"Yes—I did that with a lot of them but the ones that needed to be kept whole I left that way."

Eleanor raised a finger to caress his cheek and said, "I'm sure you will get many good memories here." Then she swung her legs down and sat straight to say, "It's time for you to experience some of what your Concordat brain can do. First, mind infiltration. Come on, down to the street."

Kolkata is a hustle and bustle city. Kolkata never slept long before New York usurped the title. They made their way to the Queen Victoria monument which at night was a gathering place for people seeking coolness after the heat of the day and for young people in the throes of love or lust.

Eleanor pointed to a couple sitting close together on the grass that surrounded the memorial. "You infiltrate into the girl and I'll take the boy, let's see what's on their minds. Focus on her mind and join with it. It isn't syncing, you won't be able to alter her thoughts but you will be aware of them. Also, you will be seeing through her eyes and feeling all the sensory events happening in her body, hearing, touch, smell etcetera. You will experience what she, as a woman, experiences. I will visit with the young man and we can compare notes after. I'll be in touch when it's time to leave them, we'll be in there no longer than five Earth minutes. Lets' do it."

"How did it go?" Eleanor enquired after they left the couple.

"Amazing the amount of sensory feedback, she was getting and was not even aware of it. And not just from her body but from him as well. I could feel the sexual urges radiating from him and she was dithering about whether to let him feel her boobs. Her body was turning cartwheels and if it had had its way she would have mounted him right there and then. I guess you must have gone through that same stage at some time and I know when I was young I felt what he was radiating and getting all horny wondering will she or won't she. What we had there were two very confused and sexually aroused kids."

"You are right. I went through that stage but was well over it by the time I met you, thankfully. The boy was almost coming in his pants and she radiated much the same sexual emotions. Like her, if his body had been in control, they would be doing it right now. Ah, the mystifying rituals of modern sexual games. Your male ancestors would just have got an erection and if a receptive female was near, they would just have gone at it. I'm glad we moved on from that stage, and that now we exercise more discretion over when and where the act is performed. Although we did push the boundaries, didn't we. Let's go back to the apartment and leave them to find their own way through the sexual maze."

Chapter 79

The whole team gathered at the diner and unable to use a booth because of their numbers helped Sherri to push two tables together and arrange sufficient chairs. Blackberry and apple crumble was the dessert of the day and at Sherri's recommendation they selected that all round with teas and coffees to follow. Sherri bustled away to get their order.

Once everyone was settled Richard spoke up, "I want to thank Emily for her work in getting me through my Meldrew period, she never missed a beat getting the right stuff to me. Thank you, Emily."

Emily, who was younger than the rest with flaming red hair, fair skin and freckles, blushed and stammered a, "Thank you."

They applauded and said, "Well done."

Sherri returned with the crumbles and asked, "A special occasion for someone?"

Richard said, "We are thanking Emily for doing a wonderful job under a lot of pressure."

"Which of you is Emily?" Sherri asked.

"I am," Emily replied quietly somewhat over awed by the attention.

"In that case Honey, make sure whoever you work for gives you something more valuable than a piece of pie and a cup of coffee," Sherri said with a wink and a laugh.

"They already have and I'm very happy to work with such good people," Emily responded with a smile.

"Then you a one very lucky young lady," Sherri said with feeling before leaving to get the coffees.

Emma took a fork and tasted the pie. "Oh wow, I have never tasted pie this good. Now I know why you come here so often. Pity we can't take some back with us."

"A small price to pay for everything else Concordat gives," Eleanor said, and which Emma acknowledged with a nod and, "True," Eleanor continued, "Before we do a full debrief and start on a nanoslice inspection of the killing memories we are going to take some private time. If anything disturbing is spotted by the Watchers or the observers we will be contacted so once we leave here head to wherever you choose but keep a channel open for emergency contact. Emma and Emily, you are part of the team now and you will be there when we do the debrief and inspection."

Over drinks they made small talk about where they were going for private time. The destinations were as diverse as their personalities and they left the diner in ones and twos. Eleanor and Richard were the last to leave. Money for the pies and coffees along with a generous tip sat on one of the tables and Sherri wondered how she could have forgotten who had sat there—but she had.

Chapter 80

At the apartment Eleanor draped a sari pallu around herself without the undergarments and Richard wrapped a lungi around his waist then they made tea and sat on the sofa drinking it.

"Is Infiltration used much," Richard asked when they were settled and comfortable.

"Usually when doing a Life Side operation. We can move from one person to another to watch or follow — it's known as 'body hopping' — without adding to numbers which happens when we go full body. When we go full body, we use our own and as soon as we pass by or leave a place, we make sure we are forgotten. It's called a momentary wipe, just that part of a person's memory that would retain knowledge of our being there."

"And I can do this 'body hopping' whenever I want?"

"No. Tonight was a demonstration. You can only do it during an operation and with approval from your section leader. Can't have naughty boys and girls hopping around like over excited voyeurs."

"See the point," Richard mused. "Now explain to me about moving from place to place and about how I am convinced that this is your apartment in Kolkata and that the pods are where analytics and programming work, and that Life Files is in a regency terrace."

"It can best be explained by you picking somewhere real or imaginary that you want us to be. Anywhere at all. If it's real all that should be there will be, but if it's imaginary you will have to outfit it. Go ahead and think about that place."

They were in a cabin on a ship. They were sitting on a day bed across from a bunk the size of a double bed. Gone were the sari and lungi and they were in western clothes suitable for hot climes, loose shirts and shorts.

Eleanor stood and exclaimed, "Your cabin on the St Albans. One of my memories. I remember the purser in the next cabin knocking and asking us to keep it down. Apparently, he was trying to take a mid-afternoon nap.

We did get noisy at times. Anyway, enough of that for now. We are both here because I accepted what was in your mind and travelled along with it. The longer you are here and the more you learn where your colleagues usually go all that needs to be said is let's go to — or meet at — such and such and you can immediately transport yourself there. The pods and the regency houses and the apartment are what I and Yuri and Alan and Jenny want them to be, they are all fabrications of our minds or from memories. For instance—because I have a memory of this cabin all you needed to say was 'See you at my cabin on the St Albans.' And I could have made my own way here but had you chosen a place you knew when I was not in your Life File then I would have had to piggy back on your mind. Try it… let's go somewhere I have no knowledge of."

A single room building built of stones with the roof long since fallen in. Where a single door and window once kept out the elements were now gap tooth openings with wood rotted to a weathered sogginess and glass dull diamond shards. All around were hummocky hills dressed in dun brown and heather green. A lingering odour of tobacco smoke tried to hide away from a stiff wind in corners terraced with cobwebs. Debris on the Earth floor showed signs of movement recently and the tracery of patterns from the soles of hiking boots was visible and not yet dry.

Eleanor wrapped her arms around herself and pulled tight the down jacket she wore, "A derelict and all but falling down bothy. Why here?"

"Twelve weeks after leaving re-hab a colleague at work asked if I wanted to go hill walking with a club he belonged to and I said 'yes'. He said all I would need was a pair of hiking boots and a backpack to carry snacks, a thermos of hot drink and some dry socks. Long story short, this bothy is the halfway point in a twelve mile walk and we stopped and sheltered from the wind to have a drink and a bite to eat. I changed my socks here, the going is pretty wet in places, and had a cigarette, a lot of the walkers smoked, and it was when I stepped outside again into the wind and looked across this barren yet incredibly beautiful land that I felt truly alive after all my years of drinking. This is the spot when one day at a time really began for me. That's why here."

Eleanor moved close to stand in the doorway beside Richard and hug him close saying, "If ever you want to share about those times, I'm here." Then tipping her head to one side she said very quietly, "If you listen really hard you can hear the history of this country being picked up from the land and carried on the wind."

Richard raised a hand to point across the glen to a ridge and said, "Watch."

Seconds passed then three stags, vanguard of a deer herd, broke the skyline and after scanning the downward slope and valley for any dangers began the descent to the glen floor followed by a large herd numbering in the hundreds that flowed over the crest and cascaded down over heather and scree to browse on the succulents growing at the sides of a burn that ran crookedly gurgling and boulder leaping along the glen floor.

They stood watching in a silent solitude broken only occasionally by the huffing sounds made by the guardian stags as they patrolled the herds perimeter until Eleanor squeezed his arm and whispered, "Time to leave Richard."

Chapter 81

Meldrew enjoyed their evening meal. He knew that Constance was a good cook but this meal tasted particularly good and he commented on the flavours in the sauce the pork chops had been cooked in. Constance, being unused to any form of compliment about her cooking from him, raised her eyebrows at his remarks and told him she'd picked the recipe up from a cooking show on television. Amy ate with the abandon of an eighteen-year-old and talked about midterms and the plans already being made about the senior prom, still months away. Meldrew amazed Amy and Constance by asking if Amy had any particular boy that she wanted to ask her to the prom. He had never asked such an intimate question of Amy before and she looked at him in surprise then answered that she thought two boys would ask her but didn't know which one to choose. Meldrew smiled and to her and her mother's surprise told her to make a statement and let both take her. Amy laughed and said she would think about that then headed to her room to complete homework. During the meal Constance had noticed his whole demeanour was of relaxed openness. Meldrew could feel a new vitality stirring inside him, something he had not felt since his late teens and early twenties. He wondered how Constance, who he now fully realised was a very attractive woman, would react to any romantic advances from him.

As was usual after their evening meal he went to his study to catch up on emails and other consultancy business. He was about to close his laptop when Constance knocked and opened the door swirling a brandy glass and offered it to him saying she thought he would enjoy a nightcap. He took it from her gratefully and suggested they have their drinks together in the living room. He put an arm around her waist as they walked from the study to the living room. Neither knew what exactly was happening, so out of the ordinary was this behaviour. Constance had decided to approach her husband with the same openness he was now displaying and to see where it led. He continued to feel an upwelling of attraction to his wife and closeness to his daughter. To him it felt like a newfound freedom, as if something momentous had changed in his life but which he could not quite put his finger on. For the first time in many years he and his wife sat in companionship and talked while sipping their drinks. Constance was prepared for this change in her husband not to last and wondered just how deep it went. She also wondered if the subject of their arrangement would arise.

They were interrupted in their conversations about their day and upcoming social engagements by Amy calling down for her mother to come to her room. Constance gave a slight shrug and with a 'what now' look on her face went to their daughter. He took the empty brandy glasses to the kitchen where he rinsed and wiped them dry and as he was taking them to the liquor cabinet Constance and Amy came down the stairs. Amy was in pyjamas and waited until he had put the glasses back before hugging him and saying, "Good night Dad." And after hugging her mother she bounded back up the stairs to her bedroom.

He smiled indulgently after his daughter and said, "That girl never does anything at half speed."

Constance replied, "Except clean her room, a snail could get to it faster." Then for the first time in many years they laughed together. Amy was happy to hear them laughing.

They were preparing for bed when from the bedroom he asked, "What did Amy want earlier on? Not problems at school I hope."

Constance who was in the en suite removing what little make-up she wore answered, "No, just girl stuff. Not something you talk about in front of your father." His reflection appeared behind her in the mirror above the vanity.

He was ready for bed in his pyjama trousers and smiled at her over her shoulder to say, "I'm a doctor, she can tell me anything."

Dropping the used make-up wipe into a bin inside the vanity she turned and smiled at him, "You are her father first and even if you are a doctor there are some things a daughter does not share with her father." They were standing close and Constance was sure that his face looked younger and less careworn. Turning back to the vanity she applied some cream to her hands and was massaging it into her arms when she felt his arms encircle her and watched in reflected fascination as his surgeon's fingers deftly unbuttoned her pyjama top. He reached up and slipped the material from her shoulders and she straightened her arms to let it fall at their feet. He moved in close behind her and her eyes opened wide in surprise as he lowered his hands to hook thumbs into the waist of her pyjama trousers and work it over her thighs to join the top already on the floor. Turning her gently by her shoulders he kissed her lips. She opened her mouth and while tongues probed and lips crushed, she let go all reservations about the change to her husband and pushed frantically at his pyjama trousers to get them over his hips. He lifted her onto the vanity and she willingly opened her legs to accept him as he moved into her.

In the early hours they at last lay sated. He said quietly, "I feel a weight has been lifted from me, but exactly what that was I have no idea. I do know that I want to be a true husband to you and a better father to Amy. I am not going to question why or how this change has come about I will simply accept it and I hope you will too. The arrangement we had is now over. How about you? Are you ready to welcome me back?"

She had turned to face him and raised onto an elbow to look down at his face in the light still burning from the bathroom and tears had fallen onto his chest as she said, "Yes, I'm ready and I'm glad whatever burden you were carrying around has gone. I did notice the difference in you and Amy did to, that's what we talked about earlier, and I will be your wife in every sense of the word. You were the only one I ever wanted from the day we met when we were students and you knew I had a high sex drive so it hurt me badly when…"

At this point he placed a finger over her lips and said, "Shush, that's all over now, let's say no more about it and move on to a happier marriage with a beautiful daughter, I've a lot of lost time to make up."

She rolled to the side pulling him on top of her and said, "What are you waiting for?"

Chapter 82

Back in the Kolkata apartment and in response to a question Eleanor explained, "Shared memories, like that of the bothy, remain only with the person or persons it or they are shared with. They cannot be accessed by third parties or retransmitted to a third party. Even memories retained from Life Files that include one or more persons that are in Concordat, like yours and mine about this apartment, can only be shared by the person whom the Life File primarily applies to. Simple terms… if I had not wanted you to know about this apartment from my memory, the primary one, I could have blocked you from coming here alone even though it's in your memory of our time together… because your memory is not the primary one."

Richard, who was stretched out on the sofa said, "Got it. Personal memories are not accessible by others and once received cannot be passed on except with permission from the primary holder of the memory."

Eleanor who was in an easy chair with feet up on a footstool threw a cushion at him saying, "All right smart arse! Put it in simpler terms than my simpler terms if you must show-off. Anything else you want answers to? I'll do my best to make my answers as complicated as I can."

"The Ether Screens seem to be everywhere." Richard commented, then, "Can you bring one up at any time? Like right now?"

"Only for a specific purpose," Eleanor responded. "We can't just bring one up to play a video game. If you want to see how Ted and Victoria are doing on the sex slave trafficking case, you can ask them for an Ether Screen connection and we can find out. Focus your mind on either Ted or Victoria and tele transmit your request asking for an Ether Screen connection to get an update on the case."

Richard had hardly finished his tele-request when an Ether Screen appeared in front of him and a smiling Ted said, "Hi, you two."

Then Victoria came to stand behind him and ask, "What are the pair of you up to on this fine night?"

Richard and Eleanor... who had moved to join him on the sofa... said, "Hello."

And Richard went on, "Eleanor is still showing me the Concordat ropes and I questioned the use of Ether Screens and she suggested I give you a call and see how your case is progressing. The human trafficking sex slave one if you have others on the go."

Victoria — having seated herself beside Ted — said, "We do have others but the one we talked about is our priority right now. Since we spoke, the retiring sergeant has spoken to the detective chief inspector in charge of the sex crime unit at his station and as we surmised he has been sworn to secrecy and the detective has set up a meeting with the assistant chief constable for the area for tomorrow morning. We expect the detective will lay all the evidence about the tattoo before him. We can only wait to see if the ACC carries the case forward or if the old boy's network closes ranks in an attempt to sweep it under the carpet. They might try to do what they and the Catholic church have done with abusers in the past which is to deny all knowledge and move him sideways or transfer. We need to wait and see."

Ted took over. "If a cover-up is attempted then we will arrange — possibly through the sergeant after he retires or a social media outlet — for certain evidence to come to light that cannot be ignored along with a social media blitz asking all sorts of tough questions about the detective involved. He's a DCI by the way. Concordat prefer we don't use social media Richard but, in this case, we think it will be granted as a last terrestrial attempt to close the trafficking down. Implicating someone that high up will force their hands and the hands of Interpol in the EU. We can keep you in the loop Eleanor, let you and Richard know how things progress. We have quite a Watchers contingent involved between here and continental Europe. It'll give you a chance to see how we operate Richard."

"Yes, please do that." Eleanor agreed, "And thanks for the update on the case and the Ether Screen demo. Much appreciated."

A synchronised, "You're welcome," came from the Watchers.

Victoria said, "Love the sari," before the Ether Screen disappeared.

"Can someone just drop in on you by a screen whenever they like? I mean what if you're doing something private?" Richard asked.

Eleanor turned and placing her mouth close to Richard's ear said in a sultry voice, "Define private, Sailor."

"Something like this," he said as he lifted the material covering her breasts and kissed them.

"I see. As of now this apartment is on lockdown from Ether Screens so shall we explore other definitions of 'private'?"

Chapter 83

The team were back together after four Earth days of private time and were pleased to see that the reports from Watchers and observers showed the Meldrews were acting normally. Meldrew continued with his work and Constance told former lovers to stop calling. Family, friends and colleagues remarked amongst themselves how Meldrew had changed and that he, Constance and Amy seemed much happier and more content. There seemed to be no residue of the other left in Meldrew and all his brain functions were normal.

Charlotte had joined them to review the reports and asked, "Any concerns from what you've seen so far? He seems to be functioning well but did you expect such a change in character and temperament Eleanor?"

"We didn't know what to expect. All the possibilities we ran before we culled pointed to some change but none gave an exact indication. We are treading on new ground here. As you know Concordat has never found a case like this and therefore no historical data exists. We will continue to monitor him closely of course and we are hopeful the dissection and scrutiny of the memory cache will provide more understanding. We are about to start looking at the killing memories now."

Charlotte left telling them she was going to report to the Solons about Meldrew's progress and would be in touch later.

Analytics and programming and Life Files arranged view screens and holographic projectors that would run the ageing of Brian Meldrew concurrently with the maturing of his absorbed twin from ten to twenty-two and the first killing. They would watch at Time Light speed and were synced into the memory at Hyper Brain to follow and understand. Alan explained that for the sake of separation Brian Meldrew would be seen in blue and killer Meldrew in red.

As they watched the years pass it became clear that Brian Meldrew knew nothing of his absorbed twin. Through puberty, adolescence and until the time of the first killing he grew and matured as any normally functioning young man would. All the preoccupations and angst of those years were clear to see. His academic record was always good and his home life secure and for the most part placid. It was he who decided to follow his father's occupation and enter medicine, family pressure was not brought to bear. During his early university years, he found the party scene was not for him. Drinking, getting wasted, and their aftermath, interfered with his studies so he distanced himself from the frat house antics on and off campus. He was twenty-one when he met Constance.

It was when Brian Meldrew had passed through puberty and adolescence that the spinal cord and nervous system of the absorbed twin showed the first signs of independent development. The second spinal cord had always been apparent but it was only when Brian Meldrew passed into adulthood that they saw the twin stealthily start feeding on Brian Meldrew's emergent maturity and for five days on an eight month and one day and one hour cycle extend the canopy across Brian Meldrew's brain all the time probing for the area where the memories of what he would use his born twin's body to accomplish could be hidden. Five days before Brian Meldrew's twenty-second birthday they saw the red outline invade and totally encapsulate the blue brain.

Brian Meldrew was not aware of the role he was about to play. The twin manipulated and dominated him so completely that he told family and university friends that he was going to take a break from his studies for a few days and hike the moors. He enjoyed hiking alone, so it came as no surprise to anyone when he announced his intention.

Chapter 84

They had come to the diner and both ordered the big breakfast then drank coffee while waiting.

"Some night huh?" from Richard.

"Some night indeed!" from Eleanor.

They smiled at each other across the table at the memory of it.

The breakfasts arrived and Richard commented that just looking at his was causing his arteries to clog then like Eleanor he started to eat with gusto.

After wiping the residue of yoke from two eggs over easy off her plate with a scrap of whole wheat toast Eleanor ate it then sat back with a sighed, "Oh boy, that was good. Great sex certainly works up an appetite, doesn't it?"

Richard forked a last piece of bacon into his mouth, chewed then swallowed before replying with a straight face, "I'll let you know after I've had great sex." Then he yelped, "Ouch," when Eleanor kicked his shin.

"You cheeky sod! You better tell me that was a joke, or you've had your last roll in the hay with me," Eleanor retorted with mock severity.

"You know very well I was joking. It was wonderful," he said reaching for her hand and giving it a squeeze.

Eleanor beamed, "It was wonderful, wasn't it? Just like when my parents were away at Sahar Ganj and we had the place to ourselves."

Before Richard could respond Eleanor held up a hand in a 'be quiet' motion and tipped her head as if listening to, or for, something. "We have to go. We're wanted at Retribution. A cull's imminent and they want you to observe. Put some money on the table and let's go." He threw some bills on the table and Denise was very happy with the tip after deducting for their breakfasts.

The team from Retribution handling the cull were in a bungalow on the outskirts of Halifax, Nova Scotia. Richard was introduced to the team,

Sonya from Retribution who would carry out the cull, Michael from Watchers and Phyllis from Life Files. They all greeted Richard with handshakes and 'pleased to meet you' and with Sonya welcoming him to Retribution section and saying she was sure Eleanor was making him comfortable in Concordat. Eleanor asked Sonya why the cull was being carried out.

"Come with me into the basement," Sonya replied.

It wasn't just a basement—four meters of it was a cell with walls formed by the concrete corners at one end and finished with metal bars running the full width and to the height of the floor joists of the room above. A door sat central in the bars. Inside the cell was a bed secured to metal plates that were themselves secured to the floor and a stainless-steel toilet like the ones used in prisons. Two lights were set into the joists of the floor above and protected with heavy duty wire mesh. Several chains which terminated in leather strapping were anchored into the walls. There was no other furniture in the cell. The floor was painted a glossy white. Two small windows set high in one wall were shuttered with dense foam padding. In the centre of the remaining space was a hospital gurney. It was the type that could be adjusted to all heights and angles and with side rails that could be raised and lowered. Numerous wide Velcro straps hung from the bed frame except for six that were being used to restrain a young woman. They were around wrists, ankles, ribs below her breasts, and at her waist above her hips. The ankle restraints were pulled tight to the side to separate her legs. Her body showed outward signs of physical harm with many bruises and shallow cuts. She appeared to be asleep.

At the foot of the bed stood a naked man. He was smiling and was fondling an erection.

Sonya began to explain, "That's Herman Oliver. He's had this one for just over two years. This is his sixth and he never kept them longer than three years. He got them off the street. Drug addicts selling sex that are easy to spot and prey on with nobody missing them for long. He lured them into his car with the promise of more drugs and a place to sleep after they had sex. He gave them money up front with the promise of more if they performed well. His words. This is a quiet street and after midnight no one's about so it was easy for him to drive into the attached garage without anyone seeing the woman. He had drinks laced with Rohypnol ready to give them. Phyllis, fill in the background please."

"Life Files picked him up when he started to erect the cage. We have an algorithm that looks for things like that in private houses. When he started fitting the restraints then anchoring the bed and installing the toilet, we started doing continuous downloads and when he took his first, we began checking the Life Files of the local police force to see if any missing person's report had been filed, none had. I won't go into the histories of the women he took, suffice to say their lives were pretty bleak. We kept tabs on him over the years and attempted through whispers and innuendo to lead the local police to his door but outside the house he was a model citizen and covered his tracks well. The police had no cause to suspect him or evidence enough for a warrant to search his home. We have now taken matters into our own hands."

Richard turned to Phyllis, "Tell me how he kept this off the police radar for so long."

Chapter 85

An observer named Samuel picked it up and flagged it to Yuri who looked at it and immediately contacted Charlotte telling her, "We have a digression with Meldrew, you should look at it."

"Why would Meldrew decide to start hiking again?" Charlotte asked. "He hasn't done that since university."

"It's not the hiking that bothers me," Yuri responded. "It's the fact that the first kill of the other Meldrew took place when he said he was going on a hiking trip on the Yorkshire moors and this Meldrew is telling his family he plans to hike the same route. The same one he said he intended to do when he was at university."

"Get Jenny and Alan here," Charlotte directed. "We need to know why he's deciding to do this hike, and tell Eleanor what's been found. It might be coincidence but best not to chance it. Oh! And tell Samuel well done for flagging this."

Alan and Jenny found something that concerned them. They asked that the original Meldrew team be brought together again to hear their concerns. Charlotte agreed.

They gathered in one of the rooms set aside at Life Files for cull teams and after the hugs and handshakes of greetings they were told to go verbal then Alan explained.

"Jenny and I asked ourselves why Meldrew would suddenly decide to start hiking again. He hasn't shown any interest in it since his university days, he hasn't done any preparation—not even short walks with a pack. Observers report his decision took his wife and daughter by surprise. The worst-case scenario we came up with — and we fervently hope we're wrong — is that it will soon be eight months since we found how Meldrew was being controlled by his absorbed brother and carried out the cull. We know the killing schedule the other used — eight months plus one day plus one hour — so perhaps he's not going hiking on the moors — suppose he goes to Accrington, or some other place, and starts the killing schedule all over again. Maybe he's going to take over where the other Meldrew left off."

A stunned silence greeted this announcement until Amber exhaled loudly through pursed lips and said, "Oh shit!"

"Oh shit indeed," came from Charlotte. "But let's not jump to conclusions. Meldrew's sudden decision to take up hiking again could be for any number of reasons. Health, exercise, break from work and family, simply wanting some alone time. You hiked a lot in life Richard, and still do here I understand, what attracts you to it?"

"Peace and quiet, solitude, pushing physical boundaries, being in nature. The simple act of *doing it* forces everything else from my mind—it's walking Zen for me, I'm always in the moment."

Yuri spoke up, "It's not the act of hiking that's so strange, there are many good reasons why he would, what is strange is the timing of his decision and the suddenness of it. Samuel flagged it because it occurred so fast. There was no lead up to it. Nothing in his downloads hinted that he was considering going for a hike, he just announced his intention over breakfast. The timing's too coincidental as is his choice of hike."

Although they were all verbal, they knew what was going through the mind of each one there. Did they miss something before or during the cull? Could this Meldrew have been complicit and they missed it? Has the absorbed Meldrew grown back after the cull? Had this Meldrew somehow found the memory cache of the other and enjoyed revisiting the killings just as the other had?

Charlotte broke into their thoughts, "Above all else we must be sure that the absorbed Meldrew has not repropagated — that somehow the cull didn't finish him off — so I want Richard and Eleanor to do a search. We need to know if any of the other Meldrew remains and to what extent. If he does, we need to find a way of getting rid of him once and for all. But, if nothing remains then we will have to follow this Meldrew very closely and see where he takes us."

"What happens if we find that this Meldrew is alone in his intentions?" Eleanor enquired. "Always assuming the hiking trip is a cover for killing. He could, after all, just be going on a hike."

"That decision will lie with the Solons," Charlotte responded. "I don't know if they will treat this Meldrew as a new find and we have to follow protocols if he starts to kill — or will they treat him as an extension of the other and order an immediate cull. The answer might come after Richard and Eleanor have done a search."

Chapter 86

Phyllis handed over to Michael saying Watchers had stayed closest to Oliver.

"At the taking of his first we began to follow him Life Side by body hopping. It allowed us to record how he functioned from a third-party view and did he cause any drawback reactions — like a sense of unease or alarm — among the persons he interacted with on a daily basis. We found none, he got along well with his neighbours and colleagues at work and paid his taxes and mortgage and the myriad other things expected of a law-abiding citizen. Outwardly mister nice guy and that is what helped him in staying hidden from the police for so long. That and the fact he never rushed things. Herman is a very patient man. Look closely at the cell bars, how they are bolted together from smaller sections, those sections match exactly those of the fencing around the property. Oliver just had the manufacturers make more than he needed for outside and assembled the rest to make the cell bars. Nobody thought anything of it when fencing started to turn up and Oliver had a contractor come to install it. The extra pieces were already in the garage. A drill, concrete anchors, nuts and bolts, brackets and hinges and he had the cell bars. He bought a new bed, again something not unusual, and secured the metal frame from his old bed to stanchion brackets and plates that match those holding his fence up. You are getting the picture now, I'm sure. Herman Oliver took great pains not to arouse any suspicion. The toilet he got from a demolition company in New Brunswick and paid cash. It's hooked up to what would have been the toilet outlet and supply already installed for a downstairs bedroom or den bathroom. The gurney came from a dealer in surplus hospital equipment in Quebec, paid for in cash, and when fully lowered and turned on its side fitted into a large SUV that he drove at the time. He took the precaution to remove the front passenger seat to allow extra room. Again, very careful and methodical. Chains and fasteners he picked up at various hardware stores, some here, and some there, and the leather strapping he fashioned from numerous belts he bought at thrift stores and all paid for with cash of course."

Michael paused as they watched Herman Oliver go to a sink beside a washer and drier that stood against the other end wall of the basement. He turned on the mixer tap and ran water into a basin and when he judged the temperature to be satisfactory, he filled the basin and carried it to a table adjacent to the gurney. Liquid soap, face clothes and towels lay on the table. Wetting a cloth Herman Oliver squeezed soap onto it and massaged it until a froth of bubbles covered his hands then he lifted the woman's right foot until it was tight against the restraints and began to wash it. The woman slept on.

Michael took up the story again as Herman Oliver began washing the woman with great care and concentration. "Food was bought at several different places and never large quantities at a time. He always bought two or three frozen dinners amongst the fruits and vegetables he got for himself. Sanitary products didn't raise any eyebrows, lots of men purchase their wives brands these days. He needed to keep the women healthy, so he fed them well until the last six months of their imprisonment. You see that this woman has lost a lot of weight recently by the way her ribs are sticking out. She is very thin, almost emaciated. He would gradually starve them until they were very weak then he would kill them. He would hang them from those hooks you see in the floor joists and exsanguinate them. He saved the blood and disposed of it in small amounts down the washer drain where it mixed with waste water and became much diluted. He would dissect the bodies into small pieces and store them in the freezer you see next to the clothes dryer then dispose of them over time by weighing them down and dropping them into the sea from a boat he owns. The disposal takes about a year and because he only takes a woman every three years, he has never had to rush the disposal. There is even a standby generator to feed power to lights and the freezer if there's a blackout. No deviation from the routine and nothing that aroused any suspicion that would bring the police to the door. Sonya—your turn. Tell Richard about the cull."

"At the moment he starts his ritualised abuse that would ultimately lead to this woman's death I will take her place and she will be isolated at Concordat until after the cull. When he is dead, she will be brought back and will believe she killed him. A scenario has been arranged that she will escape the house and will be found outside by a neighbour who will be fortuitously passing by. Her account of what happened will be very garbled but the police and EMT's will be called. The police will search the house and this room will be found along with albums full of photographs of his previous victims. This woman, who's street name is Tricia, will be judged to have partial retrograde amnesia brought on by the trauma she suffered while imprisoned and sexually abused and will have little memory of the actual killing. She will be taken to hospital and will recover her strength but will be diagnosed to have PTSD which is not unusual in cases involving sexual abuse. She will pick up her life from there."

"How do you intend to kill him?" Richard asked.

Eleanor spoke first, "Best we watch. I have a feeling that Sonya has something special for Herman."

Chapter 87

The months following the cull of Meldrew's absorbed twin were recorded as ones of harmonious married and family life in the household. Synchronous downloads were made of Constance and Amy who after having got over the initial surprise in the changes of their husband and father now accepted this much more loving and involved man. Constance had stayed true to her word and no longer sought sexual gratification outside the home—she was ecstatic with what Meldrew now provided. Amy was pleased her father took more interest in her personal and school activities but not to the point of being too nosey or involved, he kept a nice balance.

Meldrew's work at the hospital and his private practice were going well. He still consulted with various hospitals and had made several trips to oversee delicate operations and had never deviated from the travel plans he told Constance and Amy about. He and Constance now spoke on the phone several times during days he was away. It seemed to the Life File observers that the removal of his absorbed twin had released the authentic Meldrew.

Then came the announcement of the hike.

It was during a Saturday morning breakfast. Brian Meldrew was finishing a spread of marmalade on his toast when he said, "I'm thinking of doing a hiking trip in the moors. It's been years since I did anything that strenuous and it will do me good to get away from work for a few days. You two are welcome to join me if you want," he finished with a chuckle.

Amy was the first to respond, "Oh yeah, that's at the top of my 'must do' list. Tramping across the soggy moors, getting eaten alive by midges and it's sure to rain every day. That sounds lovely and not to mention sleeping in a damp tent or some wreck of hiker's hut. You go for it, Dad—I'll pass."

"Did I detect a note of sarcasm in your response Amy?" he asked with a smile and got 'mm-mm' from around a mouthful of cereal.

When she had swallowed her cereal Amy came and kissed him on the cheek saying, "You picked up on the sarcasm and here I thought I was being very subtle. I'm going to get dressed then off to the pool for training. See you later."

Constance who had gathered her plate, cup and cutlery from the table and had taken them to the dishwasher said as she placed them on the racks, "This is all very sudden. Don't get me wrong I think it's a great idea for you to get away but is this a spur of the moment thing or have you been thinking about it for some time?"

"A week or so. You know it was something I enjoyed when I was at university, so I wonder if it has the same allure. Who knows, I might turn round after the first rainy day and uncomfortable night and rush back here to my comfortable home."

Constance started to collect the other breakfast dishes and said, "Then you should go for it but I'm taking Amy's side. I didn't do it when I was younger and I'm not about to start now. I like my comfort too much. I'll put lotion on your midge bites when you get back."

Meldrew finished his coffee and handed the mug to Constance saying, "I'll have to make arrangements for someone to cover my hospital duties while I'm away and change any private appointments. I was thinking of starting next Saturday. If I can get everything arranged, will you drop me off at my start point and come collect me when I call at the end?"

"Of course. You will need to get hiking boots and a backpack and all sorts of other stuff. What you used at university are long gone," Constance said as she brushed crumbs from the tablecloth.

"No problem. I mentioned my idea to a colleague who does lots of hikes and he's offered his camping gear and backpack. All I need is boots, poles, wet weather gear and a few days' clothes along with some food. There are lots of places to leave the Pennine Way with villages close by so I can get a good meal during the day. How about we shop for boots, rain gear and poles this afternoon?"

"Good idea," Constance answered as she left the kitchen to get dressed. "I need to pick up a few things in town. Two birds with one stone."

Meldrew sat for a few moments before following his wife upstairs. He found her in the bedroom about to fasten the hooks on her bra and she could tell by the finger to his lips and the one pointing to the bathroom that he had thoughts of other than them simply taking a shower. Constance smiled and let the bra fall then removed her panties before following him into the bathroom where he was already naked and very much waiting for her.

They heard Amy thunder down the stairs shouting "Bye," and then the front door slamming.

Constance grabbed his hardness saying, "No need to be quiet now."

Chapter 88

Herman Oliver was somewhat nonplussed by how docile his woman was. (He always referred to them as 'His Woman'). Normally this far into a washing they would be coming round from the Rohypnol and moving as much as the restraints allowed. They were particularly active when he paid special attention to their vaginal area and breasts. He always lingered over those areas while massaging and exploring. He liked to look into their eyes when he touched them in those places. The padded gag fastened over their mouths deadened their entreaties but their eyes spoke volumes. But that wasn't happening with this one this time. His woman remained still and without utterance behind the gag and her eyes said nothing—just stared toward the bright lights above the gurney. It was making him angry this lack of response. He needed her to struggle. He needed her to be terrified of what he was about to do. He needed the look of fear and pleading in her eyes as he murmured softly into her ear about what he was going to do and showed her the implement he would use. It was when she screamed the loudest behind the gag and her eyes bulged from the pain that he would mount her and empty himself into her. His anger overflowed because this was not what he needed — he needed her to be terrified, he needed that power — but she lay still and calm and unblinking so he took a pair of pliers from the table and opening the jaws placed them on a nipple and crooned, "This will make you move."

A fraction of a second before the jaws closed his arm was torn away and the pliers flew from his hand and across the room to hit the wall and fall clattering to the floor. It was a moment of shocked disbelief before Herman Oliver realised that it was not the hand of his woman that was grasping his arm. Herman Oliver tried to pull away but her grip was like an iron band and as he pulled against her he saw that all of her bonds had loosened and hung empty from the gurney. A lightning bolt of pain lit

Herman Oliver's head as the woman's other hand now made into a fist struck his temple with immense force. Herman Oliver passed out.

When Herman Oliver regained consciousness, he was secured to the gurney and the woman that was not his woman was standing beside it. She held a pair of pliers which she opened and placed on one of his nipples— she closed them with great force. Herman Oliver screamed behind the gag and his eyes bulged from the agony. The woman crooned into his ear, "Not nice is it, Herman? And that's just the beginning." Reaching for one of the cords that he had used to hang his victims from in order to exsanguinate them she tied it around the scrotum and very flaccid penis of Herman Oliver and began very slowly to pull it over its pulley. He tried to arch his back to relieve the tension on the cord but she pulled inexorably and ultimately his sack was stretched to point of being torn from his body. Herman Oliver screamed behind the gag and thrashed as much as the bonds allowed — which only made it worse. The woman leant close again, "I cannot inflict all the harm and pain you did Herman Oliver because it would serve no purpose. You are going to die very soon on the floor of this place and would not remember any of it. This is just a taste and the bruise and marks on your balls will disappear but you will feel the pain while you bleed out from a cut to your femoral artery. Tricia — that's her name — will survive." Touching him on the temple Sonya told him, "Now go to sleep Herman Oliver." He did and Sonya moved him from the gurney to the floor and taking a fileting knife from the table she pressed it into the right thigh of Herman Oliver and sliced into his femoral artery. She woke him saying, "There you go Herman Oliver—try to make it out." He did but got only to the foot of the stairs before collapsing and finally bleeding out. His cries for help had gone unheard.

Afterward it happened as Sonya had said it would.

Outside a neighbour who just happened to be passing found a naked and emaciated and much bruised woman on Herman Oliver's front lawn babbling about being kept prisoner in Herman Oliver's house. The neighbour called for an ambulance and the police.

Richard, Eleanor and the others left the basement.

Tricia's story of escape by managing to pull a hand through one of the wrist restraints and undoing the rest while Herman Oliver was upstairs and then stabbing him in the leg was accepted when the photographic records of previous victims was found. Some were eventually identified as missing persons. The only fingerprints found on the filleting knife were those of Herman Oliver and Tricia.

Herman Oliver's neighbours were flabbergasted when news of what had gone on was released. They all said he had been a nice quiet man. Kept himself to himself, took good care of his property and never caused any trouble. The perfect neighbour.

Life Files would continue to observe and download Tricia's life after Herman Oliver.

Chapter 89

Yuri was surprised when Samuel showed her another aberration in Meldrews behaviour. "Take a look at this," he told her. Yuri looked then told Samuel to get Jenny and Alan while she spoke to Charlotte.

When they gathered, they looked again at what had attracted Samuel's attention. Meldrew was seen with one of the nurses at the hospital and they were obviously flirting with one another. Charlotte called a pause and asked Samuel how long the flirting had been going on. Samuel told her that this was the first time Meldrew had responded to it but that the nurse had been the instigator several weeks before. Samuel also said flirting between doctors and nurses was not uncommon and was mostly harmless banter and innuendo although some did lead to extracurricular activities.

"So this is the first time Meldrew has responded with interest to any flirty approaches?" Jenny asked.

"Absolutely," Samuel responded. "He's always laughed them off and maintained a professional relationship with all his co-workers."

Alan ran the Download from Meldrew's arrival at the hospital that day seeking the moment Meldrew started to take an interest in the flirtatious nurse. He found it and it was when Meldrew overheard the nurse telling a colleague that she had put in for some vacation time beginning in two weeks and that she was going to hike part of the Pennine Way. She expected to hike for five days. Later that download while working with the nurse Meldrew asked out of casual general interest what her hobbies were. She told him hiking was her main one and of her plans for the Pennine Way. After taking care of his patient Meldrew offered to buy the nurse a coffee in the canteen before the next patient. She was thrilled to accept. To be seen having coffee with hunky Doctor Meldrew would make her friends so jealous.

"So this is where the hiking idea started," Jenny said. "It wasn't just a random idea he came up with. Samuel, what made you go back to this download?"

"It was the reference to hiking. I was sure it had come up in a Meldrew conversation before he mentioned it to his wife, so I went back and checked and this is what I found. The thing is, since having coffee with the nurse it can be seen that Meldrew gradually withdraws from the flirty games with her and schedules his rounds for times when she is not on duty. I can bring up that download if you want."

"Yes please," came from Yuri. "And the one from the nurse covering the same time period."

It was as Samuel said. Meldrew played the game for a few days but then gradually arranged that his and the nurse's paths seldom crossed. She was disappointed but knew from experience that flirtations and affairs with doctors seldom lasted. They were good for a fling but that was all. She smiled to herself wondering if she would meet someone on her hike that she would want to fuck. Her Life File showed it had happened before.

Yuri squeezed Samuel's shoulder saying, "Good work catching that connection, Samuel. Meldrew does seem to have a plan in mind that involves this nurse and hiking. Charlotte, we need to get Richard to do a search as soon as possible."

Charlotte made the decision, "Get the Meldrew team together and we'll set up for a search."

Chapter 90

After saying goodbye to Sonya, Phyllis and Michael they went to a cabin Richard had used when hiking one of his favourite trails. They arrived just as the sun began to drop below a fringe of trees that stood on a clifftop bordering the Bay of Fundy. They made coffee without speaking and carried it outside to the veranda to sit side by side in Adirondack chairs and drink as the shadows from the trees crept silently toward and finally over the cabin and night settled its wind whisper darkness over them.

They were quiet for a long time before Richard asked, "Are all culls as violent as Herman Oliver's?"

"No. Some are remarkably gentle considering the type of persons we deal with. Sonya felt that Herman Oliver's sentencing and death suited the crimes he had committed," Eleanor responded.

"Doesn't carrying out such sentences have an effect on the Retributionist?"

"After each cull the Retributionist is wiped as are any others directly on scene." Eleanor explained, "All memory of the event is erased and in fact you will not remember anything about Herman Oliver's death when you awaken from a nap you are about to have."

"Nap? I don't need a nap. I'm not in the least bit slee…"

Eleanor handed him a mug when he opened his eyes, "Here… I made you another cup of coffee while you slept."

"Thanks. I must really have needed that… I went out like a light."

Eleanor smiled while dropping into her seat said, "Taking all the stuff in about Concordat and Retribution can tire newcomers out. Feel free to take a rest anytime."

Richard drank and then mused, "I somehow thought things like tiredness and needing sleep wouldn't apply here, what with all the super brain stuff we get to do and see. I was told natural laws did not apply."

Eleanor explained, "They don't unless we want them to and during the initiation and explanation time you are going through we've found it best not to remove all the Life Side patterns immediately. You will feel tired and require sleep for a short period. Just until your body catches up with your enhanced brain power and no longer needs statutory rest periods. Unless of course you want to take a nap or have a good sleep then that will be your choice, not your body's requirement."

Eleanor lifted her feet to rest them on the veranda railing tipped her head back and spoke to the stars, "I still like to fall into a languorous sleep after energetic activity."

"The bunks here don't lend themselves to energetic activity. Too hard, too narrow and not enough room above the top or bottom bunk."

Eleanor placed her coffee mug on the veranda planking and stretched her arms above her head while arching her back and said, "Shame about the bunks but this veranda has lots of space and it's a nice warm night. We can conjure up some nice soft sleeping pads. What do you think? Should we?"

"Oh, we should, we should," Richard answered in his best Gene Wilder impression from *Blazing Saddles*. And they did.

Both slept soundly afterward.

Chapter 91

Yuri contacted the team and had them gather again in one of the rooms set aside for Retribution teams at Life File headquarters. Charlotte, who had been reporting this latest development in the Meldrew case to the Solons, was the last to arrive. There was a lot of chatter as team members greeted one another and caught up on things. Charlotte headed straight to Eleanor and Richard.

"We have the go ahead to continue our surveillance of Meldrew by all means at our disposal and to treat this operation as an extension of the one in which we culled the absorbed twin. They are sanctioning this because we have continued to monitor Meldrew closely with continuous downloads since his twin was culled and because of this they consider the case still open. However, the Solons have put some restrictions on the personnel involved in this part of the operation. Except for us three the others are to be Wiped of all knowledge of the previous operation and all records of that operation have been sealed. Those we keep from our previous team are to think it a brand-new case and approach it without preconceived ideas about Meldrew, he is to be totally new to them. All the team plus Samuel are gathered here and on my request a wiper — Douglas — will come in and clear their minds of anything to do with Meldrew. The Watchers and observers who are presently involved will be wiped and replaced with personnel who have no knowledge of the previous Meldrew case. I have altered the downloads from Meldrew to show psychotic behaviour that our observer programs have picked up and which require investigation. The alterations show Meldrew beginning to feel urges that would bring harm to a nurse and possibly his wife. You will see the altered downloads and get the picture. As before it will have been Samuel that reported what our observer algorithms found. He has already been primed with the altered downloads. Are you clear on how we are to proceed and have I missed anything?"

These directives had been told in a closed tri-loop and to an observer it would seem a catch-up time was going on with much smiling and nodding and some laughter. Eleanor and Richard replied they couldn't think of anything missing.

Charlotte, all business, raised her voice above the chatter and silenced it, "Listen up. You've been called here because observers have found something that we feel needs to be investigated." At that moment the door opened and a man dressed as every inch the business executive entered the room. Charlotte introduced him, "This is Douglas and he is joining our team for this meeting. You can all greet him after I've outlined the case." Douglas gave a slight bow and produced a smile that brought all movement to a halt. Douglas wandered the room touching each person with the exception of Charlotte, Richard and Eleanor on the neck at the base of the skull. Yuri was the final person to be wiped. Douglas reported that all Wipes had been successful. Charlotte thanked him then he left.

As the door clicked shut behind him animation returned with Jenny from analytics and programming raising a hand asking, "What's this new case all about and why such a big team?"

"Samuel, why don't you explain what the algorithms found and what in particular attracted your attention. Bring up an Ether Screen if you need it and everyone go verbal."

All eyes turned to Samuel. "Until recently the Life File of Brian Meldrew has been pretty much same old same old. Aged fort-six a respected surgeon, married with one child and a family life that has had the usual ups and downs but overall has been happy and loving. Nothing about his life caused any alarms until a sudden switch in his behaviour. Ether Screen please. In this still, taken from third-party viewpoint, you see Meldrew sitting at a table in a hospital cafeteria beside a nurse. Nothing unusual in that, he's had coffee with nurses many times before, but watch what happens now."

The picture began to move and it became obvious that Meldrew and the nurse were flirting and a quick glimpse of him squeezing her thigh was caught and the picture froze again with Meldrew and the nurse smiling at each other.

"That had never happened before," Samuel pointed out. "And Meldrew has always shrugged off any advances with good humour and has always maintained strictly professional relationships with other doctors and nursing staff. This change in behaviour was flagged by the algorithm and prompted me to go back and look closely for a trigger point — for something that would have caused it — because it was so far out of character for Meldrew. I'm going to run what I believe to be the trigger moment."

From his Life File and through his senses Meldrew was observed attending to a patient and the nurse from the cafeteria could be heard telling a colleague she was taking vacation days to go hiking on the Pennine Way. When the nurse moved beside Meldrew to finish dressing an incision he had just inspected Meldrew asked conversationally if hiking was her hobby. She responded, "Yes," that she loved being outdoors. He then asked casually when she was leaving and from where. She answered the Monday after next for five days starting at Horton in Ribblesdale and hoping to make Greenhead before returning home on Friday. As if making small talk he let it drop that he too hiked and found it relieved the stress of long hours of work. The nurse said he looked the type who hiked being slim and obviously fit and perhaps they would meet on the trail someday. He responded that perhaps they would. The record stopped there.

"It was following this exchange that with the scene from the cafeteria the flirting started," Samuel said shutting the Ether Screen off.

Charlotte thanked Samuel for catching the anomaly in Meldrews behaviour before opening the gathering to questions and remarks.

Alan was first. "What's so special about this guy getting a little flirty? Sure, it's out of character from what's in his Life File right now but maybe it's just the start of a midlife crisis. Happens all the time."

Ted from Watchers was the next, "Why are Eleanor and Richard here at this stage? Much as it's great to see them we don't even know yet if Retribution needs to be involved."

Charlotte nodded to Yuri who spoke up, "When our observer algorithm flagged the change in Meldrew's behaviour and Samuel brought it to my attention, I gave it to Life File special cases for ultra-close scrutiny and they have found and recorded several other deviations. He has begun to search out hard core pornography and particularly that involving sadomasochism. His sexual appetite his increased markedly and has become more aggressive to the point where his wife — Constance — is becoming concerned that he will cause her physical harm. She has never seen this side of her husband before... he has always been a gentle and considerate lover. I contacted Charlotte with our findings and she has decided that a search needs to take place. Charlotte."

"Yuri was right to come to me. The changes in Meldrew and the speed at which they are escalating require that we search to find an answer. We need to know what is driving his behaviour. You are all here at the outset of our investigation to get the background for our reasoning. This might be nothing more than a passing aberration and you will not be involved after the search but if what has been recorded so far is just the tip of the iceberg then more units will need to be drawn in. That's why people from all units, including Retribution are here. Also, and this is important, Eleanor and Richard will do the search and if what they find could ultimately lead to a cull they will be prepared. This is a preparatory meeting so with the exception of Jenny and Alan, who will be needed for the search, the rest of you can return to your regular duties and I'll call on you if necessary. Thank you."

Ted was overheard to say to Victoria on their way out, "If Charlotte is involved then there is definitely something hinky going on."

Jenny raised questioning eyebrows at Richard who answered with a shrug that said, "I've no idea." Her face showed scepticism about his response.

Chapter 92

Over morning coffee Eleanor suggested they walk out from the cabin saying she could complete Richard's induction into Retribution by explaining about the regulations governing the conduct of those chosen to join Concordat.

They suitably outfitted themselves for the eighteen-kilometre hike out and stepped onto the trail leading to Red Rocks. Three strides in Eleanor began to speak.

"Throughout your transition into Concordat you have had a minder. Your minder has always had control over your thoughts and actions. I am your minder at this time. You have never had full freedom to act as you might have wanted. It is not unusual for those in transition to try to take advantage of the opportunities their activated brain brings. Some try to take advantage by acting without restraint. They become like a child in a candy store wanting to try everything. The increased sensory feedback our awakened brains provide can even overwhelm some of those who seemed promising in Life File. Those who lack control in all areas are disqualified during transition and returned to their body while some who only lack it in a certain area but have promise otherwise are adjusted to quell their specific desire or desires and we tone down the sensory feedback. You have not shown any signs of such behaviour so all those who have been your minder during transition recommend that once I've explained the regulations you will no longer have one." Eleanor reached for her water bottle and took a drink before continuing.

"Soon after you entered transition it became obvious to us that you were aware that all about you and who you met and what was happening were all creations of Concordat. That I am here is a creation of Concordat as was our love making last night. We two, this trail, these trees, that water and all our sensory responses, indeed everything in and around us is a Concordat fabrication. Our sensory world with its sight and sound and smell and touch and taste ends at the extent of our vision. All beyond that which we can see is dark emptiness. This created world copies that which exists in your Life File. The time we shared last night was created from the memories of similar times we spent together but with the heightened sensory responses our brains now afford. I'm telling you this because Concordat puts restrictions on what choices we make. Each of us brought our own world with us and we refined it during the transition process. The refinement came from retaining or disposing of memories and your world now consists of the memories you retained and I am only here in it because you allowed it. We — all those in Concordat — cannot enter another person's world without a specific invitation to do so or unless unlimited access has been granted. I advise that you keep unlimited access to a minimum. As you have seen, the various sections of Concordat have headquarters which are open to all but courtesy dictates that the section head be contacted and told of your arrival rather than just turning up. Many of the manners and niceties of the various races on Earth have been adopted by the Concordat Council responsible for the planet." Again Eleanor paused to drink then continued.

"Now please invite Sonya here and ask her to explain how a cull is decided upon and how they are generally organised. I've given her a heads-up to expect your call so go ahead and tele request she come join us."

He did and immediately spotted Sonya walking toward them waving and shouting, "Hi."

When she reached them, Sonya suggested that as there were three of them it would be better to sit somewhere while she told him about culls. They chose a maple deadfall just off the trail.

"A cull can only be sanctioned by a Concordat Council. Two Solons — the lawgivers of Concordat — and the Retribution section head of each Earth region not involved in the proposed Cull form the council. The section head, or team leader, proposing the cull must make the case that every effort has been made and failed and every avenue explored and found ineffective in bringing the perpetrator or perpetrators to justice by law enforcement means covering the section involved. If it cannot be proved that all means have been exhausted, then the council will not authorise a cull. The only records of previous culls are kept by the Solons so each new application is judged on its own merits by the other section heads. Eleanor will have told you that Retributionists and cull team members are wiped after each cull case is closed. However, if the Solons consider a lawful effort has been overlooked, they will deny the cull and send the section requesting it back to review the case with some hinted direction as to what avenue to follow. Bottom line... every lawful means has to be exhausted before a cull happens." Sonya requested Eleanor's water bottle and took a drink. "Prior to a cull it is often necessary for members from Retribution and other units such as Watchers and Life Files to go Life Side. This means taking the form you have chosen — as you look now — and operating among the population. You will be interacted with as a member of their society but once out of their sensory area they will forget you. You become a literal figment of their imagination. Experiences you have and things you learn while moving about Life Side will remain with you for future application — it is only the time immediately before and the physical act of the cull itself that is wiped. Retributionists are monitored before, during and after a cull to judge if they are secreting away all or parts of the physical act to review and perhaps enjoy as memory. If you are found to have any residual memory of a cull you will be fully wiped and assigned as a new intake to some other section. It does happen but very seldom, we screen very thoroughly. The majority of Life Filers considered for Retribution are rejected during transition. Congratulations on making it through Richard." Sonya turned towards Eleanor and said, "That about coverers it. Anything important I've missed?"

Eleanor shook her head, "No, you've covered it well. He's already been on the lead up to one cull and at the actual event on another — they are already in his Solon record — and when we leave here he will become involved in another that is in the planning stages. Thank you, Sonya, you've been a great help."

They all stood and hugged 'goodbyes' then Sonya started down the trail in the direction Eleanor and Richard had come. They watched her until she came to a bend in the trail and she waved back to them before disappearing.

Chapter 93

As far as Jenny and Alan were concerned, they were there to observe, record and report on a search designed to uncover why this Meldrew fellow whose Life File downloads had, until recently, showed him to be a responsible family man and considerate and gentle lover had very suddenly changed to one who searched out S and M porn and had begun to cause his wife concerns about the force and hurt he was beginning to inflict upon her during sex. His appetite had changed from gentle role playing and exploration to one of rough restraint and forceful penetration that was at times bordering on rape.

Eleanor and Richard were aware that the analysts thought the use of two Retributionists for what to them appeared to be a routine insertion and search was exceptional. Consideration had been given to letting Jenny and Alan retain information of the previous Meldrew case but the Solons had been definite in their instructions that they were to be wiped and have no knowledge of Meldrew's previous history.

Charlotte told them to meet at Meldrew's home at eleven that night when Meldrew would be put into a deep dreamless sleep and the insertion would take place. Eleanor would prepare Meldrew and the Analysts would record the search which this time would involve two Retributionists which was a departure from the norm. Following the search they would all gather at an analytics and programming search pod to review and give feedback on what had been found. The analysts were told to prepare a secure pod space for the review—a pod restricted to only those directly involved with the search. Another departure from the norm. Charlotte forestalled any questions from Jenny and Allan by telling them that the search results would dictate what action, if any, was needed. Charlotte said she realised it was unusual for a search be carried out under such conditions but what was found would have a direct impact on the case going forward and she told Jenny and Allan to be patient until they all saw what the search revealed.

They assembled at Meldrew's bedside at the appointed hour. The analysts reported that a pod had been prepared and made secure for the review. Shortly after eleven Eleanor judged Meldrew to be sufficiently asleep for her to sync with him and take him deep into a dreamless state. A slight twitch of Meldrew's head and a brief movement beneath the eyelids was the only sign that Eleanor had successfully synced and after a few seconds she told Richard he could join her. There was no reaction from Meldrew when Richard joined Eleanor.

Transmitting to the analysts Eleanor asked, "All ready to record Alan, Jenny?"

"Yes, ready to go," Alan responded.

"Okay. This is what I want you to do. Alan, you record me and Jenny, you record Richard. We will each start in different hemispheres and when we have completed our searches we will then cross over and do another search. We want to confirm that what one finds in each hemisphere is confirmed by the other. Keep the recordings from Richard and me entirely separate until we are in the Pod. I'm starting in the left hemisphere Alan then Richard and I will confirm our first searches are complete before we change hemispheres and resume. Please do not combine, or in any way allow the hemisphere readings to overlap. All clear on that?"

Jenny answered, "Yes. I'll stay with you Eleanor and Alan with Richard. We'll make sure no overlap occurs."

"Good. Let's get started Richard."

They were not far into the searches when Alan and Jenny became aware that it was a much more meticulous insertion and search than any they had been involved with before. The Retributionists were taking pains to explore every area and connection within Meldrews brain with care and precision and they were doing it as if looking for something in particular. As analysts they knew when certain areas were being looked at with special interest.

There was no communication between Eleanor and Richard until Eleanor communicated she had reached the end of her left hemisphere search and Richard replied he was about to complete his search of the right.

"Everything okay with the recordings so far?" Eleanor asked the Analysts.

"Fine," Alan responded.

"Richard and I will change hemispheres now."

The same meticulous care was taken with the second searches of each hemisphere and the analysts noticed that areas that had attracted special attention on the first search attracted the same attention on the second. Alan and Jenny were aware that areas containing long-term and episodic memory came in for close scrutiny as did the junction of the spinal cord to the brain proper. Of special interest to the analysts was that Eleanor and Richard each travelled the length of the spinal column separately and inspecting it closely. Three particular areas were given specific attention by both.

Richard and Eleanor conferred when their inspection of the spinal column was complete.

Eleanor queried, "Do you think we missed anything of importance?"

"No. We got everything there is to get. The analysis will show that." Richard responded.

"Even so I'm interested to see what Alan and Jenny get from the search."

"Yeah, me too. Let's go find out. Jenny, Alan, bring us out now please. We want to go verbal when we un-sync."

"Copy that, guys," came from Jenny.

Alan chimed in, "Withdrawal in three, two, one… and you're out. Welcome back."

Chapter 94

They walked on in silence for some time after Sonya left them until the trail led them through an old growth maple forest where there was space enough to walk side by side. Eleanor remarked, "This is gorgeous. Thank you for bringing me here. I'm beginning to understand the attraction it has for you. So peaceful, so perfect in its haphazardness. No landscaping involved yet everything exactly where it needs to be. Wonderful."

Richard smiled and said, "It is lovely but we must come back in the fall when the leaves turn, the colours are amazing. I've sat here in the fall and I swear I could hear the trees talking to one another as they prepared for their winter hibernation and dropped crimson and gold leaves. A magic time."

Leaving the maples, they dropped down a precipitous zigzag path that in places was only the width of a hiking boot until they reached a brook that fell in cascade steps to the beach and from there by bridge and wooden stairways followed the last of the trail to the eastern shore of the Bay of Fundy. A stroll southward along the beach brought them to a sandstone outcropping aptly named Red Rocks and they sat with backs against sun warmed rock looking out across wind rippled water and feeling the westering sun on their faces as the day drew to a close.

Richard scooped a handful of sand and then tilted his palm to let it trickle back into the depression left by his excavation. Watching the sand fall he said quietly, "tell me everything about Concordat. There has to be more to its remit than simply ridding this planet of bad people."

Eleanor hugged her knees to her chest then wiggled her backside more comfortably into the sand and began, "Concordat are the custodians of all planets that have life forms or have the necessary ingredients for life to evolve. Concordat is the collective name of a council of Solons who oversee the evolutionary progress of life forms on this and other planets. Concordat may or may not be the title used in other galaxies or on other planets. Few of us have contact with the Solons... mainly section and team leaders although none have actually seen them. They communicate by mind-speak. Concordats work, our work here, is to rid the planet of undesirables that if left unchecked would pollute the evolutionary gene pool beyond the confines placed on it by the Solons. The Solons have put certain bounds of behaviour on all sentient beings and because humans are at the top of the evolutionary ladder on this particular planet, they have been given the task of looking after the evolutionary and ecological paths the planet takes. The fate of this planet is in the hands of humankind." She paused then looked at him and said, "Go ahead, say what's on your mind."

"From what I've seen and learnt since entering Concordat this whole planet is a shitshow. Surely Concordat cannot be blind to what is happening. It seems the more the place moves ahead technologically the further behind it falls in humanitarian terms. Taking a few bad fish out of the gene pool won't alter that. That isn't even scratching the surface of all the bad things going on. It's like picking crap from a septic tank one turd at a time while toilets are still being emptied into it." He fell silent then picking up a beach stone he threw it with force into the water.

Eleanor understood, she had experienced the same emotions and frustrations. "Do you think the Solons are not aware of exactly what you just expressed? Do you think they should bring all their powers down on the heads of those you saw in the white space and wipe them out… to clear humankind of all those who cause harm? Is that what you would do?"

"I don't know. I just know that there are a massive number of humans doing harm to other humans in every way imaginable. If a mass cull is out of the question, why not alter the genetic programming and eliminate the gene that makes people want to do harm to others?"

"I want to ask Isabel to join us and explain why that doesn't happen. She is one of the few of us that is in direct contact with the Solons. She will do a better job of explaining than I can. Do you mind?"

"No, not at all but we can go to her if she prefers."

"This will do fine," came from Isabel as she rounded the rock they sat against. "I love beaches. I've brought a canvas chair with me. No, please don't get up, you look far too comfortable."

Isabel was dressed for the beach. Dark-blue knee length shorts, white tee shirt under unbuttoned white cotton blouse with sandals on her feet. Her toenails were the same colour as her fingernails. Bright purple to match her glasses.

After unfolding the canvas chair and getting settled she sighed contentedly and looked out over the water. "Such a beautiful sunset. Thank you for inviting me."

Chapter 95

Jenny and Alan exchanged a glance that between colleagues who are also close friends spoke volumes. Alan looked first at Eleanor then at Richard and Charlotte. "Okay, just what is going on here? We are not your wet behind the ears just arrived in Concordat analysts. We… and this is said with all due modesty… are the best at what we do and the search of this guy has been off from the start. Any analysis section intern could have done the job so why are three of Concordats top people so interested? You know something that Jenny and I don't. Let's face it… two Retributionists doing a neuron search on someone who's only oddball behaviour seems to be an escalating attraction to rough sex. There has to be more to it." Alan paused before asking, "Do you have anything to add Jenny?"

Jenny nodded then said, "Are you thinking of culling him because of the sex thing even before it has reached a level that will cause continual harm to his wife or others? That doesn't make sense and doesn't fit Concordat's risk boundary protocols. We haven't even been told what we should be looking for, or for that matter what you both were searching for. How can we make an analysis without some pointers as to what to look for? And, on top of that why are you here Charlotte? You manage projects and we don't see any team assembled. Somethings rotten in the State of Meldrew."

Charlotte looked at the Ether Screen that still showed Meldrew and his wife soundly asleep and tersely told the analysts, "Put your questions and suspicions aside and just do your jobs. I want you to nano-slice everything that Eleanor and Richard saw in there. You will be separated while you do this and only come together when we all gather to review your findings. You will be sequestered in places of Eleanor's and Richards choosing and have contact only with them. They will provide any resources you need." Turning from the Ether Screen she looked at the two analysts and asked, "Have I made myself clear?"

Jenny mumbled, "Sure." Alan cleared his throat before managing, "Yes." Both were obviously surprised at the forceful way Charlotte had spoken.

"Good. I'll go now. Richard and Eleanor will let me know when you have done your reviews and analysis." Nodding to the Retributionists Charlotte left.

The analysts were about to explode into criticism about the way Charlotte had spoken to them. It was apparent that their feelings had been hurt. Eleanor raised a hand to forestall them. "Don't take it personally. That's just the way she is when she has the bit between her teeth. She knows you are the best and that's why you're here. Charlotte can be very forthright in her approaches and doesn't seem to understand why her words and manner can seem somewhat waspish at times. You'll have to live with that but be assured that like you she is the best at what she does. You'll come to see that."

The righteous indignation drained from Jenny and Alan with Jenny saying, "Okay, but she could do with having her interpersonal skills worked on."

"This is how we are going to do this," came from Richard. "We have four records of the search. Each of you recorded both of us doing separate searches in both hemispheres and down the spinal cord. Jenny you will take Alan's records first and he yours and when you are convinced you have nothing more to get from them you will transfer them back and scrutinise your own recordings. You will be on sync lockdown and unable to communicate with each other throughout the review process. Take as much time as you need. Be your usual very thorough selves. Jenny, you will come with me, Alan you with Eleanor. All clear?"

Affirmative, "Yes," from both analysts.

Eleanor smiled warmly at the analysts, "We have purposely not told you anything about Meldrew's case and what led to this particular neuron search because we want you to have an open mind with no preconceived ideas about what you might find. We're not even sure there is anything to find."

Richard took Jenny to his cabin on the beach and Alan went with Eleanor to her apartment in Kolkata.

Chapter 96

Isabel had a small canvas cooler bag with her which she opened once she was settled in her chair and offered them each a bottle of iced tea which they accepted gratefully. Isabel took a drink then recapped the bottle and placed it back in the cooler. Kicking off her sandals she wiggled her toes into the warm sand and started to talk.

"It took numerous attempts to evolve a life form on this planet that had sufficient mental capability combined with the required manual dexterity to enable it through the process of natural selection to rise and become the dominant species. Throughout that evolutionary journey the original DNA markers of what are now called Homo sapiens has remained constant. But nonprogrammed abnormalities that cause the behaviour of certain persons to diverge from the norm have also appeared as the evolutionary ladder has been climbed. This was allowed to occur. It was considered necessary in order that the causes would be investigated and advances in medical and behavioural sciences would be made. The recent — in cosmological time — finding of the DNA double helix and even more recent sequencing attest to that. In some cases, these DNA markers are so radical they produce the sorts of persons you saw in the white space. These abnormalities are now considered part of the evolutionary cycle although the arguments over whether nature or nurture has most impact continues. It was never intended to create a utopia where all was perfect. Humans have to learn for themselves because if they don't, they will become extinct. Such extinctions have happened many times across many galaxies."

Isabel reached into the cooler bag for her iced tea and drank before continuing. "Now to your question Richard of 'why don't we just cull all the bad people'. In response let me ask you a question. Assuming that no bad person's DNA was allowed to develop, then at what point would you have stopped the evolutionary climb? If you can answer my question, you will have also answered your own. Take all the time you need."

Removing her spectacles, she closed her eyes and let the last of the setting sun's rays fall directly on her face. Eleanor sat relaxed with her back against the rocks.

It wasn't until all light had been swallowed by the horizon and the stars had made their appearance that Richard spoke. Isabel and Eleanor had remained still and silent throughout.

"Evolution needs rogue DNA in order for the species to evolve. A utopian society can never be achieved. How would Utopia be defined if there was nothing, no benchmark, against which to measure it. There has to be evil in order to define good. Good and bad have to exist in order to achieve movement. A utopian society would have to spring fully formed into existence without any knowledge of good or bad. It would just *be*."

Isabel stood and stretched with Eleanor following suit. "Let's take a walk along the beach. It's such a lovely night," Isabel said as she slipped into her sandals.

The moons track of reflected brilliance guided them as they walked along the shoreline. "There you have it Richard. The great contradiction or paradox if you like. Bad is needed for good to be apparent and vice versa. Power and wealth are the primary drivers that make people do bad things. Every person has the immorality gene in their DNA. Power and wealth Richard, Earth's population are slaves to it or bound by it. You were, I was, Eleanor was. Power and wealth are the carrots at the end of the stick that drives humankind. Power is the most potent driver and true selflessness as measured by perceived good done doesn't exist. Rewards are always expected from any act of charity or largesse. There is no such thing as a selfless act. Some benefit, either internal or external, must accrue to the giver otherwise the act would not take place. Power corrupts those who wield it and those who benefit from it no matter how far removed. Persons who succeed in business are as much sociopaths as those who kill. In order to succeed they have to be. The difference lies in humankind's perception. For example, business success is perceived as good, or at least tolerable, whereas causing physical and/or mental harm including murder is considered bad. Both require the same single-minded approach and both bring power either through wealth or dominance over the victim before, during and after the act. We pick and choose because up to now human evolution is dictating those we can act against. And we can only do that within the confines of Concordat protocols and directives. You are already aware of what those are."

Isabel stopped and turned to look out across the water to where lights on the New Brunswick coast could be seen.

Quietly she said, "I'm sure you had already understood or at least surmised the reasoning's when you thought about and considered your own question Richard. Concordat has to draw lines somewhere otherwise most of this planet's politicians, dictators and business persons would have to be culled."

Richard stooped to pick up a stone and threw it with all the strength he had into the night and out into the bay. It could not be seen hitting the water but the sound of it being swallowed by it carried back to them and when it faded away he said, I see. So we draw the line at sex offenders, killers, abusers and wrongdoers of all stripes and assuming they don't drive themselves to extinction before it happens we allow the rest to evolve into a more caring and inclusive humanity." "

Isabel squeezed his shoulder and murmured, "It's more complicated than that, but you're starting to get it."

Chapter 97

Alan was the first to announce his analysis was complete followed soon after by Jenny. Eleanor told Charlotte and she told the four of them to come to her cabin.

Refreshments were laid out on the dining table when they arrived with Charlotte indicating with a sweep of the arm that they should help themselves. Drinks and finger food were chosen and taken to the coffee table around which the chesterfield and easy chairs had been placed.

Charlotte waited long enough for some drink and food to be taken before telling them to go verbal and then asking the analysts, "What have you got for us? What did you find? Please keep it brief and simple enough for me to understand."

Alan took the lead. "My take is this. Meldrew's recent behaviour — the rough sex, hard core porn and flirting — is linked to memories of events that are not showing up as part of his Life File. I think these memories, wherever he's keeping them, are triggering his change in behaviour. His aggressive sexual behaviour has been escalating since the first time he became aware of the memories. However, I was unable to find where these trigger memories are being stored or get a clear picture of their content. His recent memories with sexual content overlay the stored ones. That's it." He had leaned forward to present his findings and he now sat back and Jenny gave hers.

"I agree with what Alan found. I reached the same conclusions. Saw the same things. What I'm not sure about is whether the hidden memory recall triggers the aggressive sexual behaviour or the other way round and the present behaviour triggers the hidden memories. Two other things need answers. First, how long have these memories been there? Second, why is there a broken shadow of a second spinal cord visible? It's hardly noticeable but it's definitely there." Jenny was surprised at the way the relaxed but attentive attitudes of Charlotte, Eleanor and Richard changed when she spoke these last words.

In unison they hitched forward in their seats and Richard said, "tell us more about the spinal cord shadow. Every detail."

Jenny sipped at her cola first. Her mouth had gone dry because she realised what she was about to tell them could be of great importance and she needed to collect her thoughts. "I saw the same things Alan did when I examined the brain and it's clear we arrived at the same conclusions and have the same uncertainties about the triggers. That aside, I couldn't help but notice the particular attention Eleanor and Richard paid to the spinal column and cord during their insertion. Why such attention? That wasn't usual. I was intrigued so I decided to inspect the spinal column more closely. I saw nothing unusual under our normal viewing programs, so I altered the code to give me hyper magnification. That's when it became apparent. A faint outline of what I am convinced are the vestiges of a second spinal cord. This is a first for me."

Eleanor spoke up, "Did it seem functional?"

"Do you mean was it carrying any messages to or from his brain?"

"Yes."

"No. It was inactive."

"Is there anything else you can add? Either of you," came from Richard.

The analysts glanced at each other and answered in chorus, "No."

Charlotte looked hard at the two analysts before saying, "Maybe you have nothing to add to your analytical review but there is something else you want to say so go ahead and say it."

Giving Jenny's hand a squeeze Alan spoke up. "What are you not telling us about this Meldrew fellow? You can separate us to do our analysis but the results with regards to his mind are identical. Jenny finding the vestiges of a dead second spinal cord was what really caught your attention. But this is the strange part about this whole thing. We already have a protocol and procedure for catching and dealing with hidden memory caches. It's Jenny's program that picks them out. So the question is why didn't Life Files just neutralise that part of Meldrew's retained memory? Why the flag telling the observer to contact Yuri who brought it to Charlotte and Retribution. Bit over the top for a routine hidden cache find, isn't it?"

Speaking directly to Richard and Eleanor, "We love you like brother and sister but it's usually pretty scary when Retribution gets involved and it usually doesn't happen unless the higher ups have given their okay. In order for Jenny and me to do our jobs properly and carry our analysis forward we need to know what's behind all this secrecy. Are you going to tell us or not?"

Chapter 98

The three of them walked in silence back to Red Rocks enjoying the quiet of the night.

Isabel kissed Eleanor and Richard on the cheek before folding up her chair and picking up the cooler bag along with the empty iced tea bottles and with a hushed "Goodbye," she walked out of their sight around the side of the rocks.

"Where to now?" Richard asked.

"Isabel suggested a Life File we've been keeping tabs on and in which we will have to intervene if the forces of law and order don't make a move soon. She thinks it might be a good case to get your feet wet. Let's go take a look at Life Files. I've told Yuri we're coming."

Yuri greeted them at the door. The niceties were exchanged and she guided them to one of the rooms provided for teams discussing the possibility of a cull or the actual planning of the event.

Barry, the team leader greeted Eleanor with an extravagant hug and kisses to both cheeks. Holding her at arm's length he pronounced, "As beautiful as ever. So nice to see you again. When was the last time?"

"It was the Dallas paedophile case and thank you for the compliment. You're looking pretty good yourself. Barry, this is Richard. He's new to Retribution and we'd like to sit in on your case so he can see how the decision to cull or not is made. If that's okay with you."

Barry stepped forward to grasp Richard's hand and pump it vigorously up and down saying, "Of course. The word has gone around about your new colleague. Welcome and pleasure to meet you, Richard. You're in good hands with Eleanor." Turning to the assembled team who had been watching with interest Barry theatrically spread his arms and pronounced, "Team, meet Richard—Richard, meet the team. Names can be exchanged as you meet each individual. Eleanor, how do you want to play this? Get fully involved or side-lines and observe?"

"Side-lines and observe. How far into the set-up are you?"

"Prelims. We're about to go over the subject's Life File and get feedback from all involved then if after a more in depth review a consensus to cull is arrived at I'll present it to the Solons and section heads and get the go-ahead or be told to explore more law enforcement avenues. You know the drill but this will be new to Richard, so we'll explain fully as we go along." Turning to the others in the room, "Got that folks. Give Richard as much detail as you can, all the whys and wherefores. Remember these are prelims so don't overdo the technical jargon stuff. Thanks. Right let's start with Life Files. Bring forth the Ether Screen!'

Eleanor whispered in Richard's ear, "Barry was a Thespian, mostly television. Never at the top of the profession but sought after for supporting roles. He lapses into dramatic prose and posturing at times but don't be fooled by it—he's one of the best in Retribution."

All eyes were on the Ether Screen. It showed a revolving three-dimensional image of a male Caucasian head that passed through several stages of ageing and appearance. After a number of transitions the head stopped revolving and showed the oldest iteration. Barry allowed a few moments for those in the room to absorb the image then asked Caitlynn from Life Files to give background. "No need to go back to childhood, school and the like. Just the years where he's been a bad boy."

"This is John Jones, likes to be called JJ. Age thirty-six. Independent trucker for sixteen years. Uses brokers to find him loads. More or less lives in his truck and motels. Closest thing he has to a home is his mother's place in Alabama. Mother provided down payment for his first rig, He's on his third now. Travels all over the United States and Canada. His trailer is a reefer type so he can carry frozen or chilled cargo when necessary. He's made a decent living and has a good reputation for punctuality and cargo care. Never been in trouble with the law. Keeps his log sheets up-to-date and truck well maintained. Never exceeds the allowable driving hours. His credit record is good and has never missed a payment on his tractor or trailer. Nobody is trying to track him down for any form of delinquency or misdemeanour. He's single. Never had a steady companion of any sex. Has availed himself of prostitutes at truck stops on rare occasions but the outcomes were unsatisfactory for him. Erection troubles. Known to other truckers but not friends with any. Drinks very little and doesn't smoke or do drugs. He's kept very much under the radar. Presently he's in Calgary, Alberta unloading vegetables from California then he's due to head back south empty unless his broker can get him a load to the States or somewhere else in Canada. So there you have John Jones. Quiet, unassuming, keeps his nose clean, never been in any trouble. Unremarkable and mostly unmemorable. Not someone who sticks in anybody's mind. Never in one place for very long. That's it for me."

"Thanks Caitlynn. Now over to Stanley from observers. What has JJ been up to that warrants the possibility of a cull? Again, keep it relevant. No need for a pre naughtiness biography."

A map of Canada and the United States appeared on the Ether Screen with markers at places on numerous States and Provinces. Stanley moved to stand in front of it. "The whole of North America has been his killing ground. Women frequenting truck stops his prey. Started age twenty-one when he got his first truck. Two or three on average a year. Mostly in the States. Needs the killing deed in order to get an erection. Knocks them unconscious using a lead weight wrapped in a sock. Usually one blow sufficient, two when necessary. Anchor points around the bunk in his sleeper cab keep them secure and gagged. Enters them at the same time he begins to strangle them. Their movements prior to death cause him to orgasm. Post-mortem he enters them anally. Exhibits remorse immediately following death which changes to hatred of his victims for not being able to bring him to an erection through normal sex. He blames them. Thinks of them as whores who don't deserve any better than to have him penetrate their anus. I've sanitised his thoughts for the sake of this presentation, the originals are in his Life File along with his memories of the events. We presently have live time observers in place." Stanley cleared the map from the Ether Screen and sat down.

Barry rubbed his hands together saying, "Thank you Stanley. Now let's hear from analytics and programming. Same thing Marilyn, keep it short. Just from when he started. Nothing about the neuron search."

"Our protocols and procedures programs flagged each event from the first. Jones is highly intelligent and methodical. Each victim has been transported from the event site in an insulated compartment built for the purpose in his reefer trailer. It has refrigerant coils separate to those for the main trailer area to retard decomposition. Disposal is always several hundred kilometres from the kill site. The methodology is always the same but items used to strangle vary. The age range of the victims is wide. All victims are Caucasian and of various sizes. He never mutilates or marks the bodies in any way. Those that have been found, which are in the minority, are naked and without any form of identification. Some, however, have been found in police records from fingerprints. No DNA transference has ever been found. From lubricant residue found condoms have been used during penetration. We know the kill sites but because of the distances between them and the disposal sites the police have no way of connecting one with the other. Many jurisdictional boundaries are crossed and although information may be posted there is nothing that would make one particular kill site connect with a particular disposal site. Finally, most of the girls and women were transients who turned tricks for lifts and some who were known to frequent certain truck stops but caused little enquiry when they stopped hanging around."

"Thank you, Marilyn. Now to James who carried out the neuron search."

Chapter 99

Charlotte went to the kitchen area where she started to fill the percolator asking "Anyone for coffee or tea? I'm going to have coffee and I can boil the kettle."

Eleanor, Richard and Alan asked for coffee with Jenny requesting tea. The analysts were obviously exasperated at what they saw as a delaying tactic on Charlotte's part. If Charlotte noticed their irritation, it seemed not to bother her.

It was only when she brought the coffees, tea, milk and sugar on a tray to the others that she replied to Alan's question.

"Solons were listening to your analysis, conclusions and uncertainties and they spoke to me while I was preparing this coffee and tea. It was a delaying tactic for which they apologies. You are to be told why so much interest is being shown over what appears to be the simple job of neutralising a hidden memory cache. Doing that would take care of the action or reaction question of the triggers and we'd observe what happened after that. The usual normal Life File stuff with Yuri keeping a watching brief. I'm going to hand over to Eleanor and Richard who will explain why all the secrecy."

A glance between them and a nod from Richard indicated Eleanor should begin.

"We keep this closed loop and verbal. Nothing goes beyond us five until Solons give the okay. This is the abridged version. Recently, by Earth time, there were two Meldrews inhabiting the one body. One is the surgeon you see in the Life File the other was a serial killer who took over surgeon Meldrew's body and mind to carry out the killings and then retreated back into it after the deeds. He killed thirty-six over a twenty-four-year period. It was pure good fortune that led us to find the killer Meldrew. It was the single constant program Jenny wrote and which is now part of our policies and procedures that led us to him and through a neuron search to the evidence of a second spinal cord. It took a Life Side operation to force killer Meldrew into the open and the opportunity to sever the second spinal cord by which he controlled surgeon Meldrew. Surgeon Meldrew was returned to his family and exhibited no after effects from the cutting of the second spinal card. That is until recently. Changes began to occur a few weeks ago as you saw when we held the team gathering. The aggressive sexual behaviour that is escalating and the flirting and the sudden decision to start hiking again are part of those changes. To we three that pointed to the possibility that killer Meldrew was making a reappearance. You're finding the — let's call it shadow cord — has made that likelihood more probable. That second cord was fully absorbed before Meldrew was returned to his family so why is it reappearing. We now need to mount an operation to monitor Meldrew and find out if what we suspect is true. If our suspicions are correct the cord will become more evident over time and Meldrew's behaviour more erratic. Charlotte has authorisation to bring together a team of any personnel needed and with the full resources of Concordat at their disposal. You two will be given full access to Meldrew's previous Life File and case history and we five will be the only team members that have complete knowledge of the previous operation. All others will accept this to be an original case. I'll let Richard take over while I get some fresh coffee."

Richard began, "To all intents and purposes this is to seem a normal operation to monitor a Life Sider who is beginning to step outside Concordat behavioural bounds. With the exception of us all other team members will be neural blocked so that any slip of the tongue or reference to the previous Meldrew case will pass in and out of their minds without a trace. Any remarks made at the end of the meeting between team members about Retribution and Charlotte being involved have been expunged. The altered Life File history will explain the why's of us being there. Everything clear so far?" 'Yes' and 'uh-huh' indicated it was. "Good, now you will see the previous Meldrew operation."

An Ether Screen appeared and the previous case and cull unfolded at Light Time speed.

Chapter 100

"Same thing James. Short, sweet, easy to understand please. We all know how you analysts like to lapse into mumbo-jumbo jargon far beyond the comprehension of we mere mortals."

Smiling, James stood and bowed deeply to Barry saying, "Thank you for that stirring introduction but I am sure you were speaking in the singular when you alluded to a lack of understanding by the majority of the eloquent words of explanation that are about to pour from lips. I am sure all others here will comprehend without difficulty and be happy to explain to you any words I use larger than two syllables."

Laughter rang round the room with Barry fully joining in and then saying, "You've been working on that since the last time I introduced you, haven't you. Touché, my friend."

Eleanor and Richard smiled broadly at each other with Eleanor whispering, "I've heard these two before and they always put on a good show."

"John Jones. Mister Nice Guy. Outwardly he presents himself in a quiet, almost gentlemanly, way. He's not the caricature of your average long-haul trucker. You know, all tattoos and cussing and CB radio handles talking about all the 'beaver' they've come across on the road. JJ is none of that. No tats, no swearing, no sexual innuendo. Friendly enough when approached but by no means a 'slap on the back join the group' kind of guy. He more or less passes through the ranks of his fellow truckers unnoticed. Acknowledged face to face but soon forgotten. It's a persona he has cultivated and one that has served him well."

While James was speaking a series of pictures had appeared on the Ether Screen showing Jones from childhood to the present. There had been none showing the killings.

Pointing to the screen James said, "There you have it. If we didn't know what we do about him, he would be a somewhat unremarkable man making his way in the world as best he can. But of course, we know different. He has a dark side. When I did the neural search, it was to determine if any synapses or connections were crossed or wrongly installed. This is routine when considering a cull. You all know we cull only as a last resort. I found nothing amiss in Jones' brain. He does what he does because he needs to and they are acts of revenge against his parents. You will now see what occurred that impacted so strongly on his young mind and which now drives his need, his compulsion, to kill women and do the things he does to them."

John Jones was thirteen and supposed to be playing softball but the other team was a no show, so the game was cancelled. He had heard sounds and voices as he crossed the back yard making for the porch where he would store his glove and bat. Being inquisitive as all youngsters are he stood and peered into his parent's ground floor bedroom. Jones saw it all through the crack between drapes pulled across his parent's bedroom window. What he saw would best be described as hard-core pornography. Two men, one woman. Their actions seemed enjoyable to all. The woman put up no resistance and appeared to enjoy and participate willingly. Often seeming to guide the men. The men were brothers. Father and uncle. The woman, his mother. The final image from Jones' mind was of his mother being penetrated from behind with the hands of his uncle grasping her neck and his father about to enter her mouth. The scene changed as he dropped his bat and glove and ran across the yard and into the woods that bordered the property. The Ether Screen went dark.

"That, ladies and gentlemen, is what started John on the road, literally and metaphorically, to becoming a multi murderer. Now I know without even looking at him that Barry is taking exception to my term 'multi-murderer'. I've never liked 'serial killer'. To me it's a term that says, 'tune in next week for the next exciting instalment'. It's never exciting for the victims. But that's just my idiosyncrasy."

Chapter 101

"So you think the severed spinal cord is regenerating which is causing the change in Meldrew's behaviour. Is that right?" Jenny asked.

"Yes, that's what we think," Richard answered.

"And eventually when the cord is fully regenerated the other Meldrew will reappear to continue killing," from Alan.

"Yes, that's the hypotheses," Eleanor responded.

They were in lifebrain and verbal and each went quiet as they thought things over. Charlotte moved with the tray to brew more coffee and boil the kettle for tea.

Leaning against the kitchen counter as she waited for fresh coffee to brew Charlotte started to muse out loud. "Simply culling Meldrew is out of the question. Beyond the fact that we don't actually know if he will kill, or indeed if the cord will fully regenerate, we would lose the opportunity to gather from him knowledge that could be vital to the evolutionary path humans might take. Knowledge critical to Concordat. What if Meldrew and the two cords are not an anomaly but the start of another evolutionary branch? We can't approach this episode the same way we did the first. When we found the second Meldrew he was ticking all the boxes needed to secure agreement for a cull. Culling killer Meldrew saved the life of our Meldrew and seemed to cause no harm to him. That might not be the case if our readings from his recent actions and the findings of the neural search are correct."

During her muse Charlotte busied herself with the coffee and tea things then brought the carafe of coffee and pot of tea to the others. While pouring was going on she asked, "So, what do each of you think is the best way to handle this? Let's start Jenny, then Alan then Eleanor and Richard. I'll go last. Hold any comments or criticisms until we have all had our say."

Jenny tucked her legs under her and cradled her teacup, "If we are to get the knowledge and information the Concordat want then I see no other way than to let it run its course. Put full-time Watchers on him and do regular neural inserts to check the progress of the second cord and what effects it is having on Meldrew. Precautions would have to be taken with regards to the safety of his wife and others but Eleanor and Richard's are the best ones to address that."

Time was taken to consider Jenny's words then Alan spoke.

"The cord was severed when we had Meldrew at our facility and Richard took over his role Life Side. That worked in the short-term so I'm asking myself if it would work in the longer term. If it is feasible then we would have Meldrew in the perfect spot to monitor progress of the cord and any changes that occur in his brain. I know it could mean a long-term Life Sider exchange but with proper preparation several Retributionists could do it in rotation. We would be in control and not waiting for Meldrew to make the moves."

Again, silent consideration was given to Alan's proposal before Eleanor began.

"I'm for letting it run its course. As far as any others we bring in are concerned this is a completely new phenomenon. They have no knowledge of our previous operation. This Meldrew case is to be brand new to them and we treat it as such by letting all team members have input as to its direction. I'm sure Yuri, Ted, Victoria, Emma and whoever else is involved will have opinions and suggestions as to how we handle the case. I say we don't deviate from normal protocols unless we have no other alternative than to cull in the moment before he is about to kill."

Eyes turned towards Richard.

"With the exception of Charlotte, we all should be wiped and have to approach the case as if it were any other. Charlotte can provide us with a fictitious historical Life File leading to whatever raised a flag and caught the attention of observers. From there we follow all the protocols from first observation of Meldrew's behaviour that raised a flag with observers at Life Files through to whatever conclusion the Solons sanction. If we do our jobs right the emerging second spinal cord will be found and a plan formulated that takes us forward. However, if the second spinal cord is missed then Charlotte can gently nudge in the direction of it. She would do this not by direct order but more by gentle suggestion. Maybe even bringing it to us as something coming from the Solons. I don't think any of that will be necessary because I'm sure Charlotte will bring together the team that was involved in the first case."

Richard fell silent and they waited for Charlotte to respond.

Chapter 102

"Thank you, James. We all have our idiosyncrasies but some of yours are more idiosyncratic than most," Barry said before smiling and making an exaggerated arm out leg forward bow towards James.

James turned to the room saying with laughter in his voice, "Well, well Barry, your vocabulary has certainly improved. You couldn't even pronounce those words the last time we met."

The two of them went to each other with open arms and man hugged before turning to those in the room and bowing in unison. Standing shoulder to shoulder and mimicking Porky Pig from the cartoons they both said, "Th-th-that's all folks."

Applause followed James to his seat and Barry acknowledged them before saying, "Now for the nitty gritty."

A pictorial record of Jones killings appeared on the Ether Screen running at Time Light speed. They ran sequentially and showed the details from the women being picked up then through the act and to their disposal. Synopsis of police activity relating to each case was shown. Numerous bodies had not been found. Very few missing person's reports had been filed and those that had produced no results. The distances between killing and disposal were large and the dump sites were in vast areas of wilderness. With his refrigerated storage space Jones was able to dump the bodies where they were unlikely to be found. His truck and trailer carried no identifying marks. Nothing that would make them stand out or look original. Just another truck with a reefer unit among thousands of others.

There was little Concordat could do to bring his killings to the attention of law enforcement. Some of the missing person's reports had been filed by agents of Concordat going Life Side. Clues had been dropped with regard to where the women were last seen and the possibility they had hitched a ride on a truck going to one of the destinations Jones was travelling to. Half-hearted efforts at best were made by the police. They had more important things to do than look for a missing hooker who may, or may not, have got into some sort of trouble.

The full Life File of John Jones was shown and at its most recent entry the screen went dark.

Barry began to speak, "The Solons concur that every effort has been made to bring law enforcement into the picture but without success. They agree nothing more can be done and the body count will continue to rise if Jones is not stopped. The ménage à trois he witnessed at age thirteen haunts him. He has harboured a hatred against his mother because she had — to his mind — encouraged the two men to carry out what he thought of as acts of perversion. But it is only when the women take the final position he witnessed his mother in that is he able to become fully erect and ejaculate. As we have seen his relationship with his mother turned cold from that day forward. He has never told her why despite her pleading and she has tried to compensate by giving in to his every whim. We have seen he used emotional blackmail by alluding to something he had seen his mother doing when he was a child that he couldn't bring himself to talk about it. We know from her Life File that she suspected it was something to do with her sexual exploits. We saw she gave him the money for the down payment on his first truck from insurance money collected after her husband's workplace accident. His hidden hatred towards his mother was further reinforced because after his father's death she kept on fucking his brother. The women he kills are surrogates for his mother. In his mind that's who he is really killing. And, again as we have seen, that hatred is growing with each woman he kills."

Here Barry paused and looking towards Richard he spoke to him directly.

"Richard, most of what we have just covered was for the benefit of those here that were on the case in its early stages but not throughout to its conclusion. I also added details that all of us on the team knew but would give you a better understanding of the how's and why's of the case and what brought the Solons to their conclusion that he was to be culled. I hope they served that purpose."

"Yes, thank you. The background information was very helpful in gaining an understanding of his motives."

"Good. And now you have an understanding of the case and are now part of the Retribution section, what would you prescribe as a fitting end for Mr Jones, and your reasoning for its use? I'm assuming your mentor Eleanor has no objections."

"None at all Barry. I'm confident that Richard will suggest something that suits the crime," Eleanor responded.

All eyes turned on Richard and Eleanor motioned that he should make his way to the front of the room to give his answer. Her face betrayed no emotion and she offered no encouragement.

Chapter 103

Charlotte took time to put down her coffee mug before saying, "I will take all your scenarios to the Solons who will make the final decision on which, if any, to use. All have merit but perhaps the Solons will order a totally different approach to any we present. I think that unlikely—but it's not unknown."

Alan asked, "If you had to choose which would it be?"

"Don't try and put me on the spot Alan. I'm not going to second guess them."

Stretching his arms wide Richard yawned and then said, "Well it's no good just sitting around here so I'm going to my place for a swim and a nap. Give a shout when the Solons have made their decision, please Charlotte."

"Will do. As soon as I know their answer, I'll be in touch with all of you. I'm going to contact them now but if anyone wants to hang around here then help yourself. If not, let me know where you'll be and leave a line open."

Charlotte and Richard stood together and made for the door with both saying, "See you later," as they left.

Eleanor asked, "You two fancy a piece of diner pie?"

Alan and Jenny nodded and the three rose from their chairs and left the cabin with Jenny querying "I wonder what's on the pie menu tonight?"

It turned out to be blackberry and apple. As always it was excellent.

With unspoken agreement they kept away from the subject of Meldrew and what the decision of the Solons might be. They took their time with the pie. Not much was said between them because each was weighing in their own mind the pros and cons of the plans being put before the Solons and wondering which might be chosen.

It was Alan who first noticed Richard crossing the parking lot towards the diner door. He pointed him out to the other two who raised eyebrows in query but said nothing. They waited for Richard to come to their booth.

Richard collected a cup of coffee from the counter then came and slid into the booth beside Eleanor.

"Charlotte knows where you three are because she told me to come here. She said she would be here herself very soon. And no, she didn't say anything about the Meldrew case or the Solons' decision."

Customers moved in and out of the diner while the four waited for Charlotte to arrive. None paid any attention to them, with the exception of the waitress they were seen and immediately forgotten and she would not remember them as soon as the door closed after them.

Richard's mug was almost empty when a man approached the booth. He had not been noticed crossing the parking lot or entering the diner. The fact he approached them meant he was from Concordat. Medium build, medium height, clean shaven, thinning silver hair short and neatly parted. His face was tanned and carried the contour map of ridges and creases of the elderly. He was wearing a camel hair overcoat with a velvet collar which was unbuttoned to reveal a pinstripe three-piece suit. His black brogues were highly polished. He carried a furled umbrella hooked over one arm with a pair of kid gloves in one hand and a bowler hat in the other. His most outstanding feature were his eyes. Those in the booth simply could not take their own from them. One was brilliant sapphire blue, the other an equally brilliant emerald green.

He wiped the vinyl seat where he intended to sit with a pristine white handkerchief before hanging his umbrella and hat along with his overcoat on the hooks positioned on poles that made part of the dividers to the booths. The handkerchief he folded and placed on the table before he sat down next to Jenny. Not a word was uttered by any of them while this tableau took place.

He let his mesmerising eyes fall on each of their faces before reaching a perfectly manicured hand to each of them in turn and while shaking theirs said, "Good evening," to each one. At his touch each of them felt a momentary relaxed drowsiness that vanished when he released their hand. When the handshakes had been taken care of the man announced, "My name is Winston. Charlotte sends her apologies but something has come up that demands her immediate attention. I have been sent to apprise you of a decision that has been made regarding the case of a certain Doctor Meldrew. To facilitate this transfer of information I am going to synchronise with all of you. Please indicate individually that the synchronisation is successful. Thank you. Here is the information."

Winston stood and thanked them for their time and hospitality. Donning his overcoat and bowler hat he took his gloves from a pocket then took his umbrella from the hook, picked up his handkerchief and putting it in an inside coat pocket he raised a finger to the bowler rim and said, "Goodbye Ladies and Gentlemen." Then made his way to the diner door and out into the night.

There was silence in the booth until Alan asked, "Did you three just get a message from Charlotte saying to meet at her cabin?" Nods and yeses from the others. "Then we better get there," he said as he and the rest stood with Richard throwing some bills on the table to cover the pies and drinks. Along with a sizable tip.

Chapter 104

Barry went to a seat leaving the floor to Richard.

"Barry, you and Eleanor stitched me up, didn't you?" Richard began. "Putting me on the spot like this. Obviously my mentor was not at all reluctant to throw me under the bus without a single word of guidance or encouragement. It's like being back at school. Let's stick it to the new kid."

Smiles and some gentle laughter met these remarks with Barry and Eleanor exchanging huge grins and thumbs up signs.

When the room was quiet again Richard continued, "Run him over with his own truck. Maybe he's changing a wheel or underneath it, greasing the steering when through some freak occurrence the brakes release and a wheel runs over him crushing his upper legs and pelvis area. Not enough to kill him but enough to paralyse him from the waist down. Put him in the care of his mother after he leaves hospital. His mother married and had him young. She is still sexually active. Let him listen to the sounds of his mother and uncle screwing in the next room. Use his truck because it is central to all he's done. Access to the women. A space to do his killing. Transportation to the dump sites. Those are the physical attributes. There is also an emotional component. He owes the ability to do his killing to his mother. She provided the down payment for his first truck and trailer. Symbolically he is having intercourse with, and killing, his mother. He is punishing her for the act he witnessed as a teenager. He is blaming her for the lack of potency that forces him to do what he does. I know none of this will bring any closure to the families of the missing women but I think it serves as a better punishment than simply killing him. Use his means to the killings — his truck — as the weapon of retribution. I see a certain poetic justice there." A pause before saying, "That's it, thank you."

Barry stood and catching Richard by the arm before he could return to his seat he said, "Thank you Richard. For someone put on the spot you have certainly provided an addition to what we as a team were considering as suitable retribution. I will let Eleanor and you know what the final choice is. Team please show your appreciation for Richard's contribution."

Applause followed him back to Eleanor who stood and announced, "We better be going Barry. Richard has a lot more to see and do. Thank you, and your team, for the warm welcome and I'm sure we'll be seeing many of you again once Richard gets settled in. Thanks again." As she ushered Richard to the door Barry responded with, "You're welcome, it's been a pleasure."

They stopped by Yuri's office to say their goodbyes and when they were once more on the sidewalk outside the regency terrace houses Eleanor said, "Let's go to your beach. I'd like some sun and fun before you start on your first solo case. One has come to my attention that will suit you very well I think."

He agreed and they were there.

Without discussion they shed their clothes and waded into the lagoon to swim at a leisurely pace out to the reef and then back to shore. There were towels beside the hammock and they dried themselves before climbing into it. "Ahh, this is nice," came from Eleanor as she draped an arm and a leg over him.

"Sure is. And by the way thanks for throwing me to the wolves earlier."

"That was awful of me, wasn't it? I should have warned you. I'm so sorry."

"No you're not. You're not sorry at all. You enjoyed every minute of it."

"You're right—I did. How can I make it up to you?"

Pulling her on top of him which caused the hammock to tip alarmingly he smiled broadly and said, "Oh, I'm sure you can think of something."

Chapter 105

Yuri from Life Files and Ted from Watchers were already with Charlotte when Eleanor and the others arrived. Charlotte greeted the four saying, "Sorry to bring you here on such short notice. You already know Yuri and Ted." Nods and his were exchanged. "Have a seat and I'll explain why we're having this get together."

When all were seated Charlotte told them, "Go closed loop and verbal. The Life File belonging to a Doctor Meldrew threw up a flag recently that warranted a neural search. A tech from analytics and programming carried out the search and close examination revealed traces of a second spinal cord running parallel to and in some areas integrated in what is considered to be Meldrew's original cord. This finding is so unique that the Solons directed that all those involved in the Life File compilation and neural search be wiped and access to the file be restricted to an investigative team. I am to put together that team. Its purpose is to determine if this second cord is responsible for Meldrew's recent behavioural peculiarities. All of you will be part of the team. The Solons have provided a secure pod at analytics and programming to view Meldrew's Life File. Let's go to it now."

"No! Not a Fuchsia pod," Jenny exclaimed. "Bright purplish red is not conducive to thoughtful and considered investigations and analysis. A relaxing yet inspiring colour is what is needed." Throwing her head back and placing the back of her wrist against her forehead she exclaimed in her best Nora Desmond voice, "I simply cannot work under these conditions. I'm a star. Don't you understand? A star."

The others laughed at her antics with Alan saying, "All right valley girl, get over yourself. You're the top analyst here so change it to whatever colour you want. Such a drama queen."

"No. I'm okay with Fuchsia. I just wanted you to experience my actor's range and depth," Jenny said as she led them into the pod. Behind her Alan did a silent scream and an imitation of pulling his hair out. The rest tried hard not to laugh which they knew would only encourage both Jenny and Alan. The Hollywood sign could be seen from the analytics and programming campus — Jenny's choice of location, she really was a valley girl — and the sight of it always sent her off into acting mode with Alan aiding and abetting her. Charlotte shook her head and rolled her eyes. But once they were inside the pod Jenny became the model of calm efficiency.

Looking around she commented, 'This is not one of analytics and programming pods. We've never had a Fuchsia one. Whoever put it together did a nice job. Lots of neat stuff. That looks like a mainframe direct sync portal. Wow! Probably run a whole operation from here. I assume getting in and out demands very high-level clearance. This Meldrew fellow must be one very special hombre."

Charlotte allowed some time for all of them, particularly Yuri and Ted who seldom saw such things, to take it all in before saying, "He might be. He might also be one of a kind or the start of a separate branch of evolution. We are here to find out which one. Jenny, Alan, you will see the results of a Neural Search carried out on Doctor Meldrew while Eleanor and Richard review his Life File. Rooms have been set aside, you will have noticed the doors marked A and R. All the usual paraphernalia normally needed for your work is in them. When you are finished examining and analysing, we'll get together and discuss your findings. This Pod is locked down. You cannot communicate to the outside nor can one pair share information with the other while doing your reviews. If you try you will find you are neural locked. That's it. Off you go. Take what time you need. Yuri, Ted and I will be here when you're done.'

Eleanor and Richard were the first to complete their review. They found the three waiting for them in neural hiatus and it took gentle sync prodding to waken them. Charlotte yawned and stood to stretch saying, "That was good. Nothing freshens like a hiatus nap."

Yuri and Ted went through similar motions and agreed with, "Mm's and Uh, uh."

"Other two still at it then," Eleanor remarked as she plopped into one of the easy chairs spaced around the room.

Richard followed her lead and when seated said, "You know analysts. They'll analyse their analysis then analyse that analysis. It's going to be interesting to learn what they found."

They filled the time waiting for Jenny and Alan with talk and news about recent cases they had worked on and new people they had come across. They all agreed this was the first case that their particular group had worked on together. Coffee, tea and soft drinks along with finger foods were chosen from the selection laid out in a kitchen alcove while the small talk went on. Ted was on his way to refill his coffee mug when Alan and Jenny came out from their room and flopped into easy chairs. Ted raised the coffee carafe and a questioning eyebrow. Alan accepted with a nod. Jenny asked for Diet Pepsi. When they had taken a swallow Charlotte said, "Richard and Eleanor first. What did you find from his Life File?"

Chapter 106

"It's the fellow third from the left in the back row that we've come to look at," Eleanor said as she pointed him out to Richard. "Name is Tom Donald and he abuses women. Mentally and physically. He's an asshole we've been watching for some time now and following his latest incident we have the go ahead to move on him. This is not a cull. You are just going to make sure he never abuses another woman. It's up to you how that's done but because this is your first one, I can veto it if it steps outside the bounds of Concordat protocol for this type of case. Understood?" Richard nodded in confirmation. "Good. Let's go take a look at his Life File."

The Ether Screen in Eleanor's apartment went dark and then faded away. Richard went out and stood on the balcony breathing in the warm and pungent Kolkata night. Eleanor sat on the sofa with legs drawn under her and waited. She had seen him stand in the same place soon after they first met and just before their first love making in the apartment. If she had loved anyone in life it was probably this man.

Richard turned and leant with hands in pockets against the balcony door frame. "You asked me to tell you about this man. This is a man who knows nothing but violence. Throughout his life he has been submerged in it. His father used it on him and he has used it on others ever since. Violence is the only thing he understands. His bullying childhood and street gang youth confirm that. He grew to be 'muscle' for organised crime. If you want somebody hurt, he is the one you turn to. He's undoubtedly a sociopath but one with a veneer of charm and false empathy and these are the things that get him close to the women he eventually brutalises. Of course, the most despicable thing he does is use Alcoholics Anonymous as a pick-up ground. He prays on women who are at their most vulnerable. We've seen that many of them relapsed under his domineering and controlling influence. We've also seen the mental and physical abuse he uses to subjugate and extract what he wants from them. That can be a roof over his head, sex, money, or all three. He's careful. When he uses physical violence its always in places not immediately visible. Once their money runs out or they once again become fully performing alcoholics he dumps them and seeks another mark. The women must have felt too ashamed to set the law on him. The woman he punched and broke a rib is the only one who had strength and sobriety enough to threaten him with prosecution after getting X-rays and reporting the attack. She stopped short of bringing a charge against him, wanting only to frighten him away. He was pissed and as a last metaphorical slap in the face he extorted money from her at an ATM. But he did move on from her and found another. Gutsy woman but she would have done better by her sisters by bringing a charge. I wonder how her life is progressing."

Eleanor patted the sofa beside her saying, "Come sit. That was a pretty good outline of the sleaze bag. Being an alcoholic yourself you feel deeply for the women. I know enough about the disease to say it's hard enough getting and staying sober without predators like him. And there are lots of them but most don't carry it to the extremes he has. So, what's your recommendation for a punishment?"

"I'd send a woman to give him a taste of his own medicine. Use violence against him. Let him know that if he prays on another woman, he will suffer worse. He gets pleasure, a rush, from inflicting violence so show him what it's like to be on the receiving end. Take away the rush and put the fear of pain in him."

"Mmm, and who would you send to do this?"

"I don't know. There must be women in Concordat that have had similar experiences so one of them I suppose."

"Let me see who fits the bill in Retribution."

Chapter 107

Eleanor took the lead. "We divided his Life File. Me taking the years to his change, Richard the time after. Until recently, I'm talking recently in Meldrew time, until recently his Life File could have been any one among the trillions Concordat has recorded. Nothing extraordinary happened while he grew to adulthood. Sure, there was the usual angst of the teenage years but he was single minded in his pursuit of a career in medicine and in which he has become one of the eminent practitioners in his field of neurosurgery. Married, one daughter. Marriage has been stable and he seems to be devoted to his wife and daughter. Before the flag appeared, there is absolutely nothing in his history that indicated the abrupt change his personality has taken."

Eleanor stopped and it was a beat or two before Charlotte said, "I feel a 'but' coming. What is it?"

"Let's wait until Richard says his piece and then I'll explain. Is that okay Charlotte?"

"Certainly. Go ahead Richard. What's your reading of Meldrew?"

"The change in his sexual appetite from gentle and considerate lover to one with masochistic tendencies has occurred gradually over several months. At first his wife, Constance, thought he was just taking their love making to another level of excitement and was not averse to this. The bondage games and, for them, unusual sexual positions accompanied by heartier slapping and squeezing brought her increased pleasure at orgasm. She started to become alarmed when he began to bring home a variety of sex toys and aids. Many of these were too large for her to accommodate comfortably but Meldrew became more and more aggressive in his insistence that they be used and that she should get used to them. I won't go into details but the flag appeared when it was only by watching his wife penetrate herself with various objects which obviously caused her distress that he attained full erection and ejaculated by masturbating over her. That continues to this day with Constance becoming more concerned for her own safety. Along with his change in sexual mores at home he has also started to flirt with members of the hospital staff. He is showing particular interest in a nurse who intends to go on a hiking holiday. His Life File shows he was a keen hiker during his university days. After we reviewed our individual parts of his Life File we viewed it together in its entirety. Eleanor can explain our thoughts and ideas and the 'buts' we both have."

All attention turned back to Eleanor. "We both agree that his change of character with regard to sex has been rapid but it has not affected his other professional or personal relationships. To his daughter, extended family, colleagues and friends he is the same Meldrew they've always known. Even outside the bedroom his love and affection for Constance is the same as always. Gentle and considerate. This Jekyll and Hyde persona must be deeply troubling for her. The husband she loves and knows so well outside the bedroom, the aggressive and domineering almost sadist in it. Besides that we have his flirtations with the nurse. Is he seeking an extramarital liaison with her? Perhaps. The germ of that idea is definitely in his mind. Will his masochistic tendencies lead to real harm for Constance. We are sure they will if they keep escalating."

Here Eleanor raised a hand to signal a pause and walked to the kitchen to get herself a glass of water. Dropping ice cubes into it she drank some and carried the rest back to her seat. Once settled she continued.

"Now for the 'but'. We believe that when Meldrew is forcing and performing masochistic acts on Constance he is fighting with his own mind and actions in an effort to stop himself doing those things. We detected the fight characteristic. Although we have no firm evidence, we believe there is another part of him that is controlling these actions and we also believe Meldrew is fighting it even as the acts are being carried out. We also believe this fight is going on during his flirtations with the nurse. So—we have a question for Jenny and Alan. Could he be suffering from a form of split personality where one that has been dormant is now emerging and getting stronger and that is what is bringing about these changes?"

Chapter 108

A knock on the door brought Eleanor to her feet. "That will be June," she responded to Richard's enquiring look.

The two women embraced at the threshold and Eleanor said, "Thanks for coming June. Come in and meet Richard. He recently joined Retribution."

June advanced into the room and offered her hand to Richard. Her grasp was firm and dry. Just two pumps while she looked him in the eye. "Hello," was her only greeting. Her forthright gaze which she held after releasing his hand and the mouth devoid of a smile sent him the message that she wasn't there for small talk and cups of tea. June was tall, very tall, well over six feet, slim in all areas. She wore a man style navy business suit complete with waistcoat. There were tasselled loafers on her bare feet. No shirt or blouse under the waistcoat. Dark hair short and parted on the left. Café au lait complexion. Dark eyes bordering on black. A bright green handkerchief stuffed in the breast pocket of the suit coat was the only spot of colour on her whole ensemble.

June went to a high-backed wicker chair and sat. She waited until they were seated on the sofa then asked, "So, what can I do for you?" The softness and melodiousness of her voice surprised Richard.

In answer Eleanor brought up an Ether Screen. "You are going to see the Life File of a very bad man. One the Solons want punished in such a way that he foregoes his wicked ways. You know, they want the shit scared out of him." June's mouth twitched to an almost smile. "After you've looked at the Life File Richard will outline a plan he feels can best be accomplished by a woman. That is the reason I asked you here. Take a look and then tell us if you think Richard's plan has merit."

June nodded, "Let me see the file."

When it was finished and the screen had faded away June looked directly at Richard. "Tell me your plan."

June listened without comment and when he finished, she spoke directly to Eleanor. "It's a good plan. I like the requirement for a feminine intimidator. The one who causes him pain. However, I will suggest one additional element. That is the inclusion of a male presence. This shitbag needs to know that there are men who are willing to help the women he preys on. The man won't carry out any of the Retribution. His presence in the background, the threat of male reprisal, will be sufficient to reinforce the fact that he will be hurt again by both sexes if he continues to be a naughty boy. I'm prepared to do it and I think Richard should be the male presence. His first one so let's get him up close and personal. What do you think?" June fell silent for a moment then she looked directly at Richard to say, "I don't like that son of a bitch. He needs to be stopped."

Without hesitation Richard agreed, "I'm up for it. Unless Eleanor sees any reason why I shouldn't be involved let's do it."

Eleanor shook her head, "Nope, no reason for you not being there. I'll leave the final arrangements to the both of you and you can let me know when you intend carry it out so I can be there and observe."

June stood, saying, "Good. Come with me Richard and we'll start putting it all together."

Richard caught up with her as she opened the door to leave. Eleanor gave a smile and a small wave to him as he left.

They stepped from Eleanor's apartment in Kolkata into a North American suburban split level with a style that dated to the late sixties. They were met by a woman the opposite of June in every way. She came hurrying towards them as they stepped through the front door wiping her hands on an apron saying to June, "Why didn't you let me know you were bringing a visitor. I'm in the middle of baking and must look a fright. Welcome, and in case you haven't been told I'm Helen." Short, not much over five feet was Richard's guess, pink gingham dress with flared skirt and petticoats, hour glass figure with a large bust and narrow waist, blonde hair all flicks and curls that had been hot iron and rollered to perfect symmetry then lacquered into place. Richard put her age at early thirties. He introduced himself and said the smell of fresh baking was a favourite of his.

Helen smiled in response then turned to June to say, "Go change. You know I don't like you keeping your work things on in the house." June shrugged at Richard with an amused look of resignation and walked off down a hallway leading from the living area to what Richard assumed would be one of the bedrooms. Heading into the kitchen, Helen told him to follow and have a taste of her fresh molasses cookies. As she walked ahead of him, he saw she was wearing nylon stockings with a seam down the back. On her feet she wore pink household slippers with fluffy pink pompoms. All this, the house, her clothes, even the furnishings and appliances he noticed was all very retro sixties. As he chewed on a warm molasses cookie which tasted very good, he surmised there must be a reason why two so obviously different people liked that era of psychedelia and over the top colours and fabrics. Not to mention the fashions and hairstyles. Wiping a crumb from his mouth with a paper napkin he complimented Helen on her baking. She thanked him and was obviously pleased with the compliment. A door closed and they both turned towards the hallway entrance.

Chapter 109

"Well that just ruined our grand proclamation," came from Alan as he threw up his hands and Jenny made her best attempt at a murderous glare towards the Retributionists.

The others looked perplexed and Charlotte asked, "What has ruined what? You better explain."

Jenny with exasperation edging her voice told them. "Our analysis of the neural search seems to confirm the question that Richard and Eleanor raised about a split personality. We found that Meldrew has a second spinal cord. One that is not complete in places and therefore could not be fully functional at the time of the search. We cannot state with certainty that this second cord is the cause of Meldrew's behavioural change but that possibility exists. Further observations and searches need to be carried out before a definitive answer can be arrived at. Eleanor and Richard are right that a part of Meldrew's mind seems to be fighting whatever is causing his deviant behaviour. We picked up on that too. Also, there is the possibility that the new cord will grow to completion and have more effect on Meldrew's behaviour in different ways. Ways that go beyond the present sexual preference changes. He needs to be watched very closely."

Jenny looked across at Alan who took up the telling.

"Multiple personality disorders are flagged all the time by observers and compilers and neural searches are frequently made to determine the causes." Alan paused and then with emphasis in his voice, "However, it *appears* that this is the first time that a second spinal cord has been found."

He and Jenny looked at the others and waited for the question they knew was inevitable. It came from Yuri.

"What do you mean, *appears* to be?"

Alan sat forward with forearms on thighs and hands clasped with a look on his face that portrayed the seriousness of what he was about to say. "We found what we believe to be evidence that work has already been carried out on Meldrew. To be sure of this another more thorough search needs to be done that targets particular areas of his brain and spinal cord that seem to show traces of scarring. Jenny and I need to do this search. We would focus on areas that require very detailed analysis to prove or disprove our theory. If Concordat did sanction the work, it should be in Meldrew's Life File record. There is no such record. If we are proved right and Concordat didn't sanction the work—then who did?"

Five pairs of questioning eyes turned on Charlotte.

Charlotte took time to get more coffee and to make herself comfortable before responding. They all knew it was a delaying tactic so that she could compose herself. Alan's announcement about the evidence of previous work on Meldrew had surprised them.

"I see only one way to go. Alan, Jenny, you will do a comprehensive search and analysis that gives a definite answer as to whether or not previous neural work has been carried out on Meldrew. Yuri, put your best observer on him and you scour his Life File for any hint of tampering of the file to expunge previous work. Ted, put Watchers on him, his wife, and daughter full time. I want them covered every moment in case his behaviour suddenly escalates. Richard, Eleanor, work with Alan and Jenny during their search. Monitor their movements and help direct them to any places you think need special attention. Your experience with warped minds prior to a cull might help. Yuri and Ted, make up a story between you that explains to your people why there is special interest in Meldrew. You can do that?" Nods and yes from both. "Good. When can you do the search Alan?"

Alan glanced at Jenny before answering, "Friday night. He usually sleeps later on the Saturday mornings he's not on call. This coming Saturday is one of them. Sound good to you Jen?"

Jenny said "Sure, seems like a good time. If we keep him under longer than usual no one in the family will question it."

"If the previous work and second cord are confirmed I'll have to tell the Solons but until we know for sure we keep it amongst ourselves. It's Thursday evening now Earth time so we have a little over two days to prepare. Ted and Yuri can start on their tasks and why don't you four go over his Life File and search analysis one more time. Take each other through what each pair of you found and what concerns you. Can't hurt."

Ted and Yuri made ready to leave along with Charlotte who informed, "I have some other business to attend to but I'll be back for the search."

With gestures of farewell the three of them left the pod.

Chapter 110

Helen held out her arms to the man who exited the hallway saying, "That's better Rob. Now come and give me a proper hug and kiss."

This was not June. This was a man of medium build dressed in tan slacks and a white polo shirt with a beige cardigan pulled over it. His age about forty. Head full of wavy dark hair. A face without any distinguishing characteristics. Pleasant but not handsome. An age to match Helen's probably. He had brown socks and brown plaid slippers on his feet. He did as Helen ordered then came to Richard with an outstretched hand.

"Sorry for the subterfuge. You saw me in my Retribution persona. All strength and *'in your face'* intimidation. It's what I wear when dealing with assholes like Donald. Helen and I suffered at similar hands Life Side. Lots of female to male abuse out there too. Not a one-way street. Anyway, welcome to our home. This era is not for everybody but this is what we both dreamed about at the time of our being abused. Split level in the suburbs, quiet neighbourhood, comfortable without being ostentatious. The sixties early seventies. Sex, drugs and rock and roll. Free love. We missed that scene. We weren't free."

Helen placed a hand on Rob's arm saying, "Hush now Rob, Richard isn't here to listen to our stories he's here to learn what you intend to do about Donald. Let's sit and I'll bring coffee and cookies then you boys can work on your plan."

"Okay but let's go on the deck and catch the sunset while we talk."

Helen sat with them and made points for consideration.

Eleanor was there to observe, when they confronted Donald.

"Wakey, wakey Tommy boy! Time to get your carcass out of your pit and let's take a look at you." June brought a riding crop down across Donald's bare chest at nipple level as she said this.

Eyes flying open, Donald shot to a sitting position with a grunt of pain. It took seconds for him to comprehend what had awakened him and he felt for the burning line of pain on his chest. June placed the pommel of the riding crop against Donald's throat and forced him, gagging and retching, backward onto the bed while saying, "Richard, would you be so kind as to escort that lady from the room. I believe she has friends waiting to take care of her."

The lady took the hand Richard held out and swinging her legs from the bed stood to walk with him to the door. He opened it and as she was about to pass through, she smiled into his face and asked, "Clothes?"

Richard smiled back and said, "Don't worry, your friends have others for you."

She gave a whispered "Thank you," and passed through the doorway. Richard closed it quietly behind her and went to stand in a shadowed corner of the room.

June still had the pommel against Donald's throat and as much as he struggled to remove it the harder June pushed down with the result his breathing became more ragged and his face more scarlet and lack of oxygen robbed him of strength. "Easy, Tommy boy. The more you struggle the more you'll hurt. But, of course, you won't listen. You're a big strong man used to being on the giving side of hurt and being held down like this is really pissing you off. And it's a woman that's doing it to you. I'll take this out of your neck now and let's see how you react. Let you catch your breath—so to speak."

Two gasping breathes after the crop was removed he threw the covers aside and convulsed from the bed with arms outstretched and reaching for June croaked, "You fucking bitch." She was in front of him and then he felt the searing pain of the crop as it burned across his buttocks. He spun round to find her standing on the opposite side of the bed. Enraged he uttered, "How the fuck," before scrambling across the bed on all fours. Moments before reaching her he felt the burning pain of the riding crop inflame across his shoulders. Now she was at the foot of the bed with hands on hips and smiling at him. His momentum had taken him off the bed and to a kneeling position, so he surged up and grabbing hands full of bed sheet as a shield he rushed at her in an attempt to smother any blows. He'd forgotten the man in the corner who as he rounded the corner of the bed stuck out a foot to trip him and send him crashing to the floor in a tangle of sheet. Then the foot was on the back of his neck forcing his face into the bedroom carpet. Then the crop burned across his buttocks again. Then across his back. Then across his shoulders. Then across his calves.

Richard and June could hear muffled threats coming from his bloodied lips which had been smashed when he went to the floor. Apparently, there was nowhere they could hide and no torture they wouldn't endure when he got his hands on them. All of the diatribe interspersed with a selection of profanity some of which was both original and amusing to June and Richard.

Richard removed his foot as June reached down and with ease lifted Donald's head, shoulders and torso up by his hair until he was bent upward from the waist. He tried to support himself with his arms but he found them without movement or strength. It felt like his scalp was about to be torn from his skull. Tears began to pour from his eyes and mewling words of pleading came from his bloodied mouth.

"Shh, shh, Tommy boy. Quit your cowardly babbling and listen well. We are messengers for friends of Nicole. She's been taken under their protection and if you so much as look at her again we will find you and hurt you again. But much worse. I know you understand Tommy boy but just in case you don't here's a parting gift. Richard, do the honours please."

Richards used a foot to spread Donald's legs wide enough to expose his penis and scrotum. He kicked him hard.

June let go of Donald's hair and he collapsed full length before immediately drawing himself into a foetal position and cradling his sex organs. He rocked and moaned while they watched and then June bent to one knee to say, "I forgot to tell you Tommy boy that we will be watching you all the time and visit you again if you ever take advantage of or cause harm to any other person for as long as you live. Nod if that's clear to you." Several quick short nods came from Donald. "Good."

With one last blow from the riding crop across his buttocks Richard and June left him.

Chapter 111

"Sorry about stealing your thunder," Eleanor said trying for contrition in her voice.

Jenny scowled, "No you're not. Retributionists love it when their gut tells them something we have to find through analysis. That's why you're in that job. But moving on. Now we have to prove our hypotheses. Let's do as Charlotte suggested and go over what we have from him so far. Oh, and by the way. You might be assholes for stealing our thunder but you are our assholes and we love you anyway."

Eleanor and Richard chorused, "We love you too," and the easy camaraderie was apparent as they all smiled and prepared to go to work.

They scanned all the information they had several times with each time being deeper and more intensive until eventually. "There! Do you see it?" Alan pointed to a high-def hi-mag nano sliced section of Meldrew's spinal cord. "I'd swear that's where the other cord is propagating from. Are those transparent tendrils of cord attaching themselves to the original? It's like the cutting from one plant attaching itself to another."

"Yes, and look below that point. Is that the faintest mark or residue of a previous cord?" Jenny asked.

Eleanor and Richard concentrated on the places pointed out by the analysts and Richard asked, "What do you see Eleanor? I think I see what they're talking about but I'm not sure."

Eleanor replied, "Me too but I'm used to seeing complete fully formed cords. It's far too hazy even at hi-mag nano slice for me to say for certain. Sorry guys."

Alan exhaled in frustration. "You're right. Maybe we're seeing it because we want to. We've got to go in again and target places like this."

"Agreed," came from Jenny. "And you're right when the two of you say you noticed a neural struggle going on during Mark's visit. I'll bet we find much more scarring when we go in."

Richard mused. "Okay. We go in and find all sorts of evidence that proves previous work was done. It doesn't answer the question who did it."

"Or what we do if the proof is found," supplied Eleanor.

Alan leaned back from looking closely at the three-dimensional hi-mag nano slice to stretch and ask, "Do you want to know what I'm beginning to think?"

"Was that rhetorical?" Eleanor exclaimed, "Of course we want to know."

"I think this *is* our work and the record of it has been removed from his Life File."

Richard and Eleanor stared at each other with eyes wide in surprise and it was Jenny who recovered first from Alan's shock announcement to say in hushed tones, "You're serious aren't you. You really think that."

"I do. Now we've gone over his Life File and neural search again I'm fairly certain that we will find evidence during our next insertion that one or more of we four were involved in work previously done on Meldrew. Look, each search and cull operative has a very particular style that points to them. I can tell it was Mark who did the insert we've just analysed from the way he approaches each one he does. Call it a signature. No two operatives have the same signature. I think we are going to find one or more of our signatures all over Meldrew. Let me show you." Alan brought up another high-def hi-mag image. "The neural disturbance trace just barely visible in the temporal lobe area has Eleanor's signature on it. I'd swear that's the way you search and record Eleanor, that's how you interconnect with the synapses. That area has been searched before. Searched by Eleanor. Mark's search pattern has covered up a lot of yours but you were in there Eleanor." Returning his gaze to the three-dimensional hologram of Meldrew's brain that had been slowly rotating above an Ether table throughout their review Alan murmured, "I'm sure of it."

Jenny expelled a long breath from between pursed lips then asked of the others, "What now?"

Chapter 112

Eleanor was sitting with Helen at the kitchen table when Rob and Richard returned.

"Eleanor tells me it went well," Helen said as she stood to embrace Rob.

Releasing her from the hug Rob responded, "Yes it did. Richard's plan to humiliate him and use a riding crop in the hands of a woman was perfect. Donald won't be bothering anybody in future but we'll have the observers check on him regularly. He's going to have trouble walking for the next week or so. His testicles were the size of mandarin oranges when we left and the welts from the crop will always be there to remind him to be a good boy."

Eleanor asked, "How's Nicole?"

"She's fine," Richard answered. "Once Donald had left her flat and limped back to his mother's place, we tucked Nicole back into bed and wiped all memory of Tommy Donald. She'll wake refreshed and go about her life as if Donald had never entered it. She'll seek out new AA meetings that know nothing of her time with Donald and observers will keep an eye on her from time to time. I hope she keeps her sobriety and meets someone who will cherish her. She was taken advantage of at a very stressful and vulnerable time in her life."

Helen smiled broadly, "That sounds wonderful." Then directly to Richard, "How do you feel?"

"I feel fine. I had no compassion for Donald and I think that came from having seen in his Life File how he treated vulnerable women."

A glance from Helen and Rob, who was still in his female persona, asked, "Anything you'd change? I mean about the plan. It was your proposal that a female be the main protagonist. A female as far as Donald was concerned. In retrospect would you have preferred a more active role?"

Helen interjected, "Go change while Richard considers and I'll make some coffee and tea to have with cookies on the deck. It's such a beautiful day again."

Rob headed off to change while Helen and Eleanor went about preparing things in the kitchen. Wandering out onto the deck Richard wondered why Rob didn't just change to himself in front of them. It wasn't as if he was going to stand naked in front of them while it happened. He intended to ask Rob when he got the chance. He was looking from the deck across a perfectly manicured lawn in a garden that had shrubs and flowers strategically planted along the borders which were backed by high a fence that afforded some privacy from neighbouring properties. He felt Eleanor sync with him. She told him, "Don't ask. It's none of your business and might embarrass them."

He responded with, "Understood."

Rob now shed of his female persona and dressed in a white tee shirt, dark blue shorts and flip flops came to join Richard on the deck. Laying a hand on Richard's shoulder he spoke softly, "Listen carefully and tell me what you hear." Richard turned his head slightly and tilted it to concentrate his hearing and he heard it.

"I can hear the sounds of children playing and their laughter."

Rob squeezed Richard's shoulder saying, "They are for Helen. She was unable to have children of her own but loved the sound of them playing and shouting and laughing. Another reason why we chose this type of neighbourhood at this time. It was when parents weren't afraid to let their kids out alone to play." Rob released Richard's shoulder as Helen and Eleanor walked from the house.

Eleanor had poured coffee for Richard the way he liked it as had Helen for Rob. They sat on lounger chairs around a low table to drink and chew on Helen's tasty molasses cookies.

Helen broke a small piece off her cookie and before putting it in her mouth asked, "So Richard, what's your answer to the question about having a more active role?"

"For me it was more important to observe. Eleanor brought Rob, or June if you prefer, into the picture early and I was prepared to listen and watch and learn from him. Sure, the original idea of a female meting out punishment on Donald was mine but it was Rob who polished it and brought together all the other threads needed to carry out the scheme. Things like presenting the plan to my Retribution section head for approval who then got permission from Solons to carry out a Life Side operation; there was arranging for transporter division to move and monitor Nicole; getting a wiper to clear Nicole's mind of Donald; Watchers needed to put a neural block around Rob and me so that we would not be remembered if anyone walked in on us. All this and more was down to Rob and I've learned from it. Also, I know how to use a riding crop. That part I didn't need to learn and I felt it was Rob's due to inflict the punishment. When I do all the groundwork is when I will take the lead." Smiling at Helen, "Great cookies. I'll have another one if I may." All of his mind was taken up with the enjoyment of savouring the textures and flavours of the cookie.

Rob turned to Eleanor. "He's ready."

Helen nodded in agreement and said, "Time to call in the wipers."

Richard gazed into the garden and enjoyed his cookie.

Chapter 113

Alan turned from the hologram, "We need to get Charlotte back here. She needs to be told before we go in on Friday. We need to know what was found and more importantly what was done to him. What was so strange or unusual about Meldrew that caused his Life File to be altered to hide it?"

"Back up a moment," came from Eleanor. "Before we call Charlotte let's consider who in Concordat has the authority to order the deletion or alteration of a Life File. Who in Concordat can arrange for the wiping of all knowledge of the Meldrew case from all those who were involved. We must have been wiped or we would all have some recollection of our search. It's only the actual method and time of the cull that is totally wiped. Instead, we have Alan who is *almost* sure I was involved. There is no doubt that work was done on him. The traces left confirm that. But why cover it up? None of us should go back in until we know what all the secrecy is about. Richard, what do you think?"

"I agree. The questions you've asked lead to only one conclusion. The Solons had to be involved directly. They are the only ones with enough authority to alter Meldrew's Life File. Alan's right, we need to get Charlotte back and explain all this to her. Let's contact her. You're the senior operative here Eleanor so you must have a hyper secure link you can open to reach her. Am I correct?"

"Yes. But these are links of last resort so be prepared for an ass chewing if our speculations are off the mark."

Eleanor closed her eyes and made the link. The others sat quietly until she opened her eyes to say, "Charlotte will be here as soon as she can. We are to remain on lockdown and a neural block has been thrown around the pod. Nobody can get in or out either physically or mentally. For now we just wait."

All four chose an inertia rest state including closing down their thought processes. Each retreated to a place of absolute calm and stillness. They stayed in their own moment and that moment would last until Charlotte arrived and made her presence known to each one.

Eleanor was the first to feel Charlotte's presence. It was the merest disturbance that made her aware and Charlotte took her out of her moment gently. The others were still in theirs.

"Bring the others back please. I'm going to get a coffee." Eleanor did as requested.

The others were present and alert when Charlotte sat down and took a mouthful of coffee before cradling the mug in her hands and starting to speak.

"Go verbal please. Alan, you are correct. Meldrew was the subject of a Concordat action in which Eleanor and the rest of us here were involved along with many others."

Alan noticeably relaxed at these words and smiles were directed at him from the others with Jenny mouthing, "Well done."

Charlotte continued, "The Solons have directed that the heads of departments and senior section leaders involved with Meldrew's previous case are to be given access to all records that were sealed under a Solon Executive Order. This access is to provide background for whatever future action is decided upon. I am to be team leader, as I was before. The others will be arriving soon and after I have given a brief explanation for their gathering Meldrew's file will be opened for examination."

Voices could be heard coming from the pods pedway as the others arrived. Charlotte withdrew the lockdown code from the entrance door to allow the others access and then resecured it.

There was much milling about with hellos, handshakes, hugs and air kisses as the newcomers greeted their colleagues from analytics and programming and Retribution with 'what's this all about' and 'what's going on'. "You'll see," was the only answer they got. Their greetings to Charlotte were far more restrained. Her reputation around Concordat was one of brusque efficiency. Small talk was not her forte.

Charlotte spoke up. "Let's finish the meet and greet please. You'll have time to catch up later. Get yourself tea or coffee or whatever, then take a seat so we can get on with the business at hand the subject of which is one Doctor Brian Meldrew."

Those wanting drinks gathered them and the room went silent as an Ether Screen appeared showing the face of a not unhandsome man bordering on middle age. There was a hint of a smile at his lips which reached his eyes. It was a face that said, 'trust me, I'm a doctor'.

The face on the Ether Screen dissolved and Meldrew's Life File passed across it at Time Light speed. When the Life File reached the continuous uploads that were being inserted in real time the file closed and Meldrew's face appeared again. At the first signs of movement and reaction from the gathering Charlotte stood and raised her voice to tell them, "You all have questions but what I'm about to explain will answer most if not all of them so please be quiet, be patient and listen." Silence settled over the room.

Charlotte began, "We are not here to hold an enquiry or post-mortem into why the first Meldrew case was handled the way it was nor are we here to point fingers and expound on conclusions that come from being wise after the fact. Also, we are not here to discuss or cast theories about as to why the Solons reached their decision to seal the records and wipe all personnel involved in the original case. Let us all be perfectly clear on those points."

She paused to let her words sink in.

"Having seen the unedited file, you are now aware of the individual and collective roles you played, along with others from your departments, leading to the actions taken and the final outcome. And, it was Jenny's development of the program that is now an integral part of our protocols and procedures that discovered what Meldrew had hidden for years. We are still reviewing all Life Files with the program to determine if any more like Meldrew slipped through. We are here now because analytics and programming has found what they suspect is another cord beginning to grow at the site where Retribution cut the original in order to cull Meldrew's killer alter ego. The recent behavioural change in Meldrew drew a flag in Life Files and that flag instructed Life Files to contact me. I ordered an insert search carried out and had the results handed over to me directly and I brought in your colleagues from analytics and programming and Retribution to thoroughly examine them. None of the four were aware at that time that they had been part of the original team. Their findings and suspicions resulted in the Solons agreeing to open the file and reassemble the original team. I will leave it to Alan and Jenny to explain their findings and analysis. Eleanor and Richard will give you details of their neural search and what they found."

Chapter 114

Eleanor and Richard stood to leave. "Thank you so much for having us over. It's a lovely place. So peaceful and I love your garden Helen," Eleanor said as she hugged Helen goodbye.

She then went to hug Rob after he and Richard had shaken hands with Rob saying, "Come again. It's always nice to have visitors and get free of work for a while. It's been a pleasure to meet you Richard and welcome once again to Concordat."

Rob stood with his arm around Helen's waist outside their front door as Eleanor and Richard walked toward the roadway then with a final wave they turned and entered the house.

They agreed to go back to the Concordat villa and as they stepped from Rob and Helen's world, they walked onto the balcony overlooking the sandy cove. The marquee style tent was still on the beach, so they took the winding path down and shedding their clothes onto the warm sand they walked side by side into the water. Eleanor pointed to a grotto in the headland they had visited during Richard's transition and he smiled agreement. They swam towards it. Light bounced off the clear reflecting surface of the water at the grotto's mouth and made moving rippled pictures on the golden sandstone rock that arched above and formed the headland. The seabed rose gently to a small beach below the sloping roof of the grotto which ran some ten metres further into the cliff until it came down to meet bedrock. They joined together on the firm sand and their passion and pleasure echoed around the grotto as they did all those special things only lovers who know the other's body and desires intimately can do. They lay entwined and sated afterwards and waited for strength to return to bodies drained of sexual energy before taking a leisurely swim back to the cove beach.

They dressed then lay on loungers in the shade of the marquee with cold drinks on the sand between them. Richard felt the smallest of neural shocks when Eleanor synced with him. He was getting used to the different ways of communicating in Concordat. Usually it was verbal but when large amounts of data or information had to be shared it was through neural transfer. It was faster. Eleanor lay reclined and relaxed on the cushions of the lounger and spoke to him.

"The job you did with Rob was the final stage in your transition to Concordat's Retribution section. Your plan for the chastisement of Tommy Donald was exactly what he needed. Rob and Helen were impressed that you wanted to learn from the exercise instead of glory hunting. Many applicants have been dropped from Retribution because they didn't fit well with the team dynamic. By the way, don't be fooled by Helen's folksy charms. She's one of the best and most experienced culler's we have. To impress her is quite an achievement. You now know what you can and cannot do in Concordat and the benefits having a fully functional brain bring. Do not abuse them. The Solons opened a file when you arrived and if you stray from accepted behavioural norms it will be flagged for investigation. All investigations are carried out by Solons. Most Life Side behaviour of a personal nature such as romantic interludes are acceptable. You've already experienced many of your heightened sensory responses and found how they can be modulated. Field work will expand and hone those skills. You have witnessed the cull of Herman Oliver and actively participated in the operation to alter Donald's behaviour. You sat in on the planning of an ongoing operation concerning trafficking young girls for sex and offered suggestions that may, or may not, be used. All those you have met and worked with during your transition speak highly of you and have recommended your attachment to the Retribution section. My words have gone into your Solon file and the one being kept by Retribution. Now we have to go back to the balcony where our boss is waiting."

Chapter 115

Alan cleared his throat. "We are all now fully aware of the first action taken against Meldrew and it is now obvious why the recent behavioural change in Meldrew raised a flag. They show a definite shifting towards inflicting pain on another to achieve pleasure and sexual release for himself. We saw that killer Meldrew showed the same disposition when he took over Brian Meldrew and performed his ritualised slaughters. Jenny and I were given the recent insert search of Meldrew and told to examine it minutely. This is what we found."

A holographic image in high-def hi-mag of the tendril cord attachments appeared on the Ether Screen.

"This we believe is the start of a new spinal cord to replace the one we severed. You have seen from the records that Meldrew also had a second DNA strand within that second cord but there is no sign of that from this search. Our analysis also found signs of unusual neural disturbances in the regions of long-term memory. Meldrew stored his killings in these areas but we emptied them of the memories after the cord was cut. Jenny and I are of the opinion that killer Meldrew is starting to make a return. Eleanor."

Eleanor went to the Ether Screen and brought up an image of Meldrew's brain. Circle outlines in blue appeared in places all over the image. "These are areas where Richard and I found evidence of our previous work on Meldrew." She brought up numerous red circle markers, "But these are the places where recent activity has taken place. Activity that is not ours. From the pattern of the markers, it seems a systematic search was made and over several days. The red markers are all in the areas of long-term memory. Meldrew is definitely looking for something. Perhaps a memory that we failed to empty. Or, perhaps new hiding places for future killing memories. We agree with the Analysts opinion that killer Meldrew is making a return."

Eleanor sat down as silence settled over the room as team members looked at each other or at the Ether Screen where the hologram of Meldrew's brain slowly rotated.

Charlotte stood and walked to the Ether Screen. "Thank you. Is Meldrew a singular aberration or is he on a different evolutionary track than the rest of humankind and more like him can be expected to evolve. Taking the findings and opinions you've just heard as being accurate then obviously our first attempt to get rid of killer Meldrew failed. We must have overlooked something that needed to be removed or disabled at the same time as the cord was cut, or, he is able to regenerate what we destroyed. All previous and present Life Files are being scanned with Jenny's modified program in an effort to find out if any others like Meldrew slipped through. Even at the speed we work it will take some time for the billions of files to be scanned but so far none have been found. This is what the Solons have directed. They have the same concerns that surfaced at the original case. The Solons require that we do no harm to good Meldrew unless absolutely necessary and only with their authority. They are firm that they do not want an innocent man to suffer for something outside of his understanding and knowledge. Also, and they stress this, we must use this occasion to find the root cause. Solons want to know why and how this is happening. Is it environmental evolution that's driving it, or evolutionary DNA adaptation, or something totally new and unintended? Perhaps a mutant strain?"

Charlotte scanned the room and sought the eyes of each individually before asking, "Where do we go from here?"

They all knew better than to begin a barrage of suggestions, questions and opinions. They were well aware how much Charlotte disliked that. Charlotte was silent and waited. Quiet exchanges went on amongst them with ideas being passed back and forth until Eleanor spoke up.

"How does the time frame for his change in sexual appetite fit with the eight-month periods between the killings? Yuri, can you tell us from his Life File from the time we cut the cord?"

"I can bring it up and check," Yuri answered. Meldrew's Life File took the place of the holographic brain with Yuri scanning and thought shifting dates and visual records around at Time Light speed until she slowed to assemble a chronological record.

"It's thirty months or two and a half years in Earth time since the cord was cut and from the visuals his desire for more aggressive sex began at the first eighth month anniversary. Until that time, he was a gentle and considerate lover. The dates and visuals show a steady increase in his need to abuse his wife in order to achieve orgasm whether through penetration or self-masturbation. It was at this stage when his wife was increasingly likely to suffer severe harm that his Life File was flagged. You can see that there is nothing with the exception of the first eighth anniversary to suggest that each following anniversary has caused a rapid change or escalation to its present level. It has been a steady incremental rise."

"Why did you want that information, Eleanor?" came from Victoria.

"Just wondering if this is the old Meldrew or a new one. Old Meldrew stuck to the eight-month schedule and never deviated by as much as a single day and it was based on his gestation period. Eight months, one day and one hour which was the numeric ten that brought us to his killing places. I see no pattern like that in this Meldrew, no reference to the anniversary of his so-called birth. So, has he changed his M.O. or are we seeing the emergence of a different Meldrew?"

Chapter 116

Per Lundquist was seated in the same chair he had used at the marquee on the beach. Still in a dark three-piece business suit with white shirt and a silk tie showing the star logo of the shipping company he and Richard had worked for Life Side. Black socks with black brogues polished to a high gloss. Every inch the company executive. A silver topped cane rested against the arm of the chair. He offered a brief smile and indicated two chairs identical to his in which they were to sit. A glass pitcher frosted with moisture sat on a table between him and where Richard and Eleanor sat.

"Can I offer you some iced tea?" Per Lundquist enquired, then added, "You must be warm after your climb."

Richard declined but Eleanor accepted and waited while Per Lundquist poured her a glass. His own glass was wrapped in a linen napkin to keep the moisture off his hand, so he waited for Eleanor to pick hers up before he spoke.

"Your transition has been completed and your acceptance into Retribution section approved Richard. This has happened in no small part because of those who guided you through the process. Having known and worked with you, Life Side, I admit to a degree of scepticism when I was informed of your arrival and Eleanor's recommendation that you join our section. You were considered by some within the organisation we worked for Life Side as a loose cannon and far more interested in getting things done than the business niceties and politicking that was sometimes necessary to get them approved. Better to beg forgiveness than ask permission seemed to be your style. However, I understand from those you have come into contact with here that your approach to tasks is much more measured now and Eleanor tells me that you have changed in many ways from the younger man she and I knew." Here Per Lundquist raised his glass saying, "Richard, welcome to Retribution section."

Richard smiled and nodded in acknowledgment as Lundquist and Eleanor sipped their iced teas. Placing his glass on the table Per Lundquist took hold of his cane then stood to give a slight bow to both of them saying, "Please don't get up. I'll see you as you go about your work Richard and as always, a delight to see you, Eleanor." Again the brief smile before turning to cross the balcony to enter the building. His cane tapped in time with his stride across the marble flagstones. At the threshold he paused then turned slightly to say over his shoulder, "Eleanor, take Richard back to the child trafficking case. It's about to wrap up." A further step and he was swallowed by the darkness of the room.

Reaching across the space between the chairs Eleanor took his hand and they were in the café across from the transport company depot. A waitress approached to ask for their order just as Victoria and Ted walked in and sat down with them. Even before greetings were made Ted said, "Take the all-day breakfast. Really good." Four breakfasts were ordered with coffees.

The coffees arrived as Victoria was saying, "We got Per Lindquist's message about you joining us. It's good to see you both again. We can watch what's about to happen across the street while we eat."

The breakfast plates arrived just as a number of police cars and two armoured trucks arrived at the transport yard. No sirens or flashing lights but the lead truck crashed through the wrought iron gates in the fence surrounding the yard tearing them from their hinges. People in the yard could be seen scattering or standing stunned as heavily armed police tumbled from the armoured trucks and made for the warehouse. Uniformed officers began rounding up those in the yard and herding them into a loading bay outside the warehouse. Their waitress and the other half dozen diners ran onto the sidewalk outside the café to gawk and point and talk amongst themselves. Other businesses and houses on the street emptied as others gathered to conjecture about what might be going on. The four from Concordat continued eating their breakfasts. Two dull crumps came from the warehouse along with shouting that was loud but indecipherable from a distance. A door in the warehouse wall opened and several men and one woman came staggering out followed by armed police who pushed them aggressively towards and into one of the armoured trucks. Following them came half a dozen young women looking dazed and frightened by what was going on but they were wrapped in blankets and ushered into the other armoured truck with gentleness and care. From the crashing through the gate to the armoured vehicles leaving had taken only five minutes. Police remained on the scene to gather information and question the people corralled in the loading bay. A crowd was beginning to gather at the wrecked gates and was kept back by police. A TV station had obviously been alerted and their van arrived to record the crowd and take shots of the yard and trashed gates. A presenter went and asked a policeman what was going on, he shook his head and remained silent. When they had finished their breakfasts, Ted left money to cover the bill and a sizeable tip although their waitress was still outside and did not notice them walk away.

Watchers witnessed the arrest of the head of the sex crime unit with the owl tattoo on his arm. The one who had protected the traffickers. Ted and Victoria would watch periodic downloads over the next weeks and witness the mad scramble as senior officers tried to distance themselves and go into cover your arse mode.

Such was the uproar on social media the police were forced to start an independent enquiry. The police would not be allowed to investigate the police.

Ted and Victoria kept Eleanor and Richard up to date on the case as it unfolded from the independent enquiry, which was damning, the heads that rolled and the sentencing to jail of those involved with the transport end. Arrests were also made in several European countries. Later the woman involved with the trafficking was stabbed to death in the prison showers. The retiring sergeant was feted by his brother officers as a hero for bringing 'that son of a bitch senior officer' to justice. Major changes were promised by the government to stop human trafficking. No one in Concordat was holding their breath on that promise. It came from a government after all. Governments promise much and deliver little. They all knew this from their times Life Side.

These updates came after Richard was working solo as a Retributionist. He and Eleanor met often.

Chapter 117

Richard asked, "About the tendril connections, are they showing up in the same spot the killer cord was cut?"

Jenny brought the hologram of the tendrils back on the Ether Screen. "From their position at the spinal vertebrae, it looks very close. Mark wasn't concerned about this area during his search so the clarity isn't good but yes it could be the same place."

Richard continued, "Okay. When we had Meldrew under surveillance after cutting the cord but before transporting him back Life Side we recorded that the remains of the killer cord was absorbed and disappeared. That is what we saw happen. The cord was absorbed to eventually disappear. But what if it wasn't? What if it was hidden and is now becoming apparent with the tendrils beginning to bridge the gap at the cut site?"

Emily, who had been Richard's conduit during his time Life Side as Meldrew, broke into the silence that followed his theory, "Then who hid it? In order for it to be brought back some entity had to be aware that killer Meldrew was going to be culled. Or a part of killer Meldrew was able to survive and fooled us into thinking the cord had been absorbed. But why then is attention being drawn to it by causing a red flag in the Life File? Surely it would be best to keep a low profile until the connection was complete and the cord made whole. If it is killer Meldrew again he seems not to have learned anything from his previous incarnation. He's led us right back to him."

"Emily makes a good point," came from Ted. "We watch Meldrew all the time because of his past history so does he know we're watching? Assuming it's killer Meldrew or some other iteration of him why is he inviting us in to have a look? It's as if the flag got raised on purpose. What can be gained by doing that?"

Before another opinion or theory could be voiced Charlotte called a halt, "We have lots of questions and conjecture but I've not heard any answers or any direction that we should be going. Two things are paramount. One, we do no harm to our Meldrew. Two, the Solons want to know the root cause of Meldrew's relapse. Get together and come up with a plan for going forward that fulfils these two conditions. Also, we must keep in mind that Constance Meldrew is in harm's way if her husband's behaviour continues to worsen. Perhaps she is being used as the bait to lure us into a hasty response so let's find a way to protect her until we are ready to act. Consider that." Walking to the door she said, "This place is now off lockdown, you're free to move about as normal but keep specifics of the case between yourselves. As far as anyone else is concerned this is our first Meldrew case. The file has not been opened to anyone else. Eleanor, get in touch with me when there's a plan." And with that Charlotte opened the door and left.

Silence followed Charlotte's departure until Yuri loudly asked, "Diner?"

This was greeted by a chorus of, "Diner."

They went and they pushed tables together to accommodate their number as Sherri bustled about bringing coffee, tea and cutlery. The chalk board showed that pie of the day was blackberry and apple and all agreed that's what they would have. Sherri laughed and as she headed to the counter said, "Mario's gonna love you people and you are gonna love his pie."

They talked quietly amongst themselves until the pies arrived when all conversation ceased and their full attention was afforded the pies. Eleanor waited until all plates emptied and all forks were set down.

"Let's try this and see if it gets the ball rolling. We will take five minutes by the clock above the counter to each think about this development with Brian Meldrew then each of us will write down on paper that I am about to give you one sentence that recommends how we move forward. One sentence only. No names on the paper and you will fold them and give them back to me. We will then go to my apartment and discuss them. As adjudicator I will not write anything."

Taking a notebook from a pocket in her coat Eleanor tore pages from it and handed them out. "Write so that handwriting can't be recognised. Time starts now."

Sherri was about to take a fresh pot of coffee to the table for top ups but stopped when she saw the looks of concentration on all their faces as they all stared at pieces of paper. She decided not to intrude but to come back later.

"Time's up. Give me the pages." They were handed to her. "Thank you. Now come to my apartment where we can sync and discuss each one."

The tables were empty and money for the food and drink along with a nice tip was under an empty coffee mug. As she collected the dirty plates and cups to a tray then separated the tables and returned them to their usual places Sherri wondered why she could not remember who had used them.

Chapter 118

"Everyone comfortable?" Nods and yeses of confirmation. "Good. Let's sync. Confirm connection please." All did. "A sentence will appear on the Ether Screen. Let's try not to talk over one another and please keep your comments brief. Just pros and cons of each sentence. After all views have been heard the writer will have the chance to defend his or her approach. I'll halt the discussions if it starts going round in circles. The first."

The pros and cons of each were discussed with spirited defences made by the authors. Eleanor had to step in when opposing views brought discussion to a stalemate. Approaches varied widely and even without names it would have been easy to pick the writer.

Protect wife and family and observe, Emily— sever tendrils and monitor for new growth, Ted — transport to Concordat for deep searches and replace him Life Side, Victoria — stop growth progress by inserting neural blockers, Yuri — induce selective cerebral damage to locate his area of operational cortex, Alan — observe until evidence of significant harm to others will occur then cull and autopsy — Jenny. Richard however had taken a different approach. He posed a question—is a separate entity moving against Concordat and testing for weaknesses?

Eleanor had purposefully screened Richard's question last. If such was happening a much wider threat existed than that apparent in Meldrew. When the others saw it there was no immediate responses because they all understood the consequences of such a threat.

In the quiet Emily uttered a drawn out, "Ohhh shiiit."

Eleanor responded, "Oh shit indeed. Un-sync and go verbal. Apartment is on lockdown."

Alan went to the glass doors standing open to the balcony and leaning against the frame he took a deep breath of sultry spicy Kolkata air before saying, "Richard's should have been first because if it proves true then we need to be looking much further than what is causing Meldrew's behavioural changes."

"I disagree," came from Eleanor. "It's in the right place. It proves that those of us on the front line at Concordat need to recognise that we might not hold all the cards and also realise that as the evolutionary path lengthens wrongdoers might be capable of blocking our measures against them. My proposal was going to be covert surveillance while appearing to ignore him and see what he does. Not dissimilar to others on the list and which all hold valid proposals but Richard's takes us away from what we have, Meldrew, and makes us aware that other forces could be at play within him. As Alan said we need to look beyond Meldrew. How do we do that?"

Richard stood and made his way to the kitchen asking, "Tea, coffee, soft drink anyone? I'll bring them out." Two teas, three coffees and two Diet Pepsi were requested. He would have tea.

When he returned with a laden tray the Ether Screen had gone. Emily, Alan and Yuri were out on the balcony talking while the other four were holding a murmured conversation on the sofa. Richard called the balcony trio back inside to get their drinks.

They all settled and Eleanor asked again, "How do we do that. How do we look beyond Meldrew?"

Drinks were taken while each pondered the question and sought answers. Jenny, always one for the dramatic, went onto the balcony and rested against the railing while facing into the room. Doing this she knew would draw the attention of the others to her. She drank some coffee then lowered the mug and proceeded to swirl the remaining liquid into a whirlpool which seemed to absorb her and then without looking up declared in a most casual way, "Maybe it's one of us. Perhaps someone in Concordat is manipulating Meldrew."

In the stunning moment it took for her remark to sink in she turned to look across the low roofs of the dwellings and shops across the street from Eleanor's apartment. The Wannabe actress in her loved knowing she had their full attention.

Eleanor recovered to tell her, "All right Meryl Streep, an Oscar performance so now take a bow then get back in here."

Jenny turned to face them then bowed extravagantly and with head back and nose in the air she sashayed back into the room to sit beside Alan. The others could not help but smile at her performance despite the seriousness of her allegation.

Chapter 119

Emily, who had been brought late into the team on the previous Meldrew case, looked intently at Jenny and in a voice tinged with incredulity said, "Jenny, are you serious? Why would anyone in Concordat do such a thing? For what purpose?"

Jenny answered, "I'm deadly serious and now I've said the words they bring more force to Richard's question about third party manipulation."

Richard smiled across at Jenny and said, "You have to stop doing this Jenny. You put us on track the previous case with a seemingly off-hand remark about times between killings. Now you're saying that this time we need to rule out interference from within Concordat before assuming his change in behaviour is solely down to Meldrew."

Jenny nodded, "That's what I'm saying. And—we might find similar interference was part of the original Meldrew case because if it is someone from Concordat, we have no idea how long they've been active."

Eleanor stepped into the silence following Jenny's remarks, "Charlotte needs to know about this development. Let me get hold of her."

The slightest of frowns creased Eleanor's forehead when she tele-transmitted a message to Charlotte outlining what had transpired and asking her to come to the apartment.

Soon there was a knock at the door and Richard went to let Charlotte in.

Charlotte said a general 'Hi' to the group who responded with murmured greetings of their own. Going to the kitchen she found a mug and brought it to the carafe of coffee Richard had made and poured some before settling on the arm of the sofa and saying directly to Eleanor, "Okay, what's all this about?"

"We were doing an exercise to determine the best way to find the root cause of the reappearance of the cord and of Meldrew's behavioural change while protecting Constance. Scenarios were put forward from the team that were discussed and argued over and all of which had some merit but it was when Richard posed a question and Jenny offered a theory that things changed. I'll bring up an Ether Screen and you can see for yourself."

The screen appeared with Richard's question, "Is a separate entity moving against Concordat and testing for weaknesses?" And Jenny's theory, "Maybe it's one of us. Perhaps someone in Concordat is manipulating Meldrew."

Charlotte looked at the screen for long moments then began to speak, "I'm going to have to inform the Solons about this and here's what I'm going to tell them you are doing. You will find safe haven for Constance and Amy. I want them away from Meldrew for a time. The nurse will develop appendicitis and cancel her hike because she will be recovering. Scrutinise every Concordat department and section to determine which have easiest or frequent legitimate access to Meldrew, who has used that access and if it was approved and recorded. Watchers are to be with Meldrew twenty-four hours of his day and all his movements recorded. Make all this very apparent and observe if Meldrew's behaviour changes and if so in what way. Analytics and programming are to determine if interference was going on prior to and during the previous Meldrew case and if so, why wasn't it picked up and then what needs to be in place to catch such behaviour in future. Check all peripheral personnel involved with the previous case, observers, Watchers, downloader's and suchlike. They all need to be cleared. You must take all measures to determine if anyone in Concordat is involved. Richard's question asked us to look at something new and I understand Jenny's reasoning, what better way to control Meldrew than with the tools Concordat provide. Whatever you and your team need Eleanor, I'll get it. I'll field the questions from the Solons so keep me always up to date." Charlotte returned her mug to the kitchen and then went to the door and before leaving said, "It needs to be proved one way or the other before we can move on Meldrew himself. He may be innocent."

Charlotte left and Eleanor went around collecting mugs and empty pop cans then took the loaded tray to the kitchen. As she was returning she heard Richard say "You have reason to be concerned Emily. All here are thinking the same thing. If someone in Concordat is working through Meldrew them how many more might we have missed?"

Chapter 120

Amy came slamming through the front door and dropped her school backpack at a dead run down the hallway towards the kitchen calling, "Mum, Mum, where are you?"

The answer came from upstairs, "I'm up here putting bed linens away, what's all the excitement about?"

Amy backtracked and at a two at a time charge up the stairs came to a red cheeked and dishevelled face to face with her mother at the linen closet. "Guess what Mum. The school is doing a month-long road and rail trip in Europe to see all the capitals and sail down the Rhine and climb mountains in Switzerland and visit Venice and Paris and Amsterdam and all sorts of other great stuff and it's only for my year and only twenty places and it's first come first serve and they want two chaperones to go with the two teachers so you could do that and we have to let them know soon like tonight because everyone wants to go and you're to text Mrs Bannister to book a place so do it now Mum, please."

After whirlwind Amy had been calmed down and she became more coherent Constance got more information and did contact Mrs Bannister who sent her a link that explained about the trip. Constance and Ruth Bannister knew each other from volunteer work and fund raising for the hospital where Brian worked. Ruth promised to hold a place for Amy provided Constance let her know yes or no by noon the next day. Constance promised to. She did not tell Amy of this arrangement and instead told her that they would need to talk it over with her father that evening. Amy, who had recently turned eighteen and was in her last year at school and about to enter university, was pragmatic enough to know it was best not to force the issue until she heard what her father had to say.

Watchers duly recorded and reported these events.

Brian Meldrew listened to Amy and read the information link. He agreed that it would be educational as well as mind broadening for Amy to take the trip but also argued that perhaps her time could be better spent at home preparing for university. It wasn't the cost either he said, in fact he found it very reasonable for such a trip. When the question of Constance being a chaperone came up, he seemed even more reluctant to agree. Constance knew better than to push him too hard. His behaviour towards her was getting crueller and more erratic when they were alone and she did not want to antagonise him. Amy put forth arguments he found hard to refute that it wasn't just a holiday it was a learning experience and hadn't he always said to take every opportunity to learn. Eventually he reluctantly agreed they should both go. Constance saw the look in his eyes saying she would pay for this later but she smiled as Amy rushed off to text her friends and she messaged Ruth to confirm she and Amy would be going.

During the two weeks leading to their departure Meldrew was frequently called away on consultations lasting two or three days. Constance was relieved because it reduced her husband's time at home and the painful acts he forced upon her. More and more she found it necessary to wear clothing that covered bruising on her upper arms caused by her husband's fingers. Amy was delighted and made all sorts of plans with her fellow travellers about what they would do in all the places they would visit. Constance threw herself into the role of chaperone and helped Ruth with organising all the minutia that such a trip entailed. She just wanted to be away from her husband and the man he was becoming.

Watchers were on hand when the party boarded the Eurostar headed to Paris. Many parents were on hand to wave farewell. Meldrew was not. He had said no need for him to be there when Amy's mother was a chaperone. Constance tried to conceal the bruises on her neck with makeup and a silk scarf.

Sanjeev, a Watcher, remarked to his colleague Albert, "You saw what he did last night Al, I'm sure he suspects something is going on and he did that to draw us out. Good thing we got Constance out of there today. Let Eleanor know that they are on the train and our French friends have taken over."

Al, taciturn as ever said, "Done."

Eleanor told Charlotte that Constance and Amy were safely on their way to Europe.

"Whose plan was that?"

"Yuri with help from Richard who planted the idea in Ruth Bannister's mind. Once the ball was rolling it came together quite quickly," Eleanor answered. Then continued, "We're arranging for the nurse to suffer an appendicitis attack tomorrow Earth time at the hospital. Good place for her to collapse. I'll drop in on her today and arrange for the symptoms and make it look ugly for when they remove it. That will put paid to her hiking plans for a few weeks. Now we watch for Meldrew's reaction."

"I'll tell the Solons. Let me know as soon as Meldrew makes a move."

Chapter 121

He was called Vinter and he was pissed off. He didn't mind so much that the wife and kid had fucked off to the continent on some school jolly he was pissed because he had just learned that the nurse planning a hiking trip had had an appendicitis attack and was in the recovery room after having it removed. He still intended to hike but now would have to take whoever he met up with on the trail. The nurse had taken the uncertainty out of the plan, now it was back. Plus, she was a looker. He'd wanted to see her body without scrubs. He went along with the other Meldrew as he visited her and wished her a speedy recovery. Even in a hospital Johnnie shirt her tits looked great.

With Constance away he would be forced to leave Meldrew's car at the beginning of his hike and return for it by bus or rail when he was finished. He directed Meldrew to find which section of the Pennine Way suited him best. He sustained himself with the few memories he had been able to hide before the rest were erased. It had been dumb luck that led that analytics and programming bitch to him. Her and her fucking single constant program. He was going to be stronger this time. He knew they had seen the flag and that they almost certainly had something to do with getting Constance out the way and probably the nurse as well but he wanted them to show their hand, he wanted to lure them in. He would get to know how they operated by doing things that forced them to respond. They were constrained by some shitty code of ethics and morality but he wasn't. Nor would those that followed him be. For now, he must content himself with using other Meldrew as his chrysalis.

He guided Meldrew through the preparations for the hike. Collecting backpack, tent, sleeping bag and all the other paraphernalia his friends had promised to loan him. He even wore his new boots when doing rounds as a way to break them in. He was vague about where he would hike saying he wanted somewhere relatively flat because it had been years since he had hiked at all. Easy distance was what he was aiming for with access to towns and villages along the way. A fellow doctor gave him a book about walks on the Pennine Way, both day and extended, saying she found it useful when planning her hikes. He thanked her and said it would be a great help.

Arrangements were made for colleagues to watch over his patients in the hospital and he informed his outpatients that he would be away for several days and who to call in case of emergency. They would be contacted on his return. He would not be reachable by mobile phone. He gave his nurse and receptionist paid time off.

The route he finally decided Meldrew would take was from Middleton in Teesdale to Keld. A distance of about twenty-four miles and would include the Bowes Loop if going was good and he made fast progress. He would wild camp although this was frowned upon because it was preferred that approved hostels and camping grounds were used. From experience he knew that many hikers ignored this rule. Meldrew had done so in the past during his university years. He would drive to Middleton and phone a hotel there to book a night and get permission to leave his car in the parking lot while he walked for a few days saying he would stay a further night on his return. The hotel owner was amenable to his request. He found via the internet that a daily bus could be caught in Keld which stopped at Middleton on its way to the market town of Barnard Castle.

Vinter stayed quiet throughout all the preparations. With Constance gone he felt cheated of his nightly abuse, the one time he could exert some of his power over Meldrew instead of the kind doctor persona. He was silent on the journey and thought of what he, through Meldrew, would do to the one he chose as his victim.

It was remarkable how quiet Concordat was. He'd expected more activity as they searched about to find how and why the cord was reconnecting but he was confident that he and his Despotics could outmanoeuvre anything Concordat tried to do. Concordat operatives were not immortal. Even in this world.

Chapter 122

Ted reported that Meldrew was on the move and sent Eleanor a Watcher download of him driving away from his house.

"Thanks Ted. Put someone at the hotel to monitor and report his arrival. I'd like to get inside Meldrew but can't take the chance. I think other Meldrew has a trap prepared in the event we try. It's too risky. We'll watch and wait and hope we can protect whoever crosses his path."

"You think he's hunting like the first Meldrew did?"

"No, I don't think he's hunting. I think he wants a female, any female, and do things that will force us to intervene. I believe he wants to trap one of us."

There was a long pause before Ted responded. "Damn, I don't even want to think about that possibility. Okay, I'll put people at the hotel and Life Files are recording his journey."

"Thanks Ted. Let me know when he gets to the hotel."

"Will do."

Richard had synced with Eleanor when Ted contacted her and had heard their conversation. Now he un-synced and gave a shrug along with a look of resignation.

Eleanor nodded in understanding saying, "We need a breakthrough." Then she tele messaged the other team members to tell them Meldrew was on the move.

Richard and Eleanor were in the analytic pod where Alan and Jenny were going over every search and record from the previous case and the present one trying to find how killer Meldrew had managed to convince them that the severed spinal cord had been totally absorbed and no longer operational. Amber, the Retributionist who had cut the cord, was with them and going over in detail every nanosecond of her cull. She found nothing amiss. The cord was recorded to have been cleanly and completely severed and almost immediately began to be absorbed by the surrounding tissue where over the period that Meldrew was kept at Concordat it disappeared. There had been no trace of it when Meldrew was returned Life Side.

"I'm going to my place," Richard told Eleanor. "I can think things over there just as well as I can here. Maybe the sun and sea will shake something free. I'll leave a channel open for you to get in touch."

Eleanor smiled and said, "Wish I could join you. Enjoy."

Removing his clothes, he walked into the sea and after swimming to the centre of the lagoon he rested with his back against the sea water buoyancy and closed his eyes. The residue of wave energy that had broken against the reef and washed over caused a slight swell that moved his relaxed body to its rhythm.

The voice of Takahara, his one-time guide and mentor, came unbidden to him as he cleared his mind of all but the enveloping sensation of the water. "Richard, recall your first effort taking me with you travelling and you missed the beach by many metres. I told you 'Pinpoint focus' was essential and to disregard all distractions. I repeat those words now. Not wide view Richard, pinpoint focus. Look to the very essence of Meldrew."

He let Takahara's words resonate in his mind then swam to shore where he picked up a handful of sand then let it trickle from his palm until just a single grain remained. He brought the single grain into pinpoint focus until even the background of his palm faded and the grain seemed to hang in emptiness. What in the Meldrew case was the equivalent to this single grain? What was this essence he should focus on?

It was as he widened his focus from the single grain and his surroundings once more became apparent and he surveyed the beach in its entirety that Takahara's words made sense. The beach was made up of many units and if one unit, one grain, was moved then the whole beach was changed. The grains he had picked up and then let fall had changed the beach and even the one he retained in his palm constituted change to the beach. Such a small thing, one single grain taken from it and this beach, in essence, was not the same beach he had come to.

He contacted Eleanor and told her he was returning.

Chapter 123

"What brought you back so soon?" Eleanor enquired, "Too much sun, sand and relaxation?"

"Absolutely, that stuff gets old quickly," Richard answered with a grin. "Nothing like being cooped up in an analytic pod to refresh the spirit." Then, "Can we get Amber and the other two out of their analytic den? I may have stumbled on something."

Eleanor knocked on the door leading to the analytics and programming lab then opened it and told Amber, Alan and Jenny to come out and hear what Richard had to say.

Alan went to get coffee while the two women dropped into easy chairs with Amber asking, "So Richard, what's this something you've stumbled on?"

Richard waited until Alan came back with his coffee and sat at the table then he told them about Takahara and what he could best describe as his communication to him while he had been in the lagoon. He explained about Takahara's admonition to pinpoint focus, to avoid all distractions and find the single thing that was at the core of Meldrew's behaviour. He then did an Ether Screen visual replay from his memory of his focus on the grain of sand and his thoughts that removing a single grain changed the beach radically, as would the addition of a single grain. He then tossed a question at them, "What's the absolute essence of every sentient being. The core. The guidebook?"

Alan, who was gazing into his coffee mug, answered without looking up. "DNA."

"Right, and what happens when parts of the helix are altered or disturbed?" Richard asked.

Jenny sat more upright in her chair and said, "Physical and behavioural changes occur."

Before Richard could say more Amber burst out with, "Bloody hell, we've been so focused on the cord reconnecting that we overlooked the second DNA helix we found running in tandem with Meldrew's, the one that belonged to killer Meldrew. It disappeared along with the cord and we assumed that like the cord it was absorbed because it no longer functioned. Perhaps we were wrong. Perhaps Meldrews DNA has been infected by part of the killer strain."

Alan who was now standing and paying full attention blurted, "That's what Takahara was telling Richard. Focus on the DNA, the core, because it's been fucked with. The cord is just a distraction we've been wasting time on."

Jenny chimed in, "If that's the case we need a sample of Meldrew's DNA. No. In fact we need two samples. One when Meldrew is himself and one from when the abusive one takes over. We need to be able to determine where in the chain the switch is flipped from one personality and behaviour to the other."

Eleanor who had sat quietly throughout now spoke up, "A sample from original Meldrew is easy enough. We get approval to do a Life Side operation and teleport a hair or saliva sample back here for analysis. Getting one from him while he's in abusive mode could be a problem. How do we stay close enough to collect it and at the same time not allow too much harm to be inflicted on the woman? Any suggestions?"

Richard responded "I suggest we get the whole team together. Whatever we do will require all of us. Tell them to go to my place at the beach."

Eleanor tele-transmitted to all team members including Charlotte telling them to make their way to Richard's beach cottage immediately for a meeting.

When they were all gathered on the patio Eleanor gave Charlotte a short version of what had transpired at the pod and why she had brought the team together. Charlotte voiced her understanding and told Eleanor to get things underway.

Clapping her hands to get their attention and stop the buzz of conversation she told them, "Go verbal then look at the Ether Screen. You are going to see what transpired at a meeting in the analytics and programming pod moments ago."

When the Ether Screen went blank and faded away Emily was heard to say, "Fuck me, how'd we miss that?" Which brought all eyes on her because she had never been heard to utter a single swear word before. Putting her hand to her mouth she said a muffled, "Oh dear, did I just say that out loud? Sorry." And she began to blush.

Ted told her, "It's okay. I bet a lot of us are thinking the same thing. I know I am."

Eleanor told them, "Meldrew is on his way to the hotel and will begin his hike tomorrow morning Earth time. We have to find a way of collecting a sample of his DNA while he's himself and another after his change."

"We have copies of his DNA on file from the first case, why can't we use that?" Victoria asked.

Jenny replied, "Because that won't tell us what changes or the number of them that have taken place since he was returned Life Side. We have to think of Meldrew as being brand new as far as DNA is concerned."

Charlotte spoke up, "We've agreed getting a sample from the hotel or even his car is easy. One or two go Life Side and bring or send some back. As I see it — and correct me if I'm wrong — the second sample has to come from after Meldrew changes from docile to aggressive." Sounds of agreement from the team. "So someone has to be very close to him at the time. Am I right in saying that?" Again agreement all round. "So as I see it that sample will have to come from on, or in, or near to that woman. The one that he plans to abuse." A pause and again no disagreement. "Then the woman should come from Concordat. We cannot put a stranger in harm's way in order to collect the evidence necessary to provide proof of something we overlooked. I will not permit it."

Yuri broke into the silence following Charlotte's last pronouncement. "Can I ask if you have anyone in particular from Concordat picked out? I ask because to me it points to someone already on the team. We cannot ask someone from elsewhere in Concordat to become the sacrificial lamb. That would be as cruel as using someone he meets on the trail."

Charlotte replied, "You're right Yuri. Using a woman from the team is the only option and not least because we can provide some degree of safety. We have tools that can terminate his activities if they get to the point where they threaten my life."

It took a nanosecond for Charlotte's words to sink in and before anyone spoke. It was Victoria who exclaimed, "You! You're telling us that you will be the woman. Charlotte, you have no experience in the field so what makes you think you can handle someone like abusive Meldrew in a Life Side operation?"

"That's exactly the reason Victoria. In reality the work requiring the least experience is that of the woman Meldrew takes. The rest of you are needed for other things crucial to the operation."

"Charlotte's right," came from Richard. "It will be our job to protect her as best we can without alerting Meldrew. Charlotte knows the dangers so there's no need to dwell on them."

Chapter 124

They met at the hotel bar after having dinner in the restaurant. Just two people exchanging pleasantries over a drink. They introduced themselves as Barbara and Brian. She had back story involving her love of hiking and descriptions of some of the trails she'd done. By coincidence it would turn out they intended to walk the same section of the Pennine way. Snippets of personal history would emerge from which he would learn she was a widow and this was her first hike in over a year since her husband had been killed in a car crash. Drunken driver hit him head-on. He explained this was his first serious hike since university and about his work and family. He showed no interest in her beyond the opportunity to chat and pass a pleasant hour. She was the first to leave the bar telling him she needed a good night's sleep before setting out early the next morning. They shook hands with him thanking her for her company and saying perhaps they would meet on the trail. She smiled and said it would be nice to have some company for a while if they did. He drank another scotch and soda before heading to his room.

Watchers recorded all this.

So did Vinter.

Richard visited her in her room telling her, "We got all that and it seemed harmless enough. What did you pick up from it?"

"He seemed nice. He spoke of his work with enthusiasm and family with affection. You saw he didn't make any flirtatious comments or moves. But, as I was leaving and we were shaking hands a look came into his eyes I don't think he was even aware of. It was a hard look, one that spoke of the ability to do harm. I believe that was his alter ego showing through."

In a lighter tone Richard asked, "So, how do you like being Life Side, Barbara? Did you find it a bit disorienting at first?"

"I did. It took me a couple of hours to get used to my Life Side body. So clumsy and slow, I'd forgotten what they are like."

"Yes. Not the best design by any means particularly when it's paired with a brain function as small as theirs. Amazing they've survived this long. Concordat must see something in them, and us, that warrants such a long-term evolutionary commitment."

"Mmm-mm, they have their reasons I'm sure," Charlotte said as she began to undress. "But it's time for me to sleep. Long day tomorrow and I need to be on the trail before Meldrew. Do you think it's certain he will camp next to me?"

"Not certain but highly probable. Whatever or whoever is driving alter ego Meldrew won't pass up the opportunity to be with a woman camping alone. Don't forget we believe he wants to draw us in. If he passes you by, we'll just have to see how much we can protect whoever he goes for. As planned, there will be other hikers on the trail all body hopped by the team so Meldrew will be monitored the whole way and if he goes too far with you then hopefully the plan to stop him will work."

"Right, we'll just have to see what happens but for now I'm for a long hot bath to relax then sleep," Charlotte said as she made her way to the bathroom and turned on the tap then adjusted the temperature. Taking the hotel supplied bubble bath she poured a good amount into the water streaming from the tap and instantly cloud white foam smelling of lavender appeared.

"Need a back wash before I go?" came from Richard who had been leaning against the door frame watching.

"Oh I'll need much more than just my back washed," Charlotte replied archly as she stepped into the foam.

Chapter 125

It was hardly daylight when a sleepy night clerk took her money for the room and asked if everything had been to her liking.

"Absolutely. The meal was very good, the bathtub was lovely and deep and I slept like a log. I'm up early to get a start on the trail. It's been a while since I hiked any distance, so I want to take advantage before the day starts to heat up."

The clerk watched as she slung her backpack over her shoulders and adjusted the straps then she took her hiking poles from where they rested against the reception desk. Hunching her shoulders to settle the pack she wished the clerk a nice day and smiled as she turned away and left the hotel.

When his relief came on shift at eight that morning the night clerk had no memory of a guest named Barbara Connor.

Meldrew checked out an hour and a half after her. Both Meldrew's thought about Barbara and wondered if they would see her on the trail. One because it would be nice to have company for part of the way, the other because she fitted his plan nicely. The plan the nurse had screwed up by getting appendicitis. He was still pissed about that but this one would do. They'd have to come to him if they wanted to save her. Vinter was sure Concordat was watching Meldrew.

It was mid-morning when Charlotte spotted a pair of hikers, a man and a woman, coming towards her. When they met, they exchanged pleasantries about the day and the condition of the trail and what their destinations were. As they parted to go their separate ways with 'good luck' and 'enjoy your walk' the woman of the pair turned to look over her shoulder and said without breaking stride, "Slow down or he won't catch you before nightfall."

Richard was the most experienced hiker on the team and together they had gone over the section of trail Meldrew intended to walk picking out likely camping spots at about half distance. It had been years since Meldrew had done any serious hiking and Charlotte was new to it. Richard had told her to go as much as possible into her Life Side body as represented by Barbara's Concordat age. He wanted her to feel the ache and tiredness in her muscles and the shortness of breath brought on by over a year away from the trails. He wanted her to feel the weight of the pack on her back and shoulders and how uncomfortable wet boots and socks felt. He said that hikers' hours were usually from around seven in the morning until four in the afternoon when they started looking for a suitable dry camp site not far from running water if possible. By the time she pitched her tent and set out her sleeping bag, washed and freshened up then cooked her meal it would be around six in the evening and time to relax before turning in early. He had advised her to take a book along to read.

It was three thirty when two men crested a rise in the trail ahead and raised hands in greeting. Standing on the trail they said their hellos and where they were headed. Hikers that are passing seldom exchange names or pause too long in chat, they want to get on. The two men were helpful after asking if Barbara intended to camp beside the trail by telling her of a suitable spot about a mile away. They'd used it before when hiking in her direction. Protected on three sides by large boulders and close to running water. Enough space for two or three tents actually. Charlotte thanked them and said she'd watch out for it. One of the men pointed down the trail with his hiking pole and said, "Looks like someone else going your way today. Probably forty-five minutes behind you. Just make them out on that ridge." Barbara thanked them again for telling her about the campsite and with the usual 'good luck' and 'enjoy' they parted.

Charlotte found the site and pitched her tent close beside one of the boulders. Although frowned upon by the trail minders illegal camping away from recognised campsites was never prosecuted. Hikers brought money to the local economies along the trail. This site was obviously well used with signs of tent placings and peg holes. The flattened grass beside the boulders spoke of sheltered spots for cooking stoves. Her tent was bright orange and easily visible from the trail. She was returning from relieving herself into a hole she had dug behind a large boulder a hundred yards away from the water course when she heard, "Hello Barbara. I thought it might be you when I saw the tent. Do you mind if I pitch next to you? I'm beat for the day but if you prefer to be alone, I'll find somewhere else."

Meldrew had arrived.

Chapter 126

"Oh, hello Brian. No, please pitch your tent. Plenty of room. I couldn't see a suitable place on the trail ahead, it looks pretty open."

"Me either. From the OS map the next few miles look bleak until the trail drops into the valley where it branches for the loop." As he spoke, he unbuckled his pack and dropped it to the ground with, "Aah! That's better. Now I'm thinking I should have prepared for this rather than making a spur of the moment decision. Age and the lack training are catching up with me."

Barbara smiled and said "I hear you. It's only eighteen months since I last did a multi-day but I'm feeling it now. I'm about to brew some tea, want some? It should be ready by the time you get your tent up."

"That'd be great." Pointing to a large boulder Meldrew said, "I'll pitch over there. Put some distance between us in case I snore and wake you up. Constance, my wife, has to jab me at least once a night to shut me up."

Barbara laughed, "Very considerate of you Brian. Come get tea when you're pitched."

By the time she had assembled her stove, collected water from the stream and sterilised it with her SteriStick then set the pot on the stove Meldrew was well into getting things organised in and around his tent. The water had just come to the boil when he backed out of his tent and walked over carrying a tin mug.

"I have coffee granules if you prefer," Charlotte offered.

"No thanks, tea is fine," Meldrew responded as he sat down. "I do have a flask of whisky with me, it helps me sleep, and maybe we can toast the end of the day later on."

"Thank you, I might. What I'm hoping for is that the night sky is clear and I get to see the stars without any light pollution. That's one of the best things hiking brings, that and the silence. Peter, my husband, wasn't into hiking. He tried it a couple of times but he liked his comfort too much. The beauty of the countryside and a clear night sky didn't do it for him, yet he'd go out and quite happily get beat up and broken bones playing rugby in the rain. I miss him a lot." Swallowing hard she said, "Sorry, didn't mean to bring those things up."

Barbara had been talking while the tea bags did their work and she poured tea into their mugs. She handed him a sugar sachet and a Ziplock bag with powdered milk both of which he sprinkled into his mug.

As he stirred, he said, "No need to apologise. It's good to talk about it. My psychiatrist colleagues would say it shows that you are moving on by being open about those feelings."

"So, does your wife, Constance isn't it, does she hike at all?"

"Oh no. She's a comfort bunny too. I've been away from it a lot longer than you, not since university, then out of the blue I just decided to start again. My wife and daughter, Amy, are in Europe on a final year school trip visiting a bunch of countries. Constance is one of the chaperones. At least I'll be able to limp home and recover before they get back so I can lie and tell them what a piece of cake it was." They both laughed.

They used separate stoves to cook their evening meals then Barbara carried hers to his site and they sat outside his tent and talked about all sorts of things while they ate and drank tea afterwards. The talk flowed easily about their work, families, likes and dislikes, hiking experiences. It was a typical hikers relaxing get-together at the end of the day. Meldrew took their plates and utensils to the stream to wash them while Charlotte collected food wrappers and put them in a bag to carry out when she left the trail. The leave no trash rule was observed. When everything was tidied away, he went to his pack and brought out the flask mentioned earlier.

Barbara took her clean plate and utensils from him saying, "Thank you and I enjoyed our conversation but now I think I'll go and read awhile and then if I don't fall asleep come out and see if the stars are shining later on. Sleep well."

"You too. I hope the clouds stay away. Can I interest you in that nightcap I mentioned earlier?"

"No thanks. That would really put me to sleep and I might miss the stars. Thank you all the same."

He was pouring whisky into his mug as she went back to her tent.

Barbara read until full darkness fell then turned off the headlight she was using and went outside to scan the sky. It was wonderfully clear, no clouds or haze. The dew had not started to form so she lay back on the turf beside her tent and absorbed the beauty of an infinity of stars. It was only when her eyes started to close and she felt she was about to fall asleep that she made her way back inside the tent to change into her sleeping clothes. Thermal long-sleeved top and thermal long johns with insulated ankle socks to keep her feet warm. She had a knitted hat inside the sleeping bag in case her ears and head got cold. She made sure her boots were inside the tent along with her backpack. The stove and dishes she left outside under the vestibule canopy. Satisfied all was safe and secure she slid into her sleeping bag and turned off the headlight she had hung from a loop made for the purpose.

The night was too warm to need the sleeping bag zipped closed, so she pulled it loosely over her and plumped up the down jacket she was using as a pillow then settled back to think about the day. Thoughts of Peter came into her mind and she remembered their first hike. Afterwards he told her the best part was making love to her in the tent. She remembered now how good it had been. Peter had done so many things that brought her overwhelming pleasure. Her hand was under the waistband of her long johns when a body burst through the zippered mesh that formed the tent door and fell on top of her.

Chapter 127

A hand was clamped over her mouth and the weight of the body along with the constriction of the sleeping bag made it impossible for her to move.

A voice she almost recognised whispered in her ear, "You don't have to do that now Barbara, I'll do it for you with the toys I've brought."

The hand moved from her mouth and as she opened it to scream a wad of cloth was stuffed into it causing her to choke and strain for air. She felt a loop of material being pulled quickly down over her head to be tightened over the cloth in her mouth and forming an effective gag. The weight came off her upper body and a hand went to her throat where fingers squeezed and brought her to the point of almost fainting and where her struggles inside the sleeping bag ceased.

"Good girl Barbara," the voice she almost recognised said. "Just lie still and listen. I don't have much time before they come." Letting go of her throat and grasping her hair he lifted Barbara's head and slipped a noose of fine nylon line over it and down to her neck. He pulled on the noose until it tightened and she started to convulse from lack of air. Whoever was holding the line eased the pressure and switched on a headlight that blinded her and kept his face hidden in darkness. "I'm going to get off you so you can uncover yourself from the sleeping bag then I want you to get yourself out of your long johns. You can sit up to do that and get the top up over your head. I'll handle it from there." She felt him move from straddling her hips to kneeling beside her. The pressure on the line never changed. "Sit up now and take off the long johns." She did by wiggling them down over her backside and then down over her legs. A hand came into the light, "Give them here. Now the top." When she sat up the man had moved behind her and when the top was off her arms and bunched around her neck, he pulled it over her head and along the nylon line then he changed hands to maintain pressure and let the top fall free from the line. "Very nice. Now lie back." When she hesitated to obey, he pulled the noose tighter. The light swept over her from head to toes. "Put your arms to at your sides, no good trying to hide anything." The noose tightened and she placed her arms at her sides. "Very nice indeed," the voice murmured. The light illuminated the tent walls as the man moved and she felt his knees against her thighs then it fell on her body again. She resisted again when he took hold of her hand and started to lift it, pressure on the noose made her relax and he guided it to his penis which was already in the open and hard. He stroked it using her hand and saying, "Here, you feel that. That's what you're going to get but first some toys to play with." The noose tightened as he leaned out of the tent door and brought in a bag the contents of which he emptied onto Barbara's legs. "Those opened your eyes, didn't they? Nice looking stuff there. You're going to try them all unless those assholes from Concordat come and stop me." He howled, "Do you hear me Concordat? She doesn't have much time left!"

Something in Barbara told her to relax her body and raise her hand to gently grasp his penis and start to masturbate him. It took time for him to realise what was happening and he brought the light close to her face saying, "Can't wait to get started eh? It's not going to change anything about the toys, we'll still enjoy all of those so go ahead but if you try anything I'll pull this noose so tight it will cut your fucking head off. Understand?" Barbara nodded and continued to gently move her hand. She could feel the tension in him rise as he began the climb towards orgasm, so she increased her pace and gripped a little tighter. The light illuminated the roof of the tent as his head went back and she heard his breathing deepen and become faster. Increasing the pace even more she sensed the moment as a shudder went through him and he pushed his thighs forward moments before he ejaculated onto her stomach. The noose loosened a little as he panted in release saying, "Your husband taught you well." Then he uttered, "Fuck," as lights from outside swept over the tent.

A woman's voice whispered, "Shush, the light may be on but they could be asleep."

Another voice, a male this time, whispered back, "No, the light was moving when we first saw the tent."

Again, the woman's voice, "That other tent is dark, so let's keep it quiet anyway. We can set up over there between the two. If we've disturbed anybody we can apologise in the morning."

The male voice, "Stupid idea trying a night hike anyway, I'm sick of walking into bogs and mud holes. If I ever suggest it again go ahead and slap me."

The female voice, "With pleasure. Let's get the tent up, I need to sleep."

The light in the tent went out.

Chapter 128

When the late arrivals woke the next morning and came from their tent one of the other tents was gone but the one that had been lit when they arrived was still there with a woman heating something on her stove. Whoever had been in the other must have left as dawn was breaking and done it very quietly, or, they had slept very soundly.

The woman waved and shouted, "Hi, want some coffee? I have enough water for three."

"Yes please," came from the woman. "We'll be over in a minute."

When they were settled with their coffees, they introduced themselves and apologised for any disturbance during the night. Barbara introduced herself and said no disturbance at all and that she had fallen asleep soon after they arrived. They were Bob and Carol from Barnard Castle and they explained that on a whim they decided to try a night hike from Middleton in Teesdale to Keld in two overnighters. Bob scratched at a beard he wore and said, "I don't know what possessed us to try. We've done the PW many times and know that parts of it are bad enough in daylight. We must have had brain fade."

"We are heading back now. Silly to try any more at night," came from Carol. Then, "Do you have time for breakfast. We have powdered eggs and precooked bacon if you'd like some." Barbara thanked them and said no explaining she'd had oatmeal already and was having her coffee before packing up and getting back on the trail. Having thanked her for the coffee Bob and Carol left to prepare their breakfast and Barbara began to pack things and take down the tent. Within fifteen minutes she had her pack on and after shouting a goodbye to the others who replied in kind she walked from the campsite and onto the trail.

Charlotte had been walking for only a few minutes when a hiker she had noticed when she joined the trail and who was heading in the same direction caught up with her. It was Richard.

"Good morning, Charlotte. I trust you slept well."

"I did after some earlier interruption."

"You got what we need?"

"Yes. It's dry on my stomach and protected by a gauze pad."

"Okay. Let's finish the walk together then take the bus back to the hotel and we can transport you from there."

They covered the distance to Keld without incident and arrived in plenty of time to catch the bus, so they ate a ploughman's lunch sitting outside a local pub. The barman cum waiter that served them was amazed at the size of the tip he found when he came to collect their empty plates. He stood with the money in his hand and tried to picture who had sat at that table. It wouldn't come so he shrugged and went back to serve a local shouting for another pint. Barbara and Richard watched from across the street at the bus stop. Richard remarked, "It never grows old, does it? Watching people trying to remember us."

Once on the bus, which was only half full, they took a seat at the back and Barbara asked, "What happened to Meldrew? After Bob and Carol turned in, he left me after threatening to kill me if I mentioned to anyone what had happened. He was severely angry and at one time I thought he would kill me anyway. Take a look at this." Pulling down the turtleneck of her hiking sweater she exposed the bruising made by the nylon noose. "I take it that Bob and Carol were acting under guidance from Concordat when on a whim they decided to night hike."

"They were," Richard replied. "We guided them the whole way to your campsite. We used them because we couldn't give Meldrew any idea that Concordat were involved and trying to protect you. Meldrew packed in a hurry and took off back towards Middleton in Teesdale before any of you were awake. He's not far from Middleton and being watched of course. Our Meldrew seems to have returned. Our people on the trail are reporting no sign of anger from him. He's telling them the walk he planned was too ambitious so he's heading home. He seems disappointed but friendly enough. The other one will have to make another plan because at the moment whatever's inside Meldrew it can't seem to work alone. It needs to manipulate Meldrew and needs time to do that."

"I'm looking forward to going back to Concordat and being myself again," Charlotte declared as she looked at the passing scenery.

"Not long now. Amber will come to the hotel and everything's ready at transfer so as soon as she takes a sample of his semen from your belly, we'll ship you off and we'll follow after you."

They left the bus and made their way to the hotel where they sat on a bench below a sign requesting hikers to remove muddy footwear before entering. After doing so they walked in stocking feet to reception. They paid cash for a room for one night saying they would be leaving very early the next morning.

In the room Charlotte threw herself on the bed and let out a long 'Aah' and Richard contacted Amber and told her their location suggesting the bathroom as the best point to arrive. He went into it to give Amber a locator pulse. She said she'd got it and would be right along. Moments later she stepped from the bathroom.

"Hey, you two, that's the first time I've been reassembled in a bathtub. How are you, Charlotte? It was disconcerting not being able to contact you."

"I'm fine. Just a little bruising which I'll take care of when I'm back at Concordat. I've got something for you on my stomach so let's get the sample then I can shower off the rest. He wasn't frugal in his deposit." Laying back she lifted her sweater to reveal the gauze pad covering Meldrew's deposit then released the tape and pulled the pad aside. Amber took a vile containing a sterile swab from her pocket and uncapping it took the swab and rubbed it against the patch of skin Charlotte had covered with the pad.

"I can see dried semen on your skin, so I'll lift some off and take that along. Stay still while I use my nail to scrape it off." At the first touch to her belly Charlotte giggled and Amber with mock severity told her, "Stop that! Sure, it tickles but control yourself. I can't get a decent sample while your belly's jiggling."

Stifling another giggle Charlotte said, "My belly doesn't jiggle. I'm ripped so nothing to jiggle."

Amber retorted, "Yeah, keep telling yourself that if it helps. There we go, all done."

As Amber wrapped the scrapings in a tissue and recapped the vile and Charlotte sat up Richard asked, "Won't your DNA get mixed with his by using your fingernail?"

"The lab knows my DNA and can separate the two. The swab is the main sample the other just back up."

Charlotte walked to the bathroom saying, "Shower time. I won't be long."

Chapter 129

The three of them were transmitted to the receiving room in the analytics and programming pod where the team had gathered to welcome Charlotte. After making their greetings and telling her well done Jenny and Alan took the samples from Amber and disappeared into their lab.

It took Charlotte a few moments to recover all her abilities and become her full Concordat self again then she directed a question to Yuri, "Meldrew, what's he up to?"

"He's in his car on his way home. He decided not to stay another night at the hotel. Watchers and observers report he seems perfectly normal in his behaviour. He twisted his ankle near the end of his hike, nothing serious, which slowed him down a little but all the readings coming in show him to be acting and thinking as normal Meldrew. We can't detect any movement or neural undercurrents that point to his alter ego being active."

"And what did you get from my alter ego Barbara? What were her readings like when she was under duress?"

"It worked well for a program assembled so quickly. The implant program of memories and neural responses took you seamlessly into your Barbara character whenever Meldrew was close. Barbara's mental and physical actions and reactions when Meldrew attacked her were within the program parameters and the way Barbara distracted him with masturbation was an outstanding part of the program. We'll need a full debrief but how did it feel to you? Were you in the background the whole time observing Barbara at work?"

"No, I don't think I was but I really can't be sure. The download from the program will tell us more. It was strange when Richard caught up with me and called me Charlotte because it took me a second or two realise it was me he was talking to. Even now it feels like a part of Barbara remains."

"You should mention that to Jenny or Alan and get one of them to scan and record then remove all traces of Barbara they find. They need to know any aftereffects. You should also tell Eleanor because the same or a modified program might be needed in the future." Here Yuri smiled and said, "We can't go around calling you Charbara can we."

Charlotte smiled and thanked Yuri then moved to find Eleanor who was sitting patiently waiting for the results of the DNA analysis. She told her what Yuri had recommended about the scan and reason for it. Eleanor assured her that as soon as the DNA result was known she would get Jenny or Alan to do a thorough wipe of the Barbara program. Charlotte sat on the arm of Eleanor's chair and murmured, "I'm not cut out for field work. I have all these weird residual feelings and half memories of things that went on but no clarity. I hate that."

Eleanor reached for one of Charlotte's hands and gave it a squeeze saying, "All the strangeness will pass once you are wiped." Charlotte placed her other hand on top of Eleanor's in a show of the friendship that had grown between them since their night together in Kolkata. Moments later the door to the lab opened and the analysts emerged.

Alan requested they all go verbal and lifebrain and to look at the Ether Screen at the end of the room. On the screen two DNA helixes slowly revolved in perfect synchrony. Jenny pointed to the screen, "The one on the right is our Meldrew, on the left his alter ego. They are identical. Whatever is changing Meldrew's behaviour it is not in his DNA. We were wrong in thinking that."

Absolute silence settled and all eyes were focused on the screen. The news seemed to have cast a spell where even breathing seemed to have stopped. It was Alan that broke it, "That's why I asked for verbal and lifebrain. I wanted some time for the news to sink in before all the noise started. At full brain there would have been questions from everyone ricocheting around." All attention turned to Eleanor.

"We should all take some time to think about this. What we thought was the answer turned out to be wrong so now we need a new tactic. I want us all to do the same exercise as before. Go away and think of what our next move should be and in two Earth days we will meet again. Do not use the same one you used last time. Those will be added to the new list for consideration. As before do not discuss your ideas amongst yourselves." Turning to face Charlotte, "Are you happy with that?"

Charlotte concurred, "I am. We need find to a weakness, something we can exploit, so figure out the best way to find it. I will have to report to the Solons that the DNA idea was a bust and we are back to square one. It seems Takahara got it wrong this time, Richard. Eleanor, I want to be there in two days. Let me know the place. Jenny, I want a scan, record download and thorough wipe of Barbara's program immediately by TeleWipe and we can do it all in the lab." Followed by Jenny she made her way to the lab door and said to the room at large, "I can't believe I went through all that hiking shit for nothing."

Chapter 130

Vinter was sulking and his Regulator was angry. Meldrew was deeply asleep and the two of them were hashing over the hiker farce.

The Regulator berated Vinter, "If you'd gone straight to the toys Concordat would have had to act but instead you got side-tracked by getting horny and letting her jerk you off. She knew how to distract you and you let your cock rule your brain. For fuck's sake she'd been married and you didn't think she knew grabbing most men's dicks would turn their brain off? If you'd gone straight in when she turned off her light and used the toys Concordat would have been in Meldrew long before those hikers turned up. The moment they saw Meldrew was about to cause her bodily harm they'd have swarmed all over him. What a cock-up."

Vinter trying to deflect some of the blame burst out, "Yeah, well what about those hikers. How come our lot couldn't have made them have an accident or something that made them stop or turn back? If they hadn't turned up, I'd have been able to do my thing and we'd have our Concordat asshole right now"

"Fuck's sake Vinter! You know why! We don't have the network and capabilities that Concordat have right now. There are only a few of us and if it hadn't been for the analyst bitch coming up with the single constant program you and the others would have gone on your merry way's gradually taking over your targets then jumping to the next ones as you got stronger. You were lucky to escape when they stripped Meldrew of the cord and DNA. The others have had to withdraw and lay low since Concordat put in place the new program and are scanning every file for what tipped them off to you and your damn memory store." Vinter couldn't help but look shame faced at this barb and which then changed to surprise at what his Regulator told him next, "We're transferring you to another host."

The Regulator could see Vinter was about to explode so he stepped in quickly, "Keep it down Vinter or you'll have Meldrew lit up like a

Christmas tree. The last thing we need is for them to wonder what all his excitements about." Vinter pouted and slumped in resignation and the Regulator patted him on the shoulder saying, "Good lad. Let me explain," while at the same time keeping from Vinter his thoughts of 'Dumb fucking youngsters' exasperation. He went on. "Meldrew is too hot now. They're all over him but we think they won't make a move because they suspect a trap. The hiking plan was our last go round with him and the bosses are convinced the other lot had something to do with the hikers turning up when they did. Anyway, we're backing off Meldrew and giving you a nice young sociopath to play with. He's done a few jobs for us but he wants to break out. You know, go on a spree. We want you to help him along. Teach him the ropes."

Vinter's face brightened at the idea. "Yeah, sure. Be good to have someone really into it instead of like Meldrew who needs pushing all the time. When do I do the jump? Sooner the better, I'm fed-up pushing stuff into Meldrew's missus. Him and me, two sociopaths, we'll work well together."

"That's why we chose you for him. Give you a chance to be in at the kill. A present for all the work you did with Meldrew. Stay low with Meldrew for a few days while we set things up. We need to get him and Jacob, that's his name, close together so you can make the jump. Stay hidden, don't give Concordat an excuse to come looking. Okay?"

"Okay boss, whatever you say."

"Good. I'll be in touch as soon as things are set up."

After he left Vinter, the Regulator contacted the Despots at discord. "He's all gung-ho. He can't wait to get inside Jacob. We'll just let him go this time, not like Meldrew, and once the body count is high enough the Concordat will have to act. I'll make sure the law hasn't anything to work with."

The Despots gave their approval for the plan to go ahead with the admonition that if Vinter screwed it up this time the Regulator would be held to account. They reminded him of how much time and effort had been expended on Meldrew with little to show for it because the altered DNA strand had been ripped out. The Despots were not prepared to waste more time on a slow evolutionary climb and that was why they wanted to get inside a Concordat operative. Preferably one from Retribution.

Not for the first time the Regulator cursed himself for ever bringing Vinter in but then he consoled himself with the thought that Vinter wouldn't come out of this alive. Vinter was the bait that would draw Concordat in but it would be him who returned to discord with the Retributionist.

Chapter 131

Charlotte had called her team together at Life Files. "You've all been wondering what's been going on with the Meldrew case since I told you to stand down and await further instructions. Well Yuri tells me that Meldrew has been the picture of normalcy. No abuse, no flirting and he's got rid of all the nasty toys because Constance asked him to and now he's back to being the kind and considerate husband and lover we came to like and admire before. Tell us what you've found Yuri."

"We don't know why but he's back to his old self. When Constance and Amy returned from Europe all the sexual aggression was gone. He seemed bemused about the toys and actually asked Constance if she had wanted them, she asked that they keep one and the rest he put in a skip at the hospital. We've had Watchers and observers on him full-time and we've recorded nothing that points to why the change took place. Charlotte said to do a search and that turned up nothing untoward. Cerebral activity was, and still is, normal. We took away the raised flag and watched for another. Nothing. The change in him started from the time he left the hotel after the hike. On the trail we could tell he was mad, his body language was enough to show that, then by the time he arrived home his whole demeanour had changed. Changed to the point where the ideas, plans and suggestions you all put forward two days after his return were left without discussion while we monitored if any would even be necessary. If the past six weeks are anything to go by, they might not be. Thank you all for your contributions. Some were particularly inventive and they will all be filed for possible future use. We will revert to our usual observer and compiler activity on Meldrew and act if another flag appears. You can all go back to your normal duties now. Thank you."

As they were heading to the door and talking amongst themselves about the strange turn the Meldrew case had taken Charlotte messaged Richard and told him to stay behind. Telling Eleanor that he would see her later he indicated Charlotte and gave a slight shrug. Eleanor nodded in understanding and left with the others.

When they were alone Charlotte told Richard they were going to Yuri's office.

Yuri brought up an Ether Screen and explained the still picture that appeared. "This is a corridor in the hospital where Meldrew works. I'll highlight the head and shoulders of the person on the right as we look at it. We see only the back of his head and shoulders but that is Meldrew. Now I'll highlight the head and shoulders of another man walking towards Meldrew on his left. Now I'll start the recording and you to tell me what you see."

The still image filled with movement because the corridor was busy as they typically are in hospitals and Meldrew and the man approached each other and then passed by. The other man went out of scene and the recording stayed with Meldrew until he turned into a ward. Yuri stopped the recording.

Yuri said, "You first Charlotte, go ahead and tell me what you saw."

"Mmm, the back of Meldrew's head and a busy corridor in a hospital. The other man you highlighted seemed to recognise Meldrew and Meldrew turned his head slightly towards him as they passed. Do they know each other? Did Meldrew pass some sort of greeting? That's about it. If I could look at Meldrew's face as they passed, I'd have a better idea if he did make some sort of greeting."

Yuri asked, "How about you Richard, what did you see?"

"Much the same as Charlotte except to me the look on the other's face when he passed Meldrew seemed more like a grimace than a look of recognition. Like Charlotte I'd need to see Meldrew's face as he turns his head to be sure what was happening between the two."

"We've been checking third-party records of the people who were in the corridor at the same time. This is from a nurse who was approaching Meldrew and followed him into the ward."

The back of the man's head and the face of Meldrew appeared on the Ether Screen. At the moment they drew level and Meldrew turned his head a definite look of surprise flashed across his face then was gone. Yuri brought the faces of the man and Meldrew to the screen.

"These are the looks on their faces as they passed. Seen together there does seem to be a look of recognition on the other man's face along with a slight grimace and it certainly seems to be a look of surprise on Meldrew's but it's the other man we should be most interested in. You see, we have him flagged."

Chapter 132

"Flagged. For what?" Charlotte asked.

"Sociopathic traits that are quickly escalating," Yuri replied.

"Okay but what does that have to do with Meldrew? Life Files flag sociopaths all the time," Richard remarked.

"True. But there's a back story here. What you saw was on the day Meldrew returned to work and more than two weeks before Constance and Amy returned from Europe. As we know Meldrew's personality has reverted to kind and loving, to our old Meldrew, while at the same time the sociopathic behaviour of the young man, Jacob, is becoming more and more aggressive. This is my hypothesis. As we first contemplated in the original Meldrew case I believe we *do* have a rogue operative within Concordat. I have given the idea a lot of thought since I first witnessed the incident in the corridor and it got me wondering if whoever or whatever was in Meldrew affecting his behaviour has given up on him and did a transfer to Jacob. I think something or someone left Meldrew and went to Jacob and it occurred in that hospital corridor and it wasn't by chance. From earlier observations and downloads it seems Jacob was seeking a place for an encounter. Somewhere he could get close to Meldrew without attracting attention. What better place than the hospital?" Yuri paused to take in the looks of surprise on the faces of Charlotte and Richard then said, "So, what do you think?"

"Any chance of a cup of coffee?" Richard asked. "This could take some time."

Yuri nodded and moments later a man came into the room carrying a tray with a jug of coffee and three mugs plus cream, milk and sweeteners. He placed it on a credenza at the side of the room and Yuri smiled and said, "Thank you Stan." Then asked, "How are you settling in?"

"Fine, thank you. Everyone's being very helpful. I'm assisting Cherise on the Jacob Lofthouse file."

"Tell me how's it going."

"He's a nasty piece of work. I knew there were people like him Life Side but getting up close is a whole different thing. I've not been doing the work long but I think he's going to do something really bad soon. His behaviour seems to be directed to only one thing and that's hurting others. He might even kill for his own gratification."

"Thanks for sharing your thoughts, Stan. Learn all you can from Cherise, she's very good with Life Siders like Jacob."

"I will. Enjoy your coffee."

When Stan had left Charlotte asked, "Is that the Jacob in the observer download?"

"It is. Help yourself to coffee."

Charlotte declined but the other two got theirs then sat down to talk about Yuri's hypothesis. "Yuri, tell us more about where your idea came from. What sparked it and what else are you following in Life Files that helped lead you to it."

"It started after we sent Meldrew back. We had installed analytics updated program that searches for single constants which is still looking through all past and present Life Files to see if more like Meldrew exist. None have been found so far and I don't think there will be. I think he was a one-off. That thought sent me to Jenny and Alan. We talked about the common threads that ran through the Meldrew case. The prime ones being gestation period, place names in alphabetical order and females only. This brought the realisation that only one factor never changed. The places changed over an alphabetical range and his victims, although all female, were from a variety of backgrounds, ages and ethnicities. Gestation period was the only factor that never changed. It was always eight and one and one. Arriving at this conclusion I asked Jenny and Alan to work up a program for me that looked for a single unaltered factor across all active Life Files. I should tell you that I am the only one in Life Files who has access to the program. The area of search was kept to England and as of one Earth hour ago there are forty-seven active serial murderers that are unknown to us and law enforcement. There were forty-eight but we took Meldrew out. When Meldrew was included, it meant that one serial murderer was based in each of the forty-eight counties of England. None were known to us. Each one has a distinctive factor that never changes which we'll get to but since the aborted attempt by Meldrew to force us into action on the Pennine Trail *all of them have gone quiet.*"

Charlotte stood saying "I'll have that coffee now," and went to get it. The others were silent and drank theirs until she returned to her seat and addressed Yuri, "Does going quiet mean they know we have our suspicions or are they aware of your distinctive factor program?"

"I'm not sure it's either of those. There is nothing that suggests that there is direct communication between any of the forty-eight singularly or collectively yet they all ceased their activities at the same time. As if on orders from somewhere. To me with forty-seven of them spread throughout England that points to a controlling influence of some sort."

Chapter 133

Yuri continued, "Now you've seen this I suggest we bring Eleanor in and get her input. As head of our Retribution section, she needs to know what we might be up against."

Charlotte cast an enquiring look at Richard who responded immediately, "Yes, she should be in at the start. I'll tele-message asking her to come here."

When she arrived, Eleanor was dressed in sweats and rubbing her hair with a towel, "What's so urgent you got me out of the shower? Richard said to come immediately."

Charlotte turned to Yuri saying, "It's your party Yuri, go ahead and fill her in."

"Okay. I've always thought we congratulated ourselves too much over the original Meldrew case. It was sheer good fortune that Jenny was working on her program at that time. There were no skills employed on our part that found him. A killer responsible for all those deaths over all those years that we had no idea about. After we cleaned him up and sent him home, we slapped each other's backs for a job well done. Luck brought us to Meldrew. Nothing else. He would still be killing if Jenny had not created her program. And she did it not through any direction from Solons or section heads but purely as an analytical exercise. What we found in Meldrew, the double helix, second spinal cord and the brain covering was, I believe, all bullshit to lead us away from what actually triggered Meldrew to kill. And I believe that trigger was still in him until recently. Until he passed Jacob Lofthouse in the hospital corridor." Yuri took time to drink some coffee. "The program that found Meldrew has not found another like him, past or present. That points to a one-off. This is what I am convinced will happen. Lofthouse will escalate very quickly from causing bodily harm and he will go on a killing spree. He'll do that to force us to act just as they hoped would happen on Barbara's hiking trip. The rest will stay quiet while

Lofthouse is busy. This has been forced on them by Jenny's program which is in place and by the one I'm using as an investigative tool and which I'm sure they know about. They believe these programs, and others we may be developing, have put their long-term plans in jeopardy. Their end game is to get one of us. Or more accurately *into* one of us. They think Lofthouse on a killing spree will give them that opportunity."

Eleanor broke in, "Who are these '*they*' and '*them*' you keep talking about?"

Yuri shrugged, "I don't know. Perhaps it's an '*it*' but the scale of the operation seems to indicate more than one. Perhaps the Concordat model is being used but for opposite outcomes. This is all conjecture on my part but regardless of how the operation is controlled I'm convinced they mean harm to Concordat and those inhabiting Earth."

"Please give us an example of this 'distinctive factor'," came from Richard.

Yuri considered then said, "Before I do let's go back to Meldrew. Except for now, what I am about to say, are facts. Okay?" Nods from the others. "When we lucked in with Jenny's program they — I'm sticking with they and them — they took the opportunity to front-load Meldrew with things we were sure to pick up on and follow using all the resources of Concordat. All the things we thought were triggers to him killing were bogus but the amount of information and intelligence they were able to gather while we sorted through it all would have been substantial. And, to top it all, we missed a resource they had inside Meldrew all through his episodes. That is until recently in the hospital when a transfer took place to Jacob Lofthouse. Now to Richard's request. As opposed to a single constant found by Jenny's program a distinctive factor is personal to the killer. Meldrew was found by his proximity to the killings, the single constant, whereas his distinctive factor was the gestation period. That was his trigger. Each of the other forty-seven I found in active Life Files have a distinctive factor that runs throughout their file. Ronald Gerhardt dwells on females eighteen to twenty-two with large breasts. Stella Mc Cormack is drawn to bright red fingernails. With Jimmy Marshall it's freckles. All of the forty-seven have a fixation on a particular thing. All victims show that fixation characteristic. I found them by accessing Life Files of retired and active medical examiners and selecting autopsies of unsolved murders during the time Meldrew was active. I then matched any distinctive features of all of them to the distinctive factor fixation found in Life Files. I'm convinced that each of the forty-seven I have found has a resource or asset in them that takes over at the time of the killings once the distinctive factor has been identified. Much in the same way Meldrew's mind and facial features changed when he went out to kill."

Chapter 134

"What is Lofthouse's distinctive factor?" Richard asked.

"Persons of all genders that are taller than him," Yuri answered.

"There must be something in his Life File that tells you why."

"Since childhood he has felt put down and looked down upon by persons taller than he. He blames all the misfortunes in his life on his small stature. Anything he perceives as a personal slight he blames on his being short but if you sync with the Ether Screen I'll put his Life File up and each of you can watch it and rerun whatever you like at your own speed."

"Hold off on that please," came from Charlotte. "I want to bring Jenny and Alan into this. You have recorded all we've spoken about, seen and discussed haven't you Yuri?"

"Yes, as per the protocols."

"Good, then the analysts can catch up before we all look at the Lofthouse Life File. I'll message them now."

The door opened and Jenny and Alan dressed for the basketball court entered with looks of surprise and puzzlement on their faces when they saw who was there. Before either could speak Charlotte said for them to take a seat and watch a recording that explained why they, and everyone else, was there.

At the end Jenny opened with, "So the program worked. It gave the distinctive factors of all those people. Killers that we knew nothing about and probably many more. I'm glad it did what you wanted Yuri but I feel really pissed with the way the single constant program was used against us in the Meldrew case. We found Meldrew by pure luck as you said."

Alan had helped himself to Richard's mug and then got coffee while Jenny was speaking. He sat cradling the mug and taking small sips as he looked at the screen and its image of Jacob Lofthouse. Eleanor gave a small cough and then a soft, "Alan."

Without taking his eyes from the screen he asked, "How many has he killed and over how long?"

"Ten over eight years," Yuri supplied.

"When you consider half of adult humankind is taller than him it seems a small number. It's easier for him to pick a victim than say Stella McCormack whose D-factor is bright red fingernails. Yuri's right, there's a control element and Lofthouse *will* go on a killing spree. It's easier for him because he's surrounded by his D-factor. Let's take a look at his Life File and see if gives any clue to where his trigger control is hiding." Taking his eyes from the screen and looking at the others, "I'm not very optimistic. We didn't find it in Meldrew."

He was unimpressive in stature and he certainly wasn't handsome but he had an unmistakable charm that some women found particularly attractive. He listened, he was attentive, made them the centre of conversations. Asked about them, their lives and hopes and dreams. He showed sympathy and humour when needed. He let them lead the relationship. Never pushed them. Or so it seemed to them. A lot of his success stemmed from him being unremarkable. He left no lasting impression. A short guy that left no distinct memory trace. He hated that was so, he wanted to be noticed, to be remembered, to be outstanding. That he wasn't was also his greatest advantage. He searched carefully for victims going to pubs and clubs and even bingo halls seeking out the ones sitting alone. Those that no one approached, those that no one sat down to talk to, those that arrived and left alone. Those without a wedding ring. Spotting a likely victim Lofthouse would carefully stalk them. They had to live alone. He took his time and sustained himself on how it was going to be at the end. He learned where they lived and worked, their daily routines, interactions with others, what papers they read if any, where they shopped and what they bought. When he found their name in the electoral roles, he stayed away from searches in social media not wanting to leave any trail. As an employee of one of the largest energy suppliers in the UK he used his identification card to gain access to his victims' homes on the pretence of evaluating what they could do to cut their energy costs. Most welcomed him into their homes and ultimately into their lives. How better to strike up a conversation than to walk into a pub he knew they frequented and go over to them after buying a drink and say, "Hi, remember me. We spoke at your home about saving on your energy bill."

Sometimes it took seconds for the victim to remember then, "Of course! Now I remember. How are you?"

"I'm fine. Mind if I join you or are you here with someone?"

As the Life File of Jacob Lofthouse came to an end and faded from the screen Jenny declared, "Well he has all the hallmarks. The consummate sociopath bundled in with a psychopath and sadist. We've seen how he likes to cause pain but like Meldrew the actual killings are hidden by false feedback to the observers."

"And it's the same across all of them," Yuri stepped in. "What we can call the '*courtship*' is recorded but not the act. This accounts for why flags were raised and we watch them but no actual killing or even extreme inflicting of pain has been observed that we could act on. As Richard said we watch sociopaths and the like all the time but protocols prohibit us from moving against them unless they do something heinous."

Richard leaned forward his eyes fixed on Yuri's, "So you think there's something like an Anti-Concordat controlling them and operated by someone or something within Concordat?"

Yuri answered without hesitation, "Yes, I do."

Charlotte in a voice little above a murmur said into the silence that followed Yuri's assertion, "I suppose we go to the Solons with Yuri's suspicions and get their reaction. If what she suspects is true, and from what I've just learned I see no reason to doubt her, the Solons must be told."

The others were voicing assent until Alan said, "Hold on, what if it's one of the Solons? Who is in a better position to recruit to an Anti-Concordat than one of them?"

"Are you serious?" asked Eleanor. "You really think a Solon could be mixed up in this?"

Alan shrugged and replied, "Why not? Just throwing it out there. We need to look at all the possibilities."

"Alan has a point," came from Richard. "With the exception of our team we can't rule anyone or anything out regardless of how farfetched we think it is."

"Then where do we go from here?" Charlotte asked. "Who can we trust implicitly to go to and explain all this and ask for help and guidance?"

With one voice Richard and Eleanor answered, "Takahara."

The others readily accepted their choice with Charlotte saying, "Takahara it is. Richard, please arrange a meeting with him."

Chapter 135

Eleanor's apartment was chosen. After Richard's request for a meeting on a matter of urgency that must remain secret Takahara had rightly said it was a place where Eleanor often invited friends and team members so if he was invited for a meal, as a friend, it would appear perfectly normal.

To reinforce the impression of friends gathering for a meal Eleanor provided a selection of Japanese and Indian dishes they would eat before getting down to business. If Takahara was at all inquisitive about what matter required such urgency and secrecy it did not show and he made affable conversation with them all. It was only when the last of the dishes had been cleared away and tea was being served that Takahara spoke to the matter at hand.

"Eleanor please bring up an Ether Screen. Charlotte, I prefer we use Screen Speak. I presume it must be a subject that is causing you and your team discomfort and one that you are reluctant to present through regular channels. I've placed a communication block around this apartment and Screen Speak adds another level of security with the only thing that can breech it being a Solon taking a particular direct interest in our gathering and I will know if that occurs. Please proceed Charlotte."

Synced with the screen Charlotte's explanation and the concerns of her team appeared in written format for Takahara to read. Takahara was silent throughout and betrayed no emotions even at the point Charlotte told him of their fears that there was a rogue operative within Concordat. When the words stopped and the screen went blank Takahara sat still and quiet for several moments before saying, "Yuri, I'm going to open a sync port and I want you to download all the files concerning Meldrew and this Jacob Lofthouse person to me. I'm sure you have them in a secure file that is accessible only to you so please transmit it to me. I'll sync with you now; the port is open."

After the download Takahara requested more tea and then sat silent until it had been poured and he had taken several sips. Raising his *matcha* to eye level he bowed his head to touch the rim and said, "*Arigatou gozaimasu,* Eleanor."

Eleanor smiled and bowed in response saying, "*Aapaka svaagat hai.*" Takahara drank the remaining tea, rinsed the *matcha,* dried it and placed it on the tray containing the rest of the tea ceremony paraphernalia then began to speak. "It was right that you brought your concerns to my attention, to have made them widely known would have complicated matters. You see, the Solons are already aware that Concordat has been compromised."

A chorus of incredulity greeted this pronouncement.

"Stop!" Takahara's sharp tone silenced them. "Do not talk all at once! Charlotte as team leader speak for your team."

"Why have the Solons done nothing if they are already aware?"

"Solon's will not intervene directly with the evolutionary track being taken by humankind. That is what Concordat is for. They simply started the ball rolling along this particular evolutionary path. Concordats are humankind's guardians and your jobs are to monitor them and when necessary punish the worst among them within the bounds laid down by the Solons. You have all the tools necessary to find and eradicate this threat but it must be done under the present guidelines regarding culls. You will not be allowed to take vigilante action."

"And if we fail?"

"Eventual moral decay leading to an apocalyptic end."

"You know this how?"

"It has happened many times before. It would be arrogant of you to think yours is the only galaxy, solar system or planet overseen by the Solons."

"Are you a Solon? You speak as if you are."

"No Charlotte, I am not, but I do speak for them when necessary and I am to tell you this. You must find someone who is not bound by Concordat protocols and procedures."

"Will there be other teams involved?"

"No. The infiltration began in your sector therefore it is your responsibility to eradicate it before it spreads to others."

Takahara said nothing more on the matter only stood thanking Eleanor for the meal then bowed to them all and left.

Chapter 136

Judith was on the verge of getting up and telling the receptionist that she could not wait any longer and that she'd have to go and would call about another appointment but as she was gathering her things together the nurse came into the waiting room and told her the doctor would see her now. She had no alternative than to follow the nurse.

Judith had known Geoff since high school. He'd gone off to study medicine and she had joined the police after graduating and when he came back to the city to open a practice, she signed on with him. Her visits had been few and far between and usually involved routine examinations during her yearly flu shots. She had always been a very healthy individual. She had had to force herself to visit Geoff over headaches that were becoming more frequent and more painful. An examination by Geoff resulted in her having X-rays and bloods drawn then a visit to a specialist who arranged for an MRI to be carried out. She was at Geoff's surgery to get the results of all the testing.

Geoff was at the computer when the nurse ushered her into his examination room. Smiling up at her he said 'hello' and gestured to a chair saying he'd only be a minute. His smile settled some of the nerves she was feeling about the test results. He wouldn't smile like that if there was bad news, he'd have his serious face on she thought. Like the one she'd seen at her last flu shot when he scolded her for missing yet another mammogram. She'd smiled sheepishly and claimed pressures of work. He'd just shook his head and told her they were important and not to miss another, not with her family history of cancer.

Geoff stopped moving the mouse around and turned away from the computer monitor to face her. There it was, his serious face. *Oh shit*, she thought.

When he spoke his voice was gentle, "Judith, I'm sorry but it's bad news."

An hour later she was sitting in her car allowing tears to pour down her cheeks and choking out sobs that threatened to implode her rib cage.

A year and a half, maybe a little longer, that's what he'd told her. It was in her brain and other organs. Chemotherapy could be tried but it had spread so far that it was unlikely to help and could possibly increase her discomfort. Most of what Geoff said about the cancer's progression, pain mitigation, support groups and the rest had washed over her in uncomprehending waves.

Eighteen months. She was to see Geoff once a month so he could keep track of her vital signs and general physical condition. He'd told her that towards the end she would probably be confined to bed. She knew the routine because both her father and sister had died from cancer. One cervical, the other colon. As the tears and sobs abated, she resolved not to tell anyone. Definitely not her mother who'd blame her for not taking better care of herself and then she'd play the emotional blackmail card about her not getting married and giving her grandchildren. Her mother swept all argument aside that she had yet to meet anybody she wanted to marry or even live with and admonished her with, "Your job, always your job, too busy to be a mother. You never cared about how I felt, about family, it's always been about you."

Judith wiped tears from her eyes, blew her nose then squared her shoulders before starting the car. Now the decision was made she felt better, more in control. Putting the car into gear she left the parking lot and began her drive to the police station where she worked.

Eleanor and Richard watched her struggle with her new reality.

"She's perfect," Eleanor remarked. "It was a great idea of Victoria's."

Richard agreed it was. "I'll insert into Jones tonight. Are you going to talk to Judith before inserting?"

"No, I'll run a day with her before approaching her with the offer. She seems the perfect choice but I want to have a look around just to make sure."

That night while she slept the sleep of emotional exhaustion Eleanor inserted into Judith and Richard into Detective Sergeant John Jones.

Chapter 137

Gillian Mulder was found the next morning tied to one of the pier supports below the high-water mark. A man and wife walking their dog had found her.

Judith was sent to the scene by her chief superintendent along with a detective sergeant named John Jones who had arrived that morning. The chief super had given Judith a file folder containing Jones' service record and told her to look it over when she got the chance.

Jones was waiting for her when she picked up her coat and after brief introductions, she told him to follow her. In her car she explained that Mulder had been missing ten days and they had not turned up any leads as to her whereabouts during that time. They were quiet during the remainder of the drive to the pier. Judith was happy with that, she disliked chatterboxes.

They made their way through the cordon of uniformed police keeping the gawkers and media people at bay on the promenade and made their way down steps to a lower promenade and from there to the beach and under the pier. SOCO had already erected a screen around the body and marked off a walkway to the scene with tape. Judith greeted the SOCO team leader who was hunkered down as he examined Gillian Mulders neck, "Hello Godfrey, what have you found out so far?"

Standing and arching his back to relieve tense muscles, "Good morning, Judith. Not much. Tide's done a good job of cleaning the scene but as you can see, she's tied round the neck and waist with what looks like curtain tie-backs by the material and tassels on the ends. A single one round the neck and double at the waist. Meant to keep the torso upright I assume. Arms and legs free. Also, as you can see from the way the waves have washed the skirt of her dress up to her waist and the way the wet material is clinging to her upper body she is without undergarments. I obviously can't give you a cause of death but from years of experience looking at corpses I'd say she has been very severely beaten but we'll let the medical examiner confirm that shall we. Annabelle's on her way and I'll let her in once I'm done with the scene. Report to you ASAP."

"Thanks Godfrey. By the way this is DS Jones. Joined us just this morning, showing him the ropes."

"Pleased to meet you DS Jones. Shake hands later. You're getting your feet wet already... literally and figuratively. See you both back at the station."

Retracing their steps, they met the M.E on the lower promenade. "Morning Judith. Understand it's Gillian Mulder."

"Morning Annabelle. Yes, the constable who was stopped by the couple walking their dog recognised her from the misper photos. We've just been down and I can confirm it is her. Godfrey's doing his thing. Tide's coming in so he'll have to let you at it soonest."

"Okay and yes, I know... you want the time and cause of death immediately. And this is? You really do have atrocious social skills Judith."

"Oh sorry, you're right. Annabelle let me introduce DS John Jones who joined us just this morning. Jones, this is Doctor Annabelle St. Laurent our esteemed medical examiner."

Hands were shaken and 'pleased to meet yous' made then the M.E started down the beach towards the forensics tent.

Taking steps to the upper promenade further away from the pier they made it to her car without running the gauntlet at the pier entrance. The only comment made between them during the journey back to the station was when Jones said, "I need to look at the missing persons file on Gillian Mulder."

Jones was given the other desk in Judith's office. He was provided with a computer monitor and keyboard and was connected to the network. Judith gave him the case file number for Gillian Mulder and he brought it up and when he began to read she opened his personnel file. He pushed back from the desk at the same time she closed his file.

Stretching arms above his head and extending legs out under the desk he exhaled loudly then relaxed and turned towards Judith to say, "She was reported missing ten days ago by her parents. Lived alone. No boyfriends or close friends that they knew of. They say she had no reason to run away. Kidnap seems out of it because although her parents are well off no ransom demand. Taking library studies course at community college. Instructors and classmates all state she was quiet and studious, not a social animal. Membership to local recreation centre where she used the running tracks, indoors if raining, outdoors if fine and warm. Door to door found she visited the coffee cum wine bar around the corner from where she lived every Friday evening for usually one and never more than two glasses of wine, red. People working there could not remember here meeting or sitting with anybody. Her flat was lived in but tidy with no sign of her being forcibly removed. Her car was parked in the street outside her flat. Her neighbours in the flat above say they saw her driving away in the morning and it being there when they went to bed on the night before she was reported missing. CCTV at the rec centre places her leaving the car park the evening before we suspect she went missing. Very tall and slim… six two and one ten, almost skinny. Not exactly glamorous but would stand out because of her height if nothing else. Appeals through all the usual channels… nothing. Appears to have gone home and vanished into thin air until she turns up tied to the pier support with no attempt to hide the body. In fact, quite the opposite, the body was staged. Whoever put her there is making a statement… come get me!'

Without remarking on what Jones had just said Judith tapped his personnel file and asked, "What did you do to get sent here in such a hurry. It's not in your file but something happened. Groomed for fast tracking, exemplary performance reviews and a commendation for bravery for taking a gun away from a drug dealer while he held it to the head of his crack whore. At your previous posting one day and gone the next so something happened. What was it? Don't try and bullshit me."

"One of the lifer uniform sergeants was always on my case about pretty boys from university being pushed up the ladder and getting all the plum jobs while the real work was done by the beat cop. He made it a point to screw with me in all sorts of ways until one day I had enough and held him across his desk and wrote 'asshole' across his forehead with a permanent marker. It wasn't hard, he was fat and out of shape from sitting on his arse all day and eating too many bacon sandwiches. Anyway, this was soon after the award, so it was thought best to keep it quiet rather than have the press and social media all over it by disciplining me. The fat bastard was shipped off to some village outpost for his last years before retirement and here I am."

Judith initialled his file it to signify she had read it. "Fair enough. I've come across lifers like that. I once kneed one in the balls when he asked me how many I'd had to screw to get to DCI so young. I'm going to take your file back to the chief super and when I come back, I want you to tell me which direction Gillian Mulder's case should take from what you've read and what was found this morning."

It was fifteen minutes before Judith returned and she came bearing gifts. "Here you go, coffee from the place next door… what we get from the canteen is crap… help yourself to milk and sugar. The super wasn't in his office, he's at the Mulder's giving them the bad news. They're friends according to the super's secretary." After stirring milk and sweetener into her coffee she sat back and asked, "Where would you go on the case? What's your next step?"

"Go back to the last place she was seen alive and look at the security footage again. Something happened after she got in her car at the rec centre and it being seen by her neighbours that night. Also, all the CCTV cameras on the roads leading back to her flat need to be checked for her car as well."

"You think she never made it back to her flat and that her car was dropped off by someone else?"

"I do."

"Okay. Go and get copies of the rec centre security videos and get DC Keith Moody… you'll find him in the incident room… to look for her car on traffic's CCTV footage. He's good at that sort of thing and introduce yourself to the rest of the squad while you're there. Meanwhile, I'm going to visit the Mulders to pay my respects and see if they remember anything that's not in the case file." Reaching for her coat she shrugged into it and said, "I'll bet that the autopsy says she died just hours before she was found. Somebody's held her for nearly ten days."

Jones stopped her before she got to the door, "Wait. You have an incident room and a team put together already… when did that happen?"

"As soon as the word goes round I'm senior investigating officer those that can put up working for me come together. I'm choosy and lots here would rather stick pins in their eyes than work for me. My last DS, now a DI, was exceptional so you have big shoes to fill. Oh, and one more thing, whenever you come back to the station always bring coffee from next door in with you, mine's half a sweetener and a little milk. That's about it, I'm off to the Mulders."

The 'right you are guv' from Jones followed her out the door.

He had Styrofoam cups of coffee in his hands and was backing his way into the station when Judith came from the parking lot. "Here, let me get the door. How did it go at the rec centre?"

As they walked towards the incident room, she took the proffered cup from him. "It went well, very helpful. The manager's secretary copied all the discs from all the cameras around the place. Apparently, they were only asked for a copy of the one in the parking lot showing her getting into her car and leaving. I've got ten discs all told. I did as you said and asked Keith to get onto to traffic for CCTV footage on the roads towards her home, he might have something by now."

"I'll check with Keith, you go and start on the security discs but before you do, check with SOCO and forensics and the M.E, see if they have anything for us." Judith was halfway through the doorway into the incident room when she said, "Coffee's good, thank you."

Chapter 138

Jones greeted Judith with, "You were right," when she returned to the office.

"About what? When she died?"

"Yes. Autopsy puts it at around eleven last night. Eight hours before she was found. Took some working out because she'd been in the cold water which made body temp problematic but the effects of sea water on bodies is well documented… so Annabelle tells me… so she's confident in her time of death."

"If Annabelle says she died at eleven then she died at eleven," Judith stated. "Stake your reputation on it. What else did she come up with?"

"As Godfrey remarked she had been severely beaten and over a long period but cause of death was suffocation. She also has massive penetration damage from some form of implement or implements. I got this over the phone, Annabelle wants us at the morgue, says it's pretty bad."

Judith shook her head and murmured, "Oh shit," as Godfrey the SOCO rapped on the door.

Handing Judith a file folder, "Very thin report unfortunately. Sea water did a good job of cleaning the scene. No footprint evidence except the couple with the dog, the PC at the scene and the dogs paw prints. Forensics have the cords used to tie her and her dress, maybe transfer took place that wasn't washed away. We found bottle tops, scraps of plastic, a condom and other sorts of rubbish but nothing that seems linked to the crime. Anyway, we bagged and tagged it all and gave it to forensics. It's all in the photos."

"Thanks Godfrey. We're on our way to see Annabelle. Good of you to be so quick with this, I'll get it posted in the incident room."

Godfrey held out a hand, "Here, give that back to me, I'll take it to the room. You get on and see Annabelle. Nice to see you again DS Jones and this time we get to shake hands.'"

"Good to see you too Godfrey, please call me John."

When they were in her car and heading to the morgue Jones asked, "What's the news on the traffic CCTV footage."

"Keith hasn't got to the end of the CCTV footage but he has found her car on two roads heading in the direction of her flat. Of course not every road she could have taken has CCTV cameras so there will be gaps. Keith will keep us updated on progress. What about the rec centre security discs?"

"I'm on tape two from the rec centre. I looked at the one our lot took earlier and sure enough it shows her walking to her car, getting in and driving out of the parking lot. What I'm looking for now is her before she leaves the centre and on the walkway to the parking lot then after as she drove past the entrance to the centre. I want to know if she interacted with anybody during those times or if anybody followed her or took particular interest."

"Okay. You think she might have been intercepted on the way home. It's worth looking at. Here's something else for you to do. Go into county constabulary records and look for open missing person reports and unsolved relating to women of the same body type as Gillian Mulder. You know, over six feet and thin. Start off at one ten to one thirty pounds but keep the height over six feet. I know it's a scatter shot approach but I want to see what comes up. Begin by going back ten years."

Jones responded, "Will do," and made a note on his phone.

Annabelle removed the sheet covering Gillian Mulder's body, "Fortunately she wasn't there for a full tide cycle so the sea beasties didn't do much damage. This young lady was bordering on the anorexic, at one fifteen she's far too thin. At her height and build she should be about one fifty-five. I've read her misper file and suspect she used running more as a weight control device rather than a sport or leisure activity. Gillian had been severely beaten in the time before her death and from the bruising it was inflicted by heavy objects of various sizes and also fists. Some like these indicate a broad strap of some kind was used. There are bite marks on each breast that were forceful enough to break the skin. I've got forensics coming down to take pictures for distribution to dentists, who knows we might get a match. The most severe internal damage was done to the sexual organs and anal passage by a large object being forced into these areas. I'd say she was also a virgin before the attacks." Moving to a specimen bowl Annabelle removed the cover saying, "This is the cause of her death by suffocation. This was forced down her throat to block the airways."

Both detectives made sharp intakes of breath and Judith asked, "Was that used in the other places?"

Annabelle replied, "No. Big as it is it's not large enough to have caused that damage. But, there's a maker's name on the upper edge right here so you might be able to track down who sells these things and, if the gods smile, who buys them."

Jones finished writing the manufacturer's name in his notebook then asked, "Any signs of drugs being used?"

"No, the tox screen was clean so I'd say she was aware of everything that was happening to her unless she passed out."

As Annabelle placed the sheet back over the body Judith asked, "Have her parents been to make a formal identification?"

"Not yet. Your superintendent is waiting for me to give him a call and he'll bring them in. They're friends apparently."

"Seems so, the father made that very clear when I visited them this morning. Wanted me to know that he knows lots of people in high places. He seems to be very much up his own arse."

Chapter 139

When they got back to the station, they checked with Keith who was still searching for sightings of Gillian's car on CCTV footage. "I've got her with some gaps until she turns onto Cunard but unfortunately the cameras on Cunard were down that night. The utility company was putting in new poles and the cameras were offline until the following morning. There are several streets she could take off Cunard that take her in the direction of her flat so I'm looking at all the cameras in a five-block area to see if I can catch her exiting one. Might take some time. Even with the gaps I have a pretty good timeline of her journey and so far, it doesn't seem she stopped off anywhere or was held up for any length of time."

"Okay, thanks. Let me know when you have the car on camera closest to her flat and what the time is. Be good if you can estimate travel time from last sighting to when she should have got home."

"Sure. I can do that because we know the average speed of traffic around the city at different times. It won't be dead accurate but certainly within five minutes or so."

Judith squeezed Keith's shoulder, "Thanks Keith, that would do nicely. Any new leads or developments from our people who are reinterviewing those we spoke to during the missing persons go round?" Keith whose eyes were already back on his monitor shook his head.

When they were back at their desks Jones logged into county police records and entered the search parameters suggested by Judith before asking, "How'd it go with the Mulders'?"

"All right but like I said he's all about us, the police that is, getting things done because he knows people and he gave the impression that the chief super would report every move we make to him directly. He won't of course. Gillian's mother is altogether different. She's down-to-earth and practical and sees no need to throw her weight around. She's relying on us to do our jobs and find her daughter's killer. She's the stronger of the two and I did get one new piece of information from her. A month or so ago during a visit Gillian happened to mention that a nice man from the National Power had called at the apartments in her building advising on how small things like draft proofing windows, changing to LED lamps instead of incandescent and fitting an electronic thermostat could significantly reduce electricity costs and that she had already changed her light bulbs. Her father was concerned it might be some sort of scam to check out the apartment for valuables but Gillian assured her parents that the man's credentials were in order and that he'd arrived in a National Power van. They'd forgotten about it until I asked if they knew of anyone who made regular visits to Gillian's apartment. When the father went off to answer *a very important telephone call* the mother, Gwendoline, remarked that the mention of the National Power man was the only time Gillian had referred to someone coming to her door and that Gillian had never been one for friends and social occasions, not even with other tenants. I asked if she might have become friendly with this man and had his name been mentioned and she said that *perhaps* she *might* have and *no* his name had not been mentioned. We need to check with the National Power, they're bound to have a record of house calls by their employees. I want to know who this man was."

A beep sounded and Jones turned to his computer monitor, "Hang on a second while I check this out. I have a response from county records. Hmmm, here we are. Holy shit. I'm forwarding this to you, take a look."

It was minutes before either of them spoke then in accord they looked away from their monitors and at each other with Judith declaring, "Holy shit is right. Nine missing persons over ten years and all over six feet and between one ten and one thirty-five pounds. That's on the light side. Right John, get in touch with the other divisions that handled these cases and get the files sent over here immediately then go down to our archives and get the ones that were handled by us and bring them up. If you get push back from any of the other divisions I'll get the super to light a fire under their arses."

Picking up his desk phone and reaching for the county constabulary directory Jones started in on the calls and acknowledged Judith when she said she was going to see the superintendent.

Jones was replacing the receiver after his final call requesting the missing persons file they wanted when Keith poked his head into the room,

"You better come and take a look at what I've found and get the DCI as well if she's about."

"Get me for what?" Judith who was returning from the superintendent's office asked from behind Keith.

Keith was startled, "Jesus, don't do that! Give me a heart attack creeping up like that. There's something on CCTV you need to see." Jones and Judith shared a smile as they walked to the incident room following Keith and she asked if the case files were on the way. Jones confirmed they were and no push back.

Keith pointed to a wall mounted monitor before hitting enter on his computer keyboard. A grainy black and white picture appeared and Keith began, "This is Gillian Mulder's car soon after she left the recreation centre and was on Lacewood Boulevard heading in the direction of her flat. When I enlarge the picture, we can clearly see the front number plate and if I zoom in like this, we can see that a woman, presumably Gillian Mulder, is driving and take particular notice of how high her head is above the steering wheel." Keith pressed another key and the picture was replace by one equally grainy and obviously taken on a different road. Keith zoomed in on the number plate which confirmed that it was Gillian Mulder's car then he moved to the windscreen and enlarged the image of the driver. "This was captured on Dunbrack not far from Gillian's flat and I'd bet a month's wages that the driver we see here is male and not very tall… see how low his head is behind the steering wheel compared to Gillian. From this point on Dunbrack, it would be a left then a right then another left turn onto the street where Gillian lived and if my timeline is anywhere near accurate her car was dropped off at eleven-fifteen just three minutes after this picture taken. There are no cameras in the area around her flat, so we have no evidence of the car's arrival or who dropped it off. Now, did anybody notice the time on the first picture?'

"Six twenty-two and a few seconds," came from Jones.

"Right, give the DS a prize. From other traffic cameras I managed to get four shots of the driver that are identifiable as a woman the last one being at six forty-nine on Dunbrack just six minutes from her flat at average traffic speed. That being the case she should have been picked up again at six fifty-two by the camera that shows a man driving her car much later at eleven twelve. She never got to that camera. In the distance between the cameras, she disappeared."

Judith stepped closer to the screen as if doing so would bring the man's face into focus... she was sure it was a man. "Okay. Good work Keith. Now we have an area in which she went missing. Keith, call the rest of the team in — we don't need to reinterview any more — and divide up the streets within a square kilometre of Gillian's flat and have them do a house-to-house. Somebody must have seen Gillian's car between six and eleven. I'm assuming her car never left the immediate area because it would have been picked up on CCTV somewhere else during those hours, is that right Keith."

Keith confirmed, "Last thing I did before calling you in was check on roads with cameras around where she lives. Her car never left her neighbourhood in the hours between six and eleven."

Chapter 140

Keith started calling the team in and Judith and Jones went back to their office. He slid a disc into his computer and told Judith he was going to look at the recordings from the rec centre and she told him she was going for a drive around the area near Gillian's flat to get a feel for the place, get closer to Gillian in a sense, and how about a drink after she got back to relax and go over developments. Jones smiled and gave a thumbs up.

They went to a quiet backstreet pub that was near the station but off the beaten track and used mostly as a local for those living nearby. They ordered drinks, she white wine, he a pint of bitter, she paid and Judith guided him to a secluded alcove booth away from customer traffic. When both had taken a drink, Judith opened with, "The centre's security videos, what did you find?"

"That all of the security records should have been looked at during the missing person investigation and not just those covering the parking lot. From the inside camera that covers the rear exit from the centre, doors from which you can leave but not enter, Judith can be seen talking to a man, a short man, dressed in a National Power uniform and then leaving followed by the man. His face is always away from the camera but Gillian is facing it while talking so it is definitely her. Outside the door she turns right towards the parking lot and he goes left down the service road path. Reflections from the glass in the door make it impossible to make out his face once he's outside. Gillian comes from the corner of the building and does a meandering diagonal between parked cars to get to hers where she opens the door climbs in and drives away. The camera covering the exit has her waiting for the bar to rise after she's swiped her card and it's definitely her. Turning right she heads towards Lacewood where the traffic cam picked her up but at the same time we have a recording of a National Power van leaving the centre's service road and turning onto Lacewood in the same direction. Gillian's mother told you about a visit her daughter had from a National Power man and we have her talking to someone from that company at the rec centre and then a company van leaving and turning in her direction immediately after Gillian. Coincidence? I've asked Keith to look for National Power vans on the road at the same times as Gillian and possibly following her. He says he'll have something by tomorrow morning."

Jones lifted his glass to drink and Judith asked, "Did you get the number of the van?"

"Yes, CL45 was on the back door. Should be easy enough to find out the driver's name on that day. The company will have records."

"How can you be so certain it was a man talking to Gillian? It could have been a short woman in a baggy uniform if you couldn't see the face."

"Summer uniform seems to be short sleeve shirt and shorts and from the overall build and the arms and legs I saw, it was definitely a man."

"Okay. First thing tomorrow after checking in with Keith I will hit the National Power and I want you to look over those nine misper cases and see if there's a common thread."

Drinking the last of his pint Jones pointed to Judith's glass, "Time for another?"

"Sure, why not. I've nowhere to get in a hurry. It's going to be takeout and a Netflix movie for me tonight. Same again please."

Returning with the drinks Jones asked, "How did your tour around Gillian's neighbourhood go? Did it help?"

"It was much as I expected. Older buildings most of which have been refurbished by the look of them and containing two, three or four flats by the bell name plates. Most have intercom connections above the bell pushes and several, including Gillian's, have viewing monitors as well. Very tidy neighbourhood, no old cars up on bricks or untidy gardens, no graffiti or overflowing garbage bins. I'd say mostly older people in retirement and pre family young adults and I doubt the rents are cheap, so I reckon her parents paid Gillian's."

Jones sat up straight and announced, 'Look… You mentioned a takeout meal earlier but how about a curry at that Indian restaurant on Gottingen? We can walk to it from here."

Judith considered for a few seconds then, "Yes, let's do that. Be nice to have a meal out."

During their meal they exchanged work histories and snippets of their private lives. Conversation and humour flowed easily between them. They dawdled over the meal with it being apparent neither was in a rush to bring the evening to an end and at the heart of it was the fact that Judith was not looking forward to being alone with thoughts about her diagnosis. It was after ten when they left the restaurant and Judith had insisted she pay for her own meal. Hours had passed since their last alcoholic drink, so they had no concerns about walking back to collect their cars from the station parking lot.

It was when she was cleaning her teeth that it came to her that she had not taken any pain medication since that morning and that the headache which usually grew stronger as the day wore on was no more than a dull background ache. Smiling into the bathroom mirror she allowed herself to hope the diagnosis was wrong.

Chapter 141

In bed and after entertaining thoughts about what it would have been like to have had sex with Jones sleep came quickly and then in the early hours, she was woken by the gentle shakes of a woman standing beside her bed. Judith felt no fear or concern and she did not ask the woman who she was or what she was doing in her home she simply got up and followed her into the kitchen. The kettle was already steaming and the woman was taking mugs from hooks under the cupboards. "Hello, Judith, my names Eleanor and I thought we'd have a cup of tea while I explain what is happening. Would you mind getting milk from the fridge while I pour water on the tea bags?" Judith did as asked and Eleanor thanked her before pushing a mug towards Judith and taking a seat opposite her at the breakfast island said, "Judith, I've spent today embedded in your brain and preparing it for something that will quite literally expand your mind. Strange things are about happen to you but you will suffer no harm. I'll give you the advice I heard lot's when I was Life Side... enjoy the ride."

She was about to start her car when it came to her that she had not taken her pain medication that morning and it was usually the first thing she reached for when she woke. Turning the ignition key and smiling she murmured to herself, "Maybe, just maybe, they got it wrong."

She was at her desk when Jones arrived carrying the requisite coffees. As he placed one on her desk and she handed him the money with a 'thank you' he gave her a penetrating look and she asked, "What's up? Breakfast cereal on my chin or something?"

"No... nothing like that. I need to close the door because I have something for your ears only."

"Go ahead."

Jones closed the door and then sat in the chair across the desk from Judith and began to speak but in a voice that was not that of John Jones.

"My name is Richard and I am embedded in John Jones just as Eleanor is embedded in you but I am much deeper. Jones will never be aware of me and he has many years ahead of him before Concordat might consider recruiting him as you have been recruited. I will be guiding Jones down certain paths of investigation that will, along with yours, be helpful in bringing Lofthouse to justice and his handlers into the open. Jones will have no recollection of this conversation and after he has opened the door, he will pass your coffee as if giving it to you for the first time. Eleanor and I will watch over you both." Judith nodded in understanding. She knew the Eleanor he spoke of, she had come to her during the night.

Jones opened the door then came to Judith's desk and taking a coffee he handed it to her saying, "I really enjoyed the meal last night." Accepting the coffee, she handed him money then smiled and remarked that she had enjoyed it too.

Jones was about say that Keith was still going over CCTV footage looking for National Power vans when the man himself appeared at the door saying, "Come look, I've found something."

"This is the van, CL45, leaving the service road at the rec centre as seen from the traffic camera at the junction of Dunbrack and Lacewood, the junction before the one where Gillian joins Lacewood. Now to me the van seems to wait at the service road exit until Gillian's car which is the one in the distance begins to turn onto Lacewood. The van never gets close to Gillian's car and they are never captured on the same piece of road by the same traffic cam but it does appear to follow the same route she does until it turns off about half a click from Gillian's place and where there are no cameras. Time stamps show that van is never more than two minutes behind Gillian. In the strictest sense whoever was in that van wasn't following Gillian because he already knew where she was going."

Judith stood away from the desk she had propped herself against, "Thanks Keith, brilliant work and I think you're right. The driver of the van knew where she was going. He already knew her address. Keith, keep the troops doing house-to-house… her car had to be somewhere in the area and someone must have seen it and add any sighting of a National Power van. What about lock-up garages in the area?" Keith assured her they were being checked out to see who owned them.

As they walked from the incident room Judith told Jones go over the nine missing person files looking for any statement mentioning a National Power van being in the vicinity in the days before the person went missing.

Five of the files requested were on his desk and with the two handled in-house Jones had seven to start on. He arranged them into date order from oldest to most recent. The actual date of each disappearance varied but there was never more than one each calendar year. Jones then looked at the physical description of each one and without exception they were all tall, over six feet, and very thin which was apparent from photographs and weight estimates provided to the police. It took more time to go through all the statements and at the end of two hours he had found three references to a white van and two that identified a van as being from the National Power. Judith had left the office earlier telling him she was going to see the transport manager at National Power. On his way out to get a coffee he met Judith as she entered the building carrying two coffees. Handing one across she said, "Here you go, have one on me." About to walk back into their office they were stopped by Keith calling from the incident room, "Call from foot patrol looking for you Judith. Another body. Lashed to a tree in the park. I've got the SOCO's and the medical examiner on the way."

Chapter 142

Jones stood at the entrance to the SOCO tent with Judith and gave a soft whistle before saying, "Christ, it's like being back on the beach but without the water."

Godfrey concurred, "Indeed, DS Jones. Same position, similar bruising, same lack of undergarments, same body type and I'd hazard a guess forensics will find the cords are identical to those used on Gillian Mulder. Subject to the ME's examination the only difference I can see externally is that her clothes have been purposely arranged to show her pubic and chest areas. Lots of footprints from lots of different footwear and lots of detritus from those too lazy and ignorant to use a litter bin. We'll take casts of any usable footprints get photographs then bag and tag for forensics and get back to you ASAP. Ah, I see Annabelle has arrived and is suiting up so must press on."

Judith stood silent throughout this exchange then asked, "Any bite marks you can see Godfrey?"

Shaking his head, "None that are immediately apparent but I'm sure Annabelle will find any that might be presently hidden."

Leaving the scene, they made a silent exchange of raised hands and head nods with Annabelle as she passed them.

In Judith's car going back to the station Jones enquired, "Any joy with the National Power people on who was driving van CL45?"

"Yes. On that day it was booked out to a Jacob Lofthouse and one of his calls was to the rec centre. It's a regular twice a month visit by him to check out the systems. It raised eyebrows about why we needed the info, so I told the transport manager someone had reported a traffic accident citing a van with that number being involved but obviously it hadn't been because there was no damage when the van was returned. The transport manager told me Lofthouse has never had so much as a parking ticket in the twelve years he's been employed. Lofthouse is on vacation but the manager said he would call him in if I wanted to speak to him. I told him no reason to and it was the end of the matter as far as the police were concerned."

"Well I have something from the case files we got. I'll tell you about it when we get back to the office."

There was a message slip on her desk when they got back telling her the chief superintendent wanted to see her immediately she got back. "Okay, tell me what you found in the files. Hopefully it's something positive I can take to the super."

"From the seven case files we have so far there are three references to white vans in the vicinity and two specifically stating they saw a National Power van. All were seen around the time the person went missing. The National Power vehicles are mostly white so maybe the white vans referred to were from the company. It's tenuous but it could be a link."

"Okay. Find out what happened to the files that haven't turned up yet, perhaps they'll have something about white vans. Also, find all you can about Jacob Lofthouse, you know the drill. I'm off to see the super."

Jones was finishing his search about Jacob Lofthouse and reviewing his notes when Judith returned and handed him a sheet of paper headed 'Missing Person Report'. He looked at the name and went straight to the physical characteristics somehow knowing what he would find. "Oh shit, another one. Lorna Lambert, six two and 'slender build'. Not seen or heard from for three days. So, how do we handle it?"

"We don't. Super wants it handled like any other missing person report. We don't know if this one is connected to our two bodies. The media relations people will deflect any questions... the usual stuff... at this time no connections are apparent, we are making every effort to find, anyone with information etcetera, etcetera. Anyway, we stay focused on the two we have. Anything from forensics or Annabelle about the identity of the second body? What about Lofthouse, find anything?"

"No to the first, and Lofthouse seems squeaky clean from what's on file. He had a background check done when he joined National Power, part of their hiring requirement, and it came back clean. Since then, no traffic violations, no collection agencies knocking at his door. Pays all his bills regularly and has no large debts as far as I can see. Does his taxes every year. Lives in a flat. Doesn't own a car and no expensive toys like a boat or motorcycle are registered in his name. However just give me a minute while

I bring something up on Google Earth." Judith took the opportunity to pull her chair over and sit down. "Right, this is the street where Gillian Mulder lived and that's the building where her flat is." Jones pointed to a building midway down the street. "Now if I pull out to get a wider look the street next to Gillian's comes into view and who do you think lives in that building?"

Jones was pointing to a building that was directly across a green space from Gillian's. From the image Judith judged the buildings were no more fifty meters apart and facing rear to rear. "You're going to tell me Lofthouse lives there."

"I am, and in the flat immediately opposite Gillian's."

"So we have him at the rec centre talking to Gillian… we have the van he was driving following her up to the point it appears she goes missing… he lives a street away from hers… she tells her parents about someone from National Power visiting her at her apartment… three of seven missing person reports have statements about white vans and two that say they saw actual National Power vans. Does Lofthouse come up in enquiries made about Gillian's disappearance? He should have been spoken to; he lives on the next street."

Jones cleared Google Earth and going to documents found Gillian's case file. "Here we are, the list of persons interviewed. Quite extensive… but no Lofthouse under the L's."

"Then we should go talk to him," was Judith's immediate response but then she had a change of mind. "No, you should go talk to him. Man to man sort of thing. The 'just following up because we missed you the first time round and what with recent developments we need to tick all the boxes and thanks for your cooperation' routine. He's on vacation so hopefully he hasn't taken a trip."

Jones was jotting down Lofthouse's address when Judith's phone rang. Giving her name then listening she motioned Jones to remain. "Thanks and well done. Any chance a similar thing was done with Gillian's pass card? Stuck up in the metal work under the pier perhaps? I'd appreciate you having a look when the tide is right. Okay, I'll wait to hear from you."

"What was that all about?" Jones queried.

"That was Godfrey. We have the identity of the woman in the park. Her name is Olga Petrovsky. A pass card with her picture on it was found thumb tacked in a tree a good ten metres from the one she was tied to. It was the sun glinting off the plastic laminate as the leaves moved that caught the eye of one of the techs otherwise it might have been missed. Guess where the pass card is for."

Immediately from Jones, "The rec centre!"

Chapter 143

Judith began gathering her things together preparing to leave, "Go and see Lofthouse and while you're chatting with him find out if he ever brings a work's van home overnight. I'm going to see Annabelle and find out what Olga's autopsy has turned up."

Annabelle was at her desk when Judith arrived. "Hi, just doing my report on Olga. Let's go through to the autopsy room." Removing the sheet covering the body Annabelle began, "It was strangulation this time and whoever did it took their time and tortured her. See, there are four separate ligature marks on her neck but it's this one where the skin is broken that finally closed the airway. Forensics are saying it was some type of electrical cord probably three strand braided, you'll need to talk to them. Substantial trauma to anal and vaginal areas and multiple bruises covering much of her body from severe beatings. I say beatings because there are different stages of bruising, you can see the different colours and spread, some happened days ago, some recently. Two bite marks, one on each breast. Not apparent at first glance because they are in the Areola which as you can see are very dark and quite large. All in all, very similar to Gillian Mulder."

"In many ways," Judith remarked. "Physically too. Both tall and let's face it… skinny!"

Annabelle began replacing the sheet, "Yes, both far too thin for their height. What do you think, a killer with something against tall and skinny women?"

"Maybe and we've just learned of a woman of similar build going missing. You said some of the bruising happened days ago so does that mean Gillian and Olga could have been held at the same time. That perhaps they were together when the beatings took place?"

Annabelle took time to consider, "That's possible but they definitely died at different times. Olga after Gillian."

Judith was about to get into her car when her phone rang, it was Keith. "A body answering the description of Lorna Lambert has just been found tied to a flagpole on the community college campus."

"Shit! Right, get in touch with Jones and send him to the campus, tell him I'll meet him there. You've already got SOCO's and the M.E. on the move?"

"Yes, they're on their way."

A member of campus security had found the body and taped off a perimeter using cones at the boundary and because of the pose and position of the body she had draped a heat retention blanket over it. She had also detained several bystanders and confiscated their phones in an effort to keep postings to social media to a minimum. The phones were handed over to the responding patrol officers.

Judith arrived just as the SOCO's and Anabelle pulled up with Jones following seconds behind. The first thing Judith did was to congratulate the security officer on a terrific job of securing the scene and ask her name. "Veronica, but most call me Ronnie. I know I disturbed the scene by covering her up but the position she's in I couldn't leave her uncovered for people to gawk at."

"Absolutely understand Ronnie, you did the right thing, the dead deserve dignity. But talking about people, where is everyone?"

"Midsemester break, very few students or faculty about."

"Thanks again Ronnie and I'll send my DS over to get a full statement from you if you feel up to it."

"Is your DS the good looking one over there? If it is him, he can talk to me anytime."

Judith smiled and whispered, "For goodness' sake don't let on you think he's good looking. His heads big enough as it is."

Judith thanked Ronnie again and went to Jones who was watching the SOCO's at work. "John, get a statement from Veronica. She's campus security and found the body then called it in. Go easy on her, she thinks you're good looking so she must be in shock. Seriously John, I think she's using any technique she can to stop thinking about what she saw so be gentle."

Jones nodded and confirmed, "I will. Must have been one hell of a shock for her. However, she is obviously a woman of discernment."

Annabelle came from the SOCO tent and ducked under the cordon tape then stripping off her gloves and mask went to stand beside Judith. In answer to Judith's raised eyebrows, "I'd estimate time of death seven or eight hours ago. Strangulation again but this time with hands. Finger and thumb marks are evident on the neck. Bruises everywhere and fairly recent. Clothes arranged to show vagina and breasts with bite marks that have almost severed the nipples. I'll let you know more after the post-mortem. My guess is that forensics will confirm that the cords holding the body in place are the same type as found on the other two."

Annabelle took her leave and exchanged 'Hello's' with Jones as he returned from taking Veronica's statement. Judith asked how it had gone.

"She should be in our lot. Great eye for detail and she remembers what she remembers, no maybes or I could be wrong, but little to give a clue as to who brought her here and tied her to the pole. One thing is clear, it was between six and when she called us at eight fifty-five. Her rounds take three hours when the college is closed because she has to do a foot inspection around all the buildings and she started from here at six. I asked if the timing of security rounds were common knowledge and Veronica said it wouldn't be hard to figure them out when the campus is quiet like this although they are less structured during the day when students are back for classes."

Judith interrupted him, "John, did you get to speak to Lofthouse?"

"No, he wasn't at his address. Spoke to the other tenants, they say he's quiet, pleasant and overall don't know a lot about him. He's lived there longer than any other tenant apparently. I asked about him bringing a van home overnight and none had ever seen one parked outside. Whenever he's seen coming or going it's always on foot. I'll go round again this evening, see if I can catch him then."

"Okay. One more thing… go ask Veronica if National Power people come to the campus often and if they do what's the routine about them moving about the place, do they have to sign in and out, do they get escorted to wherever they're going, that sort of thing and when you're done meet me back at the station."

She had her feet up on her desk and was staring at her monitor when Jones returned carrying the mandatory coffees and two envelopes he'd been handed at the front desk. Handing her a coffee and saying it was on him this time he took off his coat and loosened his tie before sitting and spinning his chair so that he faced Judith. "National Power people visit the campus regularly and have to sign in and out at the security office where there is always someone on duty except from nine at night until seven the next morning. It's all motor and foot patrols during those hours with an emergency number to contact them. I assumed you wanted to know if Lofthouse has been there, so I asked Veronica to check the logs for the names and dates of persons from National Power going back twelve months. She'll get back to me as soon as she has the list."

"You assumed right and I'm sure Lofthouse will be found in the log."

Jones picked up the envelopes he'd brought in and tossing one to Judith said, "These will be the files we've been waiting for, let's take a look."

Judith was the first to speak, "Mention of a National Power van is made by a woman living on the same street as the one who went missing. It was parked on waste ground at the back of the houses which she thought strange. It was followed up with the company and the driver that day said he stopped on the waste land to eat his lunch and that driver was our friend Jacob Lofthouse. This case is eight years old. What have you got?"

"Nothing in the statements about any vans. This one is ten years old. Their age is probably the reason they took a while to find and send on."

"So we have three white van and three National Power van sightings. That's six out of nine old cases that we've looked at and we have Lofthouse in a National Power van appearing to follow Gillian the night she disappeared. I think the vans are a thread through them all whether they've been remembered or not. Here's what we do, take a constable with you, DC Margaret Henry would be the best, and get down to National Power and go through their records for vans that were scheduled to be in the area in the days before the woman went missing. The log records should give you the names of the drivers. If they give you grief about privacy rights and confidentiality appeal to their social conscience and if that doesn't work give me a call and I'll get a warrant. We have enough circumstantial to do that. If Margaret isn't in the incident room tell Keith to contact her and have her meet you at the National Power offices. Transport manager's name is Richard Dick, he's the one I spoke to, earlier. Don't laugh, that really is his name, it's on his office door."

Chapter 144

They met no resistance from Richard Dick who went out of his way to explain what a good corporate citizen National Power was and that they would help the police in any way they could. Margaret and Jones were taken to an empty meeting room and given access to a computer and printer. Richard Dick asked what type of van they were particularly interested in and from their description brought up files of logs for quarter and half ton panel vans going back ten years. Margaret charmed Richard Dick by telling him how impressed she was with the record keeping of his department. Richard Dick gave Margaret authority to use a memory stick to copy the required records and using dates the week before and after the women were reported missing, she was able to quickly recover the van logs which included the driver's names. No surprise was expressed by Jones or Margaret at the number of times the name of a particular driver turned up. Richard Dick was of course intrigued as to why the police wanted records that went so far back and Jones apologised telling him he couldn't say more than its part of an ongoing investigation and usually these things turned into blind alleys but they had to be checked out. Richard Dick voiced his understanding that all due diligence had to be seen to be done. On saying goodbye Margaret's hand was held a little too long by Richard Dick but she gave him her most radiant smile and said, "Thank you Richard, you've been very helpful," in a voice that would have done justice to Marilyn Monroe herself.

Back in Jones' car Margaret with incredulity in her voice asked, "Who in their right mind with a surname like Dick would name their child Richard? What a nightmare going through life known as Dick Dick. And you, you dick, could have told me about his name before we got there."

"What would have been the fun in that? I wanted to see your reaction when you shook hands with a Dick."

Margaret harumphed, "Well obviously I did that when I met you!"

Jones with contrition in his voice asked, "Can I make it up to you by buying you dinner?" A sideways glance told him she was smiling but she took her time answering.

"All right but it has to be somewhere really nice. Somewhere I can get dressed up for. I expect to be wined and dined expensively in repayment for you not warning me about Dick Dick's name."

"It shall be so my lady. A place of exquisite food and wine in an atmosphere of luxury. Tomorrow night?"

"Yes, but not a word to anybody at work."

"Agreed. I'll make a reservation and let you know what time."

Judith who had watched their arrival from her office window gestured to them from the doorway of the incident room, "Bring what you've got in here and let's have a look at it on the big screen."

Margaret gave Keith the memory stick telling him the records went from oldest to most recent and he should skip the half ton vans and search only for Jacob Lofthouse in quarter ton vans. While Keith did the editing the other three spent their time in silence looking over the incident board and it was Margaret saying, "There's another one out there. The way it's escalating there has to be," that broke it.

"I think you're right," Judith agreed. "How much longer Keith?"

"Couple of minutes and you're going to love what's showing up."

Silence settled again until from Keith, "Here you go on the big screen. I've broken it down by location, date and driver and as you suspected Jacob Lofthouse was in the area at or about the time of the disappearance of all the women in the files."

Judith ran her fingers through her hair and let out a long breath. "John and Margaret get over to his place and if he's in do the routine enquiry bit until I give you a call that a team with a search warrant are on the way. If he's not there check with the neighbours about when he was last seen and when we have the warrant, we'll do a forced entry. My feeling is he won't be there. I think he knows we are close and wants us to find him with his next victim. He knows the end is near and wants to draw us in for some sort of grand finale. Don't ask me to explain how or why I feel this, I just do. It's something in my head and in my gut. Okay, off you go and be careful. I'll follow once the warrant is issued." Turning to Keith Judith continued, "Bring the rest of the team in and get them finding out everything they can about Lofthouse. Go way back, parents, siblings, schooling, is he on social media, mobile phone records, and bank accounts. You know what we need Keith, anything and everything, all the background we can get." Keith picked up his phone to start calling in the team and Judith was at the door when she stopped and turned back, "One more thing Keith check housing and apartment records. See if he owns any."

"He's not home. His neighbour says she hasn't seen him for a couple of days," Judith got this from Jones when she arrived after arranging for a search warrant.

"I didn't think he would be. The warrant will arrive with the forced entry team."

The building was a three-storey triplex separated from the buildings adjacent by narrow alleyways. Lofthouse lived in the middle building of three that formed that side of the street. The buildings across the street were wood framed two-storey duplexes that lacked the character and permanence of those that Lofthouse and his neighbours lived in. The three of them standing on the sidewalk was beginning to attract attention and a large busty woman with arms crossed beneath it in support came from the duplex opposite to voice in loud strident tones, "Hey, what are you lot doing hanging around? Move it or I'll call the police." Margaret took her warrant card from her pocket and walked across to the woman. Jones and Judith did not hear what Margaret said to the woman, but it appeared to have the desired effect because after some animated gesturing the woman turned on her slippered heel and went back inside slamming the door.

"Self-righteous cow. Says she needs to look after what goes on in the street because our lot don't. I can see her now, sitting all day smoking and drinking beer out of a can with one eye on the window and the other on some shit reality show or soap opera."

"Careful now, is that anyway to talk about our greatest asset in police work, a member of the public? The super will have you on a sensitivity training course if he finds out," Judith cautioned Margaret with mock severity.

It happened that the entry team were not needed. After positioning themselves to force open the door to Lofthouse's flat Judith knocked and was about to announce that it was the police when the door swung open from the force of her knock. A cautious entry was made but a look throughout the apartment confirmed that it was empty. The entry team were sent away looking chagrined that their battering ram had not been necessary. Judith called Keith and told him to send forensics immediately then the three of them retrieved bootees from their cars and donning those and gloves they began a thorough walk through of each room. The entry to the flat had been much too easy. Lofthouse had known they were coming so they went looking for a message.

The flat comprised six rooms divided by a central hallway running front to rear in the building. All rooms had connecting pocket doors that were all open which made the spaces seem airy and allowed light from large bay windows at front and rear to flood through. Although connected nothing overflowed from one space to another with each being specific to a purpose be it kitchen, bedroom, bathroom or living room. Being a ground floor flat there was a door at the rear that opened onto a small lawn that stretched the full width of the building that held several clothes lines which would be used by the tenants. Fire escapes draped down from the flats on the upper floors. A low fence marked the property line where it joined the green space Judith had seen on Google Earth. From the open back door Judith called Jones and pointing directly across the green space asked, "Is that Gillian Mulders place?" Jones confirmed it was. "Hers is the ground floor flat, right?" Jones confirmed again. "So, from Lofthouse's bedroom window here he had a very good view of Gillian's." Jones agreed and was about to suggest they look for binoculars when Judith's phone rang, and Jones went back inside while she answered it. She listened without interruption then said, "Thanks Keith, great work but keep digging into him. Forensics have just turned up, so we'll be back while they go over the place. Bye." Turning from the door she found the other two waiting expectantly for news. "Keith has found out that Jacob Lofthouse has another residence."

"The thing is," Greg explained when they returned to the station. "The other place is not in his name. I did what Judith asked and checked home and real estate records under Jacob Lofthouse and nothing came up, so I did a search for real estate listed under companies, trusts and holdings. In the records it's owned by a holding company, L.J. Holdings, and Jacob Lofthouse is registered as the principal. I passed this to Keith, and he did a probate search."

"Thanks Greg. The property was willed to Lofthouse by his mother who died fifteen years ago. It's a bungalow about ten miles along the coast. From tax records it's registered as a summer let that Lofthouse rents out during the months of May to September. It's pretty isolated, not close neighbours so great if you want a quiet get away vacation but close enough to town and beaches. We found out the rentals are handled by Coastal Cottage Rentals. I have a forensic auditor digging into Lofthouse's and his holding company bank accounts. The rest of us are still looking into his past and family history. It's coming along but taking time."

It was Jones who broke the silence when Keith finished. "You're very quiet Judith… what's on your mind?"

Judith was almost trancelike in her response with her tone even and in a voice that was barely recognisable as hers, "He's holding another woman at the bungalow. She hasn't been reported missing yet but she's there. Think about it… all this escalated very fast going from one every twelve months to three in a few days. Forensics aren't going to find anything incriminating at his flat, everything has been done at the bungalow. I think he knew that we'd eventually find out about the bungalow when we looked into his background. Something is driving him, and he wants us to come to him. We can't go in heavy handed because if he sees armed officers, he will kill the woman. He *needs to talk* because he wants something from us and the only way we are getting the woman out alive is to give him the opportunity. John you and I are going to his bungalow, Margaret will drive us there then stay out of sight." Then in a manner that quelled any dispute, "No arguments, this is not open to discussion. Keith… Margaret will call if we have not come out after thirty minutes and that's when you can bring the cavalry."

Nobody spoke during the drive. Keith's directions were exact, and they easily found the junction to the gravel road that led to the bungalow. Driving past the turn-off Judith found a place to park that was out of sight from the bungalow. "There are binoculars in the boot Margaret. Get through the hedge stay hidden and watch the house. You'll see us arrive and as soon as we enter that's when the thirty minutes start. Do not let Lofthouse see you and do not approach before thirty minutes is up and we haven't come out then wait for the rest to arrive. You'll see us if we come out before the thirty minutes. Okay John, let's go."

Margaret retrieved the binoculars from the boot then Judith turned the car around and drove to the junction then turned towards the bungalow.

They had seen a layout of the bungalow taken from the rental company online brochure. Three bedrooms, living room and kitchen with dining area. It was a picturesque setting and the building which had been a farm workers croft at one time had had extensions grafted on that blended with the original building. It looked well maintained and had a large lawn grass area encircling it with a brick barbeque on a patio that was accessible from the living room through large French doors. They were stopped on the driveway and getting out of the car while looking over the place when Jacob Lofthouse opened the front door and motioned them to come into the bungalow calling "Better hurry, she doesn't have much time left."

Margaret saw them enter and looked at her watch.

Lofthouse greeted them in a vestibule that separated the front door from the entrance door to the house proper, a space to remove muddy footwear and hang up working jackets. "Glad you could make it; we've been looking forward to your visit. Oh, by the way, Margaret won't be calling the cavalry, she appears to have fallen asleep." Lofthouse looked Judith up and down while licking his lips and fondling his crotch. "My, my Judith, you are a tall slim buxom lady aren't you. You would have suited me just fine but unfortunately Eleanor and Richard need to leave you and John here while they go inside and meet the Despot. Sit them on the bench and come forward Retributionists."

When Eleanor and Richard stood before him Lofthouse gestured toward the inner door, "Go ahead. I'm staying here to watch over these two in case your friends turn up and try to use them."

Richard pressed the handle down and pushing the door open he and Eleanor stepped through and onto the patio of Richard's beach house.

Chapter 145

A man leaning against the patio railing stood upright saying, "Welcome, I am called Maestro and I helped guide you here. A somewhat circuitous journey I admit but a necessary one." He was unknown to them. Not handsome, not plain, nothing outstanding about him, he was an average *everyman*. "The restraint both of you are showing is laudable, no shouting and histrionics, no demands or threats. Humans, your choice of classification not ours, are just the latest of many evolutionary iterations that have been tried and discarded on this planet and if they keep on their present self-destructive path of resource harvesting, pollution and excessive population then humankind will cross the tipping point to where recovery is impossible. If that happens the decision must be made whether to end this particular evolutionary experiment but Designer has decided to give them one more chance to get their shit together. Go ahead Eleanor, ask your questions. Feel free to ask me anything, both of you."

"Are we the first to meet you?"

"Yes, Eleanor, of your life form and from Concordat, you are."

"Why us?"

"Because Richard, you and Eleanor together, are greater than the sum of your minds as are the others who will be joining you; but before further explanations someone well known to you has arrived." Takahara appeared on the beach and made his way towards them. "Eleanor, Richard, so good to see you, and you Maestro, it's been a while since we got together with such promising candidates." Maestro had risen at Takahara's approach and both spread their arms wide before coming together to hug and slap backs. After their greeting they turned to face Eleanor and Richard with Takahara saying, "Maestro and I are old friends, family almost and I sense your impatience so let's get on. Such high hopes were held for the planet, it had it all. Perfectly positioned within its solar system and with all the raw materials to sustain life for billions of years. However, Designer has watched as your species has pushed the planet close to the edge of an environmental and ecological disaster. Genus Homo is ruining it because they have an exaggerated sense of self-entitlement and no self-control."

Looks of anger and deep sadness swept over Maestro's face and he shook his head murmuring, "What a mess." Then, "I have to leave and gather together the others I mentioned. Takahara will explain about Concordat and what comes next and answer any questions." Takahara walked with Maestro to the edge of the palms bordering the beach where they spoke briefly then hugged before Maestro walked into the shadows of the palms and disappeared from view. Takahara stood looking out over the lagoon for some time before returning to Eleanor and Richard who were conversing in hushed tones which stopped when he stepped back onto the patio and sat saying. "Maestro is right, it is a mess. And, it's going to get worse."

Chapter 146

"You have already determined that Concordat did not exist, that it was a simulation that ran in parallel with events taking place on your planet. The Concordat simulation was built around people, locations and events from your memory caches collected at the time of your death. The crimes you witnessed are, at this moment, happening, but, unlike Concordat outcomes, are not yet resolved. Good and evil, as humans understand the terms, are at war on the planet. Good has only one form while evil has many, and, evil is winning." Takahara stood, "Come, take a walk along the beach with me and enjoy it while it remains."

At the water's edge they began walking toward the northern arm of the bay with the sun casting long in step shadows to the west. Takahara continued, "Verbal please, I love the sound of spoken language. Hold any questions until I have finished and refrain from mind chatter, it's annoying when you talk over me. Thank you. Designer introduced a particular gene into selected humans at the moment of conception, it's called 'The Empathy Gene' because it only activated when persons with identical genes met." Three canvas chairs materialised, "Let's sit. Three hundred humans, one hundred and fifty pairs, were given the gene with each pair of genes being identical. If two humans with different genes came into contact the genes remained dormant. Because of the racial separateness and population spread the probability of these two particular humans meeting was fairly remote, but on that day in Kolkata you did meet and the connection was made. You were so in tune when together that you were sometimes disturbed by what you called your ESP gift." Takahara closed his eyes and tilted his head fully to the sun murmuring, "Solar warmth, feels so good. From the hundred and fifty pairs only sixteen connected and from those only six pairs, you included, are moving on to the next stage of Designer's opportunity for humankind to save the planet and themselves. Go ahead Eleanor."

Shifting in her chair so she could see Takahara in profile as he sat eyes closed and inscrutable. "All the hoopla we went through with transition, memory wipes, brain upgrades, Retribution cases, the Solons and all the rest was to test us, to see if we made some sort of passing grade."

"Yes, you could put it that way. A phrase once ascribed to astronauts comes to mind, it was to see if you had 'the right stuff'."

"The twelve individuals who form the six pairs all have the gene?" from Richard.

"They do," Takahara acknowledged.

"And are these individuals among those we met and worked with in the Concordat simulation?" from Eleanor.

"They are," from Takahara.

"And who are they?" from Richard.

"Work it out for yourselves," from Takahara who then opened his eyes. He added, "Enough sun, I'm going to walk in the shade of the palms, call when you've figured it out."

Takahara was sitting Zen when Eleanor called. He found them standing close and ankle deep in lagoon water holding hands. Joining them he stood beside Eleanor. "Tell me."

They spoke as one in a blended voice with the words merging seamlessly as they came from one mouth and then the other. "Six pairs selected, twelve persons. You, the Maestro and Designer. Twelve and three. A revamped version of a previous plan is being considered in a final attempt to bring harmony to the planet. Twelve and three, apostles and trinity, Christianity version 2.0. If that's the plan it won't work any better than the first time."

Takahara surprised them, "I agree. Christianity 2.0 would not work and while the twelve and three analogy to apostles and trinity appears to point in that direction you are mistaken. The premise of the first plan that all religions, faiths, beliefs and peoples should live in harmony was sound, however, the approach of letting each take a different path to their vision or version of the afterlife proved to be wrong. Too many religious leaders, saviours, call them what you will, were given the opportunity but instead of one rising above the others it became, to put it crudely, a pissing contest as to which was the one true belief. You know the outcomes, the wars, the terrorism, the ethnic cleansing etcetera. and all the while the rich got richer and the poor got shafted. Ah, here comes Maestro and your ten colleagues." Maestro led the group from the palms with the ten walking in pairs behind him. Charlotte and Ted, Victoria and Jenny, Alan and Yuri, Abigail and Amber, Isabel and Per.

Takahara and Maestro stood aside as the ten said their 'hellos' to Eleanor and Richard then Maestro nodded to Takahara who announced, "Time to get down to work and for you to give the population a final chance to save themselves and the planet. One last kick at the fur lined piss pot, so to speak. Designer still considers that twelve operatives on the planet to be an ideal number but management, the trinity, unlike last time will not appear, and, the strategy is very different. This time no 'nice guy' approach. This time if they don't listen to reason and the abundance of evidence that the planet is being destroyed you can use the powers you have been given to kick governmental, industrial, financial, criminal and corporate ass. You will be able to perform acts that they called miracles look like party tricks. What you were able to do in the Concordat simulation you can do on the planet without the population being aware, you can even visit the diner. A number of other people who worked with you in Concordat, Emma, Charles, Brian for example, were duplicates of persons still alive on the planet and who will be available to assist you if required. Of course they will not recognise you but you know their strengths. Now it is time for you to get your instructions from Designer and be told of certain restrictions placed on your activities before you head back to the planet. We must go now; the Concordat simulation is about to end. Bring your bodies with you. It's time you got down to Earth"

Part One.

THE END

www.ingramcontent.com/pod-product-compliance
Lightning Source LLC
LaVergne TN
LVHW041959060526
838200LV00038B/1288